I0822272

DUNGEONS OF DELGE

Descendants of Twilight: Book 2

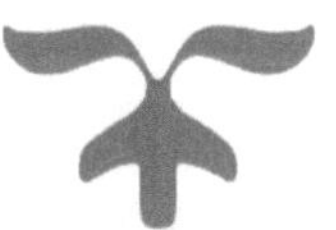

BY

C. M. SUROWIEC JR.

Dungeons of Delge is a work of fiction. Names, characters, places, and incidents either are the product of the author's imagination or are used fictitiously. Any resemblance to actual persons, living or dead, events, or locales is entirely coincidental.

10 9 8 7 6 5 4 3 2

Hardcover: 979-8-9859622-6-0

eBook: 979-8-9859622-5-3

Paperback: 979-8-9859622-7-7

Dev / Copy Line Editor: Marie Still

Cover Art Design: C.M. Surowiec Jr.

Cover Art Illustration: luv_draft

Map Enhancement: Khayyam Akhtar

CMSurowiecJr.com

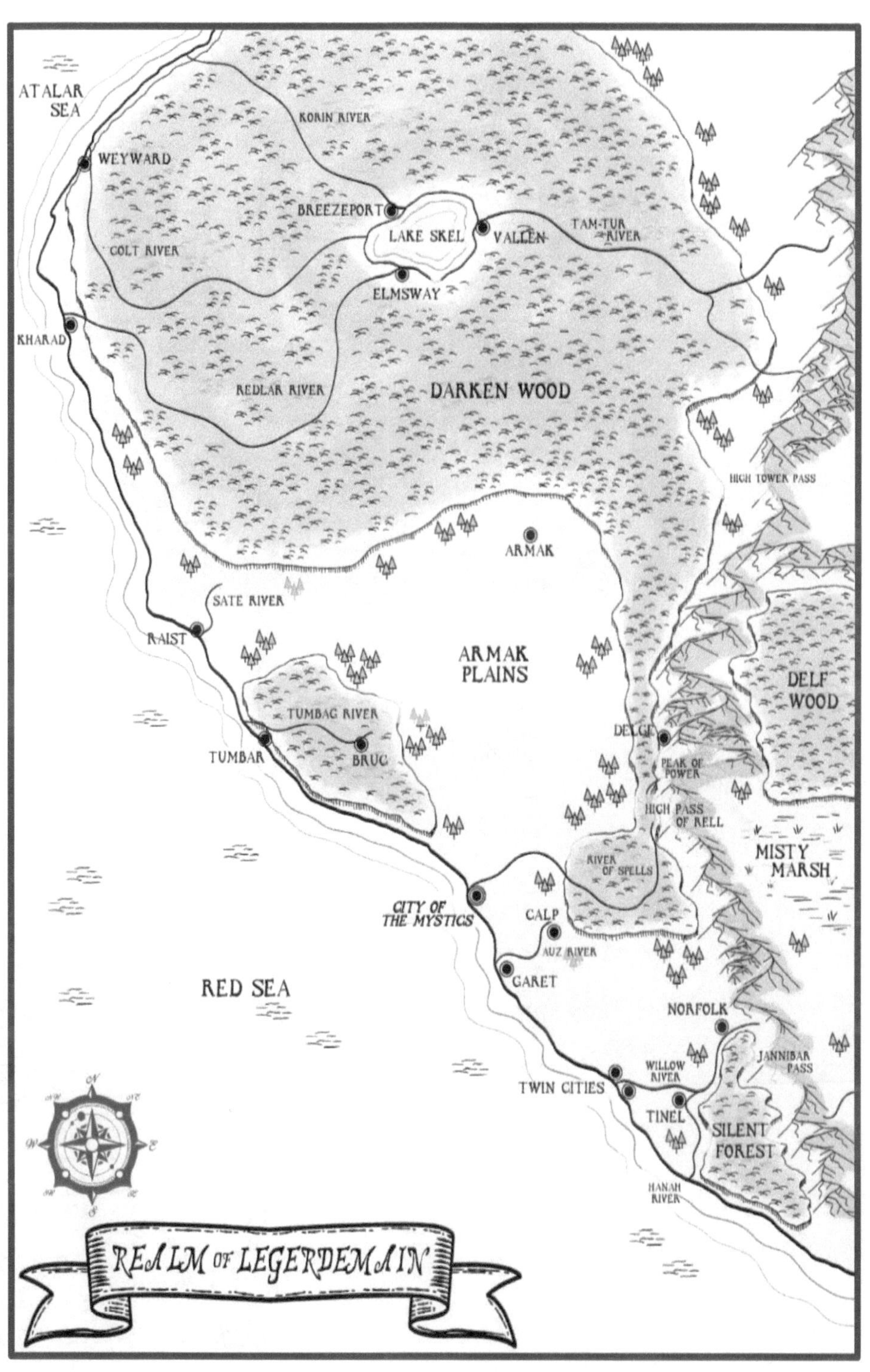
ATALAR SEA
WEYWARD
KORIN RIVER
BREEZEPORT
LAKE SKEL
VALLEN
TAM-TUR RIVER
COLT RIVER
ELMSWAY
KHARAD
REDLAR RIVER
DARKEN WOOD
HIGH TOWER PASS
ARMAK
SATE RIVER
RAIST
ARMAK PLAINS
DELF WOOD
TUMBAG RIVER
DELGE
TUMBAR
BRUC
PEAK OF POWER
HIGH PASS OF RELL
RIVER OF SPELLS
MISTY MARSH
CITY OF THE MYSTICS
CALP
AUZ RIVER
GARET
RED SEA
NORFOLK
WILLOW RIVER
JANNIBAR PASS
TWIN CITIES
TINEL
SILENT FOREST
HANAH RIVER
REALM OF LEGERDEMAIN

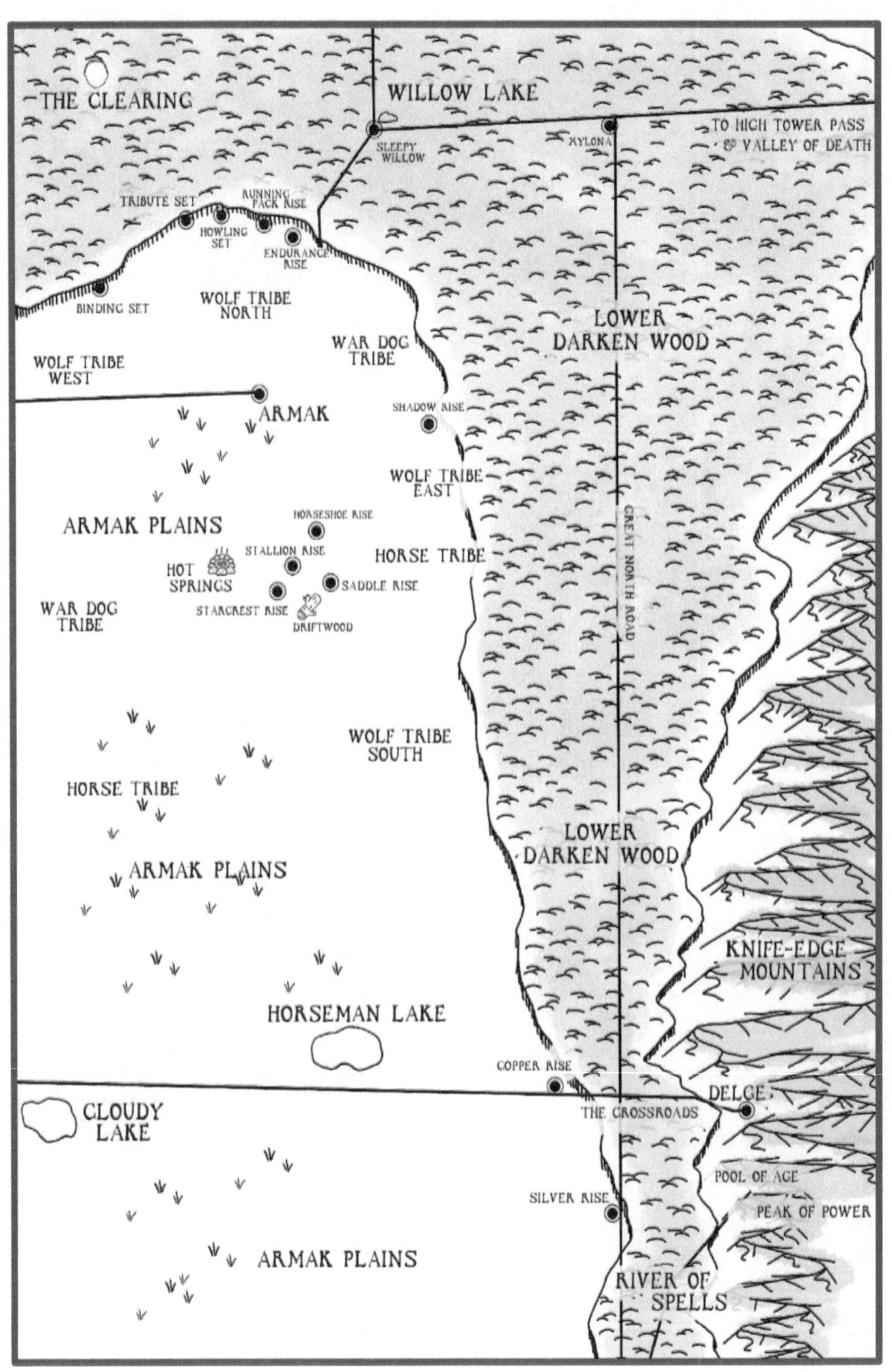
THE CLEARING
WILLOW LAKE
SLEEPY WILLOW
XYLONA
TO HIGH TOWER PASS & VALLEY OF DEATH
TRIBUTE SET
RUNNING PACK RISE
HOWLING SET
ENDURANCE RISE
BINDING SET
WOLF TRIBE NORTH
LOWER DARKEN WOOD
WAR DOG TRIBE
WOLF TRIBE WEST
ARMAK
SHADOW RISE
WOLF TRIBE EAST
GREAT NORTH ROAD
ARMAK PLAINS
HORSESHOE RISE
STALLION RISE
HORSE TRIBE
HOT SPRINGS
SADDLE RISE
STARCREST RISE
DRIFTWOOD
WAR DOG TRIBE
WOLF TRIBE SOUTH
HORSE TRIBE
ARMAK PLAINS
LOWER DARKEN WOOD
KNIFE-EDGE MOUNTAINS
HORSEMAN LAKE
COPPER RISE
DELGE
THE CROSSROADS
CLOUDY LAKE
POOL OF AGE
SILVER RISE
PEAK OF POWER
ARMAK PLAINS
RIVER OF SPELLS

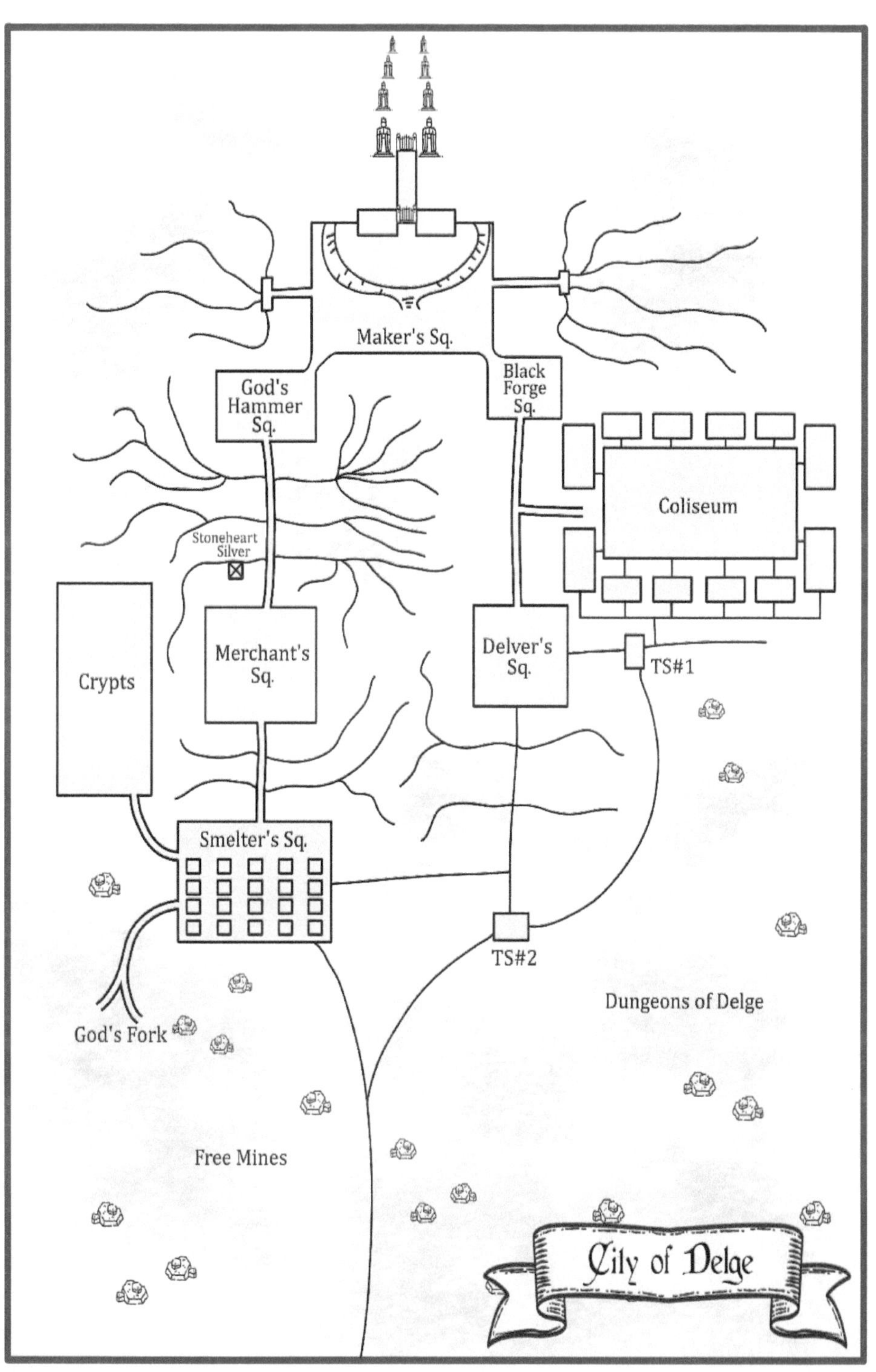
Maker's Sq.
God's Hammer Sq.
Black Forge Sq.
Coliseum
Stoneheart Silver
Crypts
Merchant's Sq.
Delver's Sq.
TS#1
Smelter's Sq.
TS#2
Dungeons of Delge
God's Fork
Free Mines
City of Delge

For:

My Brother,

who left us too soon. You will never be forgotten. Your support was always appreciated.

FROGOTHIAN CALENDAR

1. First Twilight 1/24 - Terazhan's Twilight	2. Progression	3. Breeze
4. The Initiate 4/4 - Terazhan's Twilight	5. Harvest	6. Rhomerian 6/14 - Terazhan's Twilight
7. Anuberis	8. Oderian 8/24 - Terazhan's Twilight	9. The Holy One
10. Gathering	11. Sendarian 11/4 - Terazhan's Twilight	12. Final Harvest
13. Last Twilight 13/14 - Terazhan's Twilight		14. Festival

30 days in every month

PANTHEON OF DEITIES

	Plane of Power	Color of Phylactery	Deity's Home Plane	Ethical / Moral Compass
7 Planes of Heaven	Dreams	Cobalt Blue	Melandri	Conforms to Order and Good
	Light	White	None	
	Mists	Amber	Terazhan	Law/Order and Good
	Nature	Hunter Green	Sohaleah	Law/Order and Good
	Tides	Turquoise	Feldarius	Conforms to Order and Good
	Time	Cinnamon	Vallerielle	Conforms to Order and Good
	Wind	Canary Yellow	Dilantro	Law/Order and Good
9 Planes of Hell	Ashes	Deep Hickory	Ledaedra	Chaotic and Evil
	Darkness	Black	None	
	Delights	Tangerine	Jakarrak	Chaotic and Good
	Fear	Indigo	Marekai	Chaotic and Evil
	Ice	Ice Blue	Harendread	Chaotic and Evil
	Lava	Molten Lava	Hymnoch	Chaotic and Evil
	Shadows	Violet	Malekai	Chaotic and Evil
	Spirits	Crimson	Azreala	Chaotic and Good
	Storms	Dark Silver	Bardonril	Conforms to Order and Evil

DM  Breeze

Dungeons Of Delge

Prologue

In the beginning, demons and devils fought each other in a millennium-long battle of order versus chaos known as the Age of Fire. The demi-gods and deities ousted them from power in a decade-long struggle of good versus evil, then reigned supreme for over two millennia known as the Age of Wonder. However, almost four hundred years ago, the Age of the Dragons began, when Ledaedra, a six-headed dragon god, left the Astral Plane and brought her evil horde to bear on the world. The demi-gods passively relinquished control of Erogoth. Uncontested, the dragons conquered the seven continents and subjugated all other races for the next four centuries.

1

The White Dragonfly

Cymm

Bria came running into the small clearing through the tall grass, her little legs pumping and churning the dirt beneath them. "Cymm, come quick. They're hurting it!"

A large fish struggled at the end of her brother's line. "I'm a little bussssyyyy, right now." Nine-year-old Cymm stood at the edge of the pond, teetering on the brink of an unplanned swim.

"Cymm! It's going to die!" Bria tugged on his arm, tears welling in her eyes. Although she was only three years younger, he already towered over her, an early indication of the height disparity to come.

He huffed and drove the base of the fishing pole into the mud with a satisfying *slurp*. With nostrils flaring, he stroked her hair. "Show me."

Bria ran in the direction she came from, pushing past their grazing ponies, before disappearing into the tall grass, the tassels waving above her head. Cymm lurched to keep up, following the thrashing of the underbrush and the cawing of birds. After a few hundred feet, his sister entered another clearing and came to an abrupt halt, pointing. He strode up next to her, staring at two boys he knew well.

Despite being two lifeyears younger than his nemesis, Dirk Darkmane, they stood eye-to-eye. Two altercations in the past year alone had ended with Cymm pounding him both times. The other boy, Dirk's dim-witted twelve-year-old brother Mort, could carry a two-month-old calf without breaking a sweat.

The troublemakers hunched over, dragging long reeds on the ground behind them like a plume of tail feathers.

Cymm surveyed the area in front of them and found their quarry. A large dragonfly rested on a grass tassel at the edge of the clearing. It was at least twelve inches long and pure white, even its gossamer wings were laced and lined with ivory bands.

The hooligans drew closer to the insect. With enthusiastic cries, they jumped and swatted at it. Giggling hysterically, they chased the dragonfly around the clearing.

Bria tugged on his arm again. "Do something," she whispered.

Cymm was already sprinting across the gap. "Dirk, leave it alone."

His command was ignored, and the next swing grazed the creature. It crashed to the ground among the moss on the bank. Dirk raised his foot to stomp it, and Cymm barreled into him with a flying tackle, driving him to the ground.

Mort snickered. "Get 'em Durby."

"Durby?" In confusion, Cymm let up the pressure on Dirk's shoulders.

From his prone position, the jet-black hair splayed across Dirk's contorted face did little to mask his pain. A second shadow head appeared on his right shoulder, like a two-headed monster. The new head's ethereal substance had contour. It even growled, low and spiteful. The sinister, red pulsing orbs in its eye sockets drained him of energy and was enough to give him nightmares. It vanished as fast as it arrived. Cymm glanced about in confusion.

Dirk heaved Cymm off himself with such force he went airborne, arms flailing, then slammed onto the ground a dozen feet away.

Cymm rolled to his back with his arm across his chest, gasping for air. The faint crunch of dried grass alerted him, and he lifted his head with effort. The dragonfly flopped, buzzed, and spun in tight circles, its broken wing preventing it from escaping.

Focused solely on the insect, Dirk tried to stomp on it again.

Mort charged in to join him.

Too dazed to stand quickly, Cymm crab-crawled over to place his body between Dirk and his target. The clomping of hooves echoed behind him. A rock sailed from Bria's hand, connecting with Mort's head and causing a roar of anger to escape his quivering lips.

With one swift kick from Dirk's boot, the wind rushed out of Cymm's lungs and stifled his laugh. Another blow arrived immediately, connecting with his back. He screamed in pain, not knowing which hurt worse.

"Run Cymm!" Bria plowed into Dirk with her pony and knocked him onto his back.

His sister cried out, and Cymm wobbled to his feet. Mort had tracked her down and pulled her to the edge of the saddle with a fist full of hair. He loped to his sister's defense, not realizing the insect was perched on his shoulder until after he kicked Mort in the side of his knee.

Mort released Bria with a yelp and fell to his knees.

After a loud nicker, Bria's pony lunged forward, a result of Cymm smacking it on the haunch. Its rider cast a teary-eyed smile over her shoulder, then flailed her arms wildly. "Watch out!"

Cymm barely side-stepped a crazed swing from behind, causing Dirk to lose his balance and stumble forward. He then ran in the opposite direction, shaking his arm, trying to launch the dragonfly into the air from its new roost upon his bicep.

Mort hobbled to catch up, wearing a grimace of pain.

"I'll get Dad!" Bria's pony broke into a gallop.

The insect's legs popped off his arm one at a time as Cymm frantically peeled them away, then he stopped and propelled it into the air. It flew in lazy circles to the ground. Both boys were close behind him. He whirled, taking a defensive stance.

While staring at Cymm, Dirk's left fist shot out to the side, catching Mort square in the jaw. The bigger boy collapsed like a sack of potatoes.

"What is wrong with you Dirk?" Cymm ducked under another wild punch, delivering a teeth-rattling uppercut to the ebony-haired boy's jaw.

"Not Dirk—Dego." He delivered a massive blow with his forearm to Cymm's face.

He went down again, blood pouring from his nose. It was the hardest he had ever been hit. "What in the nine hells is going on?"

"Exactly!" Dirk stepped on his back, continuing his mission to reach the dragonfly.

Cymm lunged for his ankle, securing it with both arms and his neck. His rival proceeded forward at a much slower pace, dragging him across the ground with every step. Finally, he glanced down with the eyes of a demon and shook him violently, but Cymm refused to let go.

The dragonfly flopped around frantically, as if sensing imminent danger.

Dirk's thrashing stopped abruptly, and he collapsed on Cymm.

The excitement of victory lasted only a moment. A black, wraithlike, bipedal creature with two heads loomed above him. It turned away abruptly to stalk the insect.

Cymm rolled Dirk's unconscious body off to the side and rose to his hands and knees with a gulp. The abomination in front of him made his eyes well with tears. *What in the nine hells do I do?* He glanced over his shoulder, Mort lay unmoving, still unconscious, and Bria was nowhere to be found.

The black thing continued its attack, pounding its foot into the ground. The dragonfly repeatedly evaded certain death with each slam of its foot—by only a hair.

Cymm sat back on his haunches and slapped his thighs in frustration. His mind swirled, and in desperation, he blurted, "Wait—wait, Dego."

Its blood-red orbs of death locked onto Cymm. With a snarl, it drained him again. Physically weak, his head lowered in submission to find the dragonfly had crawled up onto his thigh. He drew strength from an unknown source and defiantly returned his gaze to the demon-like creature. It was so close; he could have touched it.

Dego raised its knee, and the foot descended to crush Cymm or the insect, or both.

Cymm scooped and shielded the beautiful creature with his body, exposing his thigh to the attack. He winced in anticipation. A searing pain radiated through his leg as if a knife had been plunged into the muscle. When he opened his eyes, he found Dego's right foot buried inside his leg. Before the pain subsided, the monster slammed another foot down, penetrating Cymm's other leg.

He gasped for breath. The pain was too excruciating to endure as the thing tried to enter his body. He pounded his fist into the dirt while tremors of terror coursed through him. With a sharp gasp, he stood, drawing the creature unintentionally closer. He clutched the dragonfly to his chest and tried to disengage. He forced a battle of wills and slowly withdrew one leg.

The beast's red eyes blazed in surprise.

"No, Dego." A moment later, a tentacle-like arm clobbered Cymm to the ground. He curled his body to protect the insect, and hoped his father would arrive soon. Cymm scanned the area in haste. The insect was gone. His leg flailed about, involuntarily but vigorously.

"No!" Fear crept into the creature's voice. "You will pay for this." Dego continued his impulsive foot extrication. A burst of brilliant white light, accompanied by a thunderous *crack,* completed the exorcism, and launched Dego backward a dozen yards.

Cymm's arms drooped to his sides, and he wavered. He blinked several times and watched Dego limp back into the tall reeds with half a foot before he collapsed unconscious.

2

The Spectator

Lykinnia

Lykinnia hovered next to the teenage Cymm in her amber, ethereal form. Together, they stared at the prone body of adolescent Cymm lying on the ground next to the unconscious Dirk. The injured creature, Dego, had already disappeared.

Lykinnia's eyes misted back at the Peak of Power. "What a brave young man."

Cymm shook his head. "More foolish. I figured Dirk was messin' around." He shifted his gaze to the hologram as it disappeared. "How'd you do that?"

"Do you remember telling me about the trial, where the shaman cast Eye of the Wolf? I am using the Altar of One to cast a similar spell."

"All three of us slept for days. We woke with not a single memory and Mort babbling incoherently for a week. Those haunting red eyes weren't easily forgotten. They plagued my dreams for a year."

Cymm scratched the back of his neck. "Our fathers were planning to tan our hides publicly. I was terrified. When Dirk saw the look on my face, he put his arm around my shoulder, and said, 'Don't worry, it doesn't hurt for long.' But it wasn't the pain that worried me, it was the humiliation. I appreciated his concern and offered him my hand. We shook. Our fathers seemed to speak without words, then shook hands themselves, and canceled the discipline. We never fought again; a bizarre bond had formed between us."

Cymm's stoic expression melted away. "Bria didn't speak to my father for days, because he wouldn't help her look for the dragonfly." A smile blossomed upon his face. "Thank you, Lykinnia." He tried to grab her insubstantial hand unsuccessfully. "I have tried to remember what happened that day for eight years."

Lykinnia assumed the fond memory of his deceased family had cheered him. She bit her lip. *It has taken me four hundred years to deal with the death of my mother, and he lost his entire family only nine months ago. I wish we could hold hands, or I could give him a big hug.* "Now we need to *understand* what happened, which will take more time and research. When did you find out the dragonfly entered your body?"

Cymm turned downtrodden. "Just now. I guess that explains my *unique* aura."

"It does not make you any less special. The dragonfly chose you. I will use the altar to investigate a few events in the past to try and determine what happened. The only other person known to have your aura was Melcorac. So, I will start there and see if I can determine any similarities between the two of you."

Cymm's face brightened slightly. "I'm glad you're here." He reached for her, and his arm passed right through her. His face took on a tinge of red.

Butterflies fluttered in Lykinnia's stomach. *I am glad I had the courage to reveal myself this time.* Her smile diminished slightly, remembering her prior visit ended abruptly. She had followed him for several minutes, trying to build up the courage to reveal herself. When she had finally summoned the nerve, he entered a building full of people abruptly severing the chance for a visit. "Cymm, would it be all right if I visit again in a few—"

"Yes!" Cymm responded immediately.

Lykinnia giggled. "I need to head back. I have lingered here too long, and a headache is forming."

Cymm shuffled side to side nervously, then blurted out, "Do you have a boyfriend?"

Her body tingled with excitement. "Yes."

The young man's shoulders slumped, and he gave a half-hearted wave to her dissipating form.

"His name is Cymm Reich." The priestess merged with her physical form and slowly opened her eyes. Her palms rested on the altar, and a large feathery wing brushed against her right shoulder.

Solar regarded her from his lofty nine-foot stature, his eyes boring into hers.

Lykinnia shifted uncomfortably under her guardian's gaze. "What did you see?"

"Everything." He turned to face her. "You did well."

3

The Maverick

ZaphMordakai

ZaphMordakai loved to make a spectacle of himself. The enormous black dragon had already circled Fire Island several times, making sure the tip of his wing's shadow perfectly traced the shoreline below. He slowed his pace again as he approached the stone pebble beach where the drakaina lounged in the sun. Intentionally angling his massive body, he blocked as much of the light as possible from reaching the female dragons below.

Many of the drakaina glared up at him, but a few craned their necks, impressed. Not only the black dragons either, red, blue, white, and green; he did not care what color his consorts were, if they liked to have fun. He noted a few to engage with after his meeting with the generals.

He landed heavily near the headquarters, noting the colossal sergeant on duty. "XanChilxakxus." ZaphMordakai dipped his head in respect and motioned with his snout toward the generals. "Have they decided what city to attack next?"

The ancient blue dragon ignored him.

"Any idea if they are wrapping up soon?" The black dragon huffed, then glanced back toward the pebble beach.

"Not sure, but I wouldn't leave." The ancient blue dragon furrowed his brow. "The drakaina can wait."

"Maybe you should let the females know, Xan." The black dragon chortled as the blue shook his head.

"You will address me formally. We are not friends." XanChilxakxus paid him no heed, staring at the generals, and sighing extravagantly.

ZaphMordakai's eyes flared wide. *No respect! I bet I could kill you with two lightning bolts. Although, could I get the second one off before his first attack? One frost or steam blast from the ancient dragon would put me at Death's Door, and win or lose, Ledaedra's wrath would be brutal. Where is the Queen?* "Is that a hint of jealousy I hear? Maybe you aren't too old to try the Rainbow Run yourself."

XanChilxakxus growled ferociously. "If you touch one female in my bloodline, I will shred you to pieces."

"Who's to say I haven't? Oh look, the generals are calling me." ZaphMordakai sauntered past the big blue with a wink. The sergeant roared so loud his eardrums shook. *Hmm, I guess he doesn't like rainbows.*

The dragon generals congregated around Ledaedra's onyx ledge, but she was nowhere to be seen. The Septragons, as they were sometimes referred to, had left an opening in the semicircle for ZaphMordakai to join.

Zaph was considered a large dragon, but not compared to the seven generals: three reds, three blacks, and a shadow drake. As he assumed his position in the semicircle, his eyes darted from one colossal giant to the next. One of them would have to die for him to make general. He barely dodged the snapping jaws of his neighbor on the left.

Most of the generals leered at him, while the rest shared a mixed expression of disdain and hatred.

The largest among them—even bigger than his uncle—was a red called BrimStrakenstone, Ledaedra's chief advisor. "TetraQuerahn did not answer the summons of the Queen, you will—"

"Where is the Queen? I haven't seen her in a while." Zaph's head rocked back to meet his gaze.

"She does not report to me, and I do not report to you." Wisps of smoke escaped Brim's nostrils.

"TetraQuerahn is one of five officers who didn't report. What makes him so special?" asked Zaph.

"Silence!" Jets of fire shot out twelve feet from the red dragon's nostrils. He took an intimidating step forward, the ground rumbling in response. "You will go to Darken Wood, find the large clearing, and personally escort him back—in pieces if necessary. Do you understand?" He took another step toward him.

Zaph scratched his neck involuntarily and retreated several steps. "I will leave immediately." He did not wait for a response or permission to leave before spinning to return in the direction he came from.

The giant blue sergeant sniggered as he bounded past him and launched himself into the air. XanChilxakxus called after him, "What about the drakaina?"

4

Wedding Preparation

Cymm

Cymm bounced toward the big barn door deep in thought, almost plowing into his uncle.

"Whoa, Cymm. Who were you talking to?" Uncle Daro scanned the immediate area.

"You wouldn't believe me if I told ya. What's up?" Cymm continued walking out into the barnyard.

Uncle Daro hesitated and glanced inside the barn. "Well, I . . . well—it's Talo's wedding." He wiped his forehead, beaded with sweat.

Cymm raised his eyebrows and cocked his head. "Yes?"

Uncle Daro sighed before everything came rushing out. "We estimated three to four hundred guests, but now it looks like five to six hundred. I already spent all the coin you gave me, and even if I had coin to spare, the nearby villages have made it clear they are stockpiling for the growing season."

Cymm smirked while clapping his uncle on the shoulder. "I have plenty of coin. I will head to Armak tomorrow and be back in time for the wedding. Harvest is almost over; do you want to come?"

"Nah, we have a lot to do here. I can't afford to lose you either, but we don't have a choice. Thank you, Cymm."

They left the barn opening together, then split off toward their homes to get ready for dinner.

All I want is to spend time with Lykinnia. As soon as the wedding is over, that's where I'm heading. A forceful shove on the back of his left shoulder sent him stumbling forward, and he barely managed to stay on his feet.

His warhorse, the culprit, gave a loud whinny and pranced about.

"Very funny. We just ran out of apples for the next couple of days."

The warhorse's eyes went wide, and he croaked.

Cymm stroked his withers. "Ever since we visited Lykinnia, I swear you understand words as well as clicks and whistles. You like apples?"

The horse marched in place, causing Cymm's arms to flail high above his head.

"Are you done horsing around?" His cousin Talo jogged over, passing Uncle Daro on the way.

"Not funny. Save your coin and buy a magic potion of laughter." Cymm tilted his nose up and rolled his eyes.

Talo charged swiftly, catching him by surprise with a grappling bearhug, and the wrestling match began.

"Are you sure you want to do this?" Cymm reversed positions using an arm bar.

"Oww—when did you learn that move?" Talo disengaged, rubbing his shoulder.

"You should practice with your little sister Cela. She could teach you a few moves," Cymm sniggered.

Talo continued to massage his arm and crept closer, then charged. "You're not very funny either."

"Wow, what a great come ba—Oww!" Cymm massaged the bulging muscle on his forearm.

"You're not the only one who's learned new tricks." Talo punched him in the chest next. "You might be stronger, but I am quicker." Talo ran for the house calling over his shoulder, "And by the way, you're starting to sound like Old-Man Semper."

Cymm watched his cousin disappear into his house. He was not sure which one hurt more, the knuckle to his forearm, the punch to his chest, or the Semper comment.

ooooo

Two days later, in the late afternoon, the gates of Armak appeared on the horizon shortly before Cymm arrived at the location he had delivered the three dragon heads. Two of them were partially stripped of flesh and skin, the last, sun-bleached bone. The brilliant white dragon skull shone from a distance, a tiny sparkle against the green and tan backdrop.

The guards at the gate turned away most travelers, sending them to the north side of the city. He waited patiently for his turn, even as the two sentries thoroughly searched the large wagon in front of him.

A stoic guard motioned him forward. "What business do you have in the city?"

"I'll only be here for a day. After I buy supplies, I'll return to my village," Cymm replied.

"There is no resting or sleeping in the streets. You are permitted entry." The guard stepped to the side, waving him through.

Cymm passed through the gates with no other travelers in his vicinity, then proceeded to the first intersection. These streets bustled with activity, and it took him a few moments to merge into the flow. He nudged his warhorse with his heels to quicken their pace, fearing the vendors would be closing for the day. As he rode past the apothecary—the one he had visited several months earlier—yelling, screaming, and laughing filled the air. Despite the noise, two wolfers trying to get their snarling, circling companions under control, drew his attention.

"Watch out!"

Cymm's head whipped back around to the front, and he heaved on the lead as children cut straight across the street in front of him. His heart pounded; he had almost trampled them. He had never seen the streets this busy before, so he resumed at a slower speed, entering the market twenty minutes later. A smile slowly spread across his face while staring at the merchant he had hired two months prior to deliver supplies to his village.

The merchant finished with his current customer and their eyes met. "Cymm! What brings you back to Armak?"

Cymm extended his hand, and they shook heartily. "Hi, Forst. I have another shopping list, I'm afraid."

A grin pulled at the corners of the merchant's mouth. "Do you need a wagoneer?"

"Probably two. Can you get your hands on a rolling cage?"

The merchant scratched his head. "Yeah, and my son can drive the other wagon if it's all the same to you."

"Might need a team of four to pull the cage. It will have three large boars inside." Cymm paused, waiting for a response.

"What's in the other wagon?" asked Forst.

"You will need to use the same large wagon as last time, and it will be full. Ten bags of grain, sacks of apples, lemons, pears, carrots, potatoes, and lentils. Plus, a dozen pheasants in stackable cages and a few wheels of cheese. We can pick it all up tomorrow morning before leaving. I will let some of the vendors know tonight. We will also need guards for the caravan." Cymm scanned the market. Some of the vendors were packing up for the day.

Forst pressed on unabated, "Sounds like we need two teams of four. I'll set it up. I can also cover the carrots and potatoes, and my friend will give you a good deal on the apples and pears."

"Great, I will see you here shortly after sunrise." Cymm patted the merchant on the shoulder and continued into the market. He mentally ran through the checklist of other items he needed: S*ugar, spices, nuts, and olives. I hope I'm not forgetting anything.*

He made his way past tables and stalls, engaging with some vendors and declining the advances from others. By the time the market wound down, he had already purchased most of the spices he needed. He had varying-sized sacks of caraway, nutmeg, cardamom, ginger, cinnamon, and pepper, but could not find any saffron. He encountered another issue with his Aunt Nové's famous pottage. She needed carrots, potatoes, and lentils to complete her recipe. Hopefully tomorrow he would find someone selling lentils.

Cymm's last conversation was with a farmer who claimed he could provide three boars, but they would have to be slaughtered before entering the city. This presented a problem as the wedding was a month away and the animals would need to arrive in Stallion Rise alive. They agreed to meet outside the city gates before noon.

Satisfied with what he had accomplished, Cymm headed over to the Temple of Terazhan. The crowded streets bustled with evening activity. On his previous visit to Armak, he had requested to sleep in the temple, where horses were not allowed. Cymm had tied his warhorse to a ring mounted into the stone wall outside for the night. It had seemed safe enough back then. It felt like a lifetime, but that was only three months ago.

Two haggard women exited an alley and extended their hands toward him. "Hey, can you spare a copper?" one asked.

Caught off-guard, he stammered, "Sp-spare what?"

They furtively peeked up and down the street, then one grabbed the other, and they disappeared back into the alley.

Two town guards approached on patrol, strolling past him without a glance.

He returned to his musings. The amount of change in such a brief time concerned him. The influx of refugees was straining all aspects of the city, and although horse rustling was not common, during these hard times anything was possible. He boarded his horse in the stables attached to the Broken Horse Inn and walked the short distance to the temple.

Cymm entered and knelt before the heptagonal dais to pray. He paused, realizing something was different. Distracted, he searched his memory as he scanned the room. His brow furrowed. The once opulent room of gold and silver had been replaced by wood, even the holy symbols. All the paintings had been removed from the walls, the lace drapes were now cloth, and the velvet seat cushions, leather. Most disturbing of all, the massive holy symbol in the center of the dais had been chained to the floor.

Rising quickly, Cymm headed back into the rectory to find a priest. His progress ended abruptly at a locked door. The hallway behind it led to the private quarters of the three priests he had met before. He banged on the door and waited. After a minute, he banged on it much louder and longer.

Another minute passed and a boot scuffed against the floor followed by another before someone yelled, "It's late. Come back in the morning."

"It is Cymm Reich, First Paladin of Terazhan. I wish to speak with you."

Whispering ensued between several individuals before the same voice responded, "Cymm, it is not safe at night. Come back in the morning."

Cymm stood dumbfounded. Before he could reply, shuffling feet receded down the hallway. He scratched the back of his head, then lifted his hand to pound the door. He exhaled sharply, lowered his arm, and returned to the dais. He prayed for guidance and the health of his household and village, before heading to the Broken Horse Inn.

The street traffic had dwindled significantly. A block away, light spilled out of the tavern accompanied by a chorus of rowdy patrons. The cacophony grew louder as he approached, but it was too jumbled to make out anything specific. He entered through a propped open door and felt a sense of relief as several familiarities assaulted his senses. The pleasant aroma of bread, stew, and ale made him hesitate in the doorway so he could draw another deep breath. The owner barked out orders from behind the bar into the kitchen as she wiped down a recently vacated spot at the counter. Even Lord Barrister sat at his usual table with two of his *goons.*

Cymm headed toward the empty spot at the bar and with each step the crowd became more subdued, causing him to survey his surroundings.

Lord Barrister had risen and stared at him intently. "Is it Cymm Reich?"

The paladin could not read his deadpan face. "Yes. I see the wound on your arm healed nicely, Lord Barrister."

"Thanks to you. Please, join me." The First Sword to the King made a flourish toward his table and the open chair.

Cymm hesitated for a moment. *Is this for show? The last time I was here the townsfolk sided with me over him, and he doesn't seem like the type to forget.* The eager faces throughout the bar convinced him to accept the invitation.

"Huzzah!" yelled several patrons in succession.

"That's Cymm?" asked someone as he passed by.

A stranger stood in front of him and shook his hand.

The other two members of the King's Guard rose when Cymm pulled the chair out from under the table. It scraped loudly against the wooden floor, causing the young man to grimace.

Lord Barrister motioned toward the man on his right. "I believe you already know Lord Grom. He is originally from the Horse Clan."

Cymm extended his hand across the table, and Grom shook it heartily, causing the ring mail sleeves around his massive biceps to jangle. Although he was only a few inches shorter than the paladin, the breadth of his chest, hips, and shoulders made him look like a giant dwarf.

Barrister then pointed across the table. "And this is Lord Bostak from the War Dog Clan."

Cymm reached across his own body to shake Bostak's hand, and before the party of four sat, the noise level in the bar had already returned to normal.

Barrister grinned. "Beer?"

The paladin nodded.

The First Sword caught the attention of a serving wench as she passed. "Four tankards of Red Rye."

Cymm shifted uncomfortably. "Red Rye?"

Barrister's brow creased and lifted, while the other two snickered. "Don't mind them. You're going to like it. So, after you healed me, I heard you passed through Armak and hired a caravan to transport supplies to your village."

"Dragons attacked Stallion Rise many twilights ago, and we're still trying to recover. Those supplies will help us make it through the growing season." Cymm noted Grom's nod of approval.

"We could use a dozen more men like you," Barrister added his admiration. "I'm afraid many of those seeking refuge here in the city and along the north wall will starve to death before the next harvest."

The waitress returned with four large steins, placing them on the table in front of each man. "Can I getcha anything to eat?"

Barrister puffed like a peacock. "Let's start with a platter of meat and cheese, plus a couple loaves of bread."

She disappeared without a word as each man hoisted his beer.

Barrister offered a short, heartfelt toast, "To Cymm, for saving my life!"

Cymm gawked but tried to wipe his face clean of expression. He *clanged* his tankard into theirs, then banged it on the table, in the customary plainsmen tradition before taking a large quaff.

"Whoa, that *is* good." Cymm's mind drifted back to Warhez's special brew. *Maybe not that good, but tasty.*

Bostak finally broke his silence, "Cymm, are the rumors true? I hear you brought dragon heads to the city?"

Cymm cleared his throat.

"What he really wants to know is how you convinced the beasts to give up their heads?" Grom asked to Barrister's amusement.

"The rumors are true. The three green dragons that destroyed my village and murdered my family were dealt with. If I could slay every dragon in this world, I would!" Cymm slammed his fist on the table, making the tankards jump. "Actually, I have a genius friend, maybe she can figure out how to exterminate them before they do the same to us."

The three guardsmen glanced at each other during an awkward silence.

Bostak shrugged then whistled. "Anyone who can slay three dragons should be able to eliminate one demon."

"There is no demon!" Grom growled the words through clenched teeth.

Barrister's face screwed up, and he leaned back folding his arms over his chest. "You walked into their lair, lopped off their heads, then carried the massive things hundreds of miles to Armak?"

Cymm eyed each man. *Maybe this was Barrister's ulterior motive all along.*

The other two men continued to glare at each other, uninterested in their leader's line of questioning.

DragonSin, the sword strapped to his back, stirred. *"Be careful. The answers you give may lead to questions he never considered."*

"I only fought one at a time, and fortunately, a clan of hill giants helped me. The dragons stole their home, killing some and enslaving the rest. As for the dragon head monument, I cleared it with the King himself. Did I do something wrong?"

Bostak waved his hand at Cymm nonchalantly. "No, you're fine." He glanced quickly at Grom. "Can you help us with our demon—"

"There is no demon!" Grom's neck bulged, and he pointed at Bostak.

Barrister scanned the immediate area. In a low tone, he said, "Keep it down."

The waitress arrived with a large platter of food, placing it in the center of the table, along with loaves of bread.

Barrister continued to speak softly, "There have been unsubstantiated reports of a creature in tent city, north of the wall."

The waitress collected two empty tankards. "Not a creature, a black demon with two heads—"

"To the dungeons of Delge with you woman. Be gone!" Barrister shooed the waitress away.

"Bring another round of reds on your way back." Grom swirled his finger in the air.

Bostak smirked at the waitress, nodding his head up and down.

"A two-headed demon?" Cymm sniggered.

Bostak's expression transformed into a frown. "Yes, with red pulsing orbs in its eye sockets capable of draining your energy."

Cymm choked on a gulp of beer, then coughed repeatedly to clear his lungs. *What? How can that be? That sounds like—*

"Don't worry Cymm. We will protect you from the Bogman," cried Grom, causing everyone to burst into laughter, including Cymm.

However, Cymm's laugh was more reserved. *Maybe this creature will be able to shed some light on my aura, or at least explain why it wanted to kill the dragonfly.*

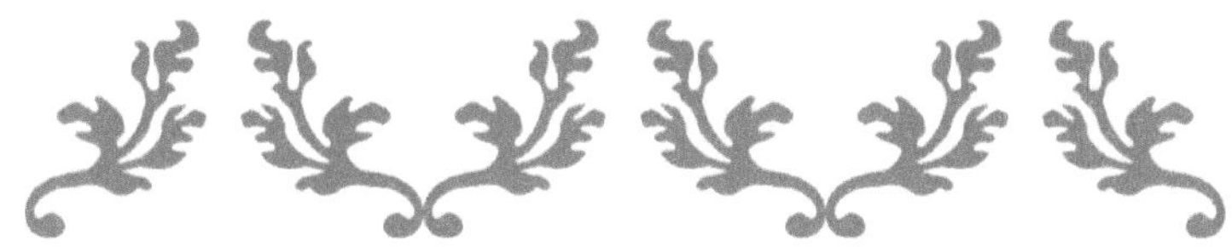

5

Time

Lykinnia

Lykinnia's palms slowly lifted off the altar, she sighed heavily, and her shoulders slumped. "I do not like having to trick Cymm."

"Do you think I enjoy lying to your father? He will be furious when he finds out." Solar tucked his wings tight to his body, the motion accentuating his physique, which was completely exposed above the shingled skirt he wore.

Lykinnia blew out a forceful breath. "You are not lying, just leaving parts of the story out."

Solar shook his head. "A lie by omission is still a lie."

"We made a deal yesterday. I help you investigate Cymm's power, and you teach me how to use the Altar of One to see my mother's death." Lykinnia placed her hands on her hips and stomped her foot.

"I have been your babysitter for a thousand years. Your millennial lifeday cannot come soon enough! What do you hope to gain from watching your mother die? It will only bring you more pain and sorrow." Solar's dour face did not relent.

Lykinnia was not ready to tell anyone her mother might be alive. *First, I need to validate the details this creature shared with me and separate fact from fiction.* "I could not possibly suffer more than I already am. This will bring me some closure."

"Fine!" Solar snapped. "Put your hands on the altar like this. They must start at this angle, then rotate both hands toward each other until your center fingers point at each other. While they are rotating, you must focus on the date or a specific image you have seen before."

"Ahh, and I questioned Cymm about his childhood to narrow down the date he gained his power." *It was more like an interrogation, which the faithful Cymm endured.* She quickly rubbed her temples. *I will make it up to him.*

Solar had been about to respond before his handsome face twisted. "Everything all right little unicorn?"

"Do not call me that! You know I do not like it."

"When you get mad, your nostrils flare like a little unicorn's." Solar pointed toward her nose.

Lykinnia fixed him with a cold stare. "Move over."

Solar yielded his spot in front of the altar as Lykinnia pushed into position. She placed her hands exactly as shown and rotated them. "Like this?"

"Yes. Perfect. Now, this time, try to focus on a recent event and see if the scrying window will appear for you." Solar stepped back a few feet with an arrogant flare, as if to say, "Good luck . . . you will need it."

Undaunted, Lykinnia focused her mind and performed the sequence as instructed. The scrying window appeared immediately. Within, an image of her golden, ethereal form stood next to Cymm. Her recent feelings of stress, anger, and sorrow melted away instantly, replaced by a deep yearning to be with him and to hold his hand. Solar's sputtering and stammering distracted her, and the window evaporated.

She scowled at the flummoxed Solar. "What is your problem?"

His eyes darted from the now empty space above the altar to her eyes, then back again. "No one has ever conjured a scrying window on their first attempt."

The intellectual prodigy flipped her dangling hair behind her shoulder with the flick of her wrist. "Well . . . not *no one.*" She feigned arrogance, then giggled.

"Lykinnia! Be serious for once. You do not understand how significant this is." Solar gazed off into the distance.

"The image appeared quickly within the window. Did you notice?" she asked.

"Yes, it is determined by how far back in time you travel. The image you recalled only happened fifteen minutes ago, so it appeared quickly. If you wanted to observe your mother's accident, it would take twenty or thirty minutes. Or to witness your own genesis would take an hour." Solar's wings flared for emphasis.

"How sweet. Every time you want to see my original lifeday, you wait for an entire hour?"

"No. If I want to see my little Unie's first breath, it appears instantly because I was there and can visualize it. And for your information, I do enjoy returning to those first couple of centuries when you were cute, adorable, and did not know everything."

His sincerity gave her pause. *He must have called me his little Unie-corn thousands of times and I used to like it.* The faint smile on her face turned into a frown. N*ow he uses it to mock me and emphasize my immaturity.* "How far back have you gone?" she asked, intentionally changing the subject.

"Not much further. It takes too long to get there, and unless it is important, my patience is limited. Do you have any questions of merit?" Solar's bored expression accompanied a glimpse at his fingernails.

She pursed her lips, then released them as an idea flitted through her mind. "It does not have to take a long time to travel backward if you create waypoints."

His brow furrowed deeply. "Waypoints? What are you talking about?"

"If you wanted to travel back to the day before my genesis, how long would it take you?" Lykinnia did a pirouette while waiting for his response.

"An hour." Solar made a curt nod of his head.

"What if you instantly travel to my first lifeday, then switch to your slow monotonous process to travel back one more day? I calculate less than five minutes." She performed a plié, into a passé, then back to a plié.

"That will not work. You would have to . . ." Solar's brow furrowed deeply. ". . . yeah, it would not work because the—" Again, he paused, his eyes arcing from one corner of his lids to the other, then finally settling on her.

Lykinnia took a bow.

Solar's chiseled features contorted. "Are we done here?"

"One more question. If rotating my hands inward goes back in time, does rotating them outward go forward?" The priestess demonstrated the movement in the air in front of her.

"Unfortunately, it does not. You cannot travel into the future."

"You cannot, or you have not figured it out yet?"

"No, I mean the device only goes in one direction—backward."

Lykinnia pondered this for a moment. "You are assuming time is linear."

Solar ruffled his feathers. "Here we go again. Please enlighten me Miss Know-it-all."

"If I head east and keep going in a straight line, do I end up back here at this same spot?"

"Your point?"

"If you go back in time far enough, even past Creation, which is also the end of the world, you can travel back through the future to the present." Lykinnia spread her arms out with both palms up.

Solar scoffed. "You cannot *possibly* know that."

"By my calculations, we are currently in the third reset of creation." Lykinnia posted a wry smile.

"Blasphemy!" Solar threw his hands up, azure bolts of electricity zipping through his wings, touching each feather. He summoned a portal while storming toward it. "You go too far! One of these days—"

The portal imploded and disappeared with a *vrrrummp*.

"One of these days I am going to pluck a feather from your wings. Now, run along and report to my father."

6

The Mission

ZaphMordakai

ZaphMordakai circled high above the clearing in the forest. Hill giants had seized it. The heat from their bodies clearly illuminated the area, even in the inky dark, and they were plentiful. A growl rumbled in his chest. *I can easily kill ten, maybe twenty, but not fifty.* He touched down in the clearing far from the cave, and on the other side of a pile of uprooted trees.

He watched from a distance, expecting the darkness to conceal him. He froze, his infra-vision picking up three heat sources on the tree mound in front of him. *Where did they come from? They must be guarding the mound of trees and living in it also.* He dug his talons into the ground subconsciously and scoffed. *There are two clans, more than one hundred giants, and I need to be gone before daylight.*

Zaph took wing. He could not walk stealthily through the clearing. He swooped in, snatching the giant up high on the stack, rending his body before he could issue more than a groan. He dropped the body in a tree outside the clearing and banked around for his second pass.

ZaphMordakai seized the second giant mid-flight as well, absconding toward the far corner of the clearing. "If you yell, I will drop you." He followed his threat with a slight loosening of his grip.

The hill giant scrambled to grab his talons but did not utter a sound.

Five feet from the ground, the dragon released his prisoner, then landed close by.

The hill giant had not relinquished his club. He gripped it tightly, with the tip pointed down in a non-threatening manner. "What you want?"

"Where are the dragons who lived in this clearing?"

The hill giant swallowed hard. "Dey dead."

"All three of them?" Zaph asked.

Now the giant cleared his throat before speaking. "Yes, but we no kill!"

"Doubtful. Where are the bodies?" ZaphMordakai opened his maw and tiny bolts of lavender lightning danced between his teeth.

The tip of the giant's club came off the ground, slowly rising toward his waist. "We ate dem."

The black dragon's neck craned up, withdrawing his massive head. His eyes widened. A temporary paralysis overcame him while he replayed the comment. A loud thunderous roar accompanied raucous laughter. He recovered his wits moments before the hill giant's club smacked him on the snout. Zaph backhanded him with closed talons, knocking him to the side like a rag doll. "Do you want me to kill you?"

The hill giant attempted to rise twice before he succeeded. "You kill anyway."

"Show me where you discarded the bones." Zaph shifted his gaze toward the pile of trees, several torches were approaching. "If you don't show me, I will kill them all."

The giant watched the torches fan out. The boldness drained from his face and limbs. "Dis way!" The giant took off running away from the torches and skirted the edge of the forest for several minutes before plunging into the woods.

ZaphMordakai followed at a distance until a nauseating smell abruptly halted his progress. The stench assaulted the olfactory glands under his tongue, and he almost retched.

The hill giant pinched his nose, creating a nasal voice. "Right der." He pointed at three rotting carcasses.

One or more of the green dragon's hydrochloric sacs had recently burst, causing the black dragon's revulsion. He turned away from the gruesome smell. A scene unfolded in his memory; one he preferred not to repeat. A much younger version of him shredded a green dragon, tearing into a sac with his teeth, which exploded all over his face. It took weeks for the smell to go away. That putrid stench had left an imprint, and now resulted in uncontrollable gagging whenever he encountered it. His infra-vision yielded no benefit, but in the limited moonlight, something caught his attention. "Where are the dragons' heads?"

"Huh?"

"Where are the heads?" ZaphMordakai repeated slowly.

The giant shrugged. "Human kill dem, chop dem, take dem."

"One human killed three dragons?"

"Yes. Clan comin'."

Not possible. Zaph scanned the clearing through the trees. Several torches were approaching in the distance. "Where did he take them?"

"Traga tell da sky."

In the sky? This one must have been bashed in his head at some point. He turned around, leaving the bewildered giant, and pushed back into the clearing. *The sky?*

Torches and yelling descended on him from all directions.

Zaph considered wiping the forest floor clear of them. Instead, he stretched his wings and slowly took flight.

7

Tent City

Cymm

Cymm yawned, the effects of a sleepless night. The conversation with the King's Guard yesterday haunted him. If this demon was in Armak, it was not to be taken lightly or used as a tale to scare children. Cymm could not dismiss these stories so easily. The description matched too closely with what he had experienced as a child.

The paladin had already met Forst and finished shopping in the market. He had even found the lentils, saffron, and met the pig farmer outside the city to take possession of three large boars.

Forst and his son joined Cymm as the pig farmer departed, and after securing their loads. "We are all set. Ready to head out?" the old wagoneer asked.

Cymm pondered his response a moment longer. "I have business to attend to north of the city. You and the guardsmen should get started. I will catch up by nightfall."

Forst hesitated before conceding. "Alright. Be careful. It can be unpredictable up there."

Cymm had already begun doling out coins to the merchants and mercenaries. "Half wages up front, the rest upon completion, and possibly extra for a successful delivery."

All four smiled and one guard clapped the other on the back, giving Cymm the impression they were satisfied with the arrangement.

Without wasting another moment, he headed north along the outside wall, for Tent City. *It can't be a coincidence Lykinnia asked me about Dego only a couple of days ago, and now he reappears in the capital city. She must know something she isn't telling me.* He rubbed the back of his neck. *But if she does, why didn't she tell me? There must be a reason.* His anticipation of their next meeting continued to mount and painted a smile upon his face.

The corner of the city wall steadily approached, and the din in the distance brought him out of his reverie. Several guards congregated below the turret built into the wall, its point reaching forty feet into the sky. They casually observed him until he attempted to pass.

One guard rose from a wooden chair and pointed at him. "No horses beyond this point."

Cymm dismounted. "Can I walk him?"

"You got grass tassels in your ears? The Cap'n said *no horses.*" A second guard pointed angrily.

"What business do you have in Tent City?" asked the original guard.

Cymm crinkled his nose. "I am looking for someone."

A horse nickered from behind the guards. Several were tied to a hitching post.

A third guard stepped forward, elbowing his cohort. "He thinks he's going to find someone in there." They rolled their eyes at each other, sniggering.

The captain's eyes glimmered, then he glanced back at the guards. "Quiet, you half-orcs." His attention returned to the front. "I think you better head back to the city."

Cymm's face reddened. "Are you saying I can't enter?"

"There is no reason to enter. In fact, you will create more work for us when we must rescue you."

"And what is your name, captain?"

"Captain Beckwith. Why?"

Cymm took a deep breath, controlling his anger, and spoke with a steady voice. "I wonder what Lord Barrister will say, or Lords Grom and Bostak, when I tell them Captain *Beckwith* denied me entrance into Tent City."

The captain attempted to speak several times and settled for placing his hands on his own hips forcefully.

"Yes. Last night, we had dinner at the Broken Horse Inn and a few red ryes. I'm intrigued by these *strange occurrences* they mentioned happening in there." Cymm jutted his chin toward Tent City.

The captain's face drained of color. "You're Cymm Reich?"

Cymm squinted his eyes and nodded slowly.

The other guards slipped away to their previous positions, leveraging physical distance to sever their involvement.

The captain gulped, then laughed nervously. "My good friend, of course you can bring your horse with you. I don't know what I was thinking." The captain turned to leave.

Cymm replied, "No."

The captain begrudgingly spun back to face him, appearing smaller than he had a few minutes ago. His shoulders were rounded, and the air had been let out of his chest.

"The rules are the same for everyone. I will leave my horse hitched to the same post as the others. Will you keep an eye on him?"

The captain's face brightened immediately. "Yes—Yes! Absolutely."

A few minutes later, Cymm rounded the corner of the wall and stopped. The land fell away revealing thousands upon thousands of erected tarps made of linen, cloth, or animal skins. Densely packed temporary homes were haphazardly strewn across his field of vision, and stretched as far as his eye could see. Most of them were not securely fastened to anything and sections drooped or flapped in the wind.

He wound his way through the first wave, but quickly realized he had no idea where he was going.

"Do you have any food? I'm so hungry," a young boy with a swollen belly cried.

"Me too!" A half-naked girl grabbed ahold of the boy's hand, moaning.

He hesitated, scanning the area. "Where is your mother?"

The little girl ran forward and hugged his leg. "Come, I show you mama."

Cymm gently peeled her arms away, knelt beside her, and produced two sticks of jerky. "One for you, and one for your brother." He craned his neck, scanning in every direction. More children were peeking out from inside the nearby tents, and from the alleyways between them. Their clothes were worn and dirty, matching their hands and faces. He sighed, then picked a direction, and forged on.

Cymm kept the city wall in view on his right side to orient himself. After several minutes, two wolfers passed by with their wolves in the lead. "Hey, what village are you from?"

They scowled and kept walking. He considered pursuing them, but a small crowd of children blocked his way. They followed him like a parade.

He picked up his pace until a light tug on his backpack alerted him. If he were fishing in his pond back home, he would have called it a nibble. He spun around quickly to identify the culprit. A mass of desperate faces stared back. His anger subsided. *Culprit? Can I blame them?*

He knelt over his satchel, securing loose items, while empty hands were thrust in front of his face. The paladin produced several more sticks of dried jerky from his pack. These meager rations disappeared in seconds, however, the hands did not. He stood with a heavy heart and continued to wind his way through the endless tents.

His gaze was constantly returned by those with dirty, sad, or angry faces. *So much pain and suffering. Why Terazhan? Why can't we help them? I could buy food from the market and bring it here.*

DragonSin stirred. *"You will have more than children swarming you. Unless there is enough food for everybody, there will be a riot."*

Cymm's eyes welled. *"There must be something I can do!"*

"There is—defeat the dragons—then everyone can go back to their homes. Everything else is a short-term fix."

"I'm going to send a wagonload of food from the city, and we're going to figure out how to eliminate the dragons."

"Please. Please help." The pleading lacked harmony and droned on. The constant murmur solidified Cymm's resolve.

More hands touched him on his legs, grasped at his arms, and even rubbed his back.

How many of these children are orphans like me? Had the dragons killed their parents too? At least I have the Reich Household. I could be one of these kids, begging in the street, not even allowed in the city.

A significant yank on his pack jerked him around to face a child of no more than ten with a firm grip on a cut strap.

Cymm grabbed his roughspun tunic, gathering a handful at the neck and chest region before lifting him a foot off the ground. "Let go!"

The would-be thief struggled and squirmed, kicked and punched. He glared at Cymm, then spit in his face, but finally released the strap.

The paladin set him down gently, then pushed him away to create some space. He hefted his pack over the top of his bastard sword and moved on.

The touching returned immediately, as well as the din of begging.

"Please!"

"Food?"

"Copper?"

"Please."

Searing pain emanated from the right side of his jaw. While palpating the area, an object whizzed past his ear. He pulled his head into his shoulders. Children were throwing stones and darting into tight alleys between tents.

Small hands groped him, searching every pocket and fold in his clothing.

"Please."

"I'm hungry."

"Leave him alone!" A robed man held a wooden staff high above his head.

The children scattered like rats before a tomcat.

"Thank you." Cymm breathed heavily.

"Where you goin'?" the man asked.

Cymm tentatively scanned the area. "I am looking for someone."

"I can help." The wrinkles on the man's face deepened as he smiled, his outstretched hand accentuating his eagerness.

The good feeling coursing through Cymm's body disappeared as quickly as it came, and he glowered at the man.

The man with the staff's congenial expression melted away, while he raised one hand above his head and flicked it around in a tight circle. The children reappeared instantly and with renewed vigor, clutching his arms and legs.

"Horseman, help us."

"Please."

"I am so hungry."

"Give us some coins."

He began jogging, dodging in and out of alleys. His speed continued to increase and the clamor behind him dropped off. He passed an old woman repairing a tarp, for the second time. *By Ledaedra's bones! I'm running in circles.* His lungs were burning; this pace was not sustainable. He scanned the vicinity for a solution.

The little girl he first met appeared a few tents away. She waved to him enthusiastically. "This way."

Cymm followed her into an enclosed tent.

"I show you mama." She walked further into the shadows.

"Shhh." Cymm dropped to one knee, pulling the flaps closed, panting like a wolf in the heat of the day.

Stomping feet approached. "Where'd he go?"

"This way!"

A low moan came from behind, and he lurched. With eyes adjusting to the dimness, he peered into the dark recesses of the tent. Three figures huddled over a prone form. The moan came again.

"We don't have food, or anything of value," a childish voice said.

"Please leave," a huskier voice added.

Cymm placed his hands up in front of him. "Shhh . . . I mean you no harm."

"Krya, what have you done?" asked the same husky voice.

"I brought help for Mama."

The cacophony outside had all but disappeared, and Cymm turned to leave. A louder, agonizing groan froze him in his tracks. "What is wrong with her?"

The man contemplated the question. "Rotten food or tainted water? Don't know. She has severe stomach pains, and her body is hot to the touch."

Cymm dropped his backpack and knelt next to her. He pulled the covers down to her waist.

"What do you think you are doing?" The man angrily returned the covers to their former position, and a tug-of-war ensued.

Grunting between words, Cymm said, "I—can—help—her."

Kyra grabbed her father's arms and pulled on them with pleading eyes. "The bad man says he has magic." She turned her gaze on Cymm. "Are you really here to kill everyone in Tent City like the bad man says?"

The father stared at Cymm with a mix of confusion and fear.

"No. Did the man with the staff say that?" asked Cymm, but no one replied. He exposed the mother's swollen belly and placed both hands on it. If he did not know better, he might have thought she was pregnant. Her skin was hot to the touch and glistened with sweat. "Terazhan, The Almighty Healer, please provide me with the power to heal this woman."

A brilliant white aura filled the tent, illuminating every corner. The father's head snapped up with a glimmer of hope etched upon his face. The woman's distended belly slowly subsided, and her moaning vanished, replaced with a content sigh before she fell asleep.

The father let out a joyous sob, leaned over to hug his wife, reconsidered, and stood to hug Cymm instead. The children cheered and danced, holding each other's hands while spinning through the cramped space.

The paladin graciously accepted the praise. "Only because Terazhan is a merciful god." He knelt. "Kyra?"

The little girl ran to him and hugged him.

"What else did the bad man say?" asked Cymm.

She withdrew shyly, shaking her head. "Please don't eat me."

"What?" Cymm jerked back in response.

The brother spoke up, "He said you eat children when you get mad."

"I am not mad," replied Cymm. "And I don't eat children."

"How can I repay you this kindness?" asked the father.

"You already have by letting me hide in your home." Cymm gathered his nerve, preparing to exit.

"Wait." The father grabbed an old, raggedy cloak from the floor, shook it out, and brought it over. He moved Cymm's backpack to the front of his body and covered him with the linen robe.

Cymm examined his new attire. "I look like a fat friar. This might fool them." The pommel of his sword stuck out above his head, giving his cowl a pointy appearance. So, he loosened the belt he wore like a bandolier, and the sword drooped lower.

"Walk slowly and drag your leg like this." The father demonstrated.

The paladin practiced the movement. "What direction is the city wall?"

"Come, I will show you." The father stepped out of the tent.

Cymm waved to the children before following.

The father pointed off to the right. "You will find the wall in that direction. What is your name, young man?"

"Cymm Reich."

"Bless you Cymm Reich and Terazhan. You have given my family new hope."

Cymm glanced around nervously. He touched the man gently on his shoulder and left without a word.

Walking in a straight line was impossible, but he walked in the direction the man had pointed, and shortly the top of the wall came into view.

What am I doing here? I have no idea where I am going, or what I would do if I found the creature. He hesitated, dejection weighing heavily on him. After considering both directions, he headed back toward his horse. *I should have heeded the guard's warning and stayed out of Tent City.*

A stone whistled past his face a moment before something much larger struck him in the back. It forced the air from his lungs and made DragonSin ring like a bell. He scanned the ground and discovered a rock larger than his fist. Another stone the size of a walnut bounced off the side of his head.

"We found you, horseman."

Cymm pulled his hood back and noticed at least six teenagers with rocks in their hands surrounding him. "I don't want to hurt you. Let me pass." He untied the robe at his neck, let it fall to the ground, and placed one hand on the pommel of his sword.

Six rocks came hurtling at him, one straight for his face. None of them came within two feet before freezing in midair and falling to the ground.

"You're welcome," DragonSin said.

Cymm picked up a rock and hefted it in his hand.

"Cymm! They are kids. Misguided kids."

"They are the same age as me and they have me surrounded. Do you have a better idea?"

The crowd continued to swell, two and three deep around him.

"A show of force, maybe they will scat—" The sword went silent.

The other boys were grinning, whooping, and hollering. A slightly larger teenage boy with jet-black hair pushed through the pack.

"Ha, ha! He's here," one boy yelled.

"Now we'll see who gets hurt," cried another.

"Cymm, I sense a powerful evil." DragonSin warned.

"I sense it too."

The boy with jet-black hair continued to approach. "I was waiting to greet you a little further in, but you turned around. You weren't planning to leave already, were you?"

A shiver surged down Cymm's spine.

"You tell 'em Dego," encouraged a teenage boy.

8

Research

Lykinnia

Lykinnia sat at the table next to her abode, capturing notes, sketching timelines, and contemplating. Her eidetic memory did not require her to take notes, but capturing nice, neat research logs in a journal, and storing it on her shelf, made her feel good.

For the past two days, Lykinnia used her time at the altar to create a series of waypoints to help her navigate through time. She relived the first day she met Cymm and lingered awhile, before returning her focus to her mother's demise. However, she had not been able to negotiate her way to that timeline yet, mentally or physically.

She closed her journal and proceeded to the altar slowly, assuming Solar was finished. *Maybe, I do not want to know.* She recalled the day her father told her about the accident. A tightness gripped her throat even though it had occurred a long time ago. *Solar and my father watched it many times. If there was evidence she was alive . . .*

But the creature knew things. She scoffed. *I still cannot call it, Mother. Sendaria Moonbeam, if that was really her, had been my mother for six hundred years. This creature knew my favorite lullaby, story, and color, and it also knew the first spell I cast, how I arranged the books on my shelves, and the first animal I created in the Lower Darken Wood. Not to mention my first pet, the first time I touched a unicorn, and my favorite fruit.*

Lykinnia sighed. *Yet she cannot remember how she met Father, or which spell caused her accident. And what happened to her arm? If she was not dead, why did she not come back to me?* She could feel the heat escaping from the nape of her neck. *Until now, because she needs me to open a portal. Her story is so outlandish. Only I can reset the portal within her abode and summon her back into her home.*

Her contemplation ended, leaving her in the mood for an argument. "Spying again?"

"I do not spy." Solar's wings flared in agitation as he stood in front of the altar.

Lykinnia ducked under a wing and peeked into the scrying window. Cymm was inside a tent with a family. The children were dancing around in celebration. *Who are you saving this time?* she thought. Aloud she said, "Not spying huh?"

"I watch over him. He has enormous potential. How is the investigation going?"

"I have not made it there yet. I am refining my process and making waypoints."

"It is not an easy thing to watch. I understand your cautiousness." Solar fixed her with gentle eyes.

The heat rekindled inside her, forcing several mean and nasty comments to come to mind, but his penetrating, compassionate gaze doused the fire. "Did my parents love each other?"

"Why would you ask such a thing? Of course, they did." Solar continued muttering to himself. "Did they love each other?" His gaze returned to her. "Have I ever told you your father used the altar to watch over—"

"Spy." Lykinnia shook her head.

"*Watch over,* your mother. He saved her life, and everyone else on the ship, including her family." Solar folded his arms over his chest.

"Yes, I have heard this story many times before. An enormous waterspout was about to engulf the ship, and my father gave them safe passage, guiding the vessel to calmer waters." Lykinnia peeked into the window, Cymm was wearing a disguise and hobbling.

Solar followed her gaze and smiled at the young man's antics. "Once you get your waypoints worked out, you should go back and watch your parents, especially before you were born."

"Ick. Can we change the subject please?"

Solar nodded. "As you wish."

Lykinnia cleared her throat. "Does my mother show any signs of—suffering?"

"No. It is over in a flash."

Lykinnia's brow wrinkled. "That is not good."

"Excuse me?" Solar's confusion disappeared upon following her gaze to the scrying window.

"Cymm is getting pelted with rocks!"

The paladin discarded his robe moments before another wave of projectiles came hurtling in.

Solar's voice fluctuated as he said, "There is no need to worry. He is very resilient." All the rocks stopped in midair and fell to the ground. "See."

"I do not like it. Something does not feel right." The young priestess rubbed her newly upset stomach. "Can you help him?"

Solar emitted a hearty laugh. "Now you condone my *watching* over him?"

Lykinnia gave him a sassy face, then returned to watching as a larger boy with jet-black hair approached.

A smaller rock-throwing boy yelled, "You tell 'em Dego!"

Lykinnia and Solar found confusion on each other's faces. Finally, they both uttered, "Dego?"

"You are in the way. Move." Solar's eyes rolled up into the back of his head and rapid tremors zipped through his body.

The young priestess sputtered a response, then balled her hands into fists and thrust them straight down by her sides. She stomped off the altar, distancing herself before turning back around.

The sky had already darkened overtop of the platform. Solar's wings were flared, and his arms spread wide. He did not flinch as lightning bolts rained down around him and the Altar of One.

Terazhan materialized beside him.

9

Dego

Cymm

Cymm slid DragonSin from its scabbard and took several steps backward.

Dego motioned with his chin. "Careful. You don't want to hurt anyone."

A boy no more than five lifeyears grabbed his leg in a bearhug. "No hurt Durby!" With a sluggish lisp, he continued, "Bad man!"

"I'm not the bad man." Cymm tried unsuccessfully to detach the boy. With one eye on his adversary, he sheathed the sword, and with two hands, peeled the boy's arms off. He stepped back and reached for his sword. The little boy charged and grabbed hold again. Cymm sighed when he found the boy sucking on his leg, then grimaced in disgust.

A crowd of over one hundred had amassed in the small clearing of tents.

Dego folded his arms. "Do you feel sorry for him? Or does he make you feel uncomfortable?"

Cymm disengaged the boy again and picked him up at arm's length. "What?"

The boy was drooling and pointing at Cymm. "No hurt Durby!"

The dark-haired demon boy pressed on. "Can you tell he is slow-witted?

Cymm shifted uncomfortably. "Well—I . . ."

"I thought as much. How do you think someone with a genius intellect feels when they speak with you?"

A wave of insecurity smashed through his wall of confidence as Lykinnia came to mind. *What does she think of me? Am I a drooling idiot hugging her leg?* He locked a wordless gaze on Dego.

"It's okay, Cymm. No one is perfect."

He remembers me.

A grinning shadow head with sharp teeth appeared next to its human one. Sinister, red orbs blazed in its sockets. The aberration vanished as quickly as it came.

A six-inch black beetle with a blue iridescent sheen landed on the head of the boy in Cymm's outstretched arms. The boy screamed in pain.

Cymm foolishly tried to blow it off. Giving up on the futile attempt, he set the boy down and grabbed the beetle with his bare hands. When he yanked it off, a chunk of scalp came with it, leaving a bloody wound. He squeezed, trying to crush it, but its rugged carapace resisted. Finally, he threw it to the ground and stomped on it. A new beetle landed on his arm, and a few more whizzed by his face to land on spectators in the crowd. A low hum filled the air as dozens entered the area. He squashed the beetle on his arm, then quickly scanned the sky. "Oh, Terazhan help us."

Thousands were descending.

Screams emanated from every direction. People bolted for cover, tripping over tent stakes and each other. A few desperately plucked beetles from their skin or off a loved one, but there were too many. The beetles were drawn to those standing out in the open, swarming them quickly.

Dego's voice rang out above the chaos. "See what this man and his false god have brought? Death and destruction! Cymm, you have brought a plague upon these good people!"

Eyes filled with hatred followed him. Before he could find an escape route, several men charged him. He punched the first one in the face, knocking him out, then grabbed the second man's swinging arm and threw him into the third. The fourth, fifth, and sixth went flying off to the side, compliments of DragonSin. However, the next two men collided with Cymm, pummeling his face and chest.

Beetles crawled on everyone, including the fighting men. Two refugees collapsed on the ground, a mass of insects covering each one. It was difficult to tell what was under the writhing pile, and Cymm fought back the urge to wretch. A searing pain shot through his right calf and thigh. Beetles chewed his leg.

"This is only the beginning, Cymm. By the time I am done, everyone will hate you and your god of nothing. He is not even a god!"

Cymm's head involuntarily rocked back, and his arms shot out to the side. He screamed in agony as twin bolts of golden lightning struck each eye socket. His bones, muscles, and skin stretched until he reached a new stature of nine feet tall.

Cymm did not remember it hurting this bad. It seemed to go on forever, both the pain and his screaming.

10

In the Sky

ZaphMordakai

ZaphMordakai flew in lazy circles high above the clearing where the green dragons had been slain. After flying all night toward Fire Island, he realized his mistake.

BrimStrakenstone's voice rang out clearly in his mind, *"You will go to Darken Wood, find the large clearing, and personally escort him back—in pieces if necessary. Do you understand?"*

If I return with a story, I'm as good as dead. If I return with a claw or a tail, will that be good enough? He recalled past experiences with the big red. None of them had gone particularly well. *I can't take the chance. I must determine how a human could kill three dragons and fly their heads into the sky.* Zaph stroked the scar on his neck, contemplating the feasibility of it all.

He considered using his innate ability to commune with the dead but shook his head. *Even the oldest and wisest black dragon can't speak with the dead if their head is missing. However, the hill giant mentioned Traga.* Zaph breathed deeply and exhaled. *And that's who I will speak with.* Acting on impulse he dove, completed one final circle around the clearing to expend the speed he had built up, and landed heavily near the green dragon carcasses. He had noticed the night before how defensible this area would be in a fight.

The alarms and pandemonium blared before he landed. He issued a primordial roar announcing his arrival anyway. The hill giants poured out of both lairs like ants and spread across the clearing like a stain.

ZaphMordakai scratched the ground and inflated his lungs to appear as large as possible. It did nothing to deter the first wave of attackers. Without warning, he opened his maw. Thunder cracked the air in response, joined by a large lavender bolt of lightning. It forked before it struck the first hill giant and blasted three others, leaving heaps of twisted, smoking flesh in its wake. He reared up on his hind legs, buffeting the air with his immense wings. The giants struggled to advance.

"Where is Traga?" he bellowed at the throng. "Deliver her to me or I will kill you all!" He immediately cast his most formidable spell, and three large balls of lightning—at least four feet in diameter—rolled off his talons. They hovered mere inches off the ground.

The giants continued to amass their strength. He had underestimated their numbers. Seventy giants stood in front of him, spanning two deep from tree line to tree line. They had backed him into a corner. For the first time self-doubt rippled through his core.

Zaph extracted a spear sunk deep in his flank, he had never felt hit him. "One last chance—I want Traga. When I am done killing you, I will root out every last child in your dens. I will spare no one!"

A minor scuffle broke out. Two large hill giants restrained a third, smaller giant.

"No kill!" yelled the giant being held.

One of the bigger ones tried to silence the smaller one by covering the mouth with its hand.

The other large giant berated the held giant in its own language.

After feigning acceptance and breaking free, the third giant proclaimed, "I Traga. What want?"

"I want you to explain the entire battle between the green dragons and the human. Every detail." ZaphMordakai left his jaws slightly ajar, allowing tiny lightning bolts to dance between his teeth.

After a few moments of silence, Zaph motioned his right talons forward, sending a ball of lightning rolling toward the right flank of the giant army.

Traga ran forward waving her arms. "Traga talk."

Zaph halted the lightning ball with a quick flick of his talon. "Everyone else can leave."

11

Avatar

Lykinnia

Anger coursed through Lykinnia's veins. Her fists remained balled from when Terazhan stepped through the portal Solar created. Lightning continued to rain down around the altar and the two nine-foot-tall men.

Two golden bolts struck Terazhan, and he shrieked in pain as he shrunk three feet in stature.

Lykinnia crept toward the platform. Both men had their hands on the altar and appeared to be in a catatonic state. "You are in the way," she said in a mocking tone. Without hesitation, she placed her hands on the altar and sent her ethereal form to find Cymm in a place she had never been before.

She arrived moments later at the epicenter of chaos and instantly located Cymm towering over everyone. Insects swarmed the area attacking indiscriminately. A man created a living shield over his daughter to protect her, while beetles devoured his flesh. Others screamed as they ran hysterically for a perceived shelter. Lykinnia raced over to help but could do nothing. She growled in frustration as her hand passed through a child.

Terazhan, using Cymm in avatar form, raised his left hand straight above his head, and his right knee came up as he lifted off the ground. He continued to levitate higher until he reached forty feet, where he hovered and chanted words in a language unfamiliar to Lykinnia.

"Tybor sha leksha. Tir'fin dubleki raemil irstas tirianel sen'heil!" commanded Terazhan.

She concentrated intensely, trying to memorize each foreign word, until her mouth fell agape.

Tiny stars the size of snowflakes fell from the sky mixed with a shimmering golden haze. The stars twinkled as they descended in straight lines and transformed a struck beetle into an equivalent sized loaf of bread. When a star touched down on a humanoid, the ugly sores began to heal.

Smoke rose from the black-haired demon boy's body. After trying to avoid them in the beginning, he gave up. His skin turned dry and cracked, and finally, the husk burst into flames, revealing a two-headed ebony creature. Dego shivered violently and the remains of the human boy sloughed off, scattering to the ground around him.

By now, the stars had ceased to fall, and Terazhan, in Cymm's body, slowly descended to the ground.

Dego placed both tentacle-like arms on his hips, standing bold and cocky. "You know you can't hurt me. Haven't we been through this before?" His attention abruptly switched to Lykinnia. "What are you?"

Her father noticed her for the first time, and shock streamed across his avatar's face.

She hesitantly backed away.

Dego's tentacle arm whipped out sixty feet and wrapped around her neck.

"This is not possible." Lykinnia struggled to free herself. "I am in ethereal form."

Dego cackled wildly, reeling her struggling form in slowly. "However, this one can be hurt."

"No!" Terazhan screamed and slammed the avatar's fists together. A massive lightning bolt exploded at the union, speeding toward Dego.

Dego's confidence never wavered until the bolt blasted a cantaloupe-sized hole in his chest. Both heads examined the damage, then turned toward each other in horror, before returning their gaze to the avatar. Too late, another bolt was incoming.

Lykinnia wriggled free after the second impact, and she raced to hide behind her father.

The common folk began throwing rocks again, not only the older boys, but the adults too. The rocks hit Dego this time.

One of Dego's heads hung limply and listed side to side. "You'll pay for this." He clutched his chest and shrank in size.

Lykinnia watched Dego transform into an eight-inch black scorpion and skitter away.

"Do not let him escape!" Terazhan bellowed. With several giant strides, he loomed over the arachnid and raised his foot to stomp on it.

"No hurt Durby!" the little boy cried. He stumbled forward and fell over the top of Dego, protecting him with his body.

The avatar's foot descended rapidly, then halted inches from the boy's head.

Cymm's voice rang out from nowhere, "No, you will not use my body to slay an innocent boy."

"Fool! That is not a boy. It is the demon's imp," Terazhan shouted with the avatar's foot suspended in the air.

Cymm remained steadfast.

"Run Durby!" The imp boy scurried away, no longer impeded by his previous ailments, with a black tar spreading across his torso.

The young man's conviction drained, leaving an emptiness inside.

"Lykinnia, you must leave now!" The avatar was only eight feet tall and shrinking fast.

I will not be told what to do. She continued to watch over Cymm, he was almost back to normal size.

"Catch him. He is going to fall!" she yelled at anyone listening, but no one came to help.

Cymm staggered one way, then the other, attempting valiantly to remain standing, before he collapsed. He struck the ground with a loud *thwack*.

Lykinnia's hands burned. *How odd, usually a pain in my head signals my time to leave.* She flew circles around the area to the same groups of people. "Help him! He saved your lives. What is wrong with you?"

The pain in her hands had intensified, and she could hardly concentrate. She approached a woman healed by the falling stars. "He saved your life. Help him."

She turned and walked away.

Two men with giant wolves came forward and knelt beside Cymm. One rolled him onto his back. "Are you sure it's him?"

Lykinnia sighed in relief. "Thank you."

Before releasing her form back to her physical body, the pain surged in her burning hands, and she screamed in agony. Instantly, she reappeared at the altar. Her hands splayed upon its red-hot surface. Smoke billowed from between her fingers, and her skin sizzled. She tried to retract them, but they were stuck, burnt onto the altar. "Help me!" she wailed.

"She is back." Terazhan rushed to his daughter's aid, using his own burnt hands.

"I will get this one!" Solar yelled, working to remove the other hand.

Lykinnia's screaming grew louder and more intense. Her hands finally ripped free from the surface, leaving most of the flesh from her palms and fingers on the altar and exposing bone in numerous locations.

With one final ear-piercing cry, she fainted.

12

Surveillance

ZaphMordakai

ZaphMordakai contemplated the battle he observed from high above. It had captivated his interest more than anything else in recent years. The cast of characters in this real-life play included a two-headed black creature, a flying golden, ethereal humanoid, and a levitating giant man, who could change size, cast powerful spells, and carried a sword with a magnificent green aura.

For a fleeting moment, he had considered entering the fray when the urge to fight had tingled beneath his scales. *Oh, the fun I'd have had, battling the golden thing. Even the black one, too.*

He pictured the unfazed creature taking the two direct lightning-bolt hits and wondered if he could have put it down. He might never know, but what he *did* know was that the generals would be extremely interested in this information.

I need to focus on my mission and avoid these distractions. Traga's story had generated more questions. He had traveled south like she had indicated. *Where would he have taken them?*

He continued to soar at a high altitude, not willing to risk an attack from a ballista or wizard. He had successfully observed the combat below from the far side of the encampment, away from the wall. *The generals have not decided on the next city to strike, but if I have anything to say about it, it will be this one. And this time I will be among the phalanxes of reds and blacks laying ruin to everything. Nothing will remain standing.* In his fury, he almost missed the white glimmer reflecting in the sun's rays.

The glare came from an object close to the gate. He banked around, approaching it from the opposite side of the city. He stared intently, consumed with validating his assumption. *Is that—a dragon skull?* A javelin came whistling in, and he barely rotated in time. *It is, and the horns indicate a green dragon's skull.* He ground his teeth as another javelin ripped through the soft, highly sensitive membrane of his right wing. He pulled up short and arced into the sky.

I will return under the cover of darkness and see what the dead have to say.

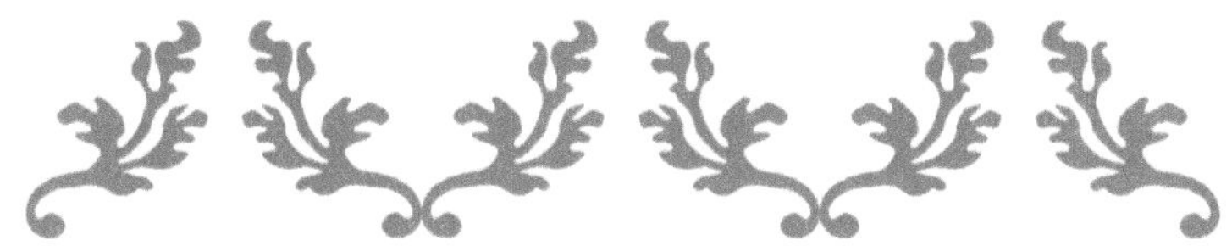

13

Balance

Lykinnia

Lykinnia awoke in her own bed with Solar pacing the room.

Solar mouthed the words, "She is awake."

Terazhan instantly appeared. "Lykinnia, what were you thinking? I told you it was time to—"

The priestess stared at her hands in horror. The flesh was no longer smoking, but it was charred black, and the smallest finger on each hand was missing. She rotated her wrists observing both sides. The center of her palms had been spared, but from her thumb to the furthest finger, the prominent ridge of each hand had been scorched and the white of bone could be seen.

She stared in disgust at the gruesome sight. Her eyes filled with tears and lifted to meet her father's angry stare. "I wanted to help."

Terazhan's visage softened, and he sighed heavily. "The healing is basic for me, but it will take some time for the finger to regenerate. Why did you not listen to me? I only want to protect you."

Lykinnia could recite this speech if necessary and had several legitimate arguments against it. She would debate vehemently about how old she was, or how smart she was, or that there was more than one way to do things. *It is easier to argue when you know you are right. How could I have been so wrong?* She nodded, not knowing what else to do. "Why did the altar get so hot? Did the demon do it?"

"Let me take care of your injuries, then we can talk," Terazhan answered.

"Okay. But why did Dego say you could not hurt him, and how did he grab me in my ethereal form? And—"

"Lykinnia, give me your hands." Terazhan reached over and snatched them out of the air. Chanting quickly followed in the same language he had used before. "Tybor istalya sen'heil laherim."

A smile tugged at the corners of her mouth. *How beautiful.* Her rumination ended abruptly with a sharp stabbing pain from her missing extremities. The bone snapped and cracked before a white bump protruded like a sapling tree erupting from the earth. A golden cross lattice appeared on her present fingers and palm, replacing the missing flesh before transforming into real skin and tissue. The garish wounds disappeared, and a skin flap formed over the missing digits.

"They will continue to grow for the next few days," replied Terazhan to his daughter's unasked question.

Lykinnia flexed her hand, wiggling the fingers she could. She formed a fist and nodded.

"I am glad you are satisfied with the outcome, *Lykinnia*! None of us will be able to use the altar for at least a day." Solar made an exaggerated motion to heal his own scarlet and blistered hands.

She scowled, realizing he had intentionally waited to heal himself in order to drive home his point. "A day of well-deserved privacy for Cymm!" she hollered back.

"I have other duties besides babysitting you and your *boyfriend*."

The priestess could feel the heat of embarrassment wash over her face. "I do not—he is not—" She stomped her foot and screamed in exasperation.

Solar smiled smugly.

Terazhan shook his head. "I thought you had a dozen questions."

She quickly accepted the lifeline from her father. "Yes, I do. Why did the altar get so hot?"

Solar jumped in swiftly, "It is designed for only one person to use at a time, not *three*, genius. Not to mention the added strain from using the ancient language of *The One*."

Terazhan shot him a glare.

"Language of *The One*?" Lykinnia studied her father.

Terazhan sighed heavily, giving Solar another sideward glance. "A thousand years, Solar. One thousand years. I wish to speak with my daughter alone. You may leave."

Solar opened a portal and disappeared without a word.

"Father, I thought you were The One? And now this strange new language . . ."

"Your mother and I decided many years ago to shield you from the atrocities of this world until you came of age. I have done my best to uphold our agreement."

"You are not making any sense. Who or what is Dego?"

"I think I better start at the beginning." He pursed his lips and paused for a moment of contemplation. "During the Age of Fire, Malekai and his army of demons fought against his twin brother Marekai and his horde of devils."

Lykinnia twirled her hand. "I know this, Father. What does this—"

Terazhan cleared his throat and fixed his gaze on her.

"Sorry. Please continue." She fidgeted with her hair.

"For a millennium, the demons and devils fought for dominion over the planes, with neither side gaining an advantage over the other. After centuries of experimenting, Malekai finally created The Ebony Shard, a talisman of immense power and malevolence. Unknowingly or uncaringly, he simultaneously created the White Shard."

"An opposite and equal reaction."

"Exactly. Dego is the Ebony Shard." Terazhan paused.

She squirmed under his intent gaze. "The dragonfly is the White Shard?"

Terazhan nodded in confirmation.

Lykinnia pondered this revelation for a moment before she gasped. "Wait a minute. If you destroy Dego—"

"I am not sure I can, but if I did, it would destroy the White Shard, which would probably kill your friend, Cymm."

Lykinnia took a deep breath and sighed. "Any more good news to share?"

"Since you like puzzles, here is another piece. Malekai used Dego to win a decisive battle over the devils, ending The Blood War. The demigods and deities formed an alliance to avoid a future ruled by Malekai, and to slay the remaining demons and devils. Using Dego to channel and magnify his power, Malekai was too powerful for us to stop. He slaughtered several of us before Dego abandoned him, allowing us to slay him and banish him from the material plane, ushering in the Age of Wonder."

"Wow. Thanks, Dego, for being a traitor," Lykinnia said.

"We searched incessantly for Malekai's phylactery of power to eradicate him permanently, to no avail, and two hundred years later he returned." Terazhan shook his head slowly.

Lykinnia tilted her head. "Is that why Dego said you already tried to kill him?"

"No. After Malekai was defeated, I came across Dego on the battlefield. He must have intentionally waited until I was alone. He attempted to make a deal with me. In my anger and arrogance, I attacked with all my power, and Dego laughed with his hands on his hips. Before he could retaliate, I created a portal—and fled."

Lykinnia knew how hard it must be for her father to admit this, and she placed her mangled hands on his forearm. "Dego said you were not a god. What did he mean?"

"By the pure definition of the word, I am not a god. In fact, there is only one God, my father. He is immortal, has no phylactery of power, no limit on his life span, and cannot be banished from any of the planes."

"Then he is *The One*, and the ancient language I have heard you use recently . . ."

"Is the only language he communicates in." Terazhan finished her thought.

"Why have I never met him?"

"You cannot meet him. Not even I have *met* him. He used to talk to me telepathically, but it has been a long time since our last conversation. I have tried to atone for whatever wrong I committed, but it has not helped. So, you should take things more seriously."

Here we go. A nice father-daughter conversation is about to morph into a lecture. She crossed her arms and scrunched one side of her face. Many seconds rolled by, feeling like an eternity to Lykinnia.

"I will assume your inquisitiveness is satiated for the moment. I have many things to attend to." With a tip of his head and a wink, he was gone.

By Melandri's good grace, what was that? No lecture. No punishment. Lykinnia scrutinized her nubs. They had already grown to the thickness of a fingernail. She abruptly reached out telepathically, "*Father! One more question?*" There was no answer. "I suppose I have exceeded my daily allotment of time. I wonder what deal Dego tried to make?"

An urge to check on the temperature of the altar forced Lykinnia from bed. She found Solar attempting to clean it when she arrived.

"Did you taste it?" Lykinnia nodded toward the cooked flesh she left on the altar. "It smelled pretty good, did it not?"

Solar cringed and shook his head disapprovingly.

"What? I would have tasted yours. My guess is *yours* tastes like chicken." She strummed the feathers on his wings. "And Father's would be dry and dusty, probably no taste at all."

This brought a smile to Solar's face.

"Oh, ho ho. The stoic Solar thinks I am funny."

"Witty at best. Go fill this bowl with water from the pool so we can boil the remnants loose."

14

Lethargic

Cymm

Cymm awoke in a tent with several strangers huddled close, inspecting him. His vision went in and out of focus. He had an extreme headache, and his body pulsed in pain with every heartbeat.

"Are you sure it's him?" asked a timid voice.

"Silak will be here shortly. He was at the trial. Whoa, look at this sword!" replied a husky voice.

"Maybe he killed him and took the necklace," the original voice said.

Cymm thought back to the battle with Dego. "I didn't . . . kill anybody." His head lolled to the side and bounced back up. He was unsure if he was lying down or standing. His eyes rolled up in his head, then back to center.

A scream startled him awake again, followed by a grunt and the clash of a sword hitting the ground.

"Father, what happened?" A young man, a couple of lifeyears younger than him, raced over to a burly, broad-shouldered man.

The large man turned; his right arm hung limp at his side. "I don't know. The sword did something to my hand."

Cymm's mind continued to swim. "Leave—my sword—alone."

Two more men came rushing into the tent through a flap with daggers in hand. "What is going on in here?" They both gave Cymm a stern look.

"I grabbed his sword and it—vibrated." He lifted his dead arm with his good one and let it fall.

The two newcomers burst out laughing.

"It's not funny, Silak! It hurts and tingles."

The last statement caused a resurgence of merriment.

Cymm tilted his head from side-to-side slowly. To his right several giant wolves were sprawled on the floor. He reached out toward them—

He could not move his arms or his legs. With blurry eyes, he discovered the rope around his ankles. He was tied to a large wooden pole buried in the ground. "Let me go."

The men were speaking in hushed tones, and even if he were not groggy, he did not think he would be able to recognize the words.

He struggled against the restraints, trying to pull his arms free, but he felt so weak.

His mind strained to understand what had happened. *Dego escaped. More like I allowed him to get away. What else?* His heavy eyelids fluttered closed for several seconds.

"Prepare him for travel. We leave before Primordian rises," Silak commanded. The sound of the tent flap and his heavy footsteps signaled his retreat.

"We should kill him and divide his stuff," whispered the man with the limp arm.

The other man carefully sheathed the sword with two hands on the scabbard and wrapped it in a cloak. "I wouldn't recommend defying his order. If he doesn't kill you, the boss will."

15

Commune

ZaphMordakai

ZaphMordakai waited until the night sky was as dark as it would get. Only the meager crimson light from Phoenix disrupted the dark shadows. The black dragon raced toward the city gate, gliding a mere ten feet above the ground. His outstretched wings were stationary, barely providing the lift he required to stay aloft. Any sound at this point could prove fatal.

He touched down as close to his target as possible with a scrape of his talons on a hidden rock in the grass. Quickly, he scanned the ramparts of the city wall, expecting a swift response. There were no alarms or movement from that direction.

Tiny lavender sparks emanated from his pupils before black shadows burst forth from the same apertures. They congealed together, then stretched to engulf the closest dragon head and the space between them. His neck craned forward, forcing his own head into the inky blackness.

Silence. In this shroud of death, nothing stirred. ZaphMordakai pushed in closer.

"Why do you disturb me?" A chilling voice shattered the stillness.

The black dragon could feel his breath rumble in his throat. "You will answer my questions, or I'll ensure your peace is disturbed for eternity. Do you understand me?"

Silence.

Zaph's anger mounted with each passing second.

The green dragon spirit wailed in agony. "Yes! Yes! I understand."

"What is your name?"

"Ennozarius."

"Ennozarius, one of the rare twin dragons?" ZaphMordakai asked, already knowing the answer.

"Yes."

Zaph's impatience boiled over, and he exerted his will. The green dragon cried out in agony again. "Quite verbose, I see. Tell me how you died."

"You don't care how I died. You're looking for the spell book TetraQuerahn—"

"Tell me how you died!"

"A human fell from above onto the bridge of my snout and slammed his sword through my eye into my brain. Even as it scorched my eyeball, it radiated searing pain throughout my mind." Ennozarius's voice reflected the pain she must have felt in her dying moments.

"The human could fly?" the black dragon asked doubtfully.

"No. I was in my lair, and he dropped from one of the tree trunks in the ceiling."

This human needs to be taught a lesson. Not only does he kill three dragons, but he takes their heads for souvenirs and displays them as trophies for everyone to see. He contemplated asking about her sister's death. The added stress and anguish could strain the link or even sever it. "How will I know this human?"

"His name is Cymm Reich, and he is from a small village called Stallion Rise. His sword is easy to distinguish. It has a large emerald and a green haze about it." Ennozarius's voice perked up a bit. "Are you going to kill him?"

"I've seen this weapon recently." *This Cymm Reich travels with some interesting company.* ZaphMordakai considered his next question carefully.

Ennozarius whispered, "It spoke to me."

ZaphMordakai's lip quivered with micro tremors. "What?"

"The sword, it spoke to me . . ."

The black dragon stifled his merriment. "You crazy drakaina."

"Do not call me that! The sword spoke to me."

"What did it say then?"

Ennozarius paused for a long moment. "Momma."

"I don't have time for this insanity. Do you know what happened to TetraQuerahn or your sister?" ZaphMordakai's head trembled. *No, not now.*

"Anekzarius? Is she all right?" asked the green dragon with terror in her voice.

The globe of darkness wavered.

ZaphMordakai growled. *If I lose this connection, it will be severed forever. I do not have time for a summons.* The black dragon resisted the pulsations again. *My Queen, please give me a few moments.*

Attend me now!

With one massive cerebral pulse, the dark sphere, and the link to Ennozarius burst into a shower of lavender sparks before disappearing forever. He growled. *Even an ancient black dragon cannot commune with the same spirit twice.*

He pushed his anger down deep before completing the summons. A shade in the form of Ledaedra instantly appeared before him. The shadow dragon protruding from her back snapped at him.

The black dragon's head bowed, almost touching the ground. "Please forgive me, my Queen. I was communing with the dead green dragons, an assignment from the Septragons."

In a raspy, echoing voice, Ledaedra said, "I don't care. First and final warning."

Voices called from the ramparts above him.

"Yes, my Queen." Zaph's legs pumped furiously.

Ledaedra floated next to him effortlessly. "I have a new assignment for you. Head south to the city of Norfolk. It lies in the foothills of the Knife-Edge Mountains, next to a large river, about three hundred leagues away. There will be further instruction when you arrive."

Arrows zipped past him, and in his current state of mind, he could not tell if he had been hit or by how many.

16

Searching

Lykinnia

Lykinnia arrived at the altar—now sufficiently cooled—two days later in the mid-afternoon to find Solar frantically pacing the width of the platform. He stopped mid-stride as soon as he saw her.

"This is your fault." He ran his hand through his hair and massaged his own neck.

Lykinnia's smile instantly disappeared. *This again.* She swallowed hard, holding her tongue.

Solar mumbled incoherently. His lined face accentuated the weariness of his appearance.

The priestess continued to approach at a much slower pace, with a wave of panic deep in her gut. "What is the matter, Solar?"

"I cannot find your boyfriend anywhere."

The muscles in her jawline quivered in response, but again, she did not retaliate. "Travel back to the battle with Dego, then follow him until you figure out where he went."

The disdain on Solar's face was obvious. "I already tried. The altar is not functioning properly, or something is distorting the view."

Lykinnia's eyes rotated slowly in a circle, pausing four separate times as they made a complete rotation. "He was heading back to his village after he bought the supplies he needed."

"I checked. The caravan recently arrived without Cymm. In fact, his uncle had to search Cymm's house for coins to pay the drivers and guards."

"Did you check the entire city?"

"Hardly. With all the refugees, Armak's population approaches that of the City of Mystics. I have been looking for over six hours. I told your father I would watch over him."

Lykinnia touched Solar's arm. "What if we work together?"

He withdrew and gave her a stern glare.

Lykinnia threw her hands up in submission. "I would not *use* the altar, merely observe over your shoulder."

Solar continued to stare, unmoving.

"Then let me use the altar to see my mother's death!"

The winged man ignored her and summoned a scrying window.

After several moments of staring from a distance, Lykinnia strode toward the altar with purpose, and placed herself off to the side behind him. Although she was tall, viewing anything over his shoulder was impossible. She giggled at the thought but cut it short with a sideways glance at Solar.

Solar rapidly wove through Tent City, barely pausing to identify the people he passed.

Lykinnia felt dizzy, and her stomach churned in retaliation. She tilted her head back and breathed in deep. *This is madness. After two days, he would not be in the same place.* She closed her eyes, reveling in the sun's rays as they warmed her face. The queasiness passed. *He likes the Broken Horse Inn, maybe he is staying there, or with the priests at the Temple of Terazhan. Wait a minute. Where is his horse?* Her eyes blinked open. "Solar, head back to the city tavern. We need to find Cymm's horse."

The frenzied pace immediately slowed, then halted. After several seconds, Solar lifted into the air, levitating high above the tents. He rotated, giving Lykinnia a panoramic view before heading toward the city wall. He skirted it, turned the corner, and hesitated for several moments, apparently studying several horses tied to a hitch.

Solar abruptly closed the scrying window and turned to face Lykinnia. "He left his horse tied to a hitching post with the other horses, and now his horse is gone." With no further comments, he created a portal behind himself and backpedaled through.

"But that was two days ago," she called after him.

ꝏꝏꝏ

The following day, Lykinnia returned to the altar in the early afternoon to find Solar back at it. She approached the platform quietly, trying not to disturb him.

Upon peering into the window, she drew a sharp breath. Solar had found Cymm's horse in a stall, part of a massive stable. The horse, recently brushed, calmly ate from the ladened troth.

Lykinnia scanned the surroundings again. The nearby stalls were occupied, but no one roamed through the area. *How did he find you?* Minor relief flowed through her. *Are you worried about Cymm too? It does not look like it.*

The scrying window disappeared, and Solar met her gaze.

"I am sorry. I was trying to be quiet."

Solar nodded to placate her. "You had a good idea to search for his horse." He even offered a smile for the first time in two days.

Lykinnia's mood brightened immediately. "How did you find him?"

"There are fewer places to look for horses in a city. I found him a couple of hours ago in the city stables, well cared for. I have been waiting for someone to appear to figure out how he got there."

She took a couple of steps backward while giving a flourishing wave toward the altar. "Thank you for the update. Is there anything I can do?"

He barely shook his head in reply before a scrying window reappeared. His attention diverted from Lykinnia to the images in the floating frame above the altar.

The priestess sauntered over to join Solar, but after staring at the horse's hindquarters for several moments, she returned to her abode to study.

17

Princess

ZaphMordakai

The black dragon had arrived near the city of Norfolk the prior afternoon but had yet to receive a summons. The city was much larger than he had anticipated. ZaphMordakai would need reinforcements to assist if before he could be expected to attack. The sun was already past its zenith in the late afternoon sky. He was taking a break from zapping a nearby boulder with lightning bolts to keep his boredom and frustration at bay when his head buzzed, and he answered the summons immediately.

Even in the midday sun, the shade of Ledaedra had minimal features. It sucked the surrounding light in like a black hole, emitting none in return.

"My Queen!" he replied with a grand genuflection.

"In the mountains, not far from here, there is a cave. It is the recent lair of a young green lieutenant. I have asked him to prepare for your arrival. Tomorrow, Princess Jenaleya returns home from the city of

Tinel, and you will capture your first descendant. Do it before the royal caravan gets too close to the city and keep her in the cave until I provide further direction."

ZaphMordakai's heart swelled. "Yes, my Queen."

Ledaedra had already disappeared.

18

Prisoner

Cymm

Cymm awoke dazed and bleary-eyed. Small tremors ran through his body. His teeth chattered rhythmically against each other. Although his hands and feet remained tied, he could lift his head to view his surroundings. A wave of nausea raced through his body, forcing him to lie back down. He was in a wagon packed with general food stores, tools, and finger-cane cages holding various birds, being pulled through the grasslands by wolves and humans. The carriage jerked to a stop causing everything around him to shift.

"Water," he begged with a raspy voice. "Please. Give me some water." Lykinnia conjuring vessels of water infiltrated his foggy mind.

The man closest to him chuckled, placing a water skin gently to his mouth. "Help yourself."

A familiarity assaulted Cymm's mind as he chugged the slightly sweetened liquid. He drank his fill, squinted up at the midday sun, and fell back asleep.

ꝏꝏꝏ

When Cymm woke again he was trussed and gagged, lying on the dirt floor of a large cage made of wooden poles lashed together. He struggled to sit up, but the rope and his pounding headache prevented it. A cool breeze whistled through the bars and buffeted his hair.

His captor approached with a laugh he recognized. "Want some water?"

Cymm shook his head, mumbling against the gag.

The jailer untied the knot securing the door and entered. "This is good water. You need to be awake for what happens next." He held up a water skin. "Want it?"

Cymm hesitated. *If he wanted me dead . . .* He nodded. *Where in the nine hells am I?*

The man removed the ball of linen stuffed in his mouth. "Don't want you dying of thirst." He poured water in his mouth one gulp at a time."

While drinking, Cymm fixated on an angry scar running from the man's ear to his chin, which he attempted to hide with a beard. However, the large fissure in his stubble could not be concealed, no matter how long his facial hair was. Cymm sighed in relief, his head feeling better already. A fire snapped and crackled in the distance, and the tantalizing scent of a roasting pig wafted past his nose. His stomach gurgled. "Can I get something to eat?"

"No need for food. Should be tomorrow or the next at most." The jailor peered into the adjoining cage. He stoppered the container and exited. "As long as I don't hear any noise, I won't cut your tongue out."

Cymm dared to scan the other pen. The wooden bars were three times as thick, the gaps twice as small, blocking parts of his view. At first, he could not penetrate the dark shadows, but eventually, a form took shape. A four-legged creature sprawled in the far corner, twitched.

Cymm assumed it was a sleeping wolf, given he was in the middle of a wolf village. He remembered what Torak had told him about the "severe punishment" a wolf would receive if it killed the livestock. *Is that why you're imprisoned?*

A pitiful moan came from the other cell, accompanied by more severe twitching.

Despite his situation, Cymm smiled, recalling the nights he slept next to Torc. He had received multiple kicks in the back while the dire wolf ran in his sleep.

The moans continued, interspersed with whines and whimpers.

Although Cymm had recently awoken, the fatigue had already returned to both his mind and body. *I have slept enough these past few days. What am I doing here?* He fought the urge to close his eyes and lost. He forced them open. There was no time to sleep. He needed to figure out an escape. Even shifting his position did not help. His eyelids fluttered, and he lost consciousness.

He awoke with a racing heart, ripped from sleep by a pack of baying wolves. He shifted his weight, allowing blood to flow into his numb arm, while listening to several wolfers yelling at each other in the distance.

A subtle noise from behind paralyzed every bit of him, except for the short hairs on the back of his neck. The creaking and cracking of the wooden poles grew louder. He inhaled deeply and turned.

The hot breath of the imprisoned wolf blasted him in the face from only a foot away. It shoved its muzzle through the cage without regard to injury. Part of its flews had already torn, and it had compressed one eyeball to the extent it bulged out toward the bridge of its snout.

Cymm scrambled back, looking more like an inchworm than a human, with his arms and legs bound.

A growl rattled and ticked in the wolf's throat, sounding like a forge overheating. The wooden poles groaned louder as they resisted the latest force applied to them.

From behind the wolf emanated a hiss; it jumped and yelped in excruciating pain. It immediately withdrew its head from the bars.

A broad-shouldered man with a large belly quickly retracted a long, red-hot poker. The wolf slammed into the wall, right where the man had stood only a moment ago.

"Easy Jalko. You'll get your chance." The man with the poker jabbed it into the dire wolf's neck.

"We may not be able to wait until tomorrow," stated the man with the scar on his face.

"I invited others to attend the show. Reinforce both cages," the man brandishing the poker commanded.

The other nodded in compliance and stepped back.

Several arguments grew louder as the participants approached. When they arrived at the wolf's cage, a shroud of silence fell over them, only to be quickly replaced by the group talking over each other.

"It's true. He has the disease."

"He must be killed and buried far from the village."

"All the wolves are at risk!"

"It's highly contagious."

"We're leaving. We'll be back in a month."

"Silence!" yelled the man with the poker, and to Cymm's surprise they obeyed. "We will destroy the creature tomorrow and burn the body."

"How can you speak of Jalko so callously?" asked a wizened old man.

The old woman standing next to him hooked his elbow with hers and quickly led him away, her eyes wide with fear.

Cymm could not tell where her fear stemmed from, the wolf or the pot-bellied man with the poker.

A huge man with a baritone voice stuttered, obviously choosing his words wisely. He inclined his chin. "We don't know what causes the disease to spread. Waiting until tomorrow will put all our bindings at risk."

A snort to Cymm's left startled him.

His jailer had noiselessly repositioned himself on the far side of the cages, away from the argument. He stared through the bars at the big man, muttering, "You might not know, but I do."

Thirty to forty wolfers now surrounded the cages, with more continuing to arrive. Cymm scanned the crowd, trying to determine if anyone cared he was bound and caged like an animal, when the mob parted like dragon flesh sliced by his sword.

Cymm's chest constricted, and a knot formed in his stomach. He had met the man currently sauntering through the newly created aisle. He was the lead elder at my trial, which means I am in Endurance Rise, and the man with the poker is—

"Brato! What is going on here?" said the elder.

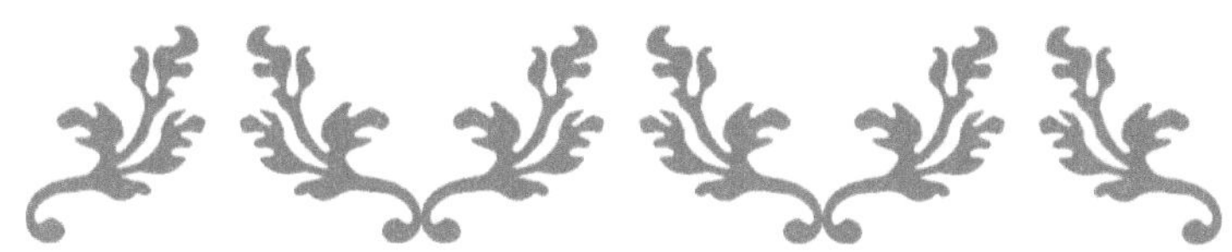

19

Mother

Lykinnia

The following morning, Lykinnia approached an unoccupied altar. Expecting to find Solar, she froze in place, scanning the area in a circle as if waiting for him to magically appear. Finally, she stepped up onto the platform and situated herself in the center.

The priestess placed her palms on the altar but hesitated. She danced a few steps to the right, closed her eyes, breathed in deep, then shuffled back to the left. She removed her hands and let them dangle at her sides while shaking out the stress and nervousness fogging her mind.

She sighed forcefully. "I wish—"

Lykinnia's hands shot out to the altar again, rotating until the window appeared. Inside, she sat at her stone table where she took her meals, and across from her was Cymm. A broad smile crossed her face, chasing away the furrowed brow and worry lines.

They both had a glass of wine, and she listened to herself brag about her research and studies.

"Do you ever get lonely up here?" Cymm asked her.

"I was not kidding before; I do not have many friends, but I do have my clerical studies. I also spend my free time learning arcane magic, like a wizard." Lykinnia rolled her eyes as she listened to herself.

He laughed. "Of course you do, because ninety-two languages and the responsibilities of a high-level priestess are not enough to keep you busy."

"Cymm Reich of Stallion Rise, I said fifty-six languages." Lykinnia giggled and wagged her finger at him.

She loved the way he made her laugh. Invigorated and bolstered by the memory, she began the time shift she had been dreading. Lykinnia had previously placed two waypoints conveniently bookending the event of her mother's death, and she *popped* into the first one. Her heart raced faster than it did around Cymm as she focused on the familiar scene in front of her.

Solar and young Lykinnia were playing her favorite game, Polymorph. Solar wore the guise of a pink goat with long braided chin hair and had the curly tail of a pig. The young priestess could not control her mirth and rolled on the ground, cackling in delight.

Solar bleated irritably, causing Lykinnia to pause momentarily before launching into more hysterical laughter. She finally dried her eyes and, with a wave of her hand, returned Solar to his proper form.

Solar cleared his throat and straightened his hair. "That is enough for today."

"One more! Please. Please. Please." Lykinnia tugged on his hand.

"I have already been a mountain dwarf, a purple worm, and now a goat. How about a new game?"

"Will you fly me around the perimeter of the Peak of Power?" asked the young lady.

Lykinnia's smile drifted away, and she turned her back on the scene. *This is it. The explosion occurs while I am in the air.* She left Solar and the little girl she once was behind and headed for their sleeping quarters on the backside of the plateau. Her heart rate accelerated again, but not from exertion since her movements required no effort. *Lykinnia, do not get your hopes up. If Father and Solar could not find any evidence, then how will you? But they are both men, maybe a woman's perspective—*

Do not get your hopes up! She gritted her teeth and clenched her fist. *If that creature lied to me . . .*

She stood in front of the door to her mother's abode, fists clenched, heart pounding. *Why am I doing this?* Her hand did not wait for a reply, the handle turned, and the door swung open.

"Mother?" Lykinnia grabbed the door frame for support. *Of course, she is here, you idiot.* She alternated between hyperventilating and body-racking sobs. She was not ready for this. She needed to leave and try again tomorrow. However, her feet did not respond.

The bouquet of floral scents and spicy aromas hung in the air, evoking happy memories of her childhood.

Her mother was arms-length away, the points of her elvish ears clearly visible, and framed by curly auburn locks. This was how she remembered her, Sendaria Moonbeam, standing tall in her jet-black robes, stern, demanding, driven, but loving. She was not one to worry needlessly, but on this day, she paced back and forth. A deep furrow creased her brow, and she was mumbling to herself.

Lykinnia shifted her perspective and her mother's face came into view. Although no wrinkles were present, overwhelming stress lines had taken a foothold between her eyebrows. *Solar said she was preparing to cast a dangerous spell or memorize one.* She ejected her emotions, and her scientific mind took over, staring and listening intently.

Her mother was muttering in Elven. *How peculiar. Arcane spells require clear annunciation, but she was mumbling. Furthermore, her mother had always used the common language to cast a spell.* After several iterations, Lykinnia picked up some of the clearer words and noticed a pattern. S*he is reciting a list or a twelve-step process. What am I missing?*

Lykinnia squeezed her temples with outstretched fingers and thumb, spinning a full circle to take in the scenery. Her mother's room was immaculate, as usual. Her bed was made, chairs pushed into the table, all her books lined up neatly on the shelves, and the material components for her spells cataloged and arranged carefully.

Sendaria continued to wring her hands while pacing.

Lykinnia examined her mother, cowl to boots, and cocked her head sideways. *What is on your robes?* She got down on her hands and knees to inspect it closer and found dashes of white and gray flecks along the bottom hem. Lykinnia wrinkled her nose. "Mother, I remember a time when I was playing tag with Solar and fell, getting green stains on my knees. You would not let me continue until I changed my clothes."

Sendaria stopped in the middle of the room, but not because she had heard her daughter. Her arms performed an intricate dance within the air, and her voice became loud and clear in the common tongue.

Lykinnia stared in amazement as her mother worked her magic, beginning her final incantation. *Is that soot on the palm of her hand?*

The room exploded in a maelstrom of hellfire, as if it were Bardonril's furnace. Although Lykinnia knew she was in no danger, her fear escalated as the inferno intensified, and the acrid stench of charred objects filled her nostrils. The density of the flames and smoke washed out everything more than a foot away. "Mother!" The surrounding cacophony swallowed any trace of her voice.

A couple of minutes transpired, and the fire disappeared as fast as it started, leaving piles of ash on the floor. Nothing else remained.

Lykinnia took a deep breath and rewound time to repeat the process, adding a waypoint as she entered her mother's abode.

Her emotions held no sway over her this time, not because she did not care, but because she did. This was her opportunity to prove decisively her mother might be alive. Her head swiveled from side-to-side taking it all in again.

A neatly made bed, books and components in order, and the rest of the room tidily kept.

Everything is in order, so why are you so disheveled Mother? Even though it has been four hundred years, I know you would never allow yourself to appear this way. There is soot on your hands, and flakes of ash on your robes before the accident. Where did the ash come from?

Lykinnia shook her head slowly. *Why would you perform such a dangerous spell indoors? Especially in your own room with so many valuable items, particularly, your spell books.*

"That is it!" She rushed over to the shelves, scanning them with her pointer finger extended and leading the way. Her eyes settled on a familiar tome with a dark brown leather binding and no discernable marking on the spine. She slid it from its resting place and scanned the front cover. With her finger she traced the lightly adorned patterns engraved into the thick leather binding. They were filled with moondust, causing it to glitter crimson red, even in the dark. Lykinnia knew the dust was from the acacia pepper, but her mother had told her she traveled to the moon Phoenix to retrieve it. There were images of a crescent moon, the sun, wandering ivy, and several geometric shapes.

It was the same spell book Cymm had brought her as a gift. Tears welled in her eyes at the implication. *If the book survived, then maybe she did.* Ecstatic, she leafed through several pages, then paused in stunned disbelief. Then the room roared to life with a fiery explosion.

The young priestess ended her reconnaissance mission and immediately returned to the altar. After taking several steps backward, she collapsed into a sitting position on the platform. Chills ran through her body. *No—it cannot be!* Her mind quickly processed dozens of permutations while beholding her new little fingers, now fully grown.

Lykinnia rose to her full height, pondering the latest information. She had much to discuss with the void creature, but first she needed a plan.

20

Assault

ZaphMordakai

Meanwhile, the green and black dragons were on a reconnaissance mission together. The royal caravan, their objective, was large enough to spot from high above. Ten knights rode in the vanguard, ten more in the rear, surrounding seven wagons, four of which were covered. The three uncovered wagons held crates, boxes, and chests presumably filled with general supplies.

The two dragons landed far from their target, and closer to the planned extraction point.

The green dragon half his size had recently been promoted to lieutenant. "I can fly over the knights and cover them in gas."

"BelCharius, what direction is the wind blowing?" asked ZaphMordakai.

"What? Who cares?" replied BelCharius, the green dragon.

"Ledaedra will if you kill the Princess in one of the middle wagons. The Queen will slit you neck to tail and turn you inside out."

The green dragon's bravado instantly evaporated, and he nodded. "Then what plan do you recommend?"

"We need to deal with the knights first, so this is what we will do." ZaphMordakai explained his plan in detail before sending him away.

"How did this halfwit become a lieutenant?" the black dragon vented aloud. He made several gestures with his talons while uttering the word "transform" in the ancient language of the dragons. A subdued *pop*, followed by the crackling of tiny violet lightning bolts, preceded the transformation of his enormous form into the body of a dark elf. ZaphMordakai continued walking down the road, heading toward the caravan, oblivious to the metamorphosis. His ears stood tall and pointy, while his eyes glowed like golden lamps. He was a few inches shy of six feet, with a barrel chest and stocky legs.

The caravan came into view twenty minutes later, and ZaphMordakai, dressed in a loincloth, proceeded toward them with no weapon.

As expected, several of the knights broke away from the group, cantering in his direction. Their full body armor glinted in the sun's rays. All four lowered their lances at the final approach.

The leader barked, "Drow, crawl back into the cave that birthed you! You are *not* welcome here."

ZaphMordakai slowly raised his arms and turned in a circle. "I am unarmed, and no threat. Let me pass."

A guard on the right thrust his lance forward, impaling him between his chest and shoulder.

Zaph stared at the leader and leaned into the weapon, driving it deeper. Although the tip tore through his bulky muscle, he felt minimal discomfort.

The leader sneered, glancing from side to side. "Tough guy wants to pass?" He laughed confidently. "I have never killed a drow before."

"And you likely never will, because I am not a dark elf."

The entire gang laughed this time.

"And I am not a human—"

"What if I were a dragon? Would you let me pass?" ZaphMordakai interrupted calmly.

The guard who wounded him replied, "If you were a dragon, I would shove this lance up your—"

"Dragon!" came the call from behind them loud and clear.

"It looks like you will get your chance, *tough guy*." ZaphMordakai pointed over the man's shoulder.

All four men turned, not noticing the miniature electrical surges pulsing in his fingers.

BelCharius roared while swooping in to snatch a rider. The man wriggled free, falling thirty feet, and landing with a loud, metallic *crunch*.

ZaphMordakai grabbed the lance and released pent-up electricity, electrocuting the wielder. He ripped the lance out of his body and sent lightning bolts racing off the end of each finger, hitting riders and their horses. The bodies of each quivered for countless seconds before collapsing into smoking heaps.

The remaining six from the vanguard had already moved to assist with the dragon, not realizing their error.

ZaphMordakai walked toward the caravan, carefully watching the wagons as they finally stopped.

The green dragon swooped again, angling his approach to avoid the wagons, and sprayed a cloud of chlorine gas. Horrendous cries escaped from several men and horses, adding to the confusion.

Two men in robes jumped out of a covered wagon, frantically scanning the sky. They fanned out once they saw BelCharius.

"There you are." ZaphMordakai raced forward with lavender balls of energy growing in his palms, a stark contrast to the charcoal color of his skin. He paused forty feet away from them and rolled the now sizable spheres at each target.

The wizards chanted, unaware of the danger approaching from behind. Their right arms dropped to their sides in synchronization, then with arms fully extended, circled back up from behind and released orange darts of plasma. The projectiles streaked toward BelCharius, as the dragon released another blast of death gas.

ZaphMordakai's fists flared open, and the balls of electricity erupted, emitting dozens of jolting arcs. The two wizards danced uncontrollably for ten seconds before bouncing off each other and falling to the ground.

The wagoneer immediately to his left, leaped from his perch toward him, two hands clenching a short sword. Twin bolts struck him at the zenith of his jump, throwing him dozens of feet off target and killing him.

Thanks to Zaph, BelCharius was prepared for a wizard's attack. The green dragon banked hard to his left, protecting his wings and exposing his underbelly. Tightly clutched in his talons flailed a guard he had snatched from a horse. The first dart struck the human in the leg, the other in the neck, and within seconds, BelCharius was carrying a stone statue, which he dropped on one of the remaining guards.

Six wagon drivers approached the black dragon in the guise of a dark elf, five with swords drawn. The unarmed man lagged behind until the others assumed defensive positions, then he continued past them. ZaphMordakai watched with amusement, static charge making audible *snaps* as it jumped from finger to finger.

BelCharius landed heavily in front of three remaining members of the vanguard and charged ferociously. He viciously swatted a warrior with his talons and decapitated and disemboweled the man with one swipe.

ZaphMordakai's attention returned to the coachmen. One knelt in front of him only ten feet away. *Hmm, finally a little respect.* "Get up and stand over here." He pointed off to his right side. To the others, he said, "Are you sure you want to do this?"

After mustering their courage, four of them charged, while the fifth threw down his sword and raced back through the wagon train.

ZaphMordakai unleashed his full arsenal of electricity on those charging him. Their smoking bodies flew backward dozens of paces, returning to the ground with a *splat* or a *crunch*.

The passengers in the covered wagons exited, attempting to flee in the same direction as the coachman.

"If you try to escape, I will kill you." ZaphMordakai stepped through the caravan line. Everyone stopped except the one wagon driver. Five spheres of pinkish-red energy, two inches in diameter, appeared instantly as he opened his hand wide. "I prefer lightning, but these never miss."

The coachman, at a full sprint, had already cleared two hundred feet when the dark elf punched the air in front of him. The balls of energy zipped forward at an incredible speed, impacting the man's back and pounding him to the ground. He quivered for a few moments before laying still.

BelCharius joined ZaphMordakai, chortling with his mouth full of horse meat. "You'll have to teach me that one."

The dark elf addressed the twelve survivors, "On the count of three, everyone will point at the Princess. If you're wrong or don't point you will die. One, two—three."

The humans hesitated only a moment before pointing at the same young woman. Even she slowly touched herself in the center of her chest.

"Load all the food and water in this wagon, and all the people in this one." Zaph nodded at each wagon. He then pointed at two random men. "You and you will drive."

The remaining coachman knelt again at his side. "Master elf, I can drive one of the wagons if you wish."

"No. What is your name, human?" asked the dark elf.

"Dyfar." He removed his hat and crumpled it with his hands, his gaze never leaving the ground.

"Do you have family in the city of Norfolk?"

"Yes."

"Then we both have something to lose if you do not follow my instructions exactly. I want you to return to the city and report this attack to the city guard. You will not mention I was here, only the green dragon. You are to tell them we headed for the mountains north of the city. Do you understand?"

Dyfar shuffled his feet. "Yes. What if they ask how I escaped?"

"Tell them you were left for dead, and when you woke, we were gone." ZaphMordakai stepped forward.

Dyfar's nose crinkled. "Left for—"

The forearm of the dark elf clobbered him on the side of his head and face. He collapsed like a rag doll.

BelCharius had wandered off to continue eating. He returned as ZaphMordakai finalized the departure preparations.

"What about the human?" BelCharius pointed his snout at the unconscious Dyfar.

"He has his assignment. He will deliver my message."

"The King will send out a search party by the end of the night. There's no need to let him return to the city. Let's nail him to the side of one of the wagons. When the King's men arrive, he can deliver the message before he dies." BelCharius's eyes grew wide with excitement.

"No! It is time to leave." ZaphMordakai turned dismissively, heading toward the front of the lead wagon.

"This is why the generals think you are weak."

ZaphMordakai whipped around, striding toward him. "What did you say?"

The green dragon gulped and searched side-to-side for an escape route.

ZaphMordakai grabbed the end of a lance stuck in the flank of the green dragon and pushed it deeper past the scales.

BelCharius moaned in pain before scampering backward, leaving a hole in his side. "I do not have such thoughts, but the generals do."

"Where did you hear this?"

BelCharius cleared his throat. "Many have heard the generals say this." He took several more steps backward.

ZaphMordakai tried to quell his fury by stroking his neck, but it was a futile attempt. The rage bottled up inside of him raced toward the lance in his other hand like a lightning rod, blasting it asunder. "Move these wagons now!"

21

Wolfbane

Cymm

Three hours past dawn, the arguing resumed. The crowd packed in tight on all sides of the cage with no wolves in sight.

Cymm's jailer sat near him on the other side of the barrier and nodded toward the adjacent cell. "Ain't long now. He's fully transformed. Not sure why the boss paid such a large bounty if he planned to feed you to the wolf."

Cymm ignored the comment. The new, thicker poles lining the cage were hard to overlook as Jalko hammered the wall between them, shaking the structure again. He took a deep breath and realized he had not prayed in quite a while. He positioned himself as best he could on his knees. "Lord Terazhan—"

A wooden staff descended upon his head, making his ears ring. "Brato said you might try to cast a spell. The next hit will be harder."

Cymm's eyes watered and his head throbbed. Anything harder and he was sure his skull would split. Another large tremor went through the walls of the cage with an audible *crack*.

The crowd went silent. Many retreated a couple of steps, even though the outer walls were much thicker than the one between him and Jalko.

Cymm glared at his warden. "Am I expected to fight him with my hands and feet bound?"

The jailer cackled in delight. "Fight him? Ten men couldn't fight him." He paused, glanced at Brato across the way, then growled, "Fine." He tossed a long dagger onto the ground next to Cymm.

The cage rumbled and creaked and there was a *crunch*.

Cymm quickly placed the dagger between his thighs with the blade pointed up and out so he could saw the ropes off his wrists. Immediately, he went to work on the ones around his legs.

The cage shook again, and poles snapped and cracked.

Jalko's head and one leg were in Cymm's cage.

The horseman cut the last bond, rolled over, stood, and fell, almost impaling himself with the dagger. He did not know how long it had been since he last stood. His legs, weak and stiff from disuse, could not support his weight and buckled.

Jalko roared and withdrew to his own cage.

Cymm stood slowly, wavering as he did. The blood and strength returned slowly to his muscles. The thudding of hooves like a galloping horse drew his attention toward the dividing wall as it exploded in a shower of wooden fragments. He fell again, shocked by the flurry of activity.

Jalko's balance, in contrast, was perfect. He shook his coat to dislodge the wood sticking to his blood-soaked fur, starting with his head, then his shoulders, right down to his tail. Wood and blood flew everywhere. The blood wolf fixed his scarlet eyes on Cymm, and a throaty growl boomed forth.

Cymm grabbed the wall for support and assumed a defensive posture with the dagger in his right hand.

Cries for Jalko's death ceased, but the macabre screams from spectators did not.

The enormous blood wolf stalked Cymm from the cage's perimeter. Jalko, formerly a dire wolf with a mixture of white and rust-brown fur, stood a full hand shorter than Torc. Now, his fur was matted and clumped with blood, his eyes bloodshot orbs, and thick strands of drool spiderwebbed between his teeth. Jalko lunged clumsily at Cymm, his newfound strength propelling him beyond his mark.

Cymm's clumsiness originated from the temporary weakness in his legs. He placed his back against an outside wall to stabilize himself, and Jalko pounced. The young man ducked, then tucked, and rolled off to the side in an awkward, lurching manner.

The blood wolf slammed into the wooden barricade with enough force to crack a beam and stagger himself for several seconds.

The crowd gasped, and pockets of dissent reappeared. A few turned to flee.

Cymm slowly regained his footing and positioned himself against a different wall, hefting the dagger in his hand.

Jalko charged.

Cymm stumbled to the side, then came back at the blood wolf, slamming the dagger into its neck, all the way to the hilt.

Unaffected, the blood wolf whirled on Cymm, ripping the dagger's handle out of his hand and sinking his fangs into Cymm's left thigh. Jalko whipped his head back and forth, eviscerating the muscle and tearing a chunk free.

Cymm collapsed to the ground with pain exploding in his mind and leg. Even with pain fogged thoughts, instinct took over, and he crawled backward away from the beast.

After swallowing the flesh and licking his jowls, tremors coursed through the blood wolf. The taste of Cymm's blood sent Jalko into a frenzy, and he leaped forward for more. As Cymm crawled backward, his hand fell upon a large wooden shard from the shattered wall. Cymm grabbed it, bringing it to bear in front of his face like a shield in the nick of time.

Jalko latched onto the broken pole, sinking one of his canines deep into the shaft.

Cymm let go and continued to scramble away. *If I can get into Jalko's cell, I might have time to heal myself.* He doubled his efforts, ignoring the bloody wound and the red trail he left behind.

Jalko shook his head frantically and chomped down hard, trying to dislodge the wood, and finally knocked it loose with his front paw. He sprang toward Cymm, who was already halfway through the broken wall. The shattered, splintered shafts protruding at weird angles kept the large wolf at bay. So, he clamped onto the young man's foot, right through his boot, piercing skin and cracking bones.

Cymm screamed in agony, and the pain heightened as the wolf dragged him back into his cell.

The jailer howled while he hammered his fist on the cage wall. "Don't worry. Humans can't catch the blood wolf disease. Not that it matters."

The paladin got his arm around the union of the lower wall beam and a thick pole, hugging it like it was his mother come back to life.

Jalko flailed, shaking his head wildly again, to extricate his prey.

The pain in Cymm's hip was excruciating. *If I don't let go, he'll rip me in half, but if I let go—*

Jalko flew backward from the force of his own pull with Cymm's dislodged boot in his mouth, and the young man wasted no time slipping through the broken wall. The blood wolf charged with a roar, bull-rushing the barrier, while Cymm began to pray.

22

Contact

Lykinnia

Lykinnia arrived at the altar mid-morning with a wry smile. She cast her invisibility spell, opening the rift to the other plane. "Creature," she called into the void. After several seconds of silence, she beckoned again, "Creature! We need to talk." Again, there was no reply.

After an extended period, a voice replied, "Maybe you should try using the word *mother*, instead of *creature*."

"Do not play games with me. There are several inconsistencies I noticed in the moments leading up to my *mother's* demise," Lykinnia replied tersely.

"And what might those be?"

"First, explain again how you survived the scorching inferno in your room." Lykinnia folded her arms over her chest and waited longer than she wanted. "This is the easy question. They get harder."

"There is nothing *easy* about it. You obviously have an issue with something I previously said, and you want me to repeat it. What is it?" replied the voice from the void.

This time Lykinnia remained quiet, except for her toe tapping on the stone platform.

A sigh of exasperation broke the silence. "Fine! I was attempting to cast a challenging spell; one I had recently learned. I must have forgotten a material, verbal, or gesture component, because the incantation accelerated uncontrollably, and a vortex opened, sucking me into it. Satisfied?"

Lykinnia performed a pirouette. "Yes. Now, where do I begin? If you were learning the spell, why did you not have your spell book out in front of you?"

The voice chuckled. "Although it was a new spell, I was not *learning* it. Where did you get that idea?"

She was about to pirouette again but stopped. "Both Father and Solar have told me you were working on a very dangerous, high-level spell."

"True. It is called Cataclysm, however, I was not trying to cast that spell."

Cataclysm? That is in the spell book I have. I will have to validate if she is telling the truth once I study the incantation further. "Do I have to ask what invocation you were attempting?"

"I was trying to teleport a fireball from—"

"What? That is insane!" Lykinnia took a seat on the stone platform and pulled her knees up close to her chest.

"Someone had to protect the Peak of Power. Did you think your father was going to?"

The fireball spell would explain the soot in the palm of her hand. Lykinnia ran her fingers through her hair. "Protect us from what?"

"Demons, dragons—unicorns."

Lykinnia giggled. "Very funny. Why do you recall so many details about me, but none about Father?"

The voice cleared her throat. "Do you have any more questions about my near death, Miss Detective?"

Evading my question about Father again? A heat wave rushed through Lykinnia's face. "What were you whispering in elvish before the spell began?"

"My dear, that was four centuries ago."

"How many times have you spoken elvish in the past four hundred years?" Lykinnia asked snidely.

The creature sighed. "This was not a good idea. Your skepticism has tainted our entire conversation. No, this entire reunion! What do I need to do or say to prove who I am?"

A devious smile appeared on Lykinnia's face, expecting the conversation to play out this way from the beginning. *Gotcha.* "Answer this one question. Why were all the pages in your spell books on the shelves—blank?"

23

Touch

Cymm

When Jalko hit the splintered prison wall, Cymm fully expected the creature to burst through it and into the cell he occupied. However, the impact rammed two wooden shards each, from the top and bottom, into the blood wolf's body. Instead of a ferocious, berserker-like response, the wolf yelped and whimpered, clinging to a vestige of its former self.

Cymm stopped mid-prayer, haunted by a loud *crack*. He could not tell if it was bone or wood. The *slurp* as the other shafts pierced soft tissue almost made him hurl. *He has the blood wolf disease,* he thought, trying to justify his emotional shift toward not caring, then it dawned on him, he had the ability to heal disease.

Any remnant of Jalko's essence faded, and he lurched forward, driving the spears deeper into his body, chomping at the air, furious he could not reach his quarry.

The blood draining from the paladin's body was taking its toll, and Cymm felt lightheaded. He ignored his own wounds and crawled toward Jalko, grabbing his paw with both hands. "Lord Terazhan, hear me, and heal this poor creature from the disease afflicting it!"

With a sharp snarl, Jalko ceased impaling himself and shook his ears like a bug had crawled inside his ear canal. The chaotic energy defining him only moments prior evaporated, and he appeared to be shrinking. The whining and whimpering returned as he attempted to retreat, but the wooden piercings held him fast.

Cymm pulled the dagger from the wolf's neck and cut the rope securing one of the massive splinters to the wall. He heaved and withdrew the spike from the wolf's lower abdomen. Blood continued to pump from his thigh and foot. He needed to heal himself quickly.
Jalko attempted to withdraw again, and with painstaking steps and whimpers, successfully retreated, removing the remaining three from his own body before collapsing next to Cymm. The wolf's head lolled to the side and crashed down, equally on the ground and Cymm's chest. The beast's long tongue flopped out smacking the young man in the neck and face. Its ragged breaths came in fits and starts. Jalko's blood-red eyes were already draining down each tear duct. As a blood wolf, he could survive the brutal damage to his body, but as he transitioned back to a dire wolf, he was dying.

Cymm pushed the slimy blood-coated tongue aside and prayed again. "Terazhan—" Cymm paused and blinked several times. His mouth had gone dry, and he fought the urge to lie down. "P-please grant me the power to heal this wolf. He did not deserve the . . ." Cymm saw the blinding white aura bloom before he passed out.

ꝏꝏꝏ

Cymm drifted along on a ragtag raft, the sun warming his face and body. The gurgling of the river interspersed with the lapping of water against the wooden slats. His small craft separated from the main flow, caught in an eddy, and gently rotated.

Splashing in the distance disrupted the tranquility—shortly after came panting. Both sounds grew louder, until a shadow fell upon him. Cymm opened tiny slits in his eyelids; an enormous beast loomed over him, but the backlight washed out most of the detail. Without a sound, the brute seized his boot with its mouth and hauled him off the raft into the water then onto the shore. He sputtered and coughed up water inadvertently trapped in his lungs and throat.

Eventually, he cleared the passage and took a deep breath, and immediately the creature mauled him. After several seconds of trying to fend off the attack, Cymm realized he had been licked a dozen times. He sat up, with the sun at his back and opened his eyes. A gigantic wolf stood in front of him, and a tall female approached.

"Can you please call off your wolf?" Cymm yelled.

"He's not my wolf." The woman reached down and patted his rump.

"Stop!" Cymm pushed the wolf away.

The wolf whimpered, then retreated several steps, where he laid down with his head on his paws. The wolf fixed Cymm with puppy-dog eyes, tail wagging.

Cymm's gaze returned to the woman. Planning to greet her, he attempted to rise but fell back to the ground with pain radiating through his leg.

"Please don't move." She rushed forward, kneeling beside him. "You've been grievously injured. The only thing keeping your soul from The Mistress is this dreamwalk you're on with your wolf."

"Dreamwalk? Who is The Mistress?" Cymm's eyes rolled up and he swooned. "This isn't my wolf!"

"Do not dismiss the wolf. He is the only thing keeping you alive right now." She gently eased his back to the ground and swiped his hair from his eyes. "I can help you if I have your consent."

Cymm popped up on his elbows. "I can heal myself—"

"Your god has no power here!" Deep lines of anger etched the woman's face before subsiding. "Do you want my help or not?"

"Fine. Please heal me."

A disturbing smile dawned upon her face. Without hesitation, she clamped onto his damaged thigh, the one missing a large chunk of flesh, with eyes blazing red and mouth chanting.

The wolf growled and slowly rose, baring his teeth.

"No!" Cymm yelled at the beast.

His new friend immediately returned to his former position with a whimper.

Cymm's leg burned with an internal fire, and he screamed in pain. However, this was nothing compared to the bone-snapping pops that came next as the hole in his leg filled with a blood-red lattice of new cells and repeated for his foot. His breathing slowed as the pain subsided.

"What in the nine hells did you do to me?" Cymm asked.

"I encased your soul and saved your life."

"I have healed myself many times, and it has never hurt before." Cymm rubbed his leg as ghost pain resurged.

"I can't *heal* you, since only your soul is present. Actually, I couldn't heal your body even in the material world."

Cymm gawked, his mouth agape.

"I am Azreala, Priestess of the Phoenix—"

"Jalko! Come back here now!" a voice called from behind Cymm.

The wolf jumped to his feet, snarling savagely toward the river.

Cymm rolled to his belly, pushed up on his knees, and stared across the river. Even at this distance, he knew immediately who it was—Brato.

Brato did everything he could to sew discord between the Clans, especially the Horse and Wolf Clans. He had tried to pin a double murder on Cymm and planted evidence to support the lie. His son, Stefo, had chased Cymm throughout the realm, intent on killing him. Fortunately, he never got the chance.

"The wolf has crossed the river to be with you. He has made his decision. Now, you must make yours," Azreala said.

Cymm thought back to when he had healed Torc and a similar event had occurred, except Torc had refused to cross the river and ran back to be with Torak. Cymm crawled on hands and knees in front of the wolf. He grabbed his jowls and forced the wolf to gaze into his eyes. "Jalko—I choose you," Cymm whispered and pushed an image into the dire wolf's mind.

Jalko replied with a lick to his face.

24

Alternate Story

Lykinnia

Lykinnia shifted her position, relishing in the silence from the void. "Do I need to ask you again?"

"The spell books were not empty," the voice finally replied.

Lykinnia scoffed. "I can tell you why they were blank if you wish to continue this charade."

"The spell books were not empty."

"You are an impressive liar. I cannot be sure you told the truth about the other questions, but regarding this one, I am confident. I recently received a gift from a friend of mine; it was a spell book. Imagine my surprise when I opened it and discovered it had belonged to my mother." Lykinnia trailed off, in no rush to complete her tale.

"Not possible," countered the voice.

Lykinnia's confidence blossomed. "Not only possible but true. In fact, the same tome rested on your shelves moments before the *failed* fireball teleportation spell. Let me propose an alternative story. Hypothetically speaking, a mage, if given enough time, could replace every book in their library with a replica, and stash the original in a safe place. The same process could be used for anything of intrinsic or sentimental value, such as rare spell components, clothing, or jewelry. If this same wizard happened to find a hidden plane of existence to conceal themselves and their belongings, a scheme could be derived to disappear—"

"And why would I want to disappear?"

"You had fallen out of love with Terazhan, or raising a child interfered too much with your studies." Lykinnia was seething by the end of the sentence. "Solar raised me! Solar kept me out of trouble. All you had to do was—love me, and you—"

Lykinnia gasped as Terazhan instantly appeared in front of her, almost on top of her. Startled, she staggered backward and almost fell off the back of the platform again.

"Solar, attend me." Terazhan paced back and forth.

Lykinnia hopped off the stone stage to avoid being trampled, a mere second before Solar arrived.

"Where is he? How did you find him?" Solar asked excitedly.

"He began praying then halted. It was so fast, I could not determine where he was located," Terazhan replied.

Cymm? "We will talk more about this later." Lykinnia immediately ended her invisibility spell without waiting for a response from the void. The priestess became visible again. Unnoticed, she circled around and stepped onto the platform. "What can I do to help?"

Solar, currently entranced by the open scrying window, did not respond.

Terazhan turned to face her. "He was north of Armak in a village—"

"Howling Set, where his friend Torak lives?" Lykinnia interrupted.

Terazhan shook his head. “Solar is checking there now, but the village looked different. There was a cage—"

“A cage? He was in a cage?” Lykinnia’s face crinkled.

The scrying window disappeared, and Solar faced them. “He is not there. I went through every home and building.”

Lykinnia rubbed her face with both hands. “He mentioned a couple of other villages where the Wolf Tribe shaman live.” The cage was weighing heavily on her mind, and a dark thought coalesced. “There is a group called Fang inside the Wolf Tribe and they hate horsemen. The same group falsely accused him of murder. Maybe they captured him.”

“Do you know where they would be holding him?” asked Terazhan.

Lykinnia shook her head.

“I do. The envoy at the trial was from Endurance Rise. We should start there,” said Solar.

Lykinnia grabbed her father’s arm and bounced on her toes. “Can I go?”

Solar’s glance made the answer obvious. He waved his arm over the altar.

Both father and daughter observed the changing scenes in the scrying window from behind Solar, as he entered Endurance Rise. On the outskirts of the community, lay a huge wooden cage, and in it the motionless bodies of a human and wolf.

Lykinnia gasped. “So much blood. Are they dead?”

Her father’s reassuring hand stroked her hair. “Solar?”

Solar raised both shoulders, intent on the scene before him. Villagers were silently hauling wood, branches, and dry grass to the cage and dumping it all along the outside edge. The people were numb, walking like zombies, and their wolves were nowhere to be seen.

Solar ended the viewing session. “They are building a pyre.”

Terazhan motioned toward the north with his hand. "Go! See what you can find out."

Solar took two steps to comply, then stopped. "There's not enough time. I can only teleport north of Armak, and I will need to—"

"Go!" Terazhan's booming voice echoed around them.

Lykinnia stepped toward the altar. "I will delay them."

"No!" exclaimed Terazhan and Solar simultaneously.

"Tera—Father! I can flash-travel there instantly. Let me do this. Please." Lykinnia hung on her father's forearm with two hands, her neck craned up, meeting his gaze with hope. The answer was obvious.

Terazhan took a deep breath. "Okay."

"What?" Solar and Lykinnia replied concurrently.

Terazhan pointed at Solar, then to the north. "Go!" Turning to his daughter, he said, "You too."

Lykinnia rushed toward the altar as Solar blinked out of view. She placed her hands on it and willed herself north.

25

Dreamwalk

Cymm

To call Azreala tall was an understatement. She stood a few inches shy of seven feet, and a half foot taller than Lykinnia, the tallest woman he had ever met before today. She offered her hand and helped him rise. She would have passed for human if not for the cloven hooves and the flicking tail. A stunning woman with exotic features. He blinked twice as if beguiled, then his thoughts shifted to Lykinnia and his planned rendezvous.

"Thank you, Azreala. I am Cymm Reich. Do you live here?"

"In the Plane of Tides? I think not. Feldarius lives here, but he does not trouble my visits."

"What or who are you visiting?" he asked.

"I came looking for you, Cymm, to guide you back to your body."

Cymm allowed her to turn him, and they began to stroll along the riverbank. "I'm confused. You came looking for *me*. I don't even know you. Do you guide *others* back to their bodies?"

Azreala huffed. "Let me start at the beginning. I am a Priestess of the Phoenix. We worship the Goddess of Death, also known as The Mistress and The Necromancer. Feldarius, her brother, is known as the Master of Souls. You have traveled into his domain, but you have nothing to worry about. I have seen other men and wolves here before. The Mistress has asked me to assist you—"

"Me? Why can't she wait until I die to claim my soul?"

Azreala chuckled. "A common misconception. The Mistress does not necessarily want death. She is the master of death. She constantly makes life and death decisions for others."

Cymm swallowed hard. "Why would she be interested in me?"

The left side of Azreala's face wrinkled. "Cymm, I have been completely forthright with you. Please return the favor. We both know you are not an ordinary human."

Cymm cleared his throat uncomfortably. "Maybe you could tell me what you think you know about me."

"If you wish to play this game, then our conversation is over, and I will take my leave without sharing two fascinating stories about you." She turned and began walking away.

Cymm's eyes shifted right and left. "Wait!"

She paused with her back to him.

"Are you referring to my white aura?"

She turned slowly and smiled. "Continue."

He eyed her for a moment. "Whenever I cast spells or heal someone, a pure white aura manifests around me. It is quite magnificent."

"That wasn't so hard, now, was it?" With three large strides, she was back, towering above him. "My first story is about your sister's visit after you killed the green dragons." Azreala's chin tilted down, and she locked her deep crimson eyes on him.

Cymm took two steps backward, as if hit in the chest, and his eyes bored into hers, seeking understanding.

"However, you must tell me what it feels like to be an avatar, when a god enters your body." She stared at him in anticipation, not hiding her feelings at all.

"I am not sure what you are talking about . . ."

Azreala frowned, then turned and walked away again.

"Okay. Okay." He jogged after her. *She must already know Terazhan has used me as an avatar, or she wouldn't be asking.* All he could think of was Bria. He must know what she knew about the apparition. "I lose complete control of my body and my vision, although my hearing is unaffected."

"Interesting. You lose *complete* control and can't resist?"

"I did resist the movement of my foot once."

Azreala leaned in, waiting for more, but Cymm did not share any details. The priestess clapped her hands together. "I promised you a story. The Mistress saw your pain and suffering and empathized with you. She asked her brother, Feldarius, to send all the lost souls from your village to parade in front of you before they departed. Do you think it is a coincidence the talisman around your neck glinted in the moonlight so you could find it? The Mistress imbued it with a memory or salutation from your sister—"

"From Bria?" Cymm grabbed the ogre ring, awkwardly scanning it on the short leather thong it was attached to.

"It will not work in this plane. When you return, take the necklace off and spin the ring around the thong as quickly as possible. If you do, you will see the gift The Mistress has given you." Azreala nodded. "It is time to leave."

"You mentioned two stories." Cymm raised his eyebrows.

"You did not earn the second story. Next time we meet, you need to trust me more and share more willingly. If you do, I will show you how Hardre died and who killed him." Azreala's hands wove an intricate pattern between them. Her gaze drifted from Cymm to Jalko and back.

"Wait! Tell me who killed him. Please."

"Next time." Azreala's hands shot forward, fingers up, palms showing.

Concentric pulses of crimson energy engulfed Cymm, and he lost consciousness.

26

Fear

Lykinnia

Lykinnia materialized high above the Armak Plains and the Village of Endurance Rise. Her unsubstantial shape twinkled like a golden star. She immediately condensed her stature to six inches. In this smaller size, she would burn through her time allotment quicker and need to return to the Peak of Power sooner.

Lykinnia zoomed down, entering the cage in her ethereal form. Cymm lay on the ground with a large dire wolf upon his chest. Both were motionless. She panicked, unable to tell if they were breathing. Her head swam with different possibilities, knowing she had to delay the bonfire until Solar arrived. She needed him there to check on Cymm.

Cymm moaned.

"Thank Melandri." Lykinnia raced ahead, scouring the vicinity for a group gathering kindling. Four hauled large branches toward her. Uncertain how to proceed, she froze momentarily, then dimmed her brightness and zipped closer to them. One man wore a hat, and she passed through the sidewall, remaining underneath. She flared her amber light in heartbeat pulses.

Flash, flash.

The procession halted.

"What in the nine hells are you gawkin' at?" asked the man whose head on which she was sitting.

Flash, flash.

"Your hat is on fire!" cried another.

The hat flew off his head, catching Lykinnia by surprise. She raced after it, trying to stay as close to it as possible, then entered the garment as it hit the ground. Next, she emitted one steady burst of light.

"My favorite hat!" The man stomped on it several times.

Lykinnia entered his boot through the sole.

The man howled and ran in a circle with his boot *on fire*. He gave his left leg—held out straight and stiff—the occasional shake. "Help, fire!" He tripped and fell to the ground, then removed his boot expeditiously.

Lykinnia peeked out from the surface of the boot while flaring. At least a dozen had gathered already, and more were coming. The young lady continued the spectacle, returning to a throbbing heartbeat.

Flash, flash.

The boot sat upright about fifteen feet from its owner.

Flash, flash.

A commotion of unintelligible content erupted. After the fourth blinking pattern, a voice boomed, "That's not a fire!"

She dimmed her light as much as possible and passed through the boot into the ground. Lykinnia anticipated the inevitable headache to remind her it was time to go. She rushed to enter the boot of the closest person, assuming they were the skeptical loudmouth. Again, she entered through the sole of the boot and immediately blazed her amber glow.

More screaming and hooting ensued until the boot was ripped off and thrown. It flopped down near the prior footwear with a *thump*. Lykinnia fought back the urge to laugh when she peeked out from the edge of the leather surface. At least twenty-five had congregated. They stood in a circle scratching their heads, staring at the discarded boots suspiciously.

The first wave of pain radiated through her head. She sighed and hoped she had bought Solar enough time. After sinking back into the ground, she headed for the cage for a final check on Cymm.

On the ground with his eyes closed, Cymm murmured softly.

Solar was nowhere to be seen.

Lykinnia floated near his ear, her eyes wide with delight. "Cymm, I am here."

"Azreala?" Cymm mumbled.

Azreala? Lykinnia frowned and flew up through the cage's ceiling. She quickly glanced around, no sign of Solar. The villagers continued to surround the mystical boots, and with a smirk, she released her ethereal form back to her material body.

Lykinnia opened her eyes.

Terazhan peered down at her from his lofty nine-foot stature. "Solar is almost there. Nice work delaying them."

"Thank you." Lykinnia stepped back, heeding the arm gesture from her father.

Terazhan opened his own scrying window on the platform, and it continued to grow until it was twelve-foot square. It blotted out the altar and everything in her peripheral vision.

Solar flew to the outskirts of the village and landed. From Lykinnia's vantage point, three feet behind him and slightly to the left, his wings folded into his back, and simply disappeared. He quickly donned a linen robe and jogged into the village as his frame shrank three feet, becoming an ordinary wolfer.

She reached out to touch Solar's back.

Terazhan seized her arm and whispered, "No, and remain silent, so no one can hear you or leave."

Solar glared over his shoulder at her, then ducked behind a hut to avoid two approaching figures.

How can he see me? The memory of his dagger-eyes a moment ago sent an eerie chill down her spine.

The commotion Lykinnia created with the boots increased in volume as Solar made his way through the village. He arrived at the cage on the opposite side from where the boots remained on the ground. A couple of wolfers had resumed stacking kindling against the cell. He peered inside. Cymm and the wolf had not moved. He grabbed two adjacent bars as if to pull them away from each other.

Someone behind him cleared his throat. "Can I help you?"

Solar flinched, and he froze.

Terazhan immediately panned the view out and dropped back ten feet. A hulking man stood directly behind Solar, smacking a club into his empty hand.

"Are you trying to take my prisoners?" asked the jailer.

Lykinnia gasped, soliciting a frown from Terazhan.

The man with the club whirled around. "Who goes there?"

Solar dove at the jailer, subduing him efficiently but not quietly. He rushed back to the cell, grasped two bars, and heaved. They both snapped, and he stepped inside.

"Hey, you shouldn't be in there." A female villager dumped an armload of kindling, then hollered over her shoulder, "Someone's in the cage!"

Solar paid no heed to the several people rushing forward.

A rock soared slightly over Solar's back. Lykinnia ducked.

This immersive experience had Lykinnia awestruck. Her father never ceased to amaze her, and she added one more thing to his list of things to teach her. Or she would figure it out herself.

Solar whispered, but Lykinnia could not determine if it were to himself or to Cymm. Finally, she realized he was trying to communicate with Terazhan. ". . . surrounded. They are repairing the broken wooden bars by lashing new ones in place."

She scanned her father's emotionless face.

Another rock streaked in and struck Solar in the shoulder, then two more barely missed. He shielded Cymm as he began to stir. "You are Cymm Reich, First Paladin of Terazhan," he stated in an angelic but authoritative voice.

Cymm cleared his throat. "Yes, I am. Who are you?"

"My name is no longer relevant. I am Solar to Terazhan. I keep an eye on his interests, in this plane and others. We need to hurry." He easily hoisted Cymm, holding him in outstretched arms. Solar glanced up, then bent both knees—

"No," Cymm commanded. "I will not leave without Jalko."

27

Jalko

Jalko

Jalko's ears perked at his newly bonded companion's call. He raced over at breakneck speed and swerved at the last moment to avoid hitting the human. He could play this game and wrestle with the other wolves for hours at a time.

Three days had already passed since they had been bound.

"Jalko, I said come here." The human pointed at the ground next to him.

Young Jalko's front end dropped low while his hind end remained high and wiggled back and forth. His companion's face darkened, and a wave of anger flooded the wolf's mind, sent from the human. His playfulness disappeared and he rushed over to the man's side.

A swift punch to the ribs greeted the young wolf. "Next time I tell you to come, you better come!"

"Hey Brato, everything alright over there?" another man called from a distance.

The human standing next to him ignored the man and grabbed him roughly by the scruff. "Let's go."

Eight months ago, Jalko had been born. He whimpered, then followed the man.

ꝏꝏꝏ

A year and a half elapsed, and Jalko had recently turned two. He was much bigger, considerably stronger, and now wore a collar. It was not comfortable, and constantly itched. His human companion had placed it on him, even though he never saw one on any other wolf.

Jalko sniffed the ground again, searching for the scent of their quarry. He shifted to smelling the air and caught it. The animal had four legs, antlers, and exuded a pungent musk, the human called them "elk."

The dire wolf dashed ahead, taking a wide arc to drive their prey back to the right where his human waited. His tormentor. The thrill of the hunt would soon be over, the one remaining joy in his life.

The elk altered its course as expected, and Jalko closed the distance slightly. The grunting and hoof-beats of his prey echoed in his ears. The glorious aroma of its musk filled his nostrils and elevated his adrenaline. He leaped a treefall in a single bound. His body felt alive.

The elk came into view ahead. Its pace had slowed, its head hung low, and its breathing was ragged. An arrow whistled past the wolf's head, grazing his ear. Jalko crouched low, but continued to run, not wanting to invoke The Tormentor's wrath. The elk let out a loud continuous cry followed by a wheeze. It collapsed to the ground, scrambled to stand back up, then bounded off in a different direction. Jalko hit it in full stride, and they fell, a twisting, rolling heap. They continued to roll around until the dire wolf clamped onto its neck and ripped it out.

"Jalko, what's this?" The Tormentor sounded angry.

The dire wolf hopped to his feet, his rear legs trembling uncontrollably. A small squirt of urine released as he made his way over in a partial walk and crawl. The Tormentor's hand raised, Jalko's ears flattened, and the wolf cowered. The hand landed on his head softly and scratched behind his ears.

"What's wrong with you?" asked the human.

Jalko's tail wagged, and he licked his hand.

A branch snapped close by, and a low growl reverberated through the woods as a giant bear rounded the trunk of the closest tree.

The Tormentor nocked an arrow and Jalko placed himself between them, then forced the bear to circle. The wolf's baritone growls stopped the bear in its tracks. It growled back, rose to almost ten feet tall on its hind legs, and swiped the air with its paws.

Jalko circled back the other way, trying to protect the human and their fresh kill. The lumbering hulk turned slow and unstable, trying to mirror his movements, and when the monster fell to all fours, the wolf attacked with lightning speed. He bit the bear's shoulder, continued past it and sunk his fangs into its rear, then proceeded back to the fallen elk, completing the circle.

Pleased with himself, Jalko glanced back craving affirmation from The Tormentor, who was no longer in sight. Confusion flooded his mind. He yelped and barely dodged a massive paw.

ꝏꝏꝏ

A few weeks later, Jalko and The Tormentor entered the city of Armak and headed straight for the market. It was pure chaos for the wolf. The numerous people, the yelling, the buffet of aromas, and the furtive movements, it all assaulted his senses.

The human pulled his collar forcefully, a clear sign to stop and wait. He proceeded to examine a clay bowl, to replace the one the human broke last week. The Tormentor had thrown Jalko's water bowl, and it had smashed against the wall in between him and the human child in their pack. He could not be certain which of them was the target.

A horseman bumped into the human. "Sorry about that."

The clay bowl he was examining shattered upon the ground. The Tormentor's face turned red from a mix of emotions. "You did that on purpose!"

"Let me pay for the bowl." The horseman immediately pulled coins out and paid the merchant.

"You don't think I can afford to pay for the broken bowl? You embarrass me, then insult me!" The Tormentor's arms flailed wildly.

"I don't want any trouble." The horseman fled and hurried to his tethered horse.

Jalko and his human hid among the crowd and followed him out of the city. The dire wolf sensed his human's emotions, and it fueled his own. It felt like they were on a hunt.

The Tormentor locked eyes with him and sent him a visual image. Jalko sprinted off, arcing wide to the left. The color of his coat provided some camouflage when the scrub and tall grass went sparse. Jalko covered a few hundred extra yards to ensure he was in front of the horseman and doubled back. The dire wolf relished the fact he was not the target of The Tormentor's ire.

The horseman came into view ahead, and he brought his horse to a stop. From the back of the horse, he craned his neck in all directions. The Tormentor jogged up from behind and the horseman's shoulders slumped, realizing his peril.

"Please, I beg you. I will pay you double the price of the bowl, and you can buy yourself two."

The Tormentor sported an evil grin, the same visage he wore before he beat Jalko. "My wolf is going to tear you apart slowly—painfully."

"You are a fiend!" the horseman sniveled.

The wolfer's grin grew even larger. "Jalko, attack."

Jalko was a well-trained killing machine. He would crush the horseman and his puny show horse in seconds. The dire wolf glared at his prey, who stared back with dread. Urine ran freely from the horse's belly, compliments of the human in the saddle. The scent of fear was invigorating. He stalked forward slowly. *Don't you have any pride? You should be embarr*—He stopped snarling and stared at his bound companion.

"I said attack, Jalko!"

This isn't a hunt. It's a slaughter. It's . . . torture. Jalko could relate to the emotions the horseman must be feeling. His hind legs quivered uncontrollably. His mouth went dry, and he panted heavily. *I can't do this, but what will he do to me if I disobey?*

The dire wolf remained frozen with indecision and blocked a forced image from The Tormentor, as he recalled the hundreds of beatings and the mental abuse he had suffered in the past. Images of the Wolf Spirit quickly replaced the traumatic memories. The apparition had appeared in his mind to punish him for what he was attempting to do. It attacked psionically, crushing his will, and damaging his mind. He howled in pain and his entire body trembled. Blood leaked from his ears. He staggered and fell, emitted a yelp driven by pain, but immediately rose. The punishment was deserved, not for refusing The Tormentor's command, but for what he desired.

The wolf shook his head vigorously, as if shaking water from inside his ears and forced his body into a calmer state. The paralysis dissipated like smoke on a windy day.

Jalko broke free of the binding ritual and took off running, followed closely behind by the horseman.

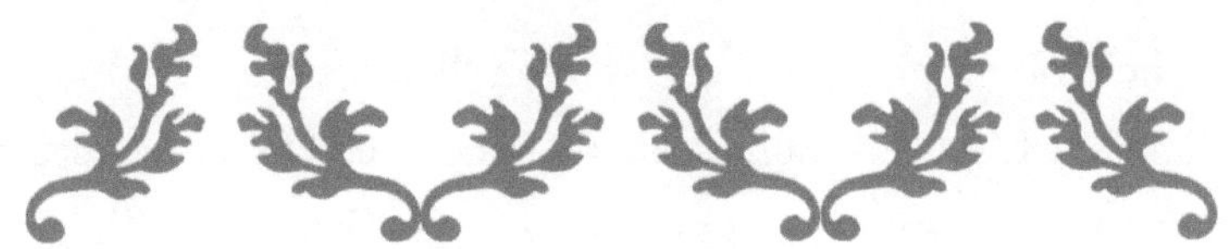

28

Friends

Cymm

The cage blazed on two sides, spreading around the corner, and racing down the third. Cymm knelt beside Jalko, shaking him vigorously. The dire wolf struggled to his feet, not completely healed.

"Follow me." Solar charged the only wall not on fire. He burst through the side of the prison sending wooden shrapnel in many directions with Cymm and Jalko on his heels.

The remaining wall ignited, and the bonfire blocked their retreat. Both men and the wolf stood frozen, highlighted by a fiery background, and surrounded by a semicircle of wolfers. A barrage of yelling ensued.

"He has charmed the blood wolf."

"Run!"

Brato's voice thundered above them all. "Kill them!"

No one moved. Fear filled their eyes.

Finally, one wolfer stepped forward. "He healed Jalko. Look at his eyes!"

"No, it's still a blood wolf."

"But his eyes are normal, and he is calm."

"Quiet!" Brato laughed slow and sinister. "Hey boy, you brought this disease with you and infected my wolf. Now—"

Cymm snorted. "I'm immune to disease, and this isn't your wolf."

With a red face, Brato strode forward. "Kill them all before they spread the infection to your wolves."

The lead elder from Endurance Rise stepped into the open semicircle with his hands in the air. "Wait! How did you cure Jalko? This disease has been a burden on our people for centuries. No wolf has ever recovered."

Before Cymm could reply, another elder joined him. "What makes you think he is cured? Look at him, he oozes blood from his pores."

Cymm glanced at Solar and rolled his eyes.

The lead elder replied, "Jalko's eyes are bright white. Don't be daft."

Brato stepped forward with his hands clenched into fists. "This is what the horseman does! He creates division, *and* he kills wolfers, including my son and several of your children!"

"More lies. Do you ever tell the truth?" Cymm retorted.

Jalko slunk behind him, then his head peeked out with a low growl.

Murmuring festered into grumbling, and soon the crowd drowned out the bonfire behind them.

"We should leave," Solar said under his breath.

"How?" Cymm waved, indicating they were trapped.

"That would hardly stop me—"

"No. Most of these people are good." Cymm shook his head with a frown. He found Jalko staring at him, but before he could send a message, a powerful image storm assailed his mind. One disturbing picture after another, until Cymm's knees buckled, and he dropped to the ground with tears streaming down his face.

"Begging for your life will not save you now," Brato crowed.

Cymm took several deep breaths before rising. He locked gazes with his wolf again and returned one image.

Jalko immediately raised his snout to the sky and bayed. The crowd slowly settled down, while other wolves joined in the distance.

Cymm's body trembled with anger. He pointed a finger at Brato. "I challenge you to a duel to the death." Solar quickly grabbed his arm, but Cymm dexterously shook it off. "You cruel, sadistic bastard!"

Brato unconsciously stepped back, scanning in all directions for support. He found plenty. Over two dozen men rushed past him to form a barrier with weapons drawn.

Cymm leaned his torso aggressively toward them. "Do you beat your wolves too? Stick a hot poker between the pads of their paws? Or maybe you put a tight collar on your wolf's neck and hang him by it?"

Several wolfers lowered their weapons and turned to face Brato.

"How could you?"

"Is it true?"

"You believe the horseman?" Brato's eyes widened with panic.

"None of this is true. Seize him," replied a village elder.

Solar stepped shoulder to shoulder with Cymm. "That is not going to happen."

"I have proof!" Cymm raised his arms, his voice booming over top of the tumult. "Inspect Jalko's paws, or look for the cut scars inside his ears, or let's summon the shaman to perform eye of the wolf."

The lead elder stepped into the small space between the opposing parties. "I will send for the shaman, if you explain how you cured . . ." He trailed off, his attention drawn by something over Cymm's shoulder.

The paladin apprehensively glanced, expecting a trick. The bonfire had collapsed upon itself revealing a small war party of heavily armed wolfers and wolves wearing studded leather armor.

At the head of the contingent stood Torak and Torc.

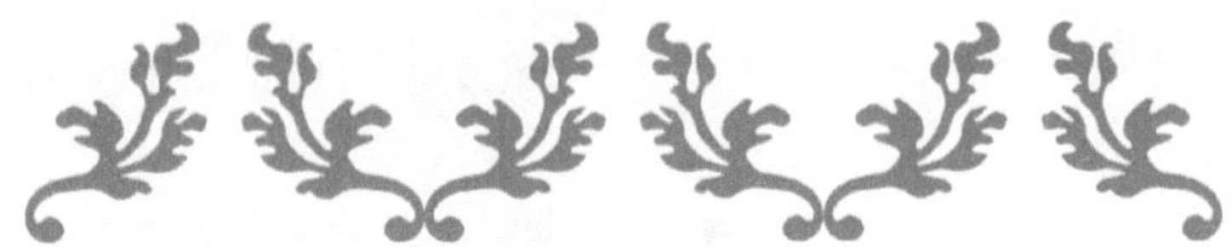

29

The Babysitter

ZaphMordakai

The two wagons wound into the foothills, following the pass for several hours. A valley opened to the left, while the road continued straight through the mountains.

BelCharius flew ahead, indicating to the wagon drivers to leave the road and follow him into the dale.

ZaphMordakai's eyes left the green dragon, inspecting the terrain before him. *How did I get selected for babysitting? The Princess, eleven humans, and BelCharius.* He could feel his heartbeat quicken. *He was a little wyrmling when I was made captain. His mother probably curled necks with one of the generals.*

They better not attack the next city without me. Maybe it will be Norfolk, and I have been prepositioned. He laughed at himself. *Wishful thinking. It will be big, like the City of the Mystics, Kharad, or Armak. Perhaps it isn't a human city. It could be the elven city of Breezeport, or Delge, where the dwarves live.*

A squirrel leaped and bounded for the closest tree, drawing Zaph's attention. A lightning bolt blasted the tree trunk inches from its fluffy tail, ripping the bark off and launching it into the air. A second bolt collided with the bothersome creature near the pinnacle of its flight, disintegrating it.

In his dark elf form, Zaph defiantly scanned the group, petitioning for a fight, but no one met his gaze. *Why did every black captain know about the last attack except me? They are afraid I will outshine them on the battlefield. That's why I wasn't selected for the attack on Bruc. I get—*

The wagons came to a halt. ZaphMordakai glanced up to find BelCharius grinning at him.

"What are you looking at?" snapped the black dragon.

"Did the squirrel attack the Princess?" The green dragon chuckled.

"One more smart comment, and these people will be eating fried green dragon with tomatoes." ZaphMordakai paused and stared. "All right humans, unload these crates into the cave. Let's go!"

Even Princess Jenaleya scurried to comply, and they worked silently.

BelCharius cleared his throat. "I have spent most of my life with other green dragons. I am not used to your straightforward speech."

"And?"

"I like it. I like you, Zaph."

ZaphMordakai bristled. "That's because you don't know me. Give it time, and you will hate me. Eventually, everyone does."

30

Torak and Torc

Cymm

Cymm's heart leaped into his throat. Torak's presence couldn't have been a coincidence, but how could he have known Cymm was here?

Torak motioned right then left, and his war party split in half. Torc was enormous and had continued to grow as Torak had outlooked. He stood at least three hands taller than the next largest wolf, including Jalko.

Solar's eyes widened. "We should not get involved. It is time to leave."

"No! My friend needs me." Cymm turned to the main crowd. "Brato, it is time to pay for your crimes."

"Good luck with that, horseman," replied Brato, the leader of Fang.

Wolfers continued to mass before him. At least fifty, then sixty, and joined by wolves. The throng swelled to eighty quickly, more than double the number with Torak.

A warm feeling filled Cymm's heart for the first time in a while. His friend stood shoulder-to-shoulder with him. He glanced to his opposite side to find Solar.

Cymm reached out to shake Torak's hand, but a sword blocked the way. It was DragonSin. Cymm gaped at the weapon, then peered at his friend. The look they exchanged made Cymm feel like they had never parted company. "Thank you."

Cymm strapped the sword on his back. "Brato, my luck has arrived. However, for the sake of honor, I will make an offer to your supporters."

Brato crossed his arms over his chest. "You are in no position to make a deal."

The sword spoke to Cymm. *"That one needs to die."*

"Yes, but Torak will deliver the judgment." Cymm scratched the stubble on his chin. "Here is my offer. Instead of pledging the life of my newly bonded companion, I will pledge my own."

Both Torak and Solar grabbed his arm at the same time.

Through gritted teeth, Solar asked, "What are you doing?"

Torak flinched. "Bonded companion?"

Cymm shook free from their grip. "I want you to summon the shaman. If I've said anything false, I will submit myself to the death penalty. However, if I tell true, then Brato will pay for his crimes."

Many shifted uncomfortably, but no one replied.

"How many sources of evil do you sense?" Cymm asked DragonSin.

"I would estimate one out of four," replied the sword.

"We must avoid needless bloodshed. We should be fighting the dragons. Not each other. So, I will challenge Brato to a duel to the death for the leadership of Fang."

A loudmouth from the crowd said, "Is the horseman trying to protect his—" He fell to his knees, clutching his head and screaming in agony.

"Is he one of the evil ones?" Cymm asked.

"No, but I admire the direction you are going. So, I will take care of this without killing him, at least for now."

When the yelling ceased, Cymm continued, "All of you should be ashamed of yourselves for following such a vile leader, and he is a coward."

"He is not an elder!" exclaimed the lead elder of Endurance Rise.

Cymm scoffed. "Do you think these people are here to defend you? Let me be clear, I know most of you are members of Fang, and if you continue down this path, you and your wolf will depart this world tonight."

"Hey horseman, my luck has also arrived. I think you've met Silak before." Brato snickered and nodded slightly.

Pain exploded in Cymm's mind, emanating from the lower part of his back. He reached around, searching, as he fell to his knees. A dagger. His head rocked back in agony, and his attacker's skull and brain exploded all over him, the aftermath of a single punch from Solar.

Torak wailed in agony next to him, drawing his attention. His friend, reduced to all fours, struggled to breathe with wheezing, rattling lungs. A dagger protruded from much higher on his back. Torak's assassin lurched for freedom and almost made it before falling to the ground, clutching his head.

Without waiting for DragonSin to finish his attack, Torc ravaged the assailant's throat so severely that his head tipped backward and lay flat on his back.

Chaos erupted. It became difficult to distinguish friend from foe, but at least Torak's men and wolves wore armor. Human and canine clashed as often as like species, and some of the wolfers from Endurance Rise had joined the resistance, attacking members of Fang.

While Cymm tended to Torak's wound, DragonSin dished out pain. Three wolfers writhed in agony, holding their heads, blood already gushing from their ears, nose, and eyes. The sentient sword was not holding back.

Torc and Jalko formed a defensive wall of teeth, giving Cymm enough time to heal his friend, but they were in the proverbial eye of the tornado.

Torak's breathing stabilized after the puncture wound disappeared.

Solar bled from several wounds as he stood stoically by Cymm's side. He swung indiscriminately at anything near Cymm, and had already killed two men, but the wolves were proving too elusive.

Torak rose. "Rally to me!"

His men cheered in response.

Cymm hoisted his sword. "For Terazhan, the One True God!" A pure white orb engulfed him and many of Torak's followers.

Men, women, and wolves were growling, screaming, and dying by the dozen, but those rallying to Torak and Cymm had renewed vigor.

Torak circled, patiently waiting for an opening. The shaggy brown kaido wolf lunged, its enormous maw open, fangs bared. His friend froze from indecision or fear. Cymm could not tell which. The wolf descended upon him, then in a flurry of movement, the wolfer's short sword thrust into the roof of its gaping mouth. The blade went deep into its brain, and before it hit the ground, the wolf was dead.

A shadow wolf sunk its fangs into Torc's shoulder, then braced its legs before lurching backward and shaking its head forcefully. Torc's yelp brought Torak to his defense within seconds. He slid his weapon between the wolf's rear legs and sliced deep into the inner thigh near the groin. The black wolf shrieked and released Torc. It rotated and backed away slowly leaving a trail of blood, before collapsing and bleeding out.

Cymm stood mesmerized by Torak's fighting prowess. There were many equally impressive wolfers on both sides, creating a savage and terrifying environment. Too far away to help, he watched a wolfer charge his friend from behind. "*DragonSin, pull him toward me!*"

The wolfer stumbled sideways, took two long steps to right himself, and received Cymm's bastard sword down through his neck into his chest. Before Cymm could withdraw his weapon, the fangs of a dire wolf sunk deep into his thigh.

Jalko ravaged the wolf's haunches before a sword descended on his back, opening a nasty gash.

Solar seized the wolf biting Cymm by the lower jaw, then grabbed the upper before he hoisted the dire wolf off the ground above his head and ripped its muzzle in half. He slammed the creature to the ground, where it took its last breath.

Cymm hurried to Jalko's side. Fortunately, the gash was not as serious as he thought.

Jalko licked his face a split second before a kaido wolf bowled them both over.

Three men fell to the ground, rolling around, clutching their heads.

The wolfers and wolves continued to capitalize on each other's weaknesses and utilize their own strengths to their advantage. Torak's group was half of its original size. Even with their armor, most of them were injured. Their enemy had taken heavy losses, losing twice as many.

Several arrows whistled in, a few finding their marks.

Solar's closed fist rose high above his head, and he chanted in a beautiful, but unrecognizable language. A shower of golden light particles rained down upon those surrounding him.

Cymm's wounds began to heal. As the paladin scanned his allies, he noticed the cuts on their bodies mending also. With his injuries disappearing he felt rejuvenated, and power returned to his attacks.

The Fang supporters pressed forward in a spearhead formation, splitting the remaining group in half. Jalko, Solar, and a few bonded pairs remained with Cymm, but the rest of their allies had been separated or driven out of sight.

"Where is Brato?" Torak yelled.

Cymm studied the enemy throng. "Brato the Coward has fled again! He has left you to die while he runs for safety!"

Several Fang wolfers paused, only to receive a forceful shove in the back from their cohorts.

"DragonSin, drop as many evil men as you can, and I will finish them off. I want to save the lives of the rest and minimize our casualties too."

Cymm lunged forward as the first man dropped to his knees, and the paladin lopped his head off. The dead man's dire wolf launched itself forward with a vicious attack.

Solar's foot landed solidly in the wolf's rib cage. A sickening crunch preceded a yelp, and the wolf was launched twenty feet into the advancing opposition.

"Brato the Coward!" a faceless voice yelled.

Many of the Fang warriors were craning their necks, searching for their leader.

Cymm quickly inspected the deep punctures on his shoulder from the wolf bite. "Brato left you to die." DragonSin had three more men writhing on the ground, but Cymm could not get at them.

A few Fang fighters threw down their weapons and slowly backed away.

Cymm smiled as he gauged the impact his words were having. "We are only looking for the leaders of Fang. Everyone else may return to their normal lives."

Many swords and spears clanged as they hit rocks and hard packed dirt. A few small skirmishes remained, but the battle was ending.

"DragonSin, you need to stop for now."

"No. The last three are on the ground."

Cymm scanned his allies. "Where is Torak?"

Several people provided empty stares; others shrugged. A knot formed in Cymm's stomach as he frantically ran through the battlefield evaluating the bodies. "Jalko, find Torak. Come on, boy. I know this is hard for you."

Jalko, having taken a defensive position the entire battle, had defended Cymm's back and flank several times. Any true aggression had disappeared with the blood wolf disease, and although he was covered in blood, most of it was his own.

The lead elder cautiously approached Cymm with his empty hands showing. "Are you happy now?"

"Not completely. Where did Brato go, and where is my friend Torak?" asked Cymm menacingly.

"This is your fault!" The lead elder madly waved his arms through the air.

Cymm's eyes flared white. "Say it again and you will join the dead. There is no war between the Horse and Wolf Clans." Jalko moved swiftly past the elder, and Cymm physically pushed him out of the way. "Get control of your village or there will be a new lead elder."

The dire wolf paused at the entrance of a wolfer's home and peeked back at Cymm with sorrow in his eyes, then entered the building.

"There is a large presence of evil ahead," said DragonSin.

Cymm dashed ahead to catch up, but before he arrived at the house the sounds of a scuffle assailed him, a wolf yelped, and a body hit the floor. Cymm crashed through the doorway.

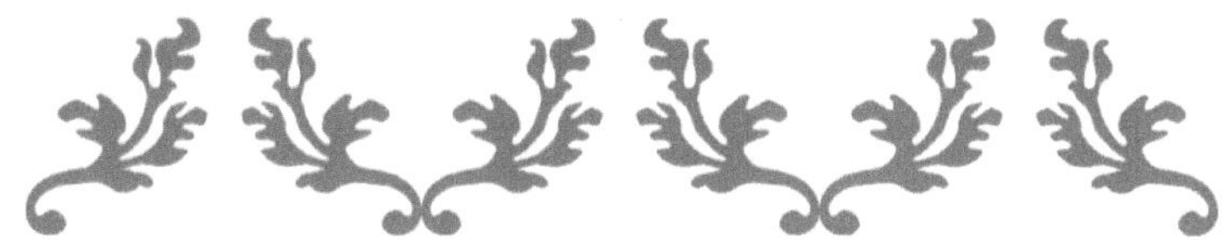

31

Retreat

ZaphMordakai

The prisoners gathered in the cave, in the area assigned to them.

"Did they all return?" BelCharius asked.

"Do I report to you?" ZaphMordakai snapped. "Count them yourself."

The green dragon scanned the group. "Why do we need so many prisoners anyway? They will be easier to count if I eat a couple."

"When the Queen contacts me, I will ask her how many we need to keep. In the meantime, pray we have enough." Zaph did not like the smug green visage, but he chose to ignore it.

BelCharius continued to stare at the prisoners.

He probably can't even count. ZaphMordakai stretched his dark elf arms above his head, then to his sides. He could not wait to lounge around in his dragon form. He had stolen away thirty minutes at a time these past couple of days to transform back and stretch his wings. Hiding his identity from the city was of paramount importance in case they mounted an attack, but the prisoners presented a different problem due to the dragon fear he naturally emanated. It was much stronger than a green, and only that of a red dragon was more formidable. If he entered the cave in his natural state, the humans would exhibit a severe reaction. The response was unpredictable, but in these tight quarters, they would either die from fear, be driven mad and blubber uncontrollably, or flee in terror. None of these would end well for the Princess.

"I haven't eaten in days. I'll be hunting. If the Queen contacts me, I will return immediately," said ZaphMordakai.

The green dragon hesitated before acquiescing.

He is getting quite bold. I will have to put him in his place when I return. The black dragon paused halfway to the exit. "Do you know where the village of Stallion Rise is located?"

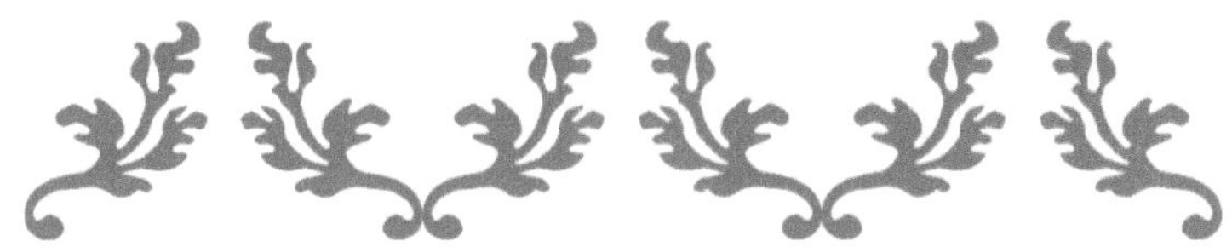

32

Brave Wolf

Cymm

Cymm struggled to comprehend the mass mayhem in front of him. How could so many people fit in this room? Shouting, stomping, and metal clanging against metal reverberated off the walls and ceiling. Even though he had burst through the front door, no one seemed to notice or care.

Jalko cowered against a side wall with a large puddle of urine beneath him. Brato stood next to him shaking a collar in front of his snout. Cymm recognized it immediately as the collar the wolf was forced to wear as a punishment, the collar he wore when Brato beat him, the collar that represented when Jalko's life changed.

Three men with crossbows and a snarling shadow wolf blocked Cymm from further entering the room. However, they were not facing him. He glanced over their shoulders and around their bodies. His heart leaped into his throat.

Two men and a dire wolf lie dead in front of Torak and Torc. His friend lay sprawled on the floor with numerous crossbow bolts protruding from his body. Torc straddled his bonded companion defensively, growling ferociously, daring anyone to attack. The wolf had three bolts buried in his fur, potentially more, and blood rained down from an unseen injury beneath him.

Cymm's eyes met Torak's for a long second, and they stared at each other through Torc's legs. A feeling of déjà vu swept through Cymm as he remembered a time not too long ago in Armak, when the roles were reversed, and Torak defended *his* fallen companion.

Cymm cried out in anguish, swinging DragonSin at the man who stood in front of him. His blade sliced through his neck with ease and the man's head dropped to the floor. His body soon followed.

The two remaining men closest to Cymm fell as if praying, gripping the sides of their heads. The paladin kneed one in the face and raised his sword to finish him.

A bedroom door opened behind the bonded companions, then another. Four more bound pairs exited each room. Two crossbow bolts struck Cymm, one in the chest, the other in his thigh. A kaido wolf barreled into Cymm, clamping its massive jaws onto his arm, and the other wolfers came in swinging. He had fallen into the same trap as his friend.

Cymm backed toward the doorway, overwhelmed by the number of attackers. He had lost visual contact with Torak and Torc. Wolf yips and yelps came from the far side of the room.

A massive fist descended on the kaido wolf's skull, and it released Cymm's arm in a daze. Solar pulled him out of the house, slammed the door, and shoved him against the wall.

Tears streamed down Cymm's face. "No, I need to help them!"

Solar brutally ripped the bolts from Cymm's body. "Heal yourself, then join me." He pointed his finger in Cymm's face. "Heal yourself!" Solar ripped the door open and trudged inside.

The thrum of crossbows firing reverberated, accompanied by grunts and moans.

Cymm hurried to comply with Solar's demand and rushed back in to join the fray. Men and wolves bore down on Solar from all sides. He had already killed a man and a wolf, but the rest drove him to a knee with his upper torso twisted to the side. He stood swiftly while uncoiling, delivering a radiant blue burst of energy in every direction. It pulsed and singed everything it touched, stopping several feet short of Cymm, Brato, and Jalko. Men and wolves flew everywhere.

At least a half dozen bolts jutted from Solar's body, and the dissipating blue glow distorted his intense visage into one of depravity.

"DragonSin, remind me to never upset Solar."

"This isn't a skit. Let's get in there." DragonSin contributed by incapacitating three more men.

"Hang on Jalko. I'm coming!" Cymm lopped the head off a wolfer attacking Solar, in a stealthy attack from behind. By the time he reached Jalko, Brato had skittered away, circling the fight in the center of the room. The Fang leader was wisely keeping the mass of bodies between them.

Jalko did not appear to be physically injured, but he now wore a thick leather collar. Cymm immediately grabbed it to rip it off, causing Jalko to yipe and bite him. Cymm withdrew his hands hastily. "Easy boy."

Jalko continued to alternate between growling and whimpering.

Cymm locked eyes and mentally blasted Jalko with an image of their bonding at the river. "I choose you, Jalko."

Jalko whined and nuzzled Cymm's chest. He grabbed the collar gently and tried to pull it over the wolf's head to no avail. Jalko yelped.

Cymm's fingers searched for a clasp while his eyes feverishly sought a glimpse of his friend Torak. Between the wolf bodies, he succeeded.

Torak had risen to his knees, and rested against his sword, with the point dug into the floor. His chest heaved as he tried to catch his breath.

Torc clamped down on a shadow wolf's throat, shook his head violently, and tossed its limp body to the side. The remaining two wolves pounced on Torc.

"I don't have time to figure this out." Cymm drew his dirk dagger, the gift from Old-Man Semper, slid it under the collar, and sliced through the leather easily. The collar remained in place, forcing him to peel it off, and revealing several long nails embedded in both the band and Jalko's neck. He threw it toward the hearth, and hugged Jalko. "Come on, let's help them."

A large dire wolf sunk its teeth into Torc's neck, while on the other side, a smaller kaido wolf bit deep into the fur covering his ribs. With their rear legs locked in place, a tug-o-war match began. The kaido wolf's head shook furiously, and the fur on Torc's ribs tore. A long, garish wound exposed the ribs and flesh below it. Torc yelped continuously, becoming frantic to escape their jaws.

Cymm charged with wide eyes.

Torak's sword descended on the kaido wolf's back in a mighty overhead chop, cutting through its backbone. It fell to the floor twitching, and Torak fell forward on top of it.

Torc staggered under the weight of the dire wolf clamped on his neck.

Cymm utilized a recently learned tactic and slid DragonSin between the wolf's legs. He cut deep into the soft underbelly, then repeated on the other side.

The wolf turned on him, back arched, bloody teeth bared.

Torc's fur hung torn and tattered, dragging on the floor. He stepped on it as he retaliated against his enemy and seized its rear leg. In a brutal display of rage, he whipped the dire wolf back around, almost ripping its leg free. Torc's face was a thing of nightmares, a bloody mess of flesh, his jowls ripped and partially missing. He took two steps toward Torak and collapsed, the bodies of five wolves and four men strewn around him.

Cymm rushed over to his friend and helped him to his knees. "I need to heal Torc before he dies." He knelt between the companions, then placed his hands on the dire wolf, glancing at Torak momentarily.

His friend forced a vague smile. A crossbow bolt pierced his eye and exploded out the back of his head. He collapsed in a heap next to his mate, their heads touching.

Cymm blinked. Time seemed to slow. He followed the trajectory back to his mortal enemy, Brato.

Brato proceeded to load the next bolt and took two steps forward.

Jalko yiped and scooted back toward the location where Cymm found him.

Haggard and bleeding profusely from many wounds, Solar was surrounded by a massive pile of bodies, and the last two living dire wolves. He staggered and almost fell.

"No, you'll pay for that!" Cymm screamed as Brato approached. "*I can still save Torak. DragonSin, take Brato down!*" He placed one foot beneath him, trying to rise. His empty hand reflexively reached for the scabbard on his back. "*DragonSin?*" Fear raced through Cymm when his eyes locked on the sword he had set down to heal Torc. He lunged for it, and a bolt tore into his side, breaking a rib and collapsing his lung. He sprawled on the floor. Even through his struggling breaths, the sharp *click* of Brato reloading rang out. Focusing his attention on the sentient weapon, he forced himself to ignore his enemy. His hand crawled toward it until Brato stepped on his fingers and raised the crossbow, pointing it at his head.

"No!" Solar groaned in pain. A wolf had fastened its jaws onto his right arm, preventing him from intervening.

"You're a vile monster." Cymm fumed through tears of fury and pain. He reached for his dagger with his other hand.

"Are you afraid of monsters in the dark? Now you know there is something much worse out there," Brato crowed with his chest puffed out.

Jalko slammed into Brato from behind with the power of a warhorse, driving him into the wall, where the crossbow or Brato's arm snapped. The Fang leader slumped to the ground, then quickly regained his feet and drew his own dagger.

Cymm grabbed hold of DragonSin, and the sentient artifact went to work.

Brato dropped the dagger and thrashed against the wall. He pulled at his hair with one hand, the other hung limp by his side.

The dire wolves attacking Solar sat back on their haunches and scratched their ears with their rear foot. One howled and bolted for the door, the other followed with a limp. Solar let them go.

With intense savagery, Jalko descended upon the prone man, his tormentor. The first bite removed his ear and three fingers, the second, his nose and upper lip, then Jalko ripped his throat out. Hyperventilating, the wolf rocked back and howled.

It struck Cymm like a thunderclap, and he covered his ears. He inspected his friends' bodies again, not knowing what else to do. *This can't be happening. They can't be dead.* His eyes shifted to Solar. "What do I do?"

Solar's eyes went out of focus, and he staggered, shook it off, then tripped over a dead body on his way to Cymm. He dropped to one knee and placed both hands on the floor to support himself.

Cymm pointed at his friends. "We have to save them."

Solar's head tilted up weakly, and he gasped and wheezed between breaths. "I—" His eyes rolled up into the back of his sockets and he lost consciousness.

33

Dark Deception

ZaphMordakai

The wind rippled his ears as he zipped from one jet stream to another. His hunting trip had yielded nothing so far, but his effort was low. Thoughts about how to find Stallion Rise swirled within ZaphMordakai's mind, consumed by the need to locate Cymm Reich. *First, I must complete the Queen's task.*

He had left BelCharius to watch over the prisoners with no regret. *I am the higher-ranking officer, and much more powerful. He should be cowering in front of me, and yet he isn't. Damn green dragons, always conniving and manipulating.*

He used his best voice imitation for BelCharius, "I like you, Zaph."

While contemplating the lieutenant's behavior, he noticed a lone figure walking on the road below, heading away from the city.

ZaphMordakai's interest piqued when the person knelt at the side of the road, inspected the ground, then quickly stood and veered off to the side where they had taken the prisoners. "Hmm, he must have found ruts from the wagon wheels. But why send a single tracker?"

Trying to keep out of sight, the black dragon descended rapidly, transforming into his dark elf form moments after landing. His agility in this shape always amazed him. The familiar bulky, heavy, dragon-feeling disappeared. He ran through the forest to intercept the tracker, like a wraith hiding in the fog.

After he broke out of the forest, a mere dozen feet from the trail, he watched the man approaching in the distance. He melted back into the tree line and waited. Several minutes passed, and he stepped back out, startling the man.

"Good morning, traveler—"

The man knelt immediately. "Master elf, I have been looking for you."

"Dyfar? Aren't you full of surprises? What brings you out into the dangerous wilds?" The dark elf rotated his hand in front of his face, watching the lightning arc between his fingers.

"I have information about the King's plans. He is sending a large contingent in two days to deal with your green friend," replied Dyfar.

"He's not my friend!" retorted ZaphMordakai and observed a twinkle in the eye of the human. "You will return at once and tell the King his daughter's life will be forfeit the moment anyone sets foot on the mountain path."

While kneeling, Dyfar cleared his throat uncomfortably. "If I do as you request, Master elf, he will know I am in league with you."

"Not my concern."

"If I may. I have an alternative suggestion. A prisoner, called Myndar, could be released to carry this message, and I can continue to inform you if anything arises." Dyfar's eyes darted up to meet his.

The dark elf shook his head. "And Myndar is your father, brother, friend, or son?"

"He is my brother, and I will counsel him on the way back to the city, concerning what information he is allowed to share."

"You play a treacherous game, and I do not like to be manipulated." ZaphMordakai took an intimidating step forward.

"No, Master elf, silence my roar if I'm lying. I have been honest the entire time." A slight tremor invaded the normally calm speech pattern of the human.

This could prove entertaining. I will let the owlbears deal with this miserable rat. "Very well. What does he look like?" asked the dragon in disguise.

"Long blonde hair, a short beard, the same height as me, and a muscular build."

"You will wait here no matter how long it takes. Understand?" asked ZaphMordakai.

"Yes."

The dark elf turned and walked up the trail. He chuckled to himself. *I wonder how long he will wait.*

ꝏꝏꝏ

ZaphMordakai extended his wings before tucking them and rolling onto his back next to the remnants of a massive cave bear. It was late afternoon by the time he decided to head back to the lair.

Every tree, root, and rock created an obstacle to his movement. The density of the forest in this area not only obstructed his travel, but also made it impossible for him to take flight. In frustration, he took the form of a dark elf once again, and his maneuverability increased immediately.

Less than an hour later, he entered the dale and slowed his pace. "What in Ledaedra's madness is going on?"

The prisoners stood huddled in the middle of the field away from the cave opening. A quick count yielded twelve humans, including the Princess.

ZaphMordakai entered the tunnel fuming. Before he could explode, voices drifted up from the lair. He crept down, staying back from the opening.

". . . ordered me to watch the prisoners and left," said BelCharius.

"You need to keep him under control. I gave you this assignment because I thought you could handle it. Contact me when he returns, and you had better figure . . ."

ZaphMordakai trembled as he backed down the tunnel quietly and exited. Both hands caressed the sides of his neck. There was no doubt in his mind who owned the other voice. It was Ledaedra, The Queen of the Dragons.

34

Breakfast

Lykinnia

"Cymm, heal Solar!" Lykinnia pleaded into the scrying window.

Cymm's head swiveled around in a daze. "Lykinnia?"

"Yes. It is me," she answered with patience she did not have.

He turned about absentmindedly. "I need to heal Torak."

"Cymm, you need to save Solar. Please. Right now."

He finally did as she requested, and Lykinnia sighed heavily when Solar sat upright.

Cymm drifted back over to his friends with Jalko by his side. He patted the wolf's sticky red rump. He spoke softly and blinked rapidly. "You need a bath."

Solar was ripping off one healing spell after another. Eventually, he joined Cymm.

Cymm met his gaze. "Help them, please."

Solar shook his head. "Their souls are beyond my reach. They have already begun their trip down the River of Tides or Binding, where they will spend eternity together as they committed to each other. Even the Mistress would struggle to bring them back."

"Maybe Azreala could help? She's a priestess of the Mistress." Cymm's head snapped to the side as two wolfers walked in the front door.

Lykinnia's brow furrowed. "Azreala? Who—"

"Quiet or leave," scolded Terazhan.

Lykinnia took one last glimpse at Cymm and chose the latter, continuing her musings as she returned to her abode. She took a mental note to ask Cymm who Azreala was and switched to an earlier conversation. *Maybe this creature from the void can invade my mind and read my thoughts. There is no other explanation. How else could she know so much about me? It could have been when I fell off the platform and awoke to her caressing my hair. That only partially makes sense, though. She could also have taken my memories about Father. I need to travel back and get current information, so I can test her.*

While all this thinking took place, she had subconsciously sat on the edge of her bed, removed her sandals, and stretched out, then promptly fell asleep.

ꝏꝏꝏ

She awoke in the wee hours of the morning famished and confused. Eventually, she realized she had passed out on her bed without eating dinner. Inadvertently, her nose passed her armpit, and she quickly turned away. Foregoing a much-needed bath, she chose food and a subsequent trip to the altar instead.

Once she arrived at the stone table, where she had her meals, she gave a quick wiggle and wave of her fingers, directing food and water to appear. While standing, she popped two strawberries in her mouth, then peered in the direction of the platform.

Lykinnia sighed heavily, dropped into a seat, and prepared a plate for herself of bread, blueberries, and more strawberries. Ten minutes later, her lengthy stride carried her toward the altar again.

I think I will start with the first time my father met my mother. It might take a while,—Lykinnia paused, staring at the altar in disbelief. A winged figure stood in front of a floating scrying window. "No." She marched onto the platform half growling. "Solar!"

The window disappeared. "Why do you disturb me? I have many hours of work to do."

She ran both her hands through her hair, trying to formulate her words into an argument, but only a childish yell came out. She tried again, but the smirk on his face only infuriated her more. "Fine!" Almost in tears, she turned to hide her face and depart.

"Lykinnia," Solar said, slow and sweet.

She gave him a death stare over her shoulder.

"I saw you eating breakfast." He let the comment linger.

"So. I was—" Alarm bells wailed inside her genius mind. She scanned his face and shook her head slowly.

Solar grinned and nodded quickly for twice as long. "I got you."

"That was mean. I thought you were going to be using the altar all day. I should have told Cymm to only cast half a healing spell on you." Lykinnia fumed in protest.

"I guess Unie is not as smart as she thinks if slow-brain Solar can fool her." He altered his speech to sound like a hill giant, "Now brain hurt, Solar need sleep."

Lykinnia put her hands on her hips. "Could you be serious for a minute?"

Solar froze, caught in the irony. "You—are asking me—to be serious," causing them both to laugh. He sobered. "Is everything okay?"

"Yeah. I am going to learn about their relationship like you suggested."

He nodded in approval. “I will let you get to it. I will be back in the early afternoon.” He summoned a portal and stepped backward into it.

35

Terazhan & Sendaria

Lykinnia

Someone else's memories drifted by as Lykinnia drove further back in time, going past her own birth. She continued to drop waypoints, never pausing for more than a few seconds. The timeline she followed was her father's, although several breaks appeared when he used a portal to travel from one plane to another. Fortunately, she already knew approximately where and when she was going. Her father had first observed her mother at her graduation ceremony from the Arcane Academy in Breezeport.

She was getting close. Her father was en route to the gathering. He had told her his interest was purely academic. Three races studying and sharing their knowledge freely intrigued him.

Terazhan landed in a glade, ended the flying enchantment, and immediately cast a polymorph spell to appear elven. A crowd walked by on the outskirts of the clearing, and he hurried to fall in with the group.

The band he traveled with merged with several others, and quickly became a pack.

The throng patiently wound its way down to the shore of Lake Skel, the location of all general assemblies in Breezeport. Two enormous vahlen trees, each one at least fifty feet in diameter, formed the bookends of the stage on which the events were already occurring.

He quickly found a seat on the ground, trying to blend in. Two regal elves wearing canonical hats and riding albino elk were the latest to parade across the stage. The next set of elves rode albino bears, wearing the same hats, but instead of tunics, stunning white dresses draped their forms. Most of the participants worshiped Sehaleah, Terazhan's sister, known for her beauty and benevolence. Out of the forty clerical representatives in the backdrop of the stage, only four of them were followers of Terazhan. Sehaleah had always scored high among the elves.

"Good afternoon, citizens of Breezeport and distinguished guests." A voice enveloped the crowd, obviously enhanced with magic, indicated the ceremony was about to begin and everyone should settle down. "I am Elennia Autumnstar, Dean of the College of Conjuring. Today we honor those who have completed their twenty-five-year program of study, and one individual who has mastered three colleges simultaneously."

The crowd roared in response.

A man joined the female presenter, also garbed in an emerald robe. "I am Sylvarest Moondown, Dean of the College of Illusion. Before the main presentation, the second term students from my school have developed a show to entertain you."

A star exploded into a dozen more and replicated the process two more times before the twinkling dust lazily rained upon the viewers. Misty stags leaped from one side of the sky to the other, and frog heads popped up from the leaves of the vahlen trees. A unicorn and a maiden stole the show as they silently reenacted their first encounter and the inevitable touch on the muzzle. Finally, an imp appeared above the stage, walking back and forth with swagger. The audience jeered, until a lightning bug emerged from the tree behind him, mimicking the way he walked. Hoots and guffaws followed. The bug hid when the imp turned then continued to imitate him in the opposite direction. Eventually, the bug was caught, and his tail flared brightly, before he collided with the imp in a massive shower of sparks across the sky.

The thunderous clapping subsided when Elennia Autumnstar assumed her position in the center of the stage. "This year, the Initiates will receive their diplomas from none other than Kazkackarus, The Master of Time, Friend to the Elves, and Headmaster of the White Towers in the City of the Mystics."

An ancient human drifted across the stage, joining her. A small dragon, no more than fifteen inches in height, trailed close behind him and perched on his shoulder when he stopped. Its gossamer wings radiated the sun's rays, creating little diamond sparkles everywhere.

The human wizard wore a grotesque mask at his hip, his rope belt looped through the eye sockets to secure it in place. Surprisingly, he did not carry a cane or a staff. In one arm, he held a glass orb in a specially designed sling. Inside it, golden, white, and lavender lights swirled with mist and raced around each other. In the other hand, he held a two-and-a-half-foot scepter with an enormous sapphire in its tip.

Lykinnia remembered her father mentioning this man. Besides Solar, he was the closest thing he had to a friend. Her impatience boiled over and she flew over to the double row of Initiates. With their hoods up, she could not tell which one was Sendaria, her mother.

Kazkackarus waved his hand while speaking a few words, and a cross between a table and a podium appeared with twenty neatly rolled and tied scrolls upon it.

The old man announced, "Tanaleal Hawksong from the College of Abjuration!"

The Dean of this school followed behind the graduate, and once she received her scroll, he gave her permission to lower her cowl. All three exchanged pleasantries and handshakes before everyone returned to their former positions.

This process continued for nineteen students in alphabetical order of the college. One hooded student remained.

Kazkackarus picked up the solitary scroll and tapped it in the palm of his hand. "Everyone here has worked diligently to achieve their diploma, and they represent only thirty percent of those who started the program twenty-five years ago. This is *not* a participation award!" He banged the scroll into his hand again and it multiplied. He laid all three of the scrolls back on the tabletop. "This has never been accomplished before and may never again. This student has mastered not two, but three disciplines within her first term. I can only imagine she will have mastered all nine before the end of her fourth term, making her the youngest to achieve the title of Archmage."

The crowd stood and cheered.

"Sendaria Moonbeam for the Colleges of Conjuration, Divination, and Invocation."

Three deans dressed in emerald robes followed her across the stage, and one at a time, they performed the hood removal tradition. Conveniently, she had worn three separate cowls, much to the delight of the audience.

When the third hood dropped, so did Terazhan's jaw.

36

Spiteful

ZaphMordakai

ZaphMordakai's eye twitched, and he barely controlled the electricity coursing through his body. The prisoners cowered at his approach.

This is my mission, not his. He shot a bolt of electricity into the ground. *I am in charge. No one needs to watch over me!*

He easily identified the man he sought. Standing nose to nose, he growled, "Are you Myndar?"

The man's brow furrowed. "How do you—"

The dark elf grabbed him by the scruff of his neck and dragged him away.

The other prisoners mewled and clung to Myndar's arms.

ZaphMordakai's voice cracked like thunder. "Shut up all of you or I will kill him. If the green dragon finds out, I will kill all of you."

Silence followed.

"Follow me. Now." The dark elf jogged toward the dale's exit. After running for half a league, he stopped and faced the human. "What is the name of your brother?"

Myndar scanned side-to-side for an escape route.

"Answer me. Three, two—"

"Dyfar! His name is Dyfar."

"Excellent. You will run down this path. Your brother is waiting for you, in a rather unsafe area. You need to find him and get back to the road before dark. Tell the King if he sets one foot on this trail, I will return his daughter in pieces."

Myndar's head bobbed up and down.

"Run."

37

Terazhan

Lykinnia

Lykinnia had minimal experience with the emotion of love. She was unsure how it felt, and even less sure what it looked like. Her parents were the only couple she knew, and they spent relatively little time together, at least with her around. They also kept separate living spaces, next to each other but not connected. Hugging was a rare event, and they never kissed in front of her. She had assumed this was normal. Now, she was not sure.

Her father continued to wind his way through the crowd toward Kazkackarus, but she knew his true destination. Many people engulfed the ancient wizard, trying to talk to him or at least shake his hand. He seemed bored and barely acknowledged the droves of people he met.

Terazhan walked by the crowd, two rows deep, and yelled, "The Peak of Power is watching."

The human wizard's eyes snapped open, and he craned his neck in wide arcs to find the speaker. He pushed into the crowd, scanning everyone. Finally, he whispered to his familiar, and the tiny dragon took wing on an obvious reconnaissance mission.

Lykinnia nodded approvingly, having always wondered from whom she received her mischievous trait. By this time, Terazhan stood among the group surrounding Sendaria. She observed her mother intently for a while. Her arms hung in front of her with hands folded neatly, and her head tilted to gaze at the floor. She never spoke unless spoken to. How could this be her mother, a demure, subservient, elf maiden?

"Congratulations Sendaria Moonbeam. Quite an accomplishment." Terazhan moved along.

For the first time, her mother's eyes came up. "Quite a unique accent, Master Elf."

"Yes—I am not from around here," replied Terazhan.

"Pray, tell." Sendaria took the smallest of steps toward her father.

She is on to you, Father. Can you not see? —Run! Lykinnia giggled.

"I hail from the Black Lake Region in the Realm of Tranquility. Are you familiar with it?" Terazhan held his breath.

"No, but I would love to hear more." Her mother put her hand into the crook of his elbow, and partially led him toward the gardens surrounding the stage.

Not so shy after all. Quite the actress, Mother. Lykinnia's eyes were drawn again to the ring on her mother's finger. This was the fourth time she had spun it in as many minutes. *Hmm, nervous?*

Her father's face was trapped between fear and happiness as he scanned the perimeter for an escape.

"Does my escort have a name?" asked Sendaria.

"Tera—" He cleared his throat. "Terataniel, would be my formal name."

Lykinnia smacked her forehead with her palm, then shook her head. *For Melandri's sake. He almost said his real name. What a half-wit.*

38

Bria's Necklace

Cymm

Cymm woke the following morning haunted by Torak's penetrating gaze before he died. He could not get the image out of his head and figured it might stay with him forever. If allowed, he would have buried his friend, but the wolfers had insisted on throwing all remains, including Torak and Torc's, into the pyre last night. Cymm watched helplessly as their bodies were cast into the fire unceremoniously.

"This is not right!" he had yelled when it happened.

"Husks." the lead elder had replied. "The body is no more than an empty shell once the spirit has moved on. I don't know what you are, horseman or wolfer, but you need to respect our beliefs. Your friends' beliefs."

Cymm had wanted to return the favor and lecture him about Fang. Instead, he left, unable to tolerate their custom because of the hole in his heart. The remnants of the rebel band had stopped him, encouraging him to learn about the battle training Jalko had been through. The past two days had been hard enough on Jalko. There would be time in the future to learn how to work together.

He sat up, rubbing the sleep from his eyes and feeling the warmth of Jalko's body against his leg. He glanced around, then jumped to his feet. Solar was gone. He shook his head in disbelief.

Jalko also rose to his feet slowly, and stretched as he did so.

Cymm scratched him behind the ears. "You're still here. Huh?"

He opened his pack and grabbed two meat sticks from Brato's pantry. He extended one to Jalko, but the wolf sniffed and turned his nose. He slung his backpack in position and headed in the general direction of Armak.

"Hey Jalko, how do you feel about horses?"

Jalko tilted his head sideways while walking next to him.

"Our next priority is to find my other friend. The three of us are going to be best friends." Cymm continued to eat his breakfast. The ogre ring from Bria's necklace thumped against his collarbone.

In the mayhem of last night's battle, he had completely forgotten about the message from Bria. With escalating excitement, he removed the necklace and held the leather thong in both hands with the ring floating in the middle as Azreala had instructed. He looped the ring around the strap slowly at first, but once he improved his coordination, the speed increased significantly.

A ghostly apparition with the visage of Bria appeared. The details of her face continuously refined as he twirled the necklace.

She sprang to life with full color. "Hi Cymm, I see you got my necklace. Please keep it safe."

"I will—"

"When you see Talo again, tell him 'hi' for me, then knock him on his butt!"

Her laughter brought a tear to his eye.

When Bria's merriment subsided, she said, "And by the way, you two still don't look like men." She giggled and faded into oblivion.

The tears ran freely down his cheek. He did not blubber or sob. These were tears of joy. "What a magnificent gift."

Deep down, he had always believed Terazhan had orchestrated the procession of souls, and the opportunity for the final farewell to his sister. Now, there was no doubt in his mind, it had been The Mistress. But why? What did she want?

He twirled the necklace again.

39

Voidwalker

Lykinnia

After a thirty-minute walk through the gardens spent droning on about the elves on the other side of the continent, Terazhan and her mother returned to the stage. Lykinnia considered jumping ahead several times. Her father exited the stage, and although she was tempted to follow, she decided to stay and observe her mother.

Sendaria glanced back over her shoulder in Terazhan's direction, then gazed down at the ring on her finger. She twisted it around with a sinister smile on her face.

Lykinnia ended her observation of past events, arriving back at the altar as the scrying window disappeared. Solar stood quietly next to her, giving her a scare.

"By Melandri's good nature, Solar. How long have you been standing there?" Lykinnia pushed Solar with two hands against his bare chest.

"Only five to ten minutes. You appeared to be making great progress, so I did not want to disturb you. However, I need the altar for a few hours."

Lykinnia nodded, then turned away with her head down, self-absorbed. *I do not need the protection of the altar anymore when I summon the creature. I can continue this back at my abode.*

She hastened to return to the wood table where she performed most of her studies. She had barely arrived when the first words of her invisibility spell came spewing forth.

"Voidwalker!" Lykinnia yelled into the pit of blackness.

"That is a step up from *creature.* Our last conversation ended rather abruptly."

"I can only listen to so much nonsense about teleporting fireballs, and disintegrated spell books, and dirty clothes." Lykinnia paused, hoping for a reaction that did not come. "Moving on to a different subject. Why do you refuse to talk about Terazhan?"

"Please stop saying his name!"

"Why?" In the silence, Lykinnia found her own answer. "Because saying a god's name gives them more power." She grunted in frustration. "Did you ever love him?"

"Obviously, dear. I—"

"No, not *obviously.* I have reason to believe your first encounter was contrived. Father fell in love with you and remains in love with you." Lykinnia's emotions bubbled over, revealing themselves in the tears streaming down her face.

"Grow up, Lykinnia. People fall in and out of love, or they move in different directions."

"He gave you half of his life force. You should have mentioned this first."

The voice snickered. "Actually, I was pregnant with you at the time. So, *we* took half of your father's life force. Several scholars have theorized the placenta would magnify the effect, and you could live well beyond the expected tens of thousands of years. You might even see the end of *The One*."

Of course, she knows about The One. I cannot win this battle with new information appearing in every other sentence. "Were you expecting Tera—my father to attend your graduation ceremony?"

"No. How would I have known?"

"Where did you get the ring worn on your right hand during the ceremony?" Lykinnia listened intently for any additional clues in the sound of her voice.

"What has your father been telling you? He is—"

"*He* does not speak of you. It is too painful for him. And why do you care?" Lykinnia shot back in anger.

"I want to rebuild our relationship. We've missed out on four hundred years. Don't you want your mother back in your life?"

"The lies and refusals to answer my questions make it nearly impossible to trust you." Lykinnia rose from the wooden bench at the table with her neck straining. "Who gave you the ring you were wearing during the ceremony?"

After a long pause, a scaly, clawed hand pushed through the aperture between the planes, right in front of the young girl's face. "Is this the ring you are referring to?"

"Yes, who gave it to you?" Lykinnia mustered as much composure as she could. *It is her!*

"My parents, as a graduation gift." The reptilian hand retracted and disappeared as quickly as it came.

"I want to know what happened to your arm. Are they both like that?"

"It is the price I paid. Now, do you believe me or not?"

"I will let you know shortly." Lykinnia ended her invisibility spell and closed the opening to the void.

40

Games

ZaphMordakai

A full day had passed, and BelCharius had not yet realized Myndar was missing. It was mid-afternoon and the prisoners were returning from a short break outside. They returned to the pen like livestock, pushing against each other.

"BelCharius, are they all back?" asked ZaphMordakai, the dark elf.

"Yeah, sure. They aren't going anywhere. There are owlbears everywhere."

"Good. I'll be back shortly. An owlbear sounds delicious right now." Zaph stepped into the tunnel.

"I don't think that is a good idea. What if—if—they come for the Princess?" The green dragon's head snapped up.

"Yes, good point. I will also do a perimeter sweep." The dark elf disappeared up the tunnel. *You want to play games? Let's play.*

"But—but—Zaph!" BelCharius yelled up the passageway.

Once out in the main clearing, he transformed into a black dragon and immediately took wing. The *whoosh* of his wings and the rippling of the skin flaps echoed in the dale. Taking off at this trajectory exerted his pectoral muscles and strained the tendons in his wings, right down to the tip of each phalanx. He circled as he gained altitude, keeping the cave entrance in sight.

BelCharius craned his neck out on the second loop and quickly retracted it.

ZaphMordakai expanded his third loop before descending. His massive bulk would not allow him to land discreetly in the dale. He located the trail, selected the widest gap in the treetops, and attempted to land on top of a large tree near it. His wings beat furiously, and his rear talons extended, seeking purchase. Every branch he touched creaked, then snapped, until he finally coasted to the ground.

He transformed back into his dark-elven form, then took off running back toward the cave.

"I need to know if he can contact Ledaedra. I can't even summon her." He growled and ran faster.

41

Sendaria

Lykinnia

The following morning, Lykinnia paced in her room. She had dreamt of this moment for almost four centuries—her mother was alive. She dressed quickly into her everyday robe, headed out the door past her wooden study table, and ended up at the stone table where she took her meals.

She conjured up her breakfast and slowly ate a hearty meal of sweet breads, cakes, and fruit. *How many lies has she told me? Definitely the book, probably the ring, and there were many questions she refused to answer. She is hiding something.* She growled. *Why do I care?*

She took several bites in mindful silence.

Why do I care? I simply want everything to return to normal, like it was before she left. She sighed. *Normal? What is normal? Mother and Father pretending to love each other? Or the five-to-ten-minute breaks from their self-interests to check on me. The fact is my childhood ignorance made those years enjoyable. Which will never happen again because I know too much.*

Four hundred years. Why did she wait so long to contact me? I have opened portals hundreds of times over the past few centuries, why did she not try to reach me sooner? What does she want?

Lykinnia finished her breakfast, then interlaced her fingers and cracked her knuckles. The desire to find out where the ring came from carried her to the altar.

The vacant platform surprised her, and she rushed to occupy it before Solar appeared. Using the marker she placed before, she easily traversed back in time to the ceremony's beginning. It was effortless with a waypoint, like finding a page in a book with tabs hanging off the edge. In this case, it pulled the scene out to the side, and as she flew past her markers, she could quickly identify each one without slowing down.

"Now, to track my mother and trace the origin of the ring." Lykinnia glanced around unsure how to proceed. "I do not even know where her abode is." She patiently waited for the ceremony to end and followed her mother as she exited the stage. As an afterthought, she added another time marker, bookending the event in case she needed to return.

"I wonder how many waypoints can be placed by an individual. I must be getting close to one hundred." Lykinnia's shoulder dance ceased when her mother stepped onto a staircase winding around a gigantic elm tree. She released a squeal of amazement. Dozens of identical pods hung from the boughs of this tree and in the hundreds of neighboring trees. Sendaria entered one near the top of the elm, with Lykinnia close behind.

A bed hung from the ceiling of the cozy room, providing enough space for a table with two chairs, a lounging chair, and a large bookshelf.

Lykinnia lingered, watching her mother's every move. She sighed deeply and ended her observation, then sent herself back one hour before the graduation ceremony. Her physical location remained unchanged; she was alone in her mother's pod. A quick glance was all she spared before jumping back another hour. Her mother sat at her table penning a letter, already garbed in her beautiful dress for the ceremony, and wearing the ring. So, she traveled back another hour. This time, Sendaria stood in her undergarments, holding a mirror in one hand, a brush in the other. Light sparkled off the ring as she stroked her lustrous hair.

Lykinnia jumped back one hour at a time until she found her mother in bed, then jumped back in increments of two hours. She was beginning to lose track of her jumps when a hand lightly rested on her shoulder.

A soft voice spoke, "Lykinnia, remember where you are. You need to end your travels."

The priestess dropped a waypoint and closed the scrying window. Solar stood within reach, and she prepared to berate him.

He took a step back. "Your body cannot take much more. You have been at it for twelve hours."

"No . . ." Lykinnia faltered. The dipping sun reinforced Solar's statement.

"Go eat and sleep. I will be done here by midnight. Make sure you drink as much as you can. This process dehydrates the user." Solar commenced his daily tasks with the altar.

Lykinnia staggered as she stepped off the platform and trudged away dejected.

42

Spy

ZaphMordakai

The dark elf ran quickly back to the cave, and he entered the dell to find the prisoners taking another break. *I knew it. The little worm can summon Ledaedra.*

Several of the captives pointed in his direction.

He glared back at them, putting his finger to his lips. His pace slowed dramatically at the entrance to the cave, and he forced his breathing under control. A voice met him halfway down the tunnel. *What are they up to?* ZaphMordakai considered his options. *I could step out and end this farce or wait till they're done and kill—What did she say?*

"Maybe you could contact him now, and ask why he is not here," offered BelCharius.

ZaphMordakai backed down the passageway, massaging his neck.

"Tomorrow! I need to meet with the generals to discuss our next attack," snapped Ledaedra.

The dark elf sighed in relief as he continued toward the exit. *Typical green dragon maneuver, contacting her to tell on me. You will pay for this BelCharius.*

43

Jakarrak

Lykinnia

Lykinnia had every intention of awakening at midnight, but her mind and body did not comply until sunrise. She raced out the door, pausing momentarily at the stone table to create food and water and to wolf it down.

She hated to admit Solar had been right, but yesterday proved she needed a new plan. When she arrived at the waypoint from the previous night, her mother was having dinner alone in her room, with the ring already on her finger.

Lykinnia attempted to fine-tune her process by moving through larger pockets of time, knowing she could be missing her mother coming and going. Frustration knotted in her back and neck. She tapped her lip with her finger until an idea came to her.

She tried counting to estimate the passage of time in her vision and discovered this process to be precise. On the fifth morning, before the graduation ceremony, Lykinnia popped in to find her mother had recently risen from bed, and without a ring on her finger. She scanned all the flat surfaces in the pod but found no trace of the item.

Lykinnia dropped a waypoint. Her stomach had been rumbling for a while. She had lost track of real time and wondered if Solar was already waiting to use the altar.

After her mother dressed and brushed her hair, she grabbed a book from the shelf and sat in the lounging chair. Lykinnia understood the morning ritual well. Her mother was memorizing spells for the day, or at least refamiliarizing herself with the nuances.

Within the hour, Sendaria Moonbeam replaced the book on the shelf, grabbed her satchel, slung it over her shoulder, and exited the pod with her daughter in pursuit. The elven mage paused to place a ward on the entrance, and soon entered an outdoor café where she met up with a large group of friends.

"Not skipping breakfast this morning Sendaria?" asked a friendly face.

Her mother took a seat at a narrow table with benches, comfortably seating six individuals per side. "Sorry Dalamar, only one breakfast for you today."

The excited group spoke over each other loudly, making it impossible to follow the conversation. Not that it mattered. Lykinnia was more intrigued by the cuisine. Bowls of puffy tan grains, mixed with a thick cream, and covered with berries, were set in front of each elf. Her stomach grumbled again, which caused her to giggle, then she clamped her hand over her mouth. She sighed in relief, remembering they could not hear her.

After breakfast, everyone dispersed, going their separate ways. Sendaria walked to a ten-story stone tower in the city's center. Although there were several other towers scattered throughout the city, this one seemed out of place and ominous.

Upon entering the building, Lykinnia found the inside much larger than the apparent outside. A large circular staircase was positioned in the center of the tower and wound its way to the top. It was a smooth black cylindrical stone, and the stairs were carved into it. The first three levels had catwalks connecting the staircase to the rooms along the outer wall, and a ceiling blocked the view beyond the fourth level.

Sendaria entered the staircase and exited to the second floor. Lykinnia could not identify any connection between station and level in the tower based on the other wizards continuing to higher floors. Her mother opened the door to her study using a skeleton key, and quickly closed it behind her. Lykinnia barely had enough time to rush through the gap. She had learned a hard lesson recently; inanimate objects have substance. The closing door would have smacked her in the forehead, and she could not open a locked door. However, there were also benefits. It had allowed her to take her mother's spell book off the shelf and examine its contents.

Sendaria lit a lamp on the desk by casting a light spell onto a large opaque sphere. The elven sorceress gasped. "What are you doing in here?"

A tall male elven hunter lounged casually in one of her chairs. His bow and quiver rested against the side within reach. "I mean you no harm."

Sendaria's spell component materialized in her hand so quickly, Lykinnia could not determine where it came from. The lump of charcoal vaporized, and red-hot flames shot forth from the palms of both hands.

The intruder waved his hand in a leisurely arc before him, and the gouts of fire burst into a stampede of butterflies with an audible *pop*.

Undeterred, Sendaria whipped a small strand of yarn in the man's direction. It transformed mid-flight into a thick hemp rope and coiled around her target from knees to shoulders.

However, with a wink and a nod, the rope transmuted into the scaly hide of a fifteen-foot boa constrictor and fell to the floor with a *thump*. The elven man and snake gazed at each other a moment before the snake slithered toward her mother.

Sendaria retreated a few steps and banged into her desk. A mask of fear engulfed her face as a hidden dagger emerged from the folds of her robes. Her mother surveyed the room for an escape route, then lunged at the serpent gliding along the floor. The dagger sunk into the wooden floor where its head had been a moment before, but now it twisted around the thigh of her closest leg. In a matter of seconds, it had engulfed her exactly as her adversary had been entangled with the rope.

"Shall we continue this game? Or you could afford me the rights of a guest," the elven hunter stated without emotion.

Lykinnia stared with her mouth agape. She dropped another waypoint.

Sendaria finally responded, "Guests do not sneak into someone's study. They knock. I will give you three seconds to explain yourself before I scream, bringing a dozen arcane wardens."

"If they could hear you." He turned the chair around, repositioned his bow and quiver, and flopped into the chair.

Sendaria's brow knit tightly together, and her lips pursed, then she screamed. "Help! There's an intruder in my room."

He demonstratively yawned, and she continued to yell and struggle against the coils of the snake.

The shouting ended when Sendaria shifted her weight too far to one side and toppled to the floor. She grunted on impact, the thickness of the snake's body preventing her head from striking the wooden planks.

"What do you want?" she asked through clenched teeth.

"I have a gift for you."

"A gift?" Sendaria said doubtfully.

"Yes. An early graduation gift." The stranger circled his index finger toward the snake, and it unwound itself, then coiled up next to her.

Sendaria sat up, right elbow on her knee. "What's the catch?"

"For now, there isn't one." He produced a ring from an inside pocket in his leather jerkin, then held it out.

Lykinnia beamed, drawing in for a closer inspection. Her vision blurred briefly, then cleared.

Her mother hesitated. "What does it do?"

"It is a ring of true seeing. If you put it on, it will be self-explanatory." He extended his hand eagerly, the ring resting in his palm only a foot from her nose.

Sendaria wiggled her fingers and recited a simple cantrip.

"First you attack me, now you insult me. I told you; I mean you no harm."

"I have no reason to trust or believe you. I don't even know who you are."

"The ring will show you." He forcefully motioned for her to take it.

She snatched it from his hand and inspected it closely. "The ring will show me?" She moved the ring into position and paused to gaze into his eyes. The enormous ring slid onto her finger, and it sized itself as it glided past her second knuckle. Her mother's eyes went wide, and she stood transfixed, staring at something two feet above the stranger's head.

Lykinnia rushed to her mother's side in excitement. "What did you see?"

No one moved for several seconds. Sendaria slid the ring off her finger, then slowly slid it back on. "How do I know this ring is not forcing me to see things falsely?"

"Fair question. Take the ring off." The stranger motioned with his chin.

"Who are you?" Sendaria removed it.

The visitor shimmered slightly, then grew to well over eight feet tall. He lost his elven features and took on an angelic glow like her father's.

"Uncle Jakarrak?" Lykinnia's mouth dropped open.

"My name is Jakarrak, God of Enlightenment."

Lykinnia remained stunned. "Uncle Jakarrak?"

"A god? What do you want from me?" Sendaria folded her arms over her chest.

"Wear the ring for a week. If you see someone like me, engage them. Find out what they want, and the ring is yours."

Sendaria nodded slowly while grinning.

Lykinnia's vision blurred again for much longer, and she swooned.

The gleam in Sendaria's eyes multiplied. "I will do it."

A firm hand shook her shoulder. "You must stop," Solar demanded.

Dazed and confused, she followed his instruction and released her control of the altar. Solar's face materialized in front of hers, and she collapsed into his arms.

44

Warhorse

Cymm

Cymm set a brisk pace, took frequent breaks, and extended the trek well into the night. The seven-day journey took him and Jalko only five days. As dusk approached, they arrived at the gates of Armak.

A guard stepped forward with his hand up. "Sorry, gates are closing. We're not admitting anyone else tonight."

"I am Cymm Reich, and—"

The guard burst into laughter. "Son, if you are going to try to impersonate someone, you should at least know the basics about them. Cymm is a horseman, not a wolfer."

"I am not a wolfer—" Cymm patted Jalko's head. "Well, I am also a horseman, and my warhorse is in the city."

"Let's go. Cap'n wants this gate closed now!" a guard yelled down from the tower.

"Nice try kid. Come back in the morning." The guard pivoted, heading for the slowly diminishing gap in the gates.

Cymm marched next to him yelling in his face. "How about we talk with Lord Barrister in the morning? I will demand he put you on patrol duty in Tent City."

"Kill him," a voice whispered from behind them.

Cymm glanced back to find no one. *"DragonSin, do not let those doors close."*

"Cymm, calm down. He is doing his job."

The guard hesitated and turned his face up to the second floor of the gatehouse.

"What's the problem?" came the same voice from above.

"He claims he is Cymm Reich and wants to see Lord Barrister."

"I'll be right down."

"I always sacrifice for everyone, including this city, and now I want a little leniency so I can find my horse. Is that too much to ask?" Cymm scratched behind Jalko's ears, which had perked to the clanging of armor and weapons.

"You might have picked the wrong occasion to make your stand," replied the sword.

Six guards with crossbows and six with long swords poured through the opening in the gates.

"Did you call for Lord Barrister?" Cymm placed his hands on his hips.

A captain stepped forward. "We won't tolerate troublemakers. Now move along or your wolf will be put down, and you will be hung from the top of the barbican."

Jalko growled low and deep.

"I don't want any trouble, but I need to find my horse." Cymm stared the leader down.

The captain stepped forward again, drawing his sword slowly and with purpose.

"Cap'n." One of the guards rushed forward, breaking rank. He whispered to the captain, whose eyes went wide.

The captain retorted loudly, "He has a dire wolf!"

The guard glanced at Cymm conspiratorially. "He's the one that entered Tent City when Captain Beckwith—"

"Yes! Captain Beckwith, I asked him to watch my horse."

The captain in front of him returned his sword to its sheath. After an awkward moment of silence, he barked out orders, "Everyone inside and close this gate." He pointed at a guard. "You, go to Northwest Tower and get Beckwith. Everyone else, back to your post."

There was a flurry of movement, and within a minute, the gate was closed and Cymm stood on the inside with only the captain.

When they were alone, the captain turned on him, shoving him against the stone wall. "You better not be lying."

"I'm not. Captain Beckwith swore to watch over my horse while I was in Tent City."

The guard leered at Jalko while pressing him against the wall and scoffed. "Beckwith is my roommate, and he has a horse, which I have fed several times, including—"

Cymm pushed the man's forearm off his chest and lunged for him, delivering a massive—hug.

45

The Wager

Lykinnia

The young priestess was sore, and her body ached all over. Her hunger and parched mouth screamed to be satiated. She struggled to sit up, and did something she had never done before, conjured food and water on the floor of her abode. A drinking and feeding frenzy ensued.

"This is—not proper," she said between gulps and slurps. "Food—should not—be in the bedroom." She had a strict code about what activities occurred at the stone table, the wooden table, and inside her abode.

Her belly now hurt worse than her body. She fought against the urge to lie back down.

She opened the door to be greeted by a brilliant sunrise and the six taviian warriors sitting at her wooden table. Their bulbous eyes glanced at her for only a moment. With their wings tucked safely away, all four arms worked diligently on their bandoliers, adding new pockets and adjusting the straps.

Gillygahpadima rose on her two-hind, grasshopper-like legs and greeted her in the shrill native voice of their kind, “Good morning!”

“Good morning, everyone. How long was I asleep for?” Lykinnia asked in the Taviian language.

Confusion was the only response.

“Solar will know.” Lykinnia held her belly and walked stiff legged to the altar, where she then waited several minutes for him to finish.

“Lykinnia, it is about time. We need to talk.” Solar beckoned her over.

“How long was I out?”

“The sun has risen and set twice since I put you to bed. It reminded me of the old days when my little Unie would fall asleep by the altar, and I would carry her to—”

“Solar, what happened to me?”

“The games you were playing with the Altar of One the past few centuries did not prepare you for the challenges of its advanced capabilities. You must train your mind and body to endure these new requirements by building up your strength and tolerance, not plunging in.” Solar paused and glared at her intently.

Lykinnia gazed up sheepishly. “You knew I was using the altar all this time and—”

“Lykinnia, are you listening to me? Forget about your mad-scientist creations in the Lower Darken Wood. You can seriously injure or kill yourself if you are not more careful,” Solar scolded.

“Does Father know?” Lykinnia waited for Solar’s face to turn tomato red. “I am kidding. I will listen and learn if you will teach me.”

“Very well. Now, tell me what you know about your mother and Jakarrak.”

Lykinnia shrugged. "Not much. I was following my mother, trying to figure out where the ring came from on her finger at the graduation ceremony. When I asked her about the—"

"When you asked her? Lykinnia, what is going on?"

Lykinnia's voice was soft, and she stared at the ground. "Solar, what if I told you my mother might be alive?"

"Not possible." Solar's wings flared and tiny bolts of electricity traced along his feathers. "You have been chasing this dream for four centuries. Stop! It is *not* possible."

"I know." She pivoted the conversation, hoping he forgot about her slip. "At my mother's ceremony, she kept playing with the ring on her finger. I could not tell if it was a nervous habit, or if she was unaccustomed to wearing it. So, I tracked her movements back in time until I discovered when and from whom she received it."

"Interesting. I was not aware they knew each other before Terazhan introduced them. I want you to take another day off from the altar, and tomorrow you can use it on a limited basis." Solar fixed her with his gaze.

Lykinnia opened her mouth to argue but decided to nod instead.

"Good. In the meantime, I will ask your father about Jakarrak's gift. I think you might have discovered an oddity."

Oddity? She scoffed. "See you tomorrow Solar. I am going to sleep a bit longer."

ꝏꝏꝏ

Lykinnia wanted to speak to her mother. There was no doubt in her mind, even though she had placated Solar earlier by denying it, her mother was alive.

She sat on the edge of her bed with the spell dancing across her lips. The void opened, and she turned invisible.

"Sendaria, I wish to speak with you," she yelled into the netherworld.

An immediate response came back. "Another improvement, however, Mother is preferred. So, you believe me now?"

"Yes. I always believed in my heart you remained alive. I have been searching for proof for almost four centuries."

"What convinced you? The ring?" asked Sendaria.

"Yes, and I know who gave it to you. It was not your parents." Lykinnia waited for a reaction.

The silence endured for a while. "Lykinnia, are you calling your mother a liar?"

"Yes, but I still want to get to know you. The real you. I am tired of all the lies and the games." Lykinnia bit her lower lip gently rolling it between her teeth.

"And who do you think gave me the ring?"

"More games! This—"

"No. If you answer correctly, the games are done," her mother interjected, her sharp tone trailing off.

"Uncle Jakarrak."

"Your father said this?" Sendaria inquired.

"No. Games are over, right?"

"Yes, my dear. You are an extraordinary young lady. I should not be surprised, and yet I am. How did you figure this out?" The tone in her mother's voice reflected her pride.

"Not yet. Explain the secretive plan you and Uncle Jakarrak organized."

"At first, I was oblivious to your uncle's plan. He asked me to wear it and report to him if I noticed anyone like him. After your father spoke to me at the graduation ceremony, I knew it was not a coincidence. Your uncle came back the following day, explained who your father was, and bet me he could force him to marry me."

Lykinnia interjected, "What was the wager?"

"If he were wrong, I could keep the ring. If he was right, the ring was a wedding gift, but I had to perform a service—"

"Eww!"

"Daughter, your immaturity is shocking. We are talking about something much more important. Power. I was positioned to win either way, I would own a powerful ring, or I would be wed to a god. Love is fleeting and requires two individuals to experience the benefit. However, power, especially extreme power, requires only one person to exert and enjoy the influence and control. Is this the type of bonding you were looking for?"

Lykinnia remained slack-jawed for several moments. "It is. So, why come to me now, after four centuries?"

"The power in this world is shifting, and I want my daughter by my side. Soon, you will be allowed to leave the Peak of Power, and together we can take over Erogoth. Good against evil, law and order in contradiction to chaos, and now the dragons versus everyone else. We do not have to pick a side. We can *break* them all and bend them to our will." Sendaria issued a light-hearted laugh. "You said no games."

Lykinnia's nose crinkled. A tornado swirled in her mind. *This has to be about my coming of age.* "How do I even fit into this grandiose plan? How would I help you achieve this?"

"Do not belittle your accomplishments. If you could have studied at the Towers of Sorcery in the City of the Mystics, or the Arcane Academy in Breezeport, you would have shattered my record for learning all nine colleges. The title of youngest Archmage would have been yours. No one I have ever met comes close to your intelligence."

She should share her perspective with Solar. Lykinnia giggled.

"Do I amuse you?" asked Sendaria, annoyed.

"Sorry, my mind drifted. Power is of no interest to me, and besides, the impact on my other relationships would be significant."

Her mother pressed, "There should be no change in the relationship with your father or Solar, and you can keep your pet—"

"Cymm is not a pet!"

"I find it interesting you knew who I was talking about. What is he then? Husband, lover—educate me," her mother pushed relentlessly.

"This conversation is over!" Lykinnia ended her spell, closing the fracture in space.

46

Frustration

Talo

An arrow zipped off the bowstring, striking the target's center-eye. Two more arrows went airborne in rapid succession, hitting the targets on each side, dead center. He did not shoot at the same target anymore, because he had damaged so many arrows from them hitting each other.

Talo stood on the line at Old-Man Semper's training grounds, working off his stress. Cymm's absence approached a fortnight, with no word.

Semper came out and joined him after he had already completed ten rounds. "Everything alright?"

"Not really. When are we going to tell Cymm enough is enough? He can't run off without letting us know." Talo backed up to the fence, ten additional paces from the line, and released three arrows. The result was the same.

"I'm worried about him too. This isn't like him, especially with your wedding coming up. He wouldn't miss it." Semper put a reassuring hand on his shoulder.

Talo's eyes met Semper's for the first time. "Do you think we should go looking for him?"

The old man rubbed his chin. "If he isn't back by your wedding, I will go find him."

"That's almost two weeks away. If he isn't back by then, I'm going with you."

"How do you think your new bride will react?" asked Semper.

"Vena will have to understand how important Cymm is to me," replied Talo. "I'm heading home. Have a good night."

Talo passed by the bell tower, weaving in and out of a large gang of adolescents, two of whom were his brothers. The children were engaged in an argument.

"I don't want to be the dragon. I was the dragon last time," yelled one of the Darkmane boys.

"Maybe someone would be the dragon, if the dragon got to win sometimes," yelled a Softtail girl in support.

"Don't be an orc-brain. Dragons can't beat paladins!" hollered Toma, his little brother.

Talo shook his head in disbelief and shocked to find most of the children agreed with him. "What are you tassel-heads doing?"

"We are playing Paladins and Dragons," replied a boy.

"Yeah! To get ready for when Cymm trains us to be paladins," added another boy.

"What?" asked Talo.

"When the girl comes to be trained by Cymm, he might as well train us too."

Talo fixed Toma with a death stare, and his brother dropped his gaze. He left the children to their games.

"What if there are two dragons instead—"

"Two dragons. We can't get one!"

"I'm going fishing."

The hubbub died out behind him, and eventually, he entered the barnyard where he found his father, Daro, cleaning a horse's hooves.

"Hey long face, what's wrong?" asked his father.

"No word from Cymm. If he's dead, I'm going to kill him," replied Talo.

His father gave him a bizarre face.

"You know what I mean. Semper and I have discussed going to find him. What do you think, Father?" Talo strode over to help keep the horse in place.

Daro scratched his head with the hoof pick. "Yeah, after the wedding we can head up to Armak and ask around."

We? Talo felt pleased they were on the same page. "I don't want to wait a fortnight, but I understand."

His father was talking about the yield of the crops this year when Talo zoned out, deep in his own thoughts. *Cymm would get in a lot less trouble if he had me to watch his back.*

47

Unexpected Information

ZaphMordakai

The forest was unusually quiet, causing the deer to pause its grazing. Its head raised, ears twitched, and tail swished, then it bound and leaped several times. An owlbear lumbered from behind an enormous tree trunk barely ten feet away. The feathers on top of its head flared, no longer lying flat against its tawny fur. The deer froze momentarily, determining an escape path, and the owlbear lunged. One ton of rage and muscle propelled it forward with six-inch talons at the ready.

The deer leaped at the last second, escaping only because a lightning bolt slammed into the bear. The hunter, now the prey, was thrown back into a nearby tree. The smell of burnt fur overpowered the sound of sizzling flesh. Not ready to surrender, the owlbear's beak snapped at the empty air, its left leg reflexively twitching.

ZaphMordakai salivated uncontrollably. He had been waiting an hour for the attack to occur. Another bolt zipped in, guaranteeing the meat was cooked the way he liked it. Extending one talon, he made several parallel slices, then peeled the fur off like a banana. He removed the upper half of the pelt and bit deep into the flesh, ripping off a large slab of meat. Gore and drool dripped from his chin and vaporized off his fangs.

Ledaedra summoned him. Fighting against his impulse to delay, he responded.

The ebony shadow of his liege appeared. She craned her neck around. "Why are you not watching over the prisoners?"

The black dragon bristled. "I required sustenance, so I assigned the lieutenant to watch over them."

"I asked you to watch over him because he is untested. His failure to keep the Princess safe would likewise be yours." Ledaedra stared in silence.

"Understood, my Queen. Is there a minimum number of prisoners you require?"

"I require only the Princess."

"Before you go, I have useful information to share with the generals."

"Speak!" she replied.

"TetraQuerahn's human killer was in Armak before you sent me south. He is in league with some peculiar individuals," said ZaphMordakai.

"Hmm. Tell me more about his companions."

"There was a golden sprite, who was almost six feet tall, and she could fly faster than anything I have seen. The enemy was a two-headed creature with skin blacker than mine, took massive lightning strikes, blasting holes in its body, and didn't die. Also, halfway through the battle, two lightning bolts struck the human, and he grew to over nine feet tall—"

"Are you certain?" asked the Queen.

"Yes. Is it important?"

"Possibly. The two you speak of reside near you at the Peak of Power. You did well. I will investigate this further." Ledaedra's form dissipated into the shadows without a farewell.

ZaphMordakai chuckled. "The Peak of Power—of course."

48

Homecoming

Cymm

Cymm strode into Stallion Rise on his warhorse, hoping to slip by unnoticed to his farm.

"Cymm's back!" A young girl yelled and fell in line behind him.

Boys and girls of all ages yelled and called to each other, and droves of children joined the procession. The shouting and excitement quickly turned to screams and shrieks of fear.

"Wolf!"

The fear quickly turned to terror and mayhem. Children ran in every direction, many screaming, the rest crying.

You fool. Cymm berated himself and swiftly dismounted. "Jalko, to me!"

The dire wolf, standing almost five feet at the scruff, charged Cymm. He side-stepped at the last second and turned to face his companion. Jalko dropped his head to the ground, raised his haunches, and vigorously wagged his tail.

Cymm locked eyes with the wolf and bombarded him with images of the children's fear. Jalko's tail stopped wagging, and his head scanned side to side, then he trotted over to Cymm.

The paladin wrapped his arms around the dire wolf's neck, hugging him. "It's alright. He won't hurt you."

No one approached.

Cymm sat on the ground, and the enormous wolf plopped down on him.

Someone tittered in the distance, then two more joined in.

"Come on. Come pet the little doggy," Cymm shouted.

The first brave soul appeared, then a few more, and within minutes over thirty kids swarmed him. Cymm stood and checked in with Jalko to make sure his temperament was good. Children pulled his fur, his tail, and stepped on his feet, and Jalko never displayed any signs of aggression.

"That isn't a little doggy."

Cymm spun to find Dirk Darkmane, the boy who had been possessed by Dego many years ago. They eyed each other for a long moment.

Dirk approached him with purpose. "You had a lot of people losing sleep. I'm glad you're alright."

They clasped hands and embraced.

Dirk collected two of the children and headed back to his farm.

"Aren't you a sight for sore eyes." Old-Man Semper walked straight into him with a hug. "Where have you been?"

Cymm slid his arm around Semper's shoulders and pulled him in the direction he was headed. "It's a long story and I would prefer to only tell it once."

"We were all worried about you, but some of us didn't handle it very well. Speak of the devil." Semper said the last part in hushed tones.

Talo, a full fence length away, was jogging toward them out of breath. As he approached, Cymm opened his arms out wide, and Talo punched him square in the chest, so hard it knocked him backward. "Where in the nine hells have you been?"

Jalko growled low and menacingly.

Cymm turned on Jalko. "No." Then he turned back again. "Never!"

Jalko slunk over and rubbed his head against Cymm's chest.

Talo's clenched fists remained by his side, his blazing eyes telling the story. "Well, what's the answer? Went looking for a new pet."

Cymm raised his open palms in surrender. "Talo, my brother—"

"Don't give me that *brother* crap. You can't keep doing this!" Talo's eyes were welling with tears.

"I plan to find our Head of Household and tell the whole story once. Hopefully, you will understand." Cymm stepped by him.

Talo followed, grumbling, "Brother? A brother wouldn't do this. Could have missed my wedding. Does he even care?"

Cymm accepted the scathing comments in stride, but they cut deep. He was glad to arrive at the farmstead where the Reich family waited in the barnyard.

"Cymm, you're back!" Cela was the first to run and jumped into Cymm's waiting arms.

The rest of the pack swarmed him, touched him, jostled him, and his Uncle Daro delivered a powerful hug.

Toma took the warhorse's lead from Cymm's hand and escorted him to the barn.

Talo chirped in the background with a mocking voice, "Welcome back. Did you have fun? Nice doggy you got there."

Cymm caught Uncle Daro giving Talo a reprimanding gaze.

Jalko's head swiveled toward him, and Talo swiftly stepped back.

"Aunt Nové, any berry bread left? I haven't eaten for a day," claimed Cymm.

"Just baked two loaves. Come on in, and we can all get comfortable."

As they all piled into the house, Cymm scanned the yard. His house and barn were still intact. Nothing had changed. He blinked slowly and sighed, before stepping inside. "There's only one thing I like better than visiting other places—coming home." A plate with a large slice slid in front of him. "And berry bread." Cymm's face took on a tinge of red. *And, of course, Lykinnia.* He glanced around quickly to see if anyone had read his thoughts.

49

Custodian

Lykinnia

Lykinnia's eyes flittered open. It was hard to tell what time of day it was, but sunlight spilled in through the circular hole in her wooden door. She sat up, rubbed the sleep from her eyes, and cast a light spell on a short stalactite in the center of her ceiling.

She grabbed a leather satchel and hurried to the altar after a quick breakfast.

Solar's arms and wings stretched wide, creating quite a spectacle as he stared into the rising sun. His eyes rolled up in the back of his head, while chanting in hushed tones for almost twenty minutes. Finally, he acknowledged her presence.

"Good morning, Solar."

"I have not seen you this cheerful in a while. What is going on?" He tucked his wings away.

She took several steps closer and studied his eyes. "Solar, I need a friend right now, not a custodian."

A wry smile appeared on his face. "Little baby sheep eyes will not work on me, you know this. However, I will endeavor to be what you need, with the right to end the trial without argument."

She performed a pirouette, then unslung the satchel from her shoulder. In one smooth move, she hoisted it up onto the altar. From the bag, she withdrew her mother's spell book. She proficiently wiggled her fingers, removing the glyph she had placed on it, and pushed it toward Solar. "Open it."

He hesitated, then shook his head knowingly.

"If I wanted to turn you into a unicorn so I could ride you, I would not need such an elaborate ruse. It is not warded. Open it," she commanded.

With a furtive glance, Solar turned the front cover in a big arc from right to left. His lips moved with silent words. He closed the book and faced her. "This is *not* possible."

Why does everyone keep saying that? "It is possible. There it is." She pointed at it.

"This is the book Cymm gave you?"

She nodded. "He does not know the significance, or even the relationship. Although, I did mention the previous owner's name. Sendaria Moonbeam." The name rolled off her tongue like a spell.

"Can you prove the providence of this artifact?" he asked dubiously.

"Yes." Lykinnia watched Solar's lower jaw fall open.

"Do it." His eyes slowly burned with inner heat.

Lykinnia removed everything from the altar and traveled back to the fire in her mother's abode. She immediately walked to the bookshelf and removed the identical book. After setting it down on a table, she leafed through numerous pages. "It is blank, and I assume the other books are too." She grabbed a second, laying it on top of the first, and opened it. It was blank, as well as a third and a fourth.

Solar leafed through a book. "All right, you proved your point."

The room burst into a ball of fire, and Lykinnia ended the vision.

No one spoke for many uncomfortable seconds. Solar attempted to repeatedly, then shook his head. Finally, he sighed. "As a friend, it appears you have been right all along. As your caretaker, and someone who knew your mother, I would strongly recommend you damper your enthusiasm. I do not believe your mother was involved in this."

"So, your theory is, a thief absconded with my mother's spell books and replaced them with exact replicas?" Lykinnia asked condescendingly.

"Why not? I could do it. I would cast a polymorph spell on each individual replacement book as I stole the original. That way, each book could be held separately without breaking the illusion." Solar replied with equal disdain.

"Impressive—and it supports my theory. My mother could have done exactly what you described."

Solar scratched his chin. "Why would she do such a thing?"

Lykinnia shook her head. "I cannot figure it out, but I think it has to do with Uncle Jakarrak and the ring he gave her. She always knew my father was a god and tricked him into falling in love with her."

Solar was intrigued. "Okay, to what end?"

A broad smile appeared on Lykinnia's face from being treated as a peer. Her dancing started anew. "Power. My hypothesis is she drained every opportunity from my father to increase her own, then left."

"Ah—I do not know Lykinnia. They loved each other. You could tell." Solar rubbed his temple briskly.

"You mean Terazhan loved Sendaria immensely, but I do not believe it was reciprocated." The young lady blew a forceful breath from her lungs.

Solar was pacing. "How could I have missed this? I need to tell Lord Terazhan—"

"No. You will not. Do you remember when I told my father I could resurrect my mother with a single hair or fingernail? When we failed to find anything but ash in her abode, it broke my father for years, and he never fully recovered. You will not say a word until we figure this out for certain." Lykinnia emphasized her last comment by pointing her finger toward his face.

Solar crisscrossed his legs and sat in the middle of the platform. "This is not good Unie." His melancholy voice was barely audible.

"It gets worse."

Solar smacked the top of his head and waited for the report.

"I have been talking to her through a summoning portal of sorts." Lykinnia cringed, waiting to be berated.

"Lykinnia, you know how convincing these devils and demons can be. What makes you so certain it is Sendaria?"

"She knows little stories about me, and many of my favorite things. The most compelling reason is her possession of the ring Uncle Jakarrak gave her. I saw it."

Solar looked like he had been trampled by a herd of buffalo. "Anything else?"

Lykinnia clasped her hands and twirled shyly. "She . . . wants to visit."

The winged man fell backward and lay on his back staring at the sky. "Hymnoch, the God of Chaos, would find this comical. I do not. If it turns out to be an archdemon or an archdevil, do you know what would happen to our home?"

50

The Story

Talo

Talo was not hungry. He was angry. No, he was furious. *Why? Why am I fuming like a madman? I should be happy Cymm is alive and home.*

He watched his cousin stuff another bite in his mouth, then folded his arms over his chest, and sat in a chair against the wall. Not at the table. He didn't understand what was wrong with everyone. They were acting like it was all some grand reunion.

The last piece of bread disappeared.

Talo scoffed. *Oh, sure. Now let's take more time to drink some water.*

His mother, father, and even Semper checked on him visually several times, but he had no intention of putting on a happy face. "Would you like another piece of bread, or maybe some pie?" Talo stomped his foot and yelled, "Can we hear the story now?"

Cymm smiled for posterity. "Yes. After I sent the caravan south with the supplies for the wedding . . ."

As the story unfolded, Talo's mood did not improve, and he crossed one leg over the other. A pang of jealousy he did not understand swept through him when Cymm described the battle with Dego and the healing mists. Talo sighed. He did not have any desire to gallivant through the plains, not with the wedding so close. He was perfectly content with a horseman's life. *We should've never trained to be in the village militia. That's what started all this nonsense.*

". . . then I fell unconscious, was taken captive, drugged, and transported north to a wolf village."

This is why he needs you to guard his back. None of this would have happened, and you would not be so upset, his subconscious told him.

Oh, shut up! I didn't know he was thrown into a cell to fight a blood wolf and almost died. Talo peered through the open door at the giant wolf lying on the porch. Light red patches stained his coat.

Tears welled in Cymm's eyes as he described the heroic battle. "Torak stared at me through Torc's legs, helpless on the ground, while the dire wolf defended him with his life. They died protecting each other, and I couldn't save them."

Cymm's body shuddered as he sobbed, but Talo remained callous and unmoved. His cousin concluded his story with the retrieval of his faithful warhorse. "It feels like this path was set before me long ago when my family was taken from me."

"It feels like a lifetime ago, but it's only been nine months," corrected Semper.

Nové, Talo's mother, reached for Cymm's hands. "We're your family."

"I know. I love you all. I thought killing the dragons would fill the void in my heart. I can't explain it, but I almost feel worse." Cymm untied the leather thong around his neck and removed the necklace. "Let me show you something."

Talo watched his cousin twirl the nose ring Bria had ripped from the ogre's dead body. A hazy mist appeared out of nowhere, swirling in circles before Cymm. It condensed into a thicker turquoise haze, and finally, an image began to form.

"Bria! It's Bria!" yelled Cymm's younger cousins. Cela, her best friend, remained silent. She moped over to her mother and hugged her tight around the neck, bawling her eyes out.

Bria sprang to life in the middle of the room. "Hi Cymm, I see you got my necklace. Please keep it safe."

Talo gasped, and his lip quivered.

Bria continued, "When you see Talo again, tell him hi for me, then knock him on his butt!"

The entire room guffawed at his expense, delivering gawks in his direction.

A lump formed in Talo's throat, and the ice-walled prison incarcerating his heart shattered. He stood and rested his hand on Cymm's shoulder, his brother, on the verge of tears.

Bria smiled and stared at them standing side by side. "And by the way, you two still don't look like men." She giggled and faded back into the mist.

Both his mother and father glanced at him and nodded, but he did not want their affirmation. *Why was I such a buffoon? I hate seeing him leave. Or maybe I hate seeing him leave without me. Was it any different when he left to fight the dragons? I wanted to go then, and apparently, I want to go now.*

51

The Warm Springs

Lykinnia

Solar and Lykinnia agreed there was no benefit to making a rash decision. With a fluffy robe in hand, the young priestess headed for the warm springs. Everything caught her attention this morning. It was the perfect temperature, the orchard colors were beyond vibrant, and the bird songs were more melodious. *I should have told Solar sooner. He accepted the news better than I expected. At least, better than the past couple of times.* She sighed. *Including the time he punished me for trying to help him organize his day more efficiently.*

The robe she was wearing fell to the ground, and she placed the clean one on a rock next to the pool. She sunk into the spring, up to her neck with a deep sigh.

She rubbed her arms, shoulders, and neck, letting the heat penetrate her muscles.

I know that is my mother. Solar will see the light. She giggled. *No pun intended.*

With her eyes closed, she slipped completely under the water and tousled her hair. Many seconds later, she emerged with her long locks slicked back, away from her face.

Am I confident enough to summon her back into her abode? She also mentioned resetting the portal with her help. Why is that necessary?

A shadow passed over the entire spring. She glanced at the sky, but the sun restricted her efforts. Using her hand to shield her eyes, she scanned the sky from horizon to horizon. *Hmm, not a cloud in the sky, and none expected for at least a month. It could have been Kamac or Camak,* she thought, considering the sphinx brothers.

She settled back into her bath, grabbing a handful of sand from the bottom and scrubbing her skin. *When the clouds do come, every mountain and valley in sight will be covered in snow—except the Peak of Power.*

Snow had never touched her home since the day her father and several others had cleaved half the peak off and cast it down the mountainside. *Sendaria and Terazhan built this home to raise me. It is my point of genesis, which is a fancy way to say my prison for a millennium.*

A herd of elephants approached, ending her contemplation. She knew the sound well, and the abrupt appearance of the sphinx brothers did not surprise her.

Lykinnia barely rotated her head. "Yes?"

"We have an intruder," replied Camak.

"What?" asked a confused Lykinnia.

Kamac growled, "We both saw it. It was black—"

"And came up the main path by the altar," finished Camak.

As if on cue, a rustling noise grew louder on the opposite side of the pool. An enormous black panther sprang onto a huge flat boulder and stared at all three of them.

Lykinnia raised one hand above the water toward the big cat, ready to blast it off the rock. She commanded the sphinxes, "Wait."

Her bodyguards had flanked both sides of the pool, holding their position as directed.

The panther's taut muscles relaxed, and it stretched before lowering itself. It settled back down on the boulder, observing them, both front paws dangling over the edge, but otherwise unmoving.

"Do you want us to chase it away?" asked Kamac.

"We could throw it off the plateau and see if it can fly?" Camak grinned, revealing his perfect teeth.

"Neither will be necessary. I will be fine. You can leave." Lykinnia returned to scrubbing her skin with a handful of sand.

Kamac grumbled and turned.

Camak hesitated. "But—"

"I will yell if I need you. I think I can handle a cat." After they departed, Lykinnia's attention turned to the panther. "You may assume your normal shape."

The feline continued to stare. If it had not blinked, it could have been mistaken for a statue.

"I will give you one last chance, then I will dispel your magic costume or blast it off of you with a lightning bolt; I have not decided which yet." Lykinnia raised her second arm out of the water.

The panther's body shimmered into a black blob before transforming into a dark-skinned elf. The humanoid sat on the rock, with its hands under its rump, and dangling its legs over the edge.

Lykinnia discreetly cast another spell, searching for an illusion. No enchantment existed. "I have never seen your kind before. What are you?"

"I am a drow, but my name is ZaphMordakai."

"I was not trying to offend you. What is your business here?"

"I observed you a fortnight ago, outside of Armak. I thought the golden sprite I saw was the most beautiful creature in the world, but I was wrong. You are much more beautiful in person and in your natural body." Zaph waved his hand down the length of her body.

Lykinnia followed his line of gaze and flushed. The crystal-clear water revealed everything. She quickly covered her chest with one arm and her lower extremities with her other. "Did you get a good look?"

The drow smirked. "I'm sorry. I wasn't trying to offend you."

"Turn around." Her face turned a deeper shade of red from anger.

ZaphMordakai did as instructed.

She hurriedly slid into her clean robe after exiting the water. "What do you really want?"

"I have given you, my name. You could introduce yourself?"

"What do you want?" she hissed.

He sighed. "This is not going well. Give me one honest chance to convince you and if I fail, I will take my leave immediately and without appeal."

She stared unblinking.

He nodded. "Think of the most magnificent creature or person in the world."

That is easy. A unicorn, thought Lykinnia.

He paused for a few seconds. "Now, imagine you see this creature for the first time. You are amazed, filled with wonder, and eager to learn more. However, you don't even know its name, and you never see it again."

She pulled the robe sash tighter and folded her arms over her chest with a huff. "My name is Lykinnia."

52

Infiltration

ZaphMordakai

ZaphMordakai found it hard to believe this beautiful creature was his enemy. Ledaedra spoke about their enemies often, which numbered in the dozens, but the inhabitants of the Peak of Power were at the top of the list. Terazhan, and his propensity to intervene seemed to be her favorite topic. He had the capability to organize the opposition and resist the Queen's dominion. Without him, the other deities would do the same thing they did four hundred years ago: nothing.

"Do you care to explain why you are *really* here?" she persisted.

Zaph remained seated. "Everything I told you is true. I was in the south near Norfolk, when I heard a story that led me here to find you. I honestly was expecting to find a golden fairy flying about. This is a pleasant surprise."

"And what do you hope to gain from this encounter?"

His brow furrowed. "Are you this tough on all your guests?"

"You are *not* my guest. You came uninvited and disturbed my solace. It was the first bath I have had in over a week, but you are deflecting."

The dark elf contemplated the color of the water. "It might come as quite a shock, but I don't have many friends. Since you aren't too far away, I was hoping to get to know you." *And get some information from you.*

Lykinnia walked back to the pool, sat at the edge, and submerged her feet and calves. "What do you want to know?"

"Why do you live up here alone?"

"I am not alone. There are a few of us, and I have several guardians, as you witnessed before." She raised her eyebrows and gave him a wide-eyed stare.

ZaphMordakai chuckled. "Yesssss. I noticed. I will be on my best behavior."

Lykinnia giggled and kicked water in his direction.

"So, what do you do up here?"

She shrugged. "I pray, study, read, and have numerous research projects."

"Sounds like fun." Zaph coughed before lying on his side and snoring loudly.

Lykinnia bristled. "And what is it you do that is so exciting?"

"Other than conversing with beautiful females, like yourself? I have significant responsibilities, crucial to the success of my civilization. For example, a few weeks ago, I was asked to investigate the deaths of three colleagues, and this week, I was assigned to be the personal bodyguard for a princess." ZaphMordakai sat up straight as he embellished his stories.

Lykinnia chortled. "Unless you think I am the princess, you are not doing your job."

Zaph folded his arms. "Don't laugh at me!"

She ceased laughing immediately. "I am not laughing *at* you. I am laughing *because* of you. You are funny."

The dark elf relaxed. "Thank you—I think. However, I wasn't attempting to be funny. This is what I've done the past few weeks. Much more exciting than reading."

"I disagree. Nothing is more exciting than opening a book for the first time and discovering what secrets lie within." Lykinnia waved him off with one hand while tossing her hair back with the other.

"Good to know. If I come across any interesting books, I know whom to gift them to." Zaph's blossoming good humor disappeared. Concern had darkened the young woman's face. "Is everything okay? What did I say?"

"You did nothing wrong. I would like to complete my bath before midday," she replied with a half-smile.

Zaph rose to his feet. "Very well. I shall take my leave, young lady. Can I—"

"Young?" A mischievous smile streaked across her face. "I am quite certain I am your elder."

"Would you bet lunch on it?" Zaph leaned in for the response.

"Yes."

"Well, *young* lady. I'm over four hundred years old," Zaph stated with pride in his voice.

"Well, *young man*, I am almost one thousand." She rose and gave a bow.

53

Arranged

Talo

The Reich family stood in the barnyard waiting. Talo's father—now the Head of Household and responsible for matchmaking—began discussing the marriage of his daughter in the month of Rhomerian with Ebor Starcrest.

Talo's mind drifted between Cymm's miraculous return about ten days ago, and his own wedding only three days away. He glanced up and found a small dust cloud in the distance. The bridal party was arriving. Talo's mouth was dry, and he gulped. It felt like a prison door was closing. Did it feel the same for Vena?

Five horses cantered into the Reich barnyard. Ebor, and his wife Essa, were side-by-side, followed by Vena, and two henchmen brought up the rear. A receiving line was formed to greet them. Daro and Nové stood at the head of the line.

Vena brought her horse to a halt abruptly, dismounted with ease, and rushed over to Talo.

Talo's eyes went wide as he awkwardly hugged her back. "Hi, Vena. Welcome."

"Vena!" her father scolded.

"Vena, etiquette, my dear," her mother tsked.

She stared up at him with doe eyes and pursed lips.

His mother and father glanced at each other and smirked. Daro offered, "It's quite all right. Better this way than dragging her here kicking and screaming."

All four parents found this amusing, but Talo did not.

"Vena, come here and greet the Reichs." Her father turned to Daro. "Recently turned eighteen and she acts like she's eleven. She hasn't stopped talking about your boy since we met up in Hot Springs three years ago."

Talo wiped his sweating palms on his pants.

"Father!" Red-faced, Vena released Talo and approached. "Hi Master Daro. Nice to see you again, and you as well Mistress Nové."

"Welcome Vena," replied Daro.

"We are going to be good friends." Nové grinned and bounced on her toes.

"Let me introduce you to the rest of the family." Daro turned with a flourish of his hand. "Of course, you know Talo." His father continued down the line in birth order. "This is Mare."

"We're the same age." Mare gave her a hug.

"Nice to meet you." Vena's gaze drifted back to Talo, but her parents pushed her along.

"Next is Toma," said Daro.

"A pleasure." Toma bent at the waist in an exaggerated bow.

His father introduced Cela, Bran, the twins (Sage and Cage), Teah, Brok, Shaw, and Sara. "Mare, please accompany Talo and Vena."

Mare nodded.

His father wrapped his arm around Ebor's shoulder. "Our nephew offered his house for you to stay in this week. I'll show you to your rooms, then we can grab an ale and find somewhere to talk."

Vena placed her arm inside her fiancée's. "Talo, how about a tour of the farm?"

"Sure. You seem very excited. Aren't you nervous?" Talo led her toward the barn.

"No. Why? Are you?"

"A little bit. Won't you miss your family?"

"Of course, but I thought our connection in Hot Springs was strong. You know, I really don't like the idea of arranged marriages. If my father had chosen anyone else, I would've left in the middle of the night for Armak." She peeked at him sideways.

"And I would've run away if I was paired *with* Talo," said Mare.

"Hey! Chaperones don't talk," scolded Talo.

Mare stuck her tongue out.

Vena switched to Mare's arm, winking at Talo. "Can my betrothed chaperone for a while? Mare, when will you be getting married?"

"I'm next in line, so probably this coming year. Could even be after first harvest."

"We have such a brief time together. Is there any chance your father might try to *castle*?" asked Vena.

Mare snorted. "My father doesn't have a lot of coin."

"Cymm does." blurted Talo.

"Hey, chaperone, quiet!" yelled Mare.

"Ha, ha. If you are interested in staying on the Reich farm, you need to tell Father. Cymm will help you."

"My father's choice of suitors will be limited, but it would be nice to raise our children together." A glowing smile filled Mare's face.

Vena hooked her index finger and put a rasp in her voice. “Yes, tell your father before the wedding. His devious plans are already in the works.”

The girls twittered.

“Although I’m enjoying this tour *immensely*, you can continue without me. Training is about to begin with Cymm and Semper.” Talo headed for Semper’s barn.

54

Partnership

Lykinnia

Ten days had passed since the unusual visit from the dark elf. Lykinnia had escorted him to the mountain path and watched him traverse the entire length. He had requested permission to return in the future but had not provided a timeline.

That same day, Solar had forbidden her from talking to her mother until he could discuss the ring and any plot with Uncle Jakarrak. In the meantime, Solar incorporated her into the search, taking turns controlling the altar. They had found his trail, but after ten days of tracking him through time, they were no closer to finding him.

Solar paced back and forth on the platform. "This is quite irritating. His constant plane jumping and teleporting are making this task impossible."

"I think our best shot is waiting on his home plane for him to return," said Lykinnia.

"No, he has been known to travel for years."

"Then what do you suggest?"

He thought deeply for several moments. "I think it is time to ask Terazhan to trace all fourteen phylacteries."

"If Father can trace them, why have we been wasting our time?"

"It is a formidable spell, making the Altar of One unusable for a day. However, the bigger concern is every deity will know he cast it, and the location of everyone else."

"I see." Lykinnia squinched up one side of her face.

"I am going to ask him now. I will let you know what he says."

55

Intervention

Cymm

The training session at Semper's farm was ending, and the three men had drawn quite the crowd. Five new recruits for the village militia reported for training today, and one of them was Toma, Talo's brother.

"The Darkmane kid missed the entire first session," said Talo.

Old-Man Semper harrumphed. "Zeke doesn't see the value. He should hope his house isn't attacked by an ogre."

Cymm quietly followed behind the two as they entered Semper's barn. The candidates were dismissed, including Toma, and not allowed in the workshop.

"Whatcha thinkin' about Cymm?" Semper finished stowing the bows.

"Hardre. It's a long story. I met a priestess up north, and she knows who killed him." Cymm slumped into his usual chair.

"Who?" Talo and Semper said simultaneously.

"She wouldn't tell me." His voice turned soprano when he said, "Next time you'll be more forthright, and I'll tell you who killed your friend, is what she said. I fear I may never see her again."

Semper cleared his throat. "I would've made her talk."

"She put me to sleep and disappeared." He paused, his vision blurring slightly as he stared into the barnyard. "I know where to start looking."

Talo and Semper exchanged glances. His cousin said, "Here we go again."

"I intend to avenge him. You might have forgotten about him, but I—"

"Hold your tongue boy!" Semper slammed his fist into the tabletop. "I haven't forgotten anyone."

"Boy? I ain't no boy!" Cymm swiftly rose to his feet.

Talo stepped in the middle. "Settle down, both of ya. Cymm, neither of us like you adventuring off on your own. It needs to stop."

Cymm replied, "I didn't have a choice. They took—"

"I'm not talking about the wolf village." Talo shook his head. "Although you did choose to go to Armak by yourself."

"And into Tent City by yourself," Semper added with raised eyebrows.

Talo continued, "I'm referring to this trip to Delge you're planning on your way to see Lykinnia."

Cymm rolled his eyes. "It's on the way. I can't see how it would hurt to pass through the city and have DragonSin scan a few people."

"You got yourself in trouble shopping for food amongst your own tribe. A city full of angry dwarves could seriously *hurt* you," replied Talo.

"There are hundreds of prisoners in the dungeons of Delge who underestimated the city's danger and corruption. The Hearth Council *will* throw you in prison." Semper's eyes lost focus, he was obviously deep in thought. "I want you both to come back here at midnight when the walls don't have ears. I need to tell you something."

With a quick peek, Cymm observed the new recruits hovering in the open doorway. He nodded and left, not waiting for Talo.

Toma fell in stride next to him, escorting him home. "How did I do today, Cymm?"

"You did great. If you keep practicing, you'll be as good as me with a bow and arrow."

Talo jogged up from behind. "Thanks for waiting."

Toma wrinkled his nose at his older brother. "What? You forgot how to get home?"

Talo tousled his brother's hair. "I was talking to Cymm, orc-brain."

ꝏꝏꝏ

Several hours after dinner, Primordian peeked up above the tall grasslands. The brilliant white moon provided plenty of light for Cymm and Talo to creep out of the Reich barnyard to meet Semper. Once in the village center, their trek became more relaxed.

"What do you think Semper wants to tell us?" Talo asked in hushed tones.

"I have no idea, but did you see his eyes? His usual crotchety anger was replaced by something much deeper." Cymm shook his head slowly.

"Yeah." Talo chuckled. "And he called you *boy*. He never called us boys even when we were, at least not like that."

In the distance, the light from Semper's workshop came into view, and the cousins picked up the pace, anxious to discover the purpose of this meeting. Cymm arrived at the barn opening first and stepped through with Talo on his heels.

Cymm scanned left to right but found no one present. "Semper, you here?"

"Yeah. Be right with you," Semper called from a corner stall.

Cymm wrinkled one side of his face as the creaking of a chest filled the silence, followed by the clanking of chains interspersed with grunts and groans. "By Melcorac's Hammer, what is he doing?"

The two young men shuffled forward.

"Let's get this over with," a strange voice grumbled.

Cymm and Talo paused and stared at each other in confusion. They reluctantly completed the walk to the last stall, pulled by an unseen force. Side by side they peered into the confined area, but Semper was not there. A solitary figure, presumably the owner of the second voice, stood in the center. A short, stocky man, wearing chainmail armor, held a two-handed warhammer across his chest. He had a long beard and a full head of hair, but the face was undeniable.

Cymm advanced. "Hardre?"

Talo pulled his dirk dagger. "Hardre's dead. I saw his body."

Cymm's hand drifted toward the hilt of DragonSin, resting above his right shoulder. "Explain yourself. Where is Semper?"

"I am Semper. Semper Ironcore, Hardre is my twin brother."

"You're who?" asked Talo.

Cymm unsheathed DragonSin. *"Time to work, my friend. Is he telling the truth?"*

"I have protected this secret for over twenty years. Only one other person knows my true identity, Daro Reich."

"Uncle Daro?" asked Cymm skeptically.

"My father?" asked Talo.

"Semper hates Uncle Daro. Now, I know you're lying." Cymm took a threatening step forward raising his sword.

"He tells the truth," DragonSin conveyed in his mind.

The stranger rested the warhammer against his shoulder, and raised one empty hand, palm out, between them. "Easy Cymm. I will explain everything, if given the chance."

Cymm immediately returned his bastard sword to the scabbard strapped to his back, then grabbed Talo's forearm. "DragonSin says he speaks the truth."

An audible sigh escaped the dwarf's lips, drawing the cousins' renewed attention. "Would you prefer I return to my Old-Man Semper form?"

"Yes!" both young men responded immediately.

Semper hung the warhammer on two large hooks in the wall and waved for them to approach. "Help me take this armor off."

Cymm hoisted the armor over his head. "Why would you tell Uncle Daro?"

"I didn't. He entered my workshop about twenty years ago, unbidden, to borrow some tongs, and caught me with my ring off." Semper stood half-naked, wearing only a loincloth.

"My father's known for twenty years?" Talo packed the armor back into the large chest against the wall.

"Yes, and he has faithfully kept my secret except for the *elf* comment, which was a drunken error and caused some friction between us." Semper retrieved a ring from a necklace, hidden from view by his long hair and beard.

"Uncle Daro doesn't owe you his allegiance. Why would he keep this information from his own family?" asked Cymm. "Better yet, why would you keep this from me?"

"Or me." Talo chimed in.

"Please sit." Semper indicated the three hay bales conveniently positioned in the stall. "Because I told him the story, I am about to tell you. This ring is what allows me to change shape." He placed it on his stubby index finger. The transformation began immediately and completed in under ten seconds. Semper grabbed at the loincloth as it fell around his thinner human frame. He cinched it tighter, then donned his usual horse-farm attire, hanging over the short stall wall.

Cymm and Talo remained unmoving with their mouths hanging open.

Semper sat on the remaining hay bale. "I had always intended to buy Hardre one of these rings. I was so close to having enough coin. He used to borrow mine to drink with everyone by the bonfire, especially during Festival. This will be the first one he's missed in over ten years."

Talo eyed three wooden mugs sitting up on a bench, drawing Semper's attention.

"Anyone thirsty?" asked Semper.

"I could use a drink." Talo cocked his neck and cracked it.

"Semper, this story better be a good one," responded Cymm.

Semper turned the spigot, filling the first mug, and delivered it to Cymm with a solemn stare.

Cymm set the ale down. "For all the lectures you two have given me, I see this as the absence of trust."

Semper poured the third mug and reclaimed his seat before taking a long pull. "When I was born over two hundred years ago, my parents and elder sister were devout believers in the teachings of Terazhan. Before my one hundredth lifeyear, Grendella, my sister, moved away from Delge to achieve the status of high priestess. Shortly after, my parents were assassinated. Hardre and I had a difficult time blending into the dwarven society, especially since my brother was becoming more vocal about his religious studies. Grendella initiated Hardre's clerical lessons before she left, and he continued advancing his understanding in private. After five years of hiding, he decided to openly heal people in the streets."

Semper took a long pull from his mug. "The day they came knocking at our door, he wasn't home, and The Red Axes arrested me for hiding him. Three days later they still couldn't find him, and I was scheduled for transfer the next day to the dungeons of Delge. A dear friend broke me out of jail that night and I fled the city. There is a large bounty on my head, and I haven't returned in eighty-five years. I spent over sixty years as a mercenary and adventurer until I had enough coin to buy this ring and this farm."

Cymm sipped his ale. "I get it. I honestly do, but neither of us would have ever betrayed you."

Semper shrugged. "Dwarves are naturally untrusting. I finally got there. Doesn't that count for something?"

Cymm pointed his finger at the old man. "No more lies, or concealing information, or hidden agendas. Say it."

"I promise." Semper thrust his hand out between them, and Talo and eventually Cymm grasped it.

Talo downed the rest of his ale. "With our new agreement, Cymm, I don't want you going to Delge alone."

The corners of Cymm's mouth curled. "I think you are stretching the meaning of our promise."

"I don't think he is," Semper piped in. "We need to look out for each other, not just trust each other. After the wedding, I can accompany you to Delge."

"Me too." Talo puffed his chest out.

"No," said Cymm and Semper simultaneously.

Talo stomped his foot. "There is no way I am staying here while you two go off on an adventure!"

Cymm ignored Talo and addressed Semper, "Do you even know how to use Hardre's warhammer?"

Semper hefted the weapon in question. "This is mine. I let my brother borrow it to keep him safe. It may not be as powerful as your sword, but it's magical, and I know how to use it. I have more reason than you to kill these assassins, to avenge my brother and parents. I want to be there in case you find them."

Cymm sighed. "Fine! After Delge, you head home. I don't need an escort to the Peak of Power."

56

The Helper

Lykinnia

Lykinnia only visited Cymm every two or three days in her amber form, not because she was afraid Solar or Terazhan would catch her using the altar, but her fear of Cymm's reaction. "He must not think I am a nuisance or have nothing better to do," Lykinnia said to herself. She placed her hands on the surface and raced to the Armak Plains.

Her nerves raced like wild horses, and she wanted to throw up. This would be the first time she met one of Cymm's friends. It took her several minutes from high above to finally locate the travelers, and the sour feeling in her stomach intensified. He had said she could visit him anytime, but nevertheless, doubt crept in. She shook it away. *No. He will enjoy the surprise.*

She landed several yards behind Cymm, using him as a visual barrier, but the old man spotted her immediately. His eyes went wide.

"What's the matter with you?" asked Cymm. "It looks like you've seen a dragon."

The old man pointed at her and Cymm whirled around, his hand instinctively going to his sword.

Lykinnia waved, biting on her lip. "Hello."

"Lykinnia! I didn't expect to see you here." Cymm's hand released his sword and his smile broadened.

She glanced past Cymm at the old man. "I can leave."

"No, please stay. This is Old-Man Semper, the one I have told you about."

She walked up next to Cymm. "Nice to meet you."

"Nice to meet you. I have heard a lot about you, young lady."

"You have?" She glanced at Cymm, beaming. She resisted the urge to perform a pirouette.

Semper stoked the tiny campfire. "Yes, many times."

Lykinnia shifted her attention to Cymm. "Are you planning to stop in Delge before you come to the Peak of Power?"

The old man chuckled.

Cymm shot him a glare that did not quell his mirth.

"What did I say?" she asked.

"Nothing wrong. He thinks it's funny that everyone knows I'm going to Delge. I'll head straight to the Peak of Power afterwards, and we can celebrate the first Twilight."

"Today is First Twilight. It is a new year," she replied.

Cymm shook his head. "No, I meant the first Terazhan's Twilight. Anyway, one of the reasons I am coming to visit you is to discuss how we can eliminate the dragons. They continue to attack cities and slaughter its people."

"Are you talking about a mass extinction? Oh Cymm, are you sure about this?" asked Lykinnia.

Cymm's countenance answered her question.

Old-Man Semper cleared his throat. "So, how did you find us?"

"I know the path Cymm plans to take. If it will help, I could search the road ahead and check for any danger."

"Lykinnia, that would be fantastic, and I would get to see you every day. Could you also check behind us to make sure Talo isn't following?" asked Cymm.

Lykinnia's heart swelled, and she spoke rapidly, "Okay, I will sweep the area and the road ahead with the time I have remaining. I will return if there is a problem. Nice to meet you Old-Man Semper."

"Nice to meet you as well."

Lykinnia zipped away.

57

The Crossroads

Cymm

Two cloaked figures—a dwarf and a human—scouted the guard station at the Crossroads from a distance, a dwarf and a human. The last two groups had passed without being detained.

"It's been eighty-five years. I think we'll be okay," Cymm whispered.

"Dwarves are like elephants. We don't forget. However, I don't recognize any of the sentries. We should go before the guard changes." Semper stood and stepped onto the road pulling Hardre's pony behind him.

"If you are worried, put the ring back on. No one will know who you are."

"After we are safely inside. I want to return to Delge as a dwarf." The muscle in Semper's jaw quivered. "Cymm?"

"Yeah?"

"If they do recognize me here or at the main gates, don't hesitate. Kill them all." Semper growled the last three words, low and menacing.

"Semper?" Cymm was appalled.

"You heard me. Kill the first wave, disable the rest if you must. Then we turn and flee. We'll regroup and come up with a new plan."

"Yes. Kill them all," whispered a voice behind him.

The shocked expression remained on Cymm's face, while he scanned the dimly lit forest behind him for the speaker. "Did you hear that?"

"What?"

Cymm turned back and focused his gaze on Semper. "I can't do that, and you know it."

"You can, and you will. If they identify me, we are both dead," snapped Semper.

"My original plan involved a little more stealth. We could—"

"Shhh." Semper motioned with his eyes toward the approaching guards.

"State your business in the great city of Delge," said a gruff guard with a battle axe in hand.

"We are only staying a couple days to pick up some supplies," replied Semper.

"If you are selling anything, you must register with the appropriate guild, including mercenaries for hire. Enjoy your stay in the great city of Delge." The guards let them pass and followed behind them, back to the outpost.

Once out of earshot, they mounted their steeds. Cymm shot a glance at his mentor. "Semper, I need to know you can handle this. You are supposed to have my back, not the other way around."

"Don't use my name again. Stick with Old-Man."

Cymm nodded. "Your pride is going to get us killed. I'm here for one day, in and out, then off to spend time with my girl."

"I can't believe you are lecturing me after you went off unprepared to face the three dragons that killed your family. You, above all others, should understand how I feel. I'm not going to jeopardize the mission, I want revenge." Semper punched his fist into his hand in emphasis.

ꝏꝏꝏ

They traveled for six more hours, passing two more guard shacks before arriving at the city entrance. Huge stone monoliths formed a walkway, increasing in size as they approached the gates. The final and largest statues were half buried in the mountain, and each one held an iron-plated gate within its grasp.

Cymm and Semper alit and walked their mounts for the final stretch, allowing them to observe the reaction of the sentries to the travelers in front of them. Semper had his cloak hood pulled up. Cymm had his down, craning his neck around and taking in the grandeur of the dwarven city outskirts. "How magnificent."

Semper elbowed him in the hip. "The guard is talking to you."

"Where are you coming from?" the guard asked, apparently for the second time.

Cymm paused his gawking. "Armak."

The guard chuckled. "Enjoy your first time in Delge."

They trekked down a tunnel, thirty feet wide by fifteen feet tall for two hundred feet, and it opened into an enormous cavern. A semi-ovular platform overlooked the main city fifty feet below, and a massive staircase off each side wound back and forth until reaching the floor.

Somehow, the dwarves had engineered light shafts in the ceiling to shine brightly on the city. It was immense, smaller tunnels in the distance exited the main square in every direction. Cymm admired the marvelous architectural craftsmanship. "What's the plan?"

"The plan is to follow me down into The Maker's Square." Semper immediately descended the first flight of stairways.

Cymm sighed, not feeling very safe. "I expected to see mostly dwarves, but there are quite a few humans and gnomes. I even saw an elf—Semper?" His friend was no longer in front of him. He turned around, and Semper disappeared into a tavern.

Cymm entered the dimly lit room to find a stone bar against the far wall with twelve wide stools sitting side-by-side and less than ten tables. A small crowd of only five patrons sat at the bar drinking, each minding their own business.

The proprietor entered the chamber from behind the bar and paused for a long moment. "Can I get you something?"

Cymm attempted to communicate with Semper telepathically about the odd expression that briefly passed over the stranger's face. Not expecting success, he tugged on his mentor's cloak, which was also ignored.

"We need a room for a couple of nights," replied Semper.

"Just one?" The dwarven barkeep took measure of Cymm.

"Yes, and we are weary from our journey, so the sooner the better."

Cymm poked Semper in the back, then repeated it when he did not respond.

"It will be five silver a night. Follow me." The innkeeper strolled to another doorway, beckoning them to follow. "What brings you here, business or pleasure?"

Cymm had to stoop and lumbered past several rooms before the hallway turned to the right.

"A little of both," replied Semper.

Halfway down the dimly lit hall, the proprietor paused and fumbled with keys at a closed door. "I hope you find this room adequate."

After entering the room and closing the door, the innkeeper attacked Semper.

58

The Meeting

Lykinnia

The following morning, Solar joined Lykinnia for breakfast at the stone table. A rare event because Solar was not fond of the concept, and commonly said, "Why should eating take any more time than it needs to?"

"Terazhan will perform the trace spell in two days. In the meantime, we are going to meet with this impersonator together." Solar bit a strawberry in half, chewing it slowly.

"You told Terazhan about Sendaria. Didn't you?" Lykinnia pointed her finger at him.

Solar raised both hands as if to surrender. "No. I have kept our agreement, and I expect you to do the same."

Lykinnia's arms flailed in excitement. "Solar, I am telling you, this is my mother."

"We shall see." Solar sported a devious grin.

Lykinnia wrinkled her brow. "What do you have in mind?"

"There are things only Sendaria and I know. I will test her with these questions."

"How is that any different than what I already did?"

"The answers to the questions you asked were commonly known."

"Pffft." Lykinnia scoffed.

"What did you ask? Favorite color, pet, or story? Go ahead. Test me." Solar leaned forward in anticipation for several seconds of silence. "Forest green, unicorns, and the Princess and the Pegasus story."

Lykinnia crossed her arms and silently pouted.

"Finish your breakfast. We are going to expose the imposter this morning." Solar nodded his head once with force.

Lykinnia jumped to her feet, stuffing a slice of bread in her mouth. With a deep voice she imitated her steward. "Eating should not take any more time than it needs to."

"Amusing. We shall do this at the altar." Solar walked in that direction with the young priestess on his heels.

With a nod from her guardian, Lykinnia cast the invisibility spell. The rift in space tore open, three feet tall and one foot wide with pitch black darkness in the middle. "Sendaria, I wish to speak to you."

"Not mother? I was beginning to think you forgot about me," the voice replied.

"The term mother implies more than genetics. I have creatures in Darken Wood who rightfully call me mother," Lykinnia snapped back.

Solar placed a hand on her shoulder.

"Are you alone? I sense the presence of another."

"Solar is with me. He would like to ask you a few questions," Lykinnia replied, undaunted.

"Of course, I am surprised you waited this long to bring him into your confidence. What would you like to know?"

"If indeed you are who you say, tell me why you forced Terazhan to select me over the other candidate to be your child's caregiver?" Solar leaned in to listen.

"Talia's desire for my husband didn't need to be encouraged."

Solar nodded skeptically. "And how did you convince him?"

The voice hesitated and cleared its throat. "I told him he could choose the child's name, and I would select the governess or governor."

Solar's mouth dropped open, and he slowly found Lykinnia's eyes.

"Father named me? Why am I learning about this now?"

After many seconds of silence, the voice asked, "Will there be anything else?"

The young priestess was trying to grasp the latest information. In a daze, she mouthed the words, "It is her."

Solar snapped out of his daze. "If you are Sendaria Moonbeam, answer this, have you ever killed anyone?"

Lykinnia gasped. "What? Why would you ask that?"

Now the voice was silent for a while. "Solar, you play a dangerous game. I have spent four hundred years trapped in a vile and corrupt place."

"Fair enough. Did you ever kill anybody before your *four-hundred-year imprisonment*?"

Lykinnia was about to put an end to this, but suddenly she wanted an answer.

The voice from the void replied immediately in hushed tones.

"What?" Solar took a step forward, cocking his head to listen.

The voice replied again, "I said . . ." and she trailed off into mumbled jargon.

The priestess shook her head. "I could not hear."

Solar positioned himself a few feet away from the rift. "Say it loud enough for Lykinnia—"

A green-scaled talon flew out of the void, grasping Solar's neck. It squeezed tighter. His gasp was cut short, and the deep blue shade in his lips slowly spread through his face.

"I warned you never to speak of this or I would kill you." The voice changed to a growl.

Solar flailed at the clawed arm feebly. Wisps of smoke escaped from between the green scales.

Lykinnia lurched forward, finally recovering from her surprise. "No! Let go of him now." She grabbed the large thumb of the assailant, trying to snap it like a twig.

A black-scaled appendage snaked out of the void, latched onto Lykinnia's neck loosely, and hauled her toward the fissure. "I know how strong you are, daughter, but you are no match for me."

"Why are you doing this? I will never trust you now." Lykinnia dug her heels into the ground and heaved. She made some headway back toward Solar, then one massive jerk pulled her halfway to the fracture, leaving deep furrows in the earth.

"Solar should have thought about his questions more carefully!" the voice screeched.

Lykinnia cried out in fear and confusion. "No! I cannot leave the Peak of—" The grip around her neck tightened, she tried to draw breath. Panic set in. She could not breathe; she could not speak. She could not close the void.

The ten feet quickly became five. Sweat beaded on her brow, her delicate muscles bulged and quivered. *I do not have a choice. "Fath—"*

A black streak of fury rocketed past Lykinnia, knocking her to the ground. Ten miniature lightning bolts struck the taloned forearm, seizing the surrounding muscle, and causing the appendage to smoke more profusely.

Jolts of energy surged through Lykinnia's neck and into her body. She ground her teeth uncontrollably while the tendons in her neck and back immobilized. No longer could she resist the pull toward the void.

A large ball of cramped muscle formed in the black scaly forearm, and she finally broke free. She lay prone on her back, struggling to breathe.

Anger flooded Lykinnia's mind as she sat up. *What in the nine—* it was ZaphMordakai.

An enormous bolt of lightning rocketed forth from the black claw intended for Lykinnia. Again, the dark elf was there, intercepting the bolt with his chest. He brought his hands up and corralled the remaining energy, swirling it into a large ball of electricity.

Lykinnia croaked the words to close the portal.

The dark elf hurled the large sphere into the void after the retreating black appendage.

The voice cried out, "I will kill—"

The rift closed, completely severing the ember-riddled, green forearm. Lykinnia returned to a visible state and stumbled to Solar's side. "I cannot believe she tried to kill us." She stood absentmindedly over his unconscious body. The feminine chant of a healing spell reverberated throughout the area, and the winged man's crushed windpipe reformed into its proper shape. A faint rise and fall in his chest became apparent, bringing her relief.

Solar's eyelids fluttered but did not open.

Lykinnia rubbed her sore neck and fell to her knees. "Why would she try to kill me?"

ZaphMordakai knelt next to her and placed his hand on her shoulder. "Are you okay?"

She peered at him in a daze. "Me? I should ask you the same."

"It's not too bad. I'm immune to most lightning bolts." Zaph shrugged off his tattered shirt.

"Why would she kill me?"

59

Delge

Cymm

Semper was not caught off guard. He had even anticipated the attack and charged into his assailant, wrapping his arms around him in a crushing bearhug. They swayed side to side, squeezing each other so tight, tears streamed down both of their faces.

"Sem—Old-Man, I'm coming!" Cymm brandished his dirk dagger.

"Shhh. Keep it down, Cymm." Semper's voice cracked under the strain.

Cymm's head tilted. *Maybe they are hugging? Or wrestling.*

The two separated. A grin stretched across Semper's face. "This is my good friend Melkerie."

Cymm noticed they were holding hands and tears flowed down both their faces into their beards.

The young man stood unmoving, his right hand frozen mid-itch on the back of his head.

Semper stared at him wide-eyed for several moments.

Melkerie shifted uncomfortably. "It's nice to meet you."

Cymm rushed forward with a red face. "It's nice to meet you too. I'm not used to Semper having friends."

"Not just any friend. Melkerie and I were betrothed before they arrested me on false charges. Her family forced her to break off the engagement because of the scandal."

Her? Cymm searched his memory and realized he had not seen a female dwarf in the crowds, and now he knew why. "It must have been difficult. Semper, can we talk?"

"I should return to the bar. Everything is the same as it was, Semper. Be careful." Melkerie rushed out of the door, not waiting for a response.

"What are we doing here, Semper? You already have a wife." Cymm placed his hands on his hips.

"Melkerie's family has owned this tavern, the Cross-Eyed Goat, for many centuries. This room connects to a secret passage which leads to another building across the square. It will conceal our comings and goings, plus provide an escape route if we need one." Semper's half-smile spoke volumes.

Cymm slumped into a cushioned chair. "Sorry for not trusting you. We need a plan, and you need to start sharing more information."

"First, we are going to the bar to have a beer. Then, we will retire to our room, loudly for everyone to hear. I plan to use the secret passage to get us out into the streets and we will head straight for the Rapscallion or the Rude Rogue. One of them is certain to be the headquarters of the Assassin's Guild. Does that work for you?"

"I'm glad you're here, Semper."

Semper donned one of his rare genuine smiles. "I told you this city was a rough one, kid. The corruption goes all the way to the top."

Two hours later, two humans walked into the Rapscallion, a tavern quadruple in size to the Cross-Eyed Goat, and took a small table near the corner.

DragonSin stirred. *You have provided me with a target rich environment. What is the plan?*

Cymm leaned into the table and whispered, "This was a bad idea. DragonSin wants to attack."

"Fine. Start on the far side of the bar and have him search their memories for info on Hardre or Terazhan." Semper's upper lip curled.

A waitress approached.

Cymm said quietly, "Are you sure?"

Semper nodded emphatically. "Kill them."

"What can I getcha?" asked the serving wench.

"Two meat platters, beers, and a transmuter," replied Semper.

"What are you changing?" she asked.

"Rubies."

She nodded and walked away.

"You are scaring me, Semper. This is not a suicide mission."

"Get on with it." Semper pounded the table, drawing attention.

Cymm shifted his bare shoulder into the crossguard and explained the plan to DragonSin. *"How many targets do you count?"*

"Eighteen."

"Eighteen!" exclaimed Cymm.

A shriek emanated from a dwarf on the other side of the room.

"I said discreetly." Cymm shot Semper a look of concern but received nothing in return.

"I agree, this is not a suicide mission. I will be more careful," replied the sword.

Two dwarves hastily walked to the exit, wearing a mask of worry, and casting furtive glances over their shoulders.

With a final convulsive jerk, the first victim's head hit the table.

The barmaid returned with their drinks.

"What is going on over there? Does he need help?" Semper feigned concern.

She walked away without responding.

"Did you learn anything useful?" Cymm asked.

"He killed someone thirty minutes ago, in the alley behind the bar. The disgusting animal had no other useful information," DragonSin replied. *"The table with two dwarves knows where the guild headquarters is located."*

Cymm spotted the dwarves, both appeared uncomfortable. One had his finger in his ear, while the other rotated his neck in a circle. "We have gathered some minor info, but I think it's time to leave."

Semper's nod was barely perceptible. He pretended to be engrossed in his ale.

A serving wench approached moments later with plates of meat, examined their drinks, and moved on.

A couple minutes passed, and the next wave of victims laid their heads down on the table one after the other.

"DragonSin, that was more subtle, but we're moving on. Scan as many of the remaining assassins as possible for information."

Semper waved to the barmaid. "Close us out."

The barmaid rushed over. "Is everything okay?"

"Yes. How much do I owe you?" Semper drained his tall mug.

"Eight silver. Will you wait for the transmuter?"

"Not tonight. There are strange happenings. We will return." Semper grabbed the last two hunks of meat and stood after paying.

Cymm downed his beer and hurried to catch up.

The streets and the city square were bustling and DragonSin spoke aloud, "Wait. Stay near the building until I am finished."

Cymm and Semper shared an uncomfortable glance but honored the sword's request.

A minute later, four dwarves burst through the door so forcefully it hit the wall fully open. One of them eyed Cymm suspiciously as he rummaged through his backpack.

Two more minutes passed before DragonSin finally spoke, "Okay, head for the Rude Rogue."

Semper took the lead. "What did you find out?"

Cymm held up his index finger. "*DragonSin, why are you speaking aloud?*"

"The street is crowded. No one will know except Semper."

"That should be used sparingly. I will relay the information. No more talking unless it is necessary," Cymm scolded.

"Fine! I killed another assassin while we waited. He planned to murder a mother and child tonight. I also discovered there is a bounty on all believers of Terazhan and doubled for dwarves. Also, their headquarters is near the Rude Rogue, and there is a secret passage from the kitchen."

Flabbergasted, Cymm relayed the info to Semper.

They had traversed most of the square when Semper called out, "By Bardonril's beard, look at the size of him."

Cymm followed his gaze. The man in question would be a giant among humans, but he was a titan among dwarves. "Wow. He is as big as—wait I know him!"

"Keep moving. That can't be a coincidence." A worried expression darkened Semper's face.

"I saved him from the gnoll cages. His best friend was a dwarf, and they headed south. I don't think there's a conspiracy here." Cymm was agitated he could not greet his friend.

They exited the city square, following a main tunnel for several hundred feet. It opened in a smaller cavern square, and on the far side was a sign for the Rude Rogue.

"There it is." Semper motioned with his chin.

"Can we try this one from the street? We're dealing with assassins, if they discover us, we're dead."

"I don't think it will matter, but let's give it a try. Tell DragonSin not to attack this time until he searches everyone's memory," replied Semper.

The two humans picked a spot close to the building, but far enough away to be inconspicuous. Cymm lightly grasped the scabbard behind his back, and DragonSin went to work.

The congestion in the first square made walking difficult without bumping into someone. In the current square, there were pockets of citizens or travelers with large gaps between them.

"What is taking so long?" Semper gazed at the building over his shoulder.

"I'm sure he's being thorough. Let me check."

DragonSin replied, "*There are over eighty humanoids in the building, with close to twelve thousand lifeyears. If I did a thorough search, I would need a couple of hours. I did, however, find something that will send your friend over the edge.*"

"*What is it?*" asked Cymm.

"*The dwarf who murdered Semper's mother.*"

60

Intruder

ZaphMordakai

ZaphMordakai helped Lykinnia to her feet with a smile on his face.

"How did you know I needed help?" asked Lykinnia.

"I didn't. I came to visit again, and I saw you were in trouble," replied Zaph.

She flinched. "You saw me? I was invisible."

"You know what I mean. The black arm was holding something, and I knew it was you."

"I am glad you were here. Thank you." Lykinnia gave him a quick hug.

The two sphinx creatures landed nearby, watching him with dreadful stares.

"Is your friend all right?"

"I think so. Thanks to you, *young* man." She bit her lip and grinned.

Zaph rolled his eyes. "What was that thing anyway?"

Solar stirred and his eyes popped open.

Lykinnia knelt by the winged man. "Solar, I am sorry. I should have listened . . ."

Solar swallowed hard a few times before he found his voice. "No, I should have listened to you. You may be on to something. We have more investigating to do." He sat up slowly, then his eyes locked on ZaphMordakai. Solar pointed his finger at him. "Who are you?"

Zaph stared down at him. "The one who saved your life."

Solar labored to his feet. "And who will save yours?"

Lykinnia stepped between them. "He saved our lives. You should be thankful he was here."

Tiny lightning bolts arced throughout the wings of the upset man. "I am not. How is it possible for a dark elf to set foot on the Peak of Power?"

Zaph took two apprehensive steps back, involuntarily rubbing his neck. *If he attacks, my lightning will be useless.* He glanced back over his shoulder at the sphinx. "It would appear I am surrounded."

The young lady stomped her foot. "You are not surrounded. You are my guest."

"Lykinnia, do not be foolish. What do you know of this dark elf?" asked Solar.

"I know he saved our lives, and I am offering him free passage to visit me."

Zaph tried to paint an innocent smile upon his face, but inside a wicked smile bloomed.

61

Vigilante

Cymm

Old-Man Semper trembled like he was standing buck-ass naked in an ice-cold pond. Cymm had relayed that his mother's assassin, Thalras Hammerfist, was currently in the Rude Rogue.

Semper rolled his shoulders and stormed toward the building.

Using DragonSin's power, Cymm pulled him back ever so slightly to avoid making a scene. The young man stepped around him and met his gaze. "Are you a fool? There are eighty thieves and assassins in there right now. Even if you manage to kill him, you're dead, and Hardre's and your father's killers will never be punished. He will die tonight in a more suitable location."

Semper stared at him through the tops of his eyelids. "We'll follow him when he leaves."

"I am scanning the rental rooms for potential targets," DragonSin stated.

"If you ruin his chance for revenge, I'll wrap you in a blanket until we are far from this city."

An hour passed, and DragonSin's singing resonated in Cymm's cranium. He closed his right eyelid and massaged the closest temple. *"Please stop."*

"Are you okay?" Semper placed a hand on Cymm's shoulder.

"I am now. DragonSin was singing."

"Singing?" Semper's brows knitted in confusion.

"He sings when he's happy. Don't ask. Neither of us wants to know what he did."

"The assassin is on the move. He is heading for the back door," said the sentient weapon.

Cymm dashed ahead, pulling Semper with him toward a narrow alley running alongside the Rude Rogue. "He is leaving through the back door."

Semper stumbled, trying to keep up. "Keep going! I'm right behind you."

They arrived at the corner of the building and slowly entered the back alley. It was empty.

"I knew it!" fumed Semper. "Where'd he go?"

"Quiet," Cymm whispered.

"Don't tell me—"

Cymm hushed Semper with a glare, then scanned in every direction.

Water dripped further down the alley.

Thalras appeared from the shadows of the wall like a stone wraith. So perfectly blended with his surroundings, Semper could have reached out and touched him.

"Watch out!" Cymm yelled.

Thalras plunged his dagger into Semper's back. "Who are you looking for? Human scum."

DragonSin rang against the scabbard walls as Cymm withdrew it.

"Easy. I am the only one with the antidote to help your friend," the arrogant dwarf said.

"I have my own remedy, and it doesn't involve you." Cymm's hand shot out and the dwarf flew backward, slamming against the stone wall.

Semper fell to one knee. "No. He is mine." His voice was low and raspy.

The rowdy patrons in the Rude Rogue masked the noise from the alley. He rushed the assassin pinned against the stone and slammed his head into the wall. The dwarf crumpled to the floor. "Semper, pull up your jerkin now. We need to get the poison out."

Semper struggled to comply.

Cymm helped to lift the boiled leather. *"DragonSin, remove the poison like you did for Barrister."*

The poison puffed from the wound as a mist and coagulated into a thick gel. DragonSin discarded it on the floor of the alley.

Cymm healed the deep puncture wound and pulled his armor back into place.

A slow, deliberate clap echoed down the alley, startling them. Another dwarf materialized from against the stone wall, his cloak providing absolute camouflage. "Quite impressive. Thalras is a high-ranking guild member, but of course you already knew that. Apparently, many in my guild have died tonight."

Cymm rose to a defensive posture, two hands on the hilt of the sword guarding his face, with the blade pointed down across his body.

The new arrival raised his hands in submission. "I have seen your work, but tell me, who sent you?"

"What? Who sent me?" Cymm asked in confusion.

"Yes. Who is paying you to complete this job? I will pay you double if you tell me and leave the city."

Cymm and Semper shared a glance and chuckled.

The dwarf's pleasant face filled with hatred. "I make you a great offer and you laugh in my face?"

Cymm fixed Semper with a stare, hoping he would follow his lead. "No. Our employer sent all of us to extract information. Not to kill."

"*All of us*? That would explain the other killings." The dwarf smirked.

Old-Man Semper backhanded him in the shoulder, playing along.

"If we get the information we need, we'll leave," said Cymm.

"There are two behind us, and three more in front," DragonSin reported.

"Take care of the two behind us; drop them in front of me on their knees," Cymm replied.

Cymm glanced over his back as two dwarves appeared out of the wall. They stumbled toward him holding their heads and fell on their knees in front of him. They squirmed and moaned.

Thalras twitched several times.

The dwarf's eyes moved from Thalras back to Cymm's, and he hissed, "What information?"

Cymm and Semper glanced at each other again, and Semper nodded.

"Who is responsible for killing the members of the Ironcore Clan?" asked Cymm.

Now the dwarf chuckled. "That's what this is about?"

With an open palm, Cymm waved before him. "Time is wasting. These two will be dead shortly."

"I assume you already know who killed the mother." The dwarf half motioned toward Thalras. "The father is not dead, nor the children."

"Liar!" Semper could hold his tongue no longer.

"I am not lying. The father has been in the dungeons of Delge for almost eighty-five years, and the sister for twenty."

Semper's agitation grew exponentially. He paced back and forth in a two-foot square box. "How can that be?" he mumbled.

With a clenched jaw, Cymm placed his hand on Semper's shoulder.

"Two more approach from behind," said the sword.

"What about the brothers? Hardre or Semper? Quickly, or there will be a bloodbath. The others are about to enter the headquarters," pressed Cymm.

"They are still alive. The bounty on each of their heads is over twenty thousand gold, and neither reward has been collected. Now call the attack off!" The dwarf turned to his unseen companions. "Go and report back."

The two in front of Cymm fell to their sides. *"Pull the next two behind us forward."*

DragonSin did as instructed.

"You can save these two, but I am not sure about them. However, this one"—Cymm pointed at Thalras— "dies."

Semper smashed his warhammer into the face of his mother's murderer, killing him with a single blow.

"No! You will pay for this. We will root out every last one of you," exclaimed the dwarven assassin.

Cymm and Semper turned and fled.

62

Traitor

ZaphMordakai

ZaphMordakai banked from one airstream to the next, attempting to maximize his speed as he returned to BelCharius's lair. His stomach rumbled, and he realized he had not eaten in days. The thought of smokey owlbear monopolized his thoughts briefly. It was replaced by his experience on the Peak of Power.

A chortle reverberated deep in his throat. "I thought I was dead for a moment. Lykinnia must be desperate for friends. Her risk-taking is unwarranted, even if I did save her life and the winged man's." He thought about how many friends he had. "Friends are overrated, who needs friends."

Lightning jumped between his teeth and his eyes narrowed. "Some of the drakaina like me."

His subconscious disagreed. *They don't like you. They laugh at you.*

"No one laughs at me!" he screamed.

He continued in self-reflection. *How many black dragons respect you? How many of the generals?*

"They will after this. All the drakes will recognize my strength and power." Zaph released a massive bolt of lightning into the clouds, illuminating them. "Now we will see if BelCharius is the favorite."

He was halfway back to the green dragon's lair when he received the summons.

"Yes, my Queen."

The jet-black form of Ledaedra floated next to him, keeping pace. "Well?"

"I saved the young girl's life, and they gave me permission to come and go as I please," replied Zaph.

"In dragon form?" Ledaedra asked skeptically.

He paused momentarily to rub the scar on his neck, the only blemish on his otherwise pristine scales. "Yes," he lied.

"You have done well. I will be in touch shortly." The Queen's embodiment dematerialized.

ZaphMordakai found it difficult not to smile.

63

Trace

Lykinnia

A solitary figure stood at the altar deep in concentration, emitting a pulsing hum every three seconds. Terazhan's hood rested on his back and shoulders, a rare occurrence. Lykinnia watched from twenty feet away, at the edge of the platform. The sun had passed its zenith a few hours ago, making it almost two full days since Solar had almost died.

Lykinnia clutched her forehead with both hands as a massive wave of pain shot through her mind. It buckled her knees. She wavered but remained standing.

"Another one?" Concern filled Solar's face.

Lykinnia lightly tapped the front of her forehead. "It hurts right here. It is payback for severing her arm."

Solar placed his arm around her shoulders. In hushed tones he said, "Maybe, but it is unlikely. I am almost convinced that was her, with what she knew, including the promise of death."

Lykinnia cringed. "Not so fast. Now I am confused. My mother would not have tried to kill me. What if she extracted information from my mother?"

Solar shook his head. "You do not understand. I have kept your mother's secret for many centuries, and she promised to kill *me* if I told anyone."

"What did she do?"

"It is a story you deserve to hear at a later time. Lord Terazhan is almost ready to begin. When we are done here, I want to examine your head. The creature should not be able to attack you with the portal closed." Solar motioned for her to pay attention to her father.

A three-dimensional hologram appeared of their planet Erogoth, encompassing the entire space above the Pool of Age, in front of the altar. It rotated slowly about its axis. Four distinctly colored, brilliant lights twinkled.

Solar whispered to her, giving her live commentary of what was transpiring. "Each of the sparkling lights represents one of the fourteen beings possessing a phylactery. The gold is your father. He knows the other colors for certain, but I believe the dark silver closest to us is Bardonril, the ice white with a tinge of blue at the north pole is Harendread, and the deep hickory is . . ."

Lykinnia glanced at Solar in confusion, but the map reformed, forcing her attention to return to the trace spell. Erogoth became a small portion of the new map, and tiny gemstones popped across the entire image.

Solar counted aloud, ending at fourteen.

Lykinnia gazed up at him, expecting a smile, but instead found a scowl. "What?"

The hologram dissipated and Terazhan turned toward them with a frown. "He is dead."

Lykinnia regarded her father, then Solar and back. "Who?"

Both men answered in unison, "Phindazar."

“I do not know who that is. What about Uncle Jakarrak? Is he alive?” spouted Lykinnia without taking a breath.

Terazhan returned his cowl to its usual position. “Yes. I saw Jakarrak on the Plane of Ashes.”

Solar shifted from one foot to the other. “The deep hickory light is new, and on our planet. Is it—”

“Yes. I believe so. I plan to investigate further.” Terazhan pursed his lips and blinked.

Lykinnia’s head swirled with new information, and she endeavored to capture everything for future consideration. “What did I miss? Who is it?”

Solar glanced at Terazhan. “Ledaedra. She killed Phindazar, and now has a phylactery of her own.”

“Now she is immortal?” asked Lykinnia.

Solar deferred to Terazhan for guidance with a flourish.

Terazhan blinked twice. “None of us are truly immortal. Ledaedra killed Phindazar, then found and destroyed his phylactery of power, and killed him again on his home plane.”

She stepped close to her father, feeling small for the first time in a while. “How does this affect us?”

Terazhan put his hand on her shoulder and bent at the waist. “Phindazar was my brother, and the balance of power has shifted significantly.”

64

Help

Cymm

Semper closed the door to the secret passage and leaned against it, chest heaving with every breath.

Cymm took a seat in a plush chair. "Did they follow us?"

"I don't know. I doubled back twice. Those stone cloaks are tough to see. Do you think he told the truth about my family?" Semper made his way over and sat across from Cymm.

"According to DragonSin, everything he said about your family was true, or at least the dwarf believes it. There is no way you could have known." Cymm's head lulled back against the cushion.

Melkerie burst through the front door. "Semper, what did you do? There are guards swarming through God's Hammer Square."

Semper rose and hugged her. "I'm sorry. I shouldn't have brought my problems to your door."

She held one of his hands with both of hers. "Your problems are my problems. How can I help?"

"We are going to hide until morning and try to sneak out of the city. They are looking for two humans, so I will take my ring off—"

"What a horrible plan. Why not turn yourself in now and get a good night's rest?" Melkerie's eyes were welling with tears.

"Do you have a better idea?" asked Semper.

"You could hide out here and leave in a few weeks when the patrols return to normal." She gazed into his eyes, pleading.

"My father and sister are in the dungeons, and the Guild knows we are searching for them. It will be expensive, but I know who can get them out. The longer I wait, the greater the chance of something happening to them."

"You could leave through the mines. They won't expect humans to go deeper into the mountain, or believe they could find their way," Melkerie said.

"What a great idea." Cymm sat upright.

"Except how long it will take to exit the mines and return for my family." Semper folded his arms over his chest.

Cymm rested his hand on Semper's shoulder. "Once we collect the gems we need from my stash, we will come right back to free them."

Melkerie's eyes pleaded with Semper.

Semper said through clenched teeth, "Fine."

Melkerie stood to leave. "I'll contact my brother. He works in the Free Mines. He'll know the best route to take and any potential issues with the plan."

ꝏꝏꝏ

Cymm awoke from a dream by the slamming of a door. The memory of his visit with Lykinnia dissipating from his mind. He shielded his eyes as candlelight brightened the room.

"You don't have much time. Guards are searching through every building, room by room, and the Cross-Eyed Goat is next. My brother will meet you at the iron vein near God's Fork." Melkerie rushed forward to hug Semper, already in dwarven-form.

Cymm gathered his belongings and waited by the entrance to the secret passage.

Within moments the doorway closed, and the blackness swallowed them. Semper would not risk any light until they were far from the room, so Cymm ducked low and held onto the dwarf's backpack.

Finally, they paused, and Semper lit a hooded lantern. "They are looking for two humans. One of them is as tall as a damn tree and carries a magnificent sword." The dwarf slowly, grudgingly, held out his hand to Cymm and opened it. Semper's prized possession laid in his palm—his ring.

Cymm's eyes widened, but he did not move.

"Take it. A dwarf and an average sized human will draw much less attention."

Cymm did as instructed and slowly placed it on his finger. The ring sized itself and transformed him into Old-Man Semper.

"Don't get used to looking so good. I want the ring back." Semper smacked his knee and sniggered.

Cymm punched him. "If only Talo could see me now."

They continued to the end of the passageway and extinguished the lantern. Minutes rolled by while they listened for movement.

Semper finally pulled the catch release and ushered them into the small chamber. "Wait here." He opened the real door on the opposite wall and stepped out with the hood of his cloak in place. He returned moments later, beckoning Cymm to follow.

From the shadows of the doorway, Cymm observed the numerous sentries in the Maker's Square. Most of these guards swarmed near the Cross-Eyed Goat.

"Hunch down like an old man and follow me." The real Semper turned his back on the scene and led them to a side-street exit. The bustling crowd engulfed them, and the noise from the guards faded into the distance. "Keep your hood pulled forward. We will be passing through the same square as last night."

"Can't we go around?" asked Cymm.

"No, not if we are heading to the mines."

Although his back and shoulders stooped forward, Cymm was a foot taller than the crowd. He scanned forward and grabbed Semper's arm. "They are searching everyone as they enter the square."

Semper shook his head. "Too late to turn back now. It would be obvious we are avoiding the checkpoint."

Eight people stood between the guards and them.

The crowd stopped and lurched forward as people cleared the screening.

Three people in front of them.

Cymm's heart raced; it was pounding in his ears.

The last person stepped forward. They were next.

Cymm's mouth went dry. He swallowed hard, then stepped up to the guards.

"Keep moving." The captain of the guards waved them through.

Semper's sigh of relief, after they passed the final guard, was quite telling.

A dwarven guard in the square pointed a gnarled finger at them. "The old human is one of them. Seize him!"

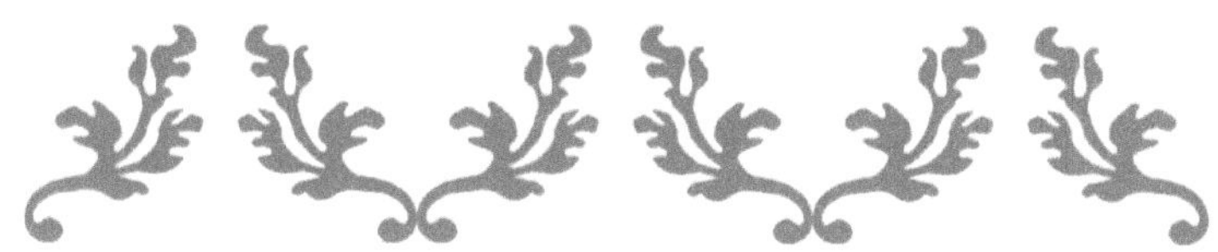

65

Wasting Time

Lykinnia

Solar had been gone for over two weeks. He left the day after the trace spell to locate Uncle Jakarrak on the Plane of Ashes. During his absence, Lykinnia had been plagued by more intense and frequent headaches. In the confusion caused by the discovery of Phindazar's death, her malady had been completely forgotten.

Lykinnia was unsure how long he would be gone, so she spent her time at the altar, traveling back in time to set waypoints. She continued to search for the beginning of time so she could wrap around into the future. At her current pace, she had no idea how long it would take.

She used Solar's responsibility as an excuse to observe Cymm for a half-hour each day. However, once he arrived in Delge, her apprehension elevated. It gave her a compelling reason to watch over him more frequently until he was on his way to see her. While observing him, a disturbing thought occurred to her, *how is it Cymm can receive a*

Vision or Divine Quest? Both are examples of seeing into the future. So, why did Solar tell me it is not possible, if Terazhan already does it? Why did I not realize this sooner?

Her head flared with pain for the third time that day. As it subsided, she noticed movement forty yards off the backside of the platform.

"What is that?" Lykinnia hopped off the back and walked toward it.

A rift in space had torn open. It was larger than normal, at least five feet tall and two feet wide. The pitch-darkness in the middle emitted the faint sound of a crackling campfire.

"Where did this come from?" The portal closed when she spoke, and her headache immediately vanished.

Lykinnia's heart thumped rapidly, a wave of fear crashing over her. "*Father, come quickly!*"

Terazhan replied almost immediately, "*What is wrong?*" He appeared a moment later.

She pointed at the empty space in front of her. "It was right here a second ago."

"What was there?" her father asked.

"A large rift in space . . ."

"A large—Lykinnia, your mother and I cast powerful spells to prevent anything like that from happening."

"It was right there. I saw it."

"I believe you saw something. How is your head feeling?" Her father rubbed her shoulder.

"But I saw it. A strange noise was coming out. It should never come out," she mumbled.

"You are pushing yourself too hard with the altar. A lack of sleep, nutrition, or hydration can cause hallucinations."

"I know what I—" She took a deep, steadying breath. "Have you heard from Solar?"

"Two days ago. He found Jakarrak on the Plane of Ashes, but he could not talk for fear of giving his position away."

"He could be in trouble. Should we check on him?"

"I am not worried yet. Time there passes much slower. I am returning to my tasks. Please take some time off to recover." Her father smiled at her.

"I know you are not fond of deal making, but I will take a couple of days off from the altar if you show me how to use it to travel forward in time." Lykinnia smirked back at him.

"It only goes backward in time."

"Then how do you use it to send Visions or Divine Quests to Cymm?"

"Ahh. You are confusing activities. First, I cast a spell to divine potential outcomes for a specific event. Then, I use the altar to design the vision or quest before sending it to an individual. When you called for me, I was running through multiple scenarios for what is about to happen in the south." Terazhan's face was inviting.

Lykinnia found her father's politics uninteresting. "Hmm. Okay." Her face went tight; she was deep in thought. "Father, I think it is time for you to teach me the language of The One. I have not made any significant advancements in my clerical studies for a century."

Terazhan scratched above his eyebrow, contemplating. "Your mother and I agreed to wait until after your millennial lifeday, but I do not see a reason why we cannot start a few months early."

Lykinnia launched into a ballet recital.

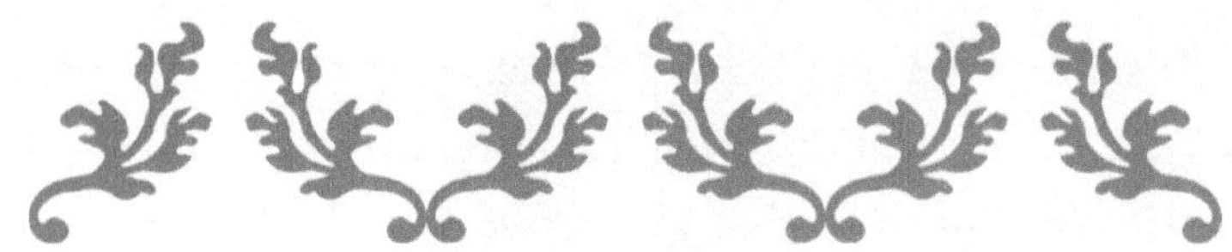

66

Escape

Cymm

Out of the corner of his eye, Cymm followed the dwarven guard pointing and walking straight for him. He knelt and bent low. The ring slipped off his finger, and he handed it back to Semper. "Take it and go. They don't recognize you. Lead the way. I will create a diversion then follow." Back to his normal form, he stood, towering over everyone nearby.

The dwarf skidded to a stop, no longer calling for reinforcements that were already descending on their position.

"DragonSin, drop this dwarf so he can't identify us," instructed Cymm.

"He was one of my targets anyway."

Cymm glanced back briefly, satisfied the dwarven whistleblower was on his knees unable to talk to the guards surrounding him. His smile dissipated as he ran into a wall. At least it felt like a wall. Once his vision unblurred and his ears stopped ringing, he realized a giant man had spun him around, wrapped his massive arms around him, and secured him tightly. His hand was no longer in contact with DragonSin.

"Let go—you oaf!" While struggling, Cymm's hood fell back.

"Brogan, let go." The dwarf next to him stared at him in wonder.

"Are you kiddin'. We could use the bounty." The one called Brogan turned to the side and carried him toward the guards.

The dwarf rushed around in front and kicked him in the shin. "It's Cymm!"

Brogan spun him around and their eyes met. It was the Big Man from the gnoll cages. "Karaz, take him to your shop. I will redirect the guards then meet you there."

His sleeve yanked hard, and Karaz pulled him toward one of the square exits.

A dwarf came roaring in, blocking their path.

Cymm sighed in relief. It was Semper barreling toward them. Cymm stepped in front of him with hands raised. "Stop! He's helping us."

Semper came to a screeching halt and fell in line.

They ran out of the square into a main street where the traffic slowed their pace considerably. Cymm stayed close to his benefactor. After a few crossroads, the fugitives turned right and entered a shop one hundred feet down on the left. A sign on the door read "Stoneheart Silver."

Cymm assumed the shop owner was a silversmith. There were forks, spoons, plates, bowls, candelabras, and more—all made from silver. He tried to catch his breath, along with eight dwarves—Semper, Karaz, and six others that he had no idea where they had come from. Cymm inched closer to Semper. "Why didn't you leave?"

"Don't be foolish. I would never leave you. You're like a son to me," Semper smacked him on the backside.

Brogan burst through the door, clipping his shoulder on the frame. "I got rid of them. Sent 'em to Black Forge Square." He closed the door and held his arms out wide. "Cymmmm!"

Cymm extended his hand to shake. "How do you know my name?"

Brogan pushed his hand aside and pulled him into a bearhug. "Cymm Reich of Stallion Rise."

His charismatic smile set Cymm at ease. "Zecarius. Did all three of them make it through the hill giant country?"

"Yeah, we went around. Too many giants and spiders. Me and Karaz have been talking about coming to find you and thank you properly. Let's start over. I'm Brogan of the Cragstrike Clan, this is Karaz Stoneheart, and this is—"

There was a pounding at the door. "Brogan, we know you're in there! Are you harboring the outlaws?"

Karaz glared at Brogan in disgust. "I knew I should have done it myself." His gaze rotated to Cymm. "You got any luck left, or is it all used up?"

"We are fighting, then? Shouldn't we see what they want first? They could be delivering a key to the city gates." Cymm chuckled alone.

Brogan hung his head. "You stepped on a hornet's nest, Cymm, and they're pissed. You and your friend are being accused of seventeen murders last night."

Cymm glanced at Semper. "Seventeen?" *"Seventeen?"*

"I tallied eighteen. Most of them in the Rude Rogue, while we were waiting for the assassin to leave the building," replied DragonSin.

"By Ledaedra's bones!" blasted Cymm. *"How many assassins await us in the streets?"*

"Only three or four, but there are many guards out there."

"Yes. If caught, the Hearth Council will have you hanged over the Great Forge and slowly lowered into the lava pit. If it were anyone else, I'd turn you over in a second," fumed Brogan.

"Oh, quiet. Many are silently praising him this morning." Karaz wagged his finger in chastisement.

"Brogan, you have ten seconds to open the door!" the same booming voice demanded.

Cymm took a deep breath and grabbed the handle. "Let's try diplomacy first." He opened the door halfway and stood in the breach with DragonSin hidden behind the door. At least forty guards surrounded him in a semicircle fifteen feet away, with their leader in the center. "Captain, I believe you are looking for me. If you intend to arrest me, I must demand to know the charges."

"Demand? You insolent scoundrel. Are you surrendering or not?" barked the captain.

"Will I be given a fair trial? Will there even be a trial?" Cymm could feel everyone crowding him from behind the door.

The captain was silent.

"You're an honorable dwarf, captain. Thank you for not lying to me. May I ask, what is your responsibility to the city and its people?" asked Cymm.

The captain flinched, then cleared his throat. "To keep the city and its people safe, to protect them."

"And do you think you are doing a respectable job? Seventeen assassins died last night. Many of them had contracts to kill. I could have saved your life or someone in your family." His pointer finger swept the arc of soldiers.

"I thought he said diplomacy, not insults," whispered Brogan.

"Sometimes they are one and the same." Semper smacked Brogan's massive thigh.

Karaz nodded in agreement.

A roar came from the crowd. "I have heard enough!" A dwarf pushed through the guards forcefully. "Captain, your orders were to capture or kill the fugitives. Not drink a beer with them." He raised the crossbow in his hands and fired at Cymm. The crossbow bolt streaked toward Cymm's face. A foot away it halted, hovered in the air with poison dripping from it, and fell to the floor with a clatter.

"Drop him!" Cymm conveyed, referring to the dwarf with the crossbow. He shook his head at the captain. "Do you take your orders from the King or the Assassin's Guild?"

"You will be reprimanded to the dungeons of Delge, by my order, loudmouth!" Spittle flew from the captain's contorted face.

The assassin who fired at Cymm dropped to his knees, shrieking in pain. The guards, including the captain, swiveled their red-streaked helms back and forth, uncertain what to do.

A score of dwarves without uniforms pushed through the guards. Each with a crossbow raised and released their package for Cymm in unison. He closed the door a moment before the first thumped into the wood, which was followed by the remaining barrage.

"If we can get to the mines, we have a guide to show us out. Is there a back door we can use to avoid the sixty dwarves waiting for us out there?" asked Cymm.

"Sixty!" Karaz's jaw dropped.

Several other dwarves moaned, and Brogan sighed heavily.

Semper laid his hand on Cymm's forearm. "If we fight, many of us will die. If anyone can escape the dungeons, it's you."

Brogan snapped out of his reverie. "Follow me. Before they can reload."

"No. Semper's right. Brogan, you're not going to like this." Cymm paused a second to reconsider. *"DragonSin, drop him."*

While Brogan screamed and thrashed on the floor, Cymm approached Karaz. "Here's the plan."

ꝏꝏꝏ

A few minutes later, Brogan opened the door, blood leaking from his eyes, ears, and nose. He carried an unconscious Cymm on his shoulder and dragged Old-Man Semper by the scruff of his cloak. The big man stumbled, and Cymm thought he was going down. Somehow, he caught himself and managed to recover.

"There's at least six more bodies in there." Brogan nodded back over his shoulder. He pulled hard on Old-Man Semper's collar and threw him down at the captain's feet. With a heavy boot, he half kicked and rolled the dead assassin over. "He almost got me too. Look at my eyes!"

An unknown voice said, "Ah, Brogan, we owe you a great debt. We will take—"

"No, you won't. They're both going to the dungeons as the King instructed," replied the captain.

Brogan slammed Cymm down on the dead assassin as planned, and the paladin let out a pitiful moan.

"Get these two in chains," the captain yelled.

"You may regret going against the guild, captain. They are not beyond our reach in the dungeons," said the unknown voice.

Cymm continued the charade but desperately wanted to open his eyes to identify the speaker.

"Once I have delivered them to the dungeon warden, my responsibility ends, so I doubt I will regret it. Or are you threatening me?" snapped the captain.

There was no response.

The shackles snapped into place on his ankles and wrists, and Cymm was hauled to his feet. He feigned a groggy recovery and opened his eyes.

"Brogan, you will pay for your treachery!" Cymm yelled. He glanced quickly at Old-Man Semper to validate everything went as planned and received a brief nod. Cymm breathed a sigh of relief, happy his weapons and necklace had been stashed inside. *Now, hopefully the rest goes as planned.*

67

Fifty-Seven Languages

Lykinnia

Lykinnia closed the scrying window. Cymm's progress toward the Peak of Power had been delayed longer than she anticipated, and he was playing a dangerous game. He was safe for now, but would he remain so?

Lykinnia reached out telepathically, *"Father."*

"Yes, Lykinnia?" answered Terazhan.

A giant smile crossed her face at his quick response. *"I have been watching over Cymm in Solar's place, and—"*

Terazhan appeared at the altar immediately. "And?"

"He needs our help. The dwarven guards in Delge arrested him and threw him in the dungeons. Can you possess him again so he can escape?"

Terazhan rolled his eyes. "I do not possess him. I enter the body of a willing host, and they become my avatar. There are many actions he can resist if he chooses. However, I can only enter the same body once between Twilights."

"But Father, he needs help, and it *is* a new cycle of the moons."

Terazhan pondered this for a moment. "So, it is. Continue watching over him. If he needs help, we will figure out what needs to be done. Let us not forget, my power is more defensive and in the realm of healing."

"Is that why you did not help when he fought the blood wolf?"

"I did help. I sent you and Solar. However, the cycle of the moons definitely needs to be kept in mind." Terazhan diverted the conversation to a new subject. "Before we begin with the lesson for today, I want you to understand it will be to learn the basics of the language, not how to cast higher level spells."

"Okay, but if there is an easy—"

"No, Lykinnia. I know how you think. We are going to take this slow and lock in the fundamentals. The language is simple to learn if you build off the basics."

"Did Mother know the language of The One?" She held her breath, hoping this would not upset her father.

"No. Not many do. I am aware of only my sisters, Melandri and Sehaleah, and my brother Dilantro. Our father taught us, so we could communicate with him. The access to more complex spells was an inadvertent benefit."

And very advantageous, she thought.

Terazhan locked eyes with his daughter. "Let us begin."

68

Dungeons of Delge

Cymm

More than two weeks transpired, and Cymm's concern about the plan escalated. By his estimation, today was Terazhan's Twilight. He would miss his commitment to Lykinnia—not the best way to start a relationship. The dungeons were slave camps for mining. The few prison cells they encountered held starving troublemakers. Chain gangs of ten to twelve were created, and the shackles were never removed from their feet. Not for sleeping, eating, working, or even a call of nature.

Most of their valuables had been wisely left in the silversmith's shop. When they arrived at the processing station, they were searched, and their belongings confiscated, except for a ring. The hair on Semper's toes had successfully hidden it.

The clanging of pickaxes and shovels constantly rang throughout the caverns, grottos, and tunnels. Each taskmaster ran their crew as they saw fit, but the schedule most commonly followed was six hours on, six hours off. Twelve-hour days of hard labor, seven days a week. Most non-dwarfs did not survive very long.

The picks and shovels were collected at the end of every shift, and their hands were re-shackled. Cymm shifted uncomfortably on the ground, his back against a wall. He whispered from the end of the line to Old-Man Semper in front of him, "I can barely feel my arms and legs, and there's a knot in my back. How are you doing?"

"I'm fine. Dwarves are built for this sort of thing."

"Do you think they are coming?" moaned Cymm.

Another mining team trudged past them, and Semper scrutinized every individual. "I do. Be patient and enjoy the food."

Cymm did not know whether to laugh or cry, but his thoughts lasted a fleeting moment before he fell asleep.

ꝏꝏꝏ

Cymm sensed movement to his left. A bleary-eyed glance revealed a dwarf sitting next to him. He was no longer at the end of the chain gang. Unlike a dwarf, he had a difficult time making out any details in the low light, but the wild eyes and the low growl warned him to mind his own business.

The taskmaster drifted over. Cymm groaned. *It can't be time already.*

Chains rattled at the head of the line and slogged its way toward Old-Man Semper. Cymm's arms were pulled to the right as his friend was unlocked, but he felt no resistance from the new prisoner.

The warden shuffled toward Cymm. "Hey, what are you doing here?" He was not talking to Cymm, but to the new dwarf.

Semper clobbered the warden from behind, knocking him to the ground. A second blow rendered him unconscious.

"Nice job Semper," the new dwarf whispered.

Brogan lumbered through an opening into the tunnel, banging his head on an outcropping. "By the nine hells!"

Karaz came next, dragging chains. "Keep it down, you fool."

"Thank Terazhan. What took you so long?" Cymm asked in a restrained voice.

Eight more shackled dwarves followed.

"Do you know how big these mines are? We've been searching for days," replied Brogan.

The manacles on Cymm and Semper fell to the floor, allowing the old man to unlock the rest of his group.

"You were caught?" Cymm asked Brogan.

Karaz pushed past the big guy. "What are you talking about?"

Cymm pointed at the chains. "What are those?"

"These are for show. They were my cousin's idea. He is our taskmaster and dungeon guide. Cymm, meet Ibor Stoneheart." Karaz made a flourishing wave toward the growling dwarf.

Brogan scanned through the group. "Gather what you need. We leave in one minute. I'll take care of the taskmaster."

Cymm stepped to intervene. "No, you won't. Do we have any rope?"

Brogan hesitated. "Cymm."

The young man blocked the way. "He's been firm, but fair. We're not going to kill him. Tie and gag him, then throw him in a side tunnel. We'll be long gone before he causes any trouble."

Karaz pushed up next to the big guy. "We don't have time for—"

"I'll make time. Go on ahead," Cymm cut in.

"Stubborn blockhead. Get the damn rope!" yelled Brogan.

"This is why we didn't end up in the gnoll pits." Karaz nodded with respect and walked away issuing orders. "Grab a shovel or a pick for a weapon, and clasp one shackle to your ankle or wrist. We will be carrying the chain."

Ibor and Brogan secured the taskmaster, and the party of over twenty hastily evacuated.

Cymm's satisfaction wavered. "You brought my sword, right?"

Karaz nodded. "Yes, of course. All our weapons are in the ore carts. Let's hope we don't need them."

Ibor set a brisk pace through the twisty tunnels and after two hours, they had managed to avoid running into anyone.

Cymm's feet were sore. "Semper, are we sure he knows where he's going?"

"He was a taskmaster for over forty years. Now he runs rescue and escape missions. He agreed to help me find my father and sister, even though he doubts they're alive."

The tunnel's gradient abruptly increased.

Cymm labored under the stress of the past three weeks, the pace, and the weight of the chain. "How much—is he—charging?"

Old-Man Semper sighed. "He doesn't want coin. He asked for—"

Ibor stopped. A hushed message rolled through the crew to remain silent and still. Their guide disappeared ahead.

The minutes clicked by, and the tension mounted. Every shift of position or accidental rattle of a chain seemed loud as thunder.

Ibor finally returned with flailing hands, beckoning them forward. "The transfer station has a squad of city guards, and they don't appear to be in a hurry to move on."

"By the nine hells, I knew we should've eliminated the taskmaster," Brogan grumbled.

Cymm pushed back on Brogan's shoulder. "There's no way he beat us here."

"The kid's right. Those guards have been there awhile. Maybe they found out we entered the dungeon." Ibor scratched his head. "We can try the other transfer station, but it will take us several hours to get there."

Cymm sighed.

Karaz shook his head. "Can we wait them out?"

"No. The next patrol will pass through within the half hour. We need a plan," replied Ibor.

"How many guards?" asked Brogan.

"Six city guards and three jailers. Most of us won't fit in the room." Ibor's eyes flitted anxiously from one person to the next.

Cymm glanced at Old-Man Semper, then puffed to speak. "I—"

Brogan laid his hand on Cymm's back. "We need to fight."

Semper and Karaz nodded in agreement, and Cymm reluctantly conceded a few moments later.

Brogan turned to those behind them. "Get the chains off quietly and fall back in line with a weapon."

They crept forward soundlessly without the shackles on. There was no hesitation at the entry. Brogan crashed through the doorway and into the soldiers. Some of them faltered and dove out of the way, the others went flying.

Cymm and eight dwarves followed in his wake. They formed a semicircle with their backs to the tunnel opening. The battle commenced in earnest, and bodies struck the stone floor.

"For Terazhan, the One True God!" A globe of shimmering white light detonated around the paladin with such force, it rocked his enemies back on their heels. The aura was large enough to encompass his entire group, except for Brogan on the far side of the room.

A crossbow bolt sailed through the open space, ripping through a defender's throat. Karaz and another dwarf also went down. Both tried to rise, but only his friend succeeded. Two dwarves rushed forward from the tunnel to take the place of their fallen comrades.

DragonSin and Brogan did the greatest damage to the enemy ranks trapped between them. Escape was not possible past the giant man blocking the other exit.

Only four enemies remained when Karaz went down again. Cymm straddled him, shielding the dwarf. He regained his feet at the same time Semper took a massive blow that staggered him. Cymm could only watch in slow motion, unable to assist, as the next swing barreled in.

DragonSin knocked the attacking dwarf off balance, causing him to swing wide, but the damage had already been done. Cymm watched in horror as Semper collapsed.

Brogan, Karaz, and the others surrounded the remaining foes, making quick work of them. The final two threw down their weapons.

Cymm lunged to Semper's side. "Terazhan, Almighty Healer, bless me with the power to heal my friend." The pure white aura blazed forth and Semper's breathing regulated.

Karaz oversaw the remaining guards bound and gagged. "We need to keep moving. A patrol could come from either direction."

Cymm counted five dwarfs not continuing with them.

Ibor joined him. "Most of them had been falsely accused and didn't deserve to be imprisoned. It is the same story for many of the prisoners."

"For what reason?" asked Cymm.

"Free labor. If there aren't enough miners to meet the King's demand, the Red Guard arrest citizens and send them to the dungeons."

Cymm shook his head, staring at the bodies in dismay.

"This is why I quit being a taskmaster and will do anything I can to free the prisoners. The entire system needs to change." Ibor left Cymm standing there staring at the dead bodies.

"Most of the dwarves I took down are not dead and will rouse shortly," said the sword.

"Why?" asked Cymm.

"Evil leadership doesn't make one evil."

Cymm hauled Semper to his feet, then turned to Brogan. "We have to go now."

Brogan followed Cymm's gaze to a guard that was stirring. His head snapped back around. "You two, set up one hundred feet down the hall. Now!"

They did as they were instructed, and the rest of the group gathered up.

Brogan picked two more dwarves. "One hundred feet past the first two. Go."

Ibor pushed to the front. "If we can make it past Smelter's Square . . ."

Brogan pulled two more dwarves roughly to him. "All the way to Smelter's Square and guard the entrance of the free mines."

The last of the escapees left the transfer station; they were on the move, but not before Brogan jammed two axes between the floor and the bottom of the door. He tapped Karaz on the chest and nodded. "Ibor, continue ahead at this pace. I'll send word if there's a problem."

They ran ahead.

Cymm smiled despite the situation, and his admiration of the big man grew. "We're going to get through this," he whispered to Semper, who leaned on him heavily.

They passed a couple of side tunnels branching in different directions and one cutting across their path, but they did not encounter resistance.

After ten minutes, Ibor announced, "Smelter's Square is straight ahead."

The dim light of the tunnels brightened as the passageway widened, and a warm breeze drifted past them. Metal clanked against metal, and gruff voices called to each other.

Old-Man Semper walked on his own now, barely, and Cymm kept a watchful eye on his every step. *I should heal him again*, thought Cymm. Having used his paladin power to heal already, only his two priest spells remained. His contemplation ended when they emerged from the corridor into Smelter's Square, with Ibor in the lead.

The ceiling in this square was thirty feet high with several shafts cut into it for proper ventilation. Huge bellows pumped, each with its own cadence, creating a relaxing rhythmic beat.

"Spread out and meet on the far side by the tunnel." Ibor melted into the crowd without another word.

"Where in the nine hells is Brogan?" Cymm whispered to Old-Man Semper. There was no reply. "Should I carry your hammer for you?"

"Should I hit you in the face with it?" growled the old man.

"Ah, you're alive. Pick up the pace. We're falling behind." Cymm scanned over his shoulder.

Another blast furnace loomed before them, the final obstacle in this cavern.

Karaz materialized out of a small crowd and joined them. "Keep moving. The city guard is on alert and a patrol of Red Axes entered the far side of the square."

Brogan appeared at the edge of the tunnel, their destination, draped in shadows. He peered around both corners, then his eyes went wide with shock. Frantic hands indicated they should hurry to join him.

They passed the furnace and entered the wide-open space running the length of the square. Now, clearly visible in the causeway, a platoon of Red Axe Guards approached.

For all his bluff and bluster, Old-Man Semper struggled to run. He tripped, sprawled, and hit the ground hard.

Cymm rushed back and knelt beside him. Above the din of the bellows, the clanging of weapons rang out from the tunnel behind Brogan. The noise grew rapidly, and the entire escape party burst into the square pursued by another squad of Red Axes.

Cymm yanked his mentor to his feet and turned to head back in the direction they came, but a large group of gray cloaked figures barred the way: The Assassin's Guild.

His group congregated and pushed down the causeway in the only remaining direction toward the next blast furnace. The assassins shadowed their movement on the far side of the structure, blocking their escape. They continued to the last furnace, effectively trapping themselves in the corner of Smelter's Square.

69

Kindred Spirits

Talo

Almost two fortnights had passed since Cymm and Semper left Stallion Rise. Talo was in a barn with the two-year-old colts and fillies. He clicked and whistled, moving the youngsters into the correct position.

Mare scratched a colt behind his ear. "See what your sister did? Now it's your turn."

Talo moved to assist with the maneuver.

"I really like Vena. You're fortunate." Mare held the colt in position.

"Father will find a nice match for you as well."

"What's the matter? You've been moping around for days." Mare gave the colt a chunk of carrot. "Talo? Talo!"

"Yeah?"

"Agghh! Never mind. Are you and Vena going to the bonfire tonight?"

Talo shrugged. "I don't know."

"It's Terazhan's Twilight. Don't be a pimple on an orc's butt." His sister giggled.

He threw a carrot at her. "Can you finish up here without me? I need to set up the training field at Semper's for today's lesson."

"Fine, as long as you and Vena are at the bonfire tonight." Mare grabbed both sides of the colt's head, making their eyes meet. "See what I did there? Does your sister have to trick you to have fun?"

Talo huffed and exited the barn, almost tripping over Jalko. He knelt and scratched the wolf behind the ear. "Still here?"

Jalko, lying in the spot where Talo told him to stay before entering the barn, cocked his head.

Talo continued petting him. "I was wrong about you. You're a good boy. Do you miss Cymm?"

Jalko's whine mutated to a moan, then he flopped to his side.

"I miss him too. If we stick together, next time we can both go. No more getting left behind."

Jalko sat up with a bark.

Talo chuckled and motioned for Jalko to follow. "Come on."

70

A Dire Situation

Cymm

Cymm's escape party formed a defensive arc two rows deep, with their backs to the corner.

Old-Man Semper stumbled ahead of the group, hefting his warhammer. Cymm and Ibor stepped out to retrieve him.

Cymm reached for him. "What are you doing?"

Semper's warhammer swung in a high sweep, but there were no enemies within twenty feet. His weapon crashed into the iron-reinforced wall of the furnace with a *clang*. A warbling sound pulsated through the area.

Cymm grabbed his arm and pulled his mentor back toward the group.

Semper shrugged off Cymm's hand with renewed vigor. "No!" The warbling grew to a head-pounding shriek.

Ibor fell where he stood, unconscious or dead, Cymm could not tell. Cymm closed his eyes and covered his ears instinctually, feeling relieved as the pain subsided.

Semper swung again, striking the furnace wall harder.

Cymm's hands squeezed the sides of his head. He cried out and examined the defenders behind him. Everyone gaped at him in perplexity. When he faced forward again, a dozen assassins lay on the ground unmoving, and at least a score of Red Axe Guards were amid toppling over.

The old man listed side to side.

"Semper, back up!" Cymm brought his hands up, then froze, afraid to touch him. Semper fell back onto his rump, and Cymm dragged him to the group.

Crossbow bolts came whistling in from the remaining assassins before DragonSin could drop three more of them. The corner of the blast furnace protected all of them except Brogan, and two found their mark.

"For Terazhan, the One True God!" A globe of shimmering white light surrounded the paladin and his allies.

Twenty guards and ten assassins charged, clashing in a grand melee. Four dwarves on each side fell dead within seconds, only to be replaced by the next in line. Shouted commands and screams of pain echoed throughout the cavern.

Cymm glanced at the big man next to him and noticed poison dripping from the bolts. "By Ledaedra's bones!" He ripped one out. *"DragonSin, he needs our help."* Cymm could not reach the other. "Take it out, Brogan!" The enemy pressed in hard, but Cymm successfully protected his flank.

The poison coagulated in the air, then DragonSin hurled it into the face of a guard. The sword went back to work on the assassins.

Swords and battle axes rang against each other.

Semper's warhammer lay on the floor next to him, and he was propped up in the corner.

"Captain! I don't want to kill your soldiers. Only the assassins should die. Help me cleanse your city!" bellowed Cymm.

The last two assassins dropped to their knees writhing in pain, along with one of the guards. One of the defenders fell, and Brogan decapitated another Red Axe.

Every dwarf trapped in the corner was wounded and breathing heavily. Out of the twenty-one original escapees, only eleven remained, including Semper sitting on the floor.

Another defender collapsed, while Brogan and Karaz each killed a Red Axe. Bodies lay strewn across the blood-soaked floor. The blood oozing from the dead made the surface slick and one's footing treacherous.

"Captain!" roared Cymm. *"DragonSin, throw the attackers away from us. I need time!"*

The captain and several of his remaining dwarves wavered.

DragonSin walked the guards back three at a time, until all eight guards had been pushed more than two horse lengths. A temporary armistice ensued. No one dropped their defense as they eyed each other suspiciously.

Cymm took a hesitant step forward. "Although we outnumber you, I do not wish to fight you. The Assassin's Guild started this problem, and I intend to exterminate them, root and stem. The people of this fine city deserve better than cowering in their homes at night, hoping to live another day."

The captain's chest heaved, and he glanced side-to-side at his fellow guards, uncertain.

DragonSin moved on to hurling assassin bodies against the walls.

"What are you doing?" asked Cymm angrily.

"They are only asleep, not dead," replied the sword.

Cymm quickly found Ibor's body and dragged him inside the circle.

DragonSin sang as he launched the assassins and their henchmen into the rock walls so forcefully, most of them died on impact.

The rhythmic sound of marching boots filled the air, and to Cymm's dismay, another captain approached with a contingent of forty more Red Axe Guards.

The defenders tightened their line, Brogan, Karaz, three dwarven fighters, three dwarven convicts, and Cymm. Even Semper staggered to his feet and joined them. The party members bled from numerous gashes, and four were on the brink of death.

Without thinking, the paladin grabbed Semper and Karaz simultaneously, with separate hands. "Holy Terazhan, provide me with the power to heal these friends!" The flow of power was both exhilarating and rejuvenating. The light manifestation radiated in every direction, forcing many to shield their eyes.

The new captain alone stood against the onslaught of light. "Do not say his name in these halls!"

The light faded as quickly as it came, and smiling faces gawked back at him. Everyone in his party had been healed.

The last sleeping assassin hit the wall with an audible *crunch*.

The new captain's face turned red with fury. "Red Axes, bring me their heads!"

Forty new soldiers charged, along with the original captain and his seven men. They crashed into the defender's meager wall, causing it to falter.

"Semper, use your magic," cried Cymm.

"I must hit metal, and no one can be in front of me."

"Push to the flank and hit the furnace. I'll make an opening for you." Cymm cleaved another Red Axe.

DragonSin dropped three attackers in the front line, relieving some of the pressure up front.

Two more defenders fell, as well as four more guards from the heavy swings of Brogan, Cymm, and Karaz.

Ibor joined in line next to Cymm. "What happened to me?"

The paladin's face blanched and he quickly glanced at their fallen enemy. "By the nine hells! Terazhan protect us!" Cymm watched in horror as twenty fallen Red Axe Guards awoke and joined their comrades in the fight.

Another defender fell next to Karaz.

The chaos of battle surrounded them, but Cymm could sense a new form of bedlam. Shrieks and screams emanated from the back of their enemy line. *"DragonSin, are you doing this?"* Many seconds transpired. *"DragonSin!"*

A battle axe came in high, aimed at Karaz's neck. He leaned back barely escaping the blow. A second battle axe swung in low at his newly exposed flank. The force almost amputated his leg below the knee, causing him to pitch forward, where he took the first battle axe in the side of his head on the backswing. He tumbled to the floor, dead.

"No!" Cymm's roar fueled his next few swings.

A tall woman, the same height as Brogan and dressed in flowing red robes, walked among his enemy. She touched each dwarf she passed on the shoulder, causing the combatant to scream with fear and bolt in the direction they were facing. Their eyes radiated terror and they ran into walls, dead bodies, and each other.

The new captain roared in frustration. "Azreala, this is not your concern!"

She made her way swiftly toward Cymm with the new captain in pursuit.

"Azreala? Yes, it's her." Cymm's face screwed up in confusion. *How does the captain know her? "DragonSin, protect her."* Again, there was no response.

When the Priestess of the Red Phoenix was twenty feet away, she yelled, "Cymm you must trust me!" Her tall lanky body collapsed to the ground as if struck from behind. When she hit the ground, a wraith with crimson eyes hurtled toward Cymm like a spear. It bifurcated a foot from his nose and struck him in both eyes.

Cymm's head rocked back, and he screamed in agony. The more he fought, the more it hurt. He continued to resist, until a feminine voice rang out in his mind, ". . . next time we meet, maybe you will trust me more . . ." Cymm accepted her into his body. A burning pain seared deep into his bones. The throbbing agony dredged up memories of when Dego tried to possess him.

He grew over six inches, and crimson liquid pooled in his eyes, running down his cheeks like bloody tears. His eyeball turned the color of a blood wolf's. The most terrifying change was his forearms and hands. From the emaciated appendages grew two-inch long blood-red talons.

The captain arrived at Azreala's body and raised his foot to stomp on it. Brogan hit the much smaller dwarf with a flying tackle, and the sickening sound of bones breaking filled the air. Brogan slumped to the floor, wheezing.

The captain proceeded with the stomp and moved to kick Brogan. "Cymm, I'd say there's a bit of me father in ye boy."

Cymm lacked control of his voice to respond aloud. *We are far from related. "DragonSin, where are you? Take this arrogant fool down."*

Azreala's avatar strode forth confidently. The captain puffed his chest and stood unflinching. She rubbed his arm, and the smug expression upon his face changed to terror. He ran five steps to the right, his teeth chattering, screaming nonsensical words, then immediately turned and ran three steps in a different direction.

"Did I scare you, brother?" Azreala closed her avatar's eyelids.

Fear and confusion ran through Cymm's heart and mind. His arms involuntarily lifted above his shoulders and twirled in circles independently. When his eyes opened twenty seconds later, the battleground had transformed into a nightmare.

71

A Little Late

Lykinnia

Lykinnia stood transfixed for several minutes, staring into the recently opened scrying window. Cymm was at the epicenter of a brutal battle, surrounded by dead bodies.

Lykinnia's heart raced as she inspected him. "Oh Melandri, what happened to his eyes? And his hands?"

The blood-soaked floor continued to accumulate fresh bodies, and the groans and moans of the dying grew in volume.

Cymm touched every enemy within reach, and they ran off screaming like madmen. He closed his eyes and raised his grotesque hands.

Lykinnia had witnessed gruesome battles before, but not like this, and within moments, the scene became even more terrifying and hellacious. She closed the scrying window with a gasp. *I need to help him.*

Preparing to flash travel to the gates of Delge, the last place she visited Cymm, she positioned her hands on the altar. *Or should I call*

Father? Her indecision cost her valuable seconds. She nearly screamed aloud. After drawing a deep breath, she reached out telepathically, *Father, Cymm's in trouble!*

Terazhan appeared immediately. "What happened?"

"There is a massive battle in the streets of Delge and many have died already. Cymm has been disfigured or cursed, and his allies are few," Lykinnia summarized as best she could.

With the wave of one hand, Terazhan opened a scrying window so large it blotted out the altar again.

Lykinnia peeked in tentatively, and for her, the battle resumed.

72

Bardonril

Cymm

The crimson liquid pooling in Cymm's eyes blocked most of his vision, and made it difficult to see the living, but not the dead. A cold hand gently grabbed his knee. It was Karaz, trying to stand on his broken leg. The hideous gashes covering his body had not healed and continued to ooze. The abomination's eyes bulged between lids thrown insanely wide. He knew that look of depravity would haunt his dreams for years to come.

The new captain and his men continued to run in terrified loops, hitting walls, or tripping and falling, only to rise and resume.

Moans and groans from the dying and the dead filled the air, and corpses were rising, or at least attempting to, while others were starting to twitch. The undead creatures were sluggish and clumsy, as if sleepwalking.

The new captain paused, his chest heaving from exertion. His face twisted in rage. "I am going to enjoy killing you, Azreala!"

Azreala, in avatar form, did not waver. The arms she had been twirling shot forth and pointed toward him. "Ghouls, ghasts, and zombies attack!"

The walking cadavers unexpectedly woke up and sprinted at the captain howling, screaming, and moaning. The first wave of dead hit him with a berserker-like frenzy, latching on to him with tooth and talon. He collapsed under the weight. As they eviscerated his body, he bellowed and rose in an explosion of power, flinging a dozen undead creatures in every direction.

He bled from multiple lacerations. His stare of visceral hatred bore into Cymm's mind, and he panted like a rabid dog. "Sister, do not do this."

"Sister? Bardonril, you have never treated Feldarius and I as peers, and now you will pay for it." Her taloned avatar hands shot forth again, and a second wave of death bore down on him.

"I will hunt you down and kill you. All of you!" Bardonril wailed.

"Not if I kill you. Two hundred years you will be banished to your home plane. Oh wait, this will be your second death." Azreala's sinister laugh sent shivers through his avatar body. "Four hundred years."

"I don't think you should antagonize him. What if he comes looking for me or my friends?" asked Cymm.

"Shhh," replied Azreala.

The captain's strength surged again, and he hurled two dozen bodies off him. "You do not have enough to kill me." He stared back defiantly, chest heaving. His armor lie around him in shreds. A significant amount of skin had been flayed from his face and body.

Azreala pulled her fisted hands back to her hips. "How many dead do you think rest in the crypts?"

"No!" he howled. Bardonril stepped backward, then turned to flee.

Many of Azreala's undead legion had been damaged or slain when they hit the rock walls, but at least twenty pursued and caught him.

They sunk their fangs and claws into him, weighing him down, holding him fast.

In the distance, a wailing of ghostly hyenas reached Cymm's ears, followed by the clatter of bones. Cymm's heartbeat raced. Terror took over his mind, and his instincts begged him to run. He had no control of his body. It grew louder and more terrifying with each passing second.

Bardonril pounded another creature, its head exploding like a melon, then another. He continued to scan the distance, as if he knew what was coming for him. His sense of urgency doubled, and a third and a fourth cadaver returned to a motionless state.

It was too late. Death had arrived.

Hundreds of skeletons poured into the area from every avenue in Smelter's Square, each one in a different stage of decay. Some had weapons, even armor, while most had tattered robes or loincloths. Wave upon wave of skeletons joined the remaining ghouls in the attack.

Bardonril's strength and fighting prowess with a battle axe were impressive, but for every five he slew, two got through his defenses.

This isn't right? Should I allow this to happen? Old memories flooded his mind. Warhez and his village of diseased dwarves. Warhez told him, 'This village is plagued by a flesh-eating disease from Bardonril, The Maker.' *Could Bardonril have infected his own people? Even little children?*

Azreala's voice sounded in his mind, "*Do you know why Bardonril infected all those innocent dwarves? Because Warhez beat him fairly in the annual blacksmithing competition held here in Delge.*"

Cymm's blood boiled. *"You're joking, right?"*

"No."

"How could you possibly know this?" While he waited for an answer, another memory of the first time he met Azreala rushed forward. After she saved him, she had said, 'The Mistress is the master over death. She constantly makes life and death decisions for others.' *I should let her decide*

the fate of Bardonril. And gradually it dawned on him, *Azreala is The Mistress. I am such an idiot.*

"You may be naïve, but not an idiot. Besides, your innocence makes you quite charming. Get ready to leave." Azreala moved her avatar toward her own body.

A sword plunged through Bardonril's back and out of his chest, piercing his heart. A guttural sound emanated from his mouth before a dagger sank into his neck. The battle axe dropped from his hands and clanged on the floor. Immediately, a swirling vortex of dark silver and crimson opened above his body. It dragged a wailing apparition from the corpse of the demi-god and imploded upon itself.

"He's dead?" Cymm asked hopefully.

"Not exactly. He is confined to his home plane for the next four hundred years. Long enough for you to never see him again." Azreala picked up her own lifeless corpse and slung it over one shoulder.

"We were planning to escape through the mines. You should go back to your own body."

"Not yet." "We are leaving Delge through the front gates. Come with me if you're leaving," Azreala said to the remnants of Cymm's escape party, Semper, Brogan, Ibor, a former prisoner, and two dwarven fighters.

Everyone cowered in the corner, trying to appear as small as possible. He was not completely surprised, given the atrocities the avatar had performed at the end of the battle.

"Going through the mines would be the safer escape route. We have lost enough lives today," said Cymm.

Azreala chuckled. Scores of undead soldiers fell into rank before her, awaiting her command. "*Yes. The front gates.*"

Semper approached him slowly, cowering, and flinched when Azreala gazed at him. "What are you?"

Cymm could not tell if he was talking to him or Azreala, but he hoped it was the latter.

"Cymm?" asked DragonSin.

"Where have you been? I needed you!" replied Cymm angrily.

"I was trapped in the captain's mind. You won't believe this, but he was Bardonril, the dwarven demi-god."

Cymm had to laugh at the late delivery of the information. *"You were what?"*

"The reunion can wait. It is time to leave." Azreala walked her avatar forward, carrying her own body, and leading a procession of dead bodies.

"Cymm, please help me." Brogan coughed, then choked, and spit out a blood clot.

Azreala turned her back on him. "We do not have time."

Cymm thought back to the battle with Dego, and how he had resisted Terazhan's call to crush the demon-imp boy. His body froze mid-step like a rusted hinge, his foot hanging in the air. Then he took control of the rest of his body and turned back to kneel next to Brogan. He instructed Azreala, *"Ask if he can walk. I will heal him outside."*

Cymm grabbed Brogan's arm, causing him to yelp in pain.

"Can you stand on your own?" asked the avatar voice.

Moaning and quivering, Brogan worked himself up on hands and knees, using only his left arm. His right dangled loosely, hanging in a pool of his own blood. His labored breaths came out in high-pitched wheezes.

Semper rushed forward assisting him to rise. He nodded toward the avatar. "I knew you were in there, lad. The big guy won't survive long. Let's get moving."

Brogan leaned heavily on Old-Man Semper.

Ibor sidled up beside them. "His collarbone and shoulder are broken, and probably a punctured lung. If you can heal him, then Semper is right. You can help me."

Cymm assumed Ibor was talking about the deal Semper made to free his family. *"Wouldn't you prefer to walk out of Delge in your own body, so everyone may witness who truly defeated Bardonril?"* Cymm intended to heal his friend as soon as he evicted Azreala.

"Where do I dare to start? I could never have defeated him on my own, in fact he would have killed me, but together it was an easy feat. Plus, I am enjoying being inside your body, which is ironic, because you have been thinking about returning the favor," Azreala replied.

"I have not. I—I—have a girlfriend already!" Cymm fumed.

"Anyway, tolerate me a short while longer and I will share the second story with you." Azreala took the avatar's hand and caressed the buttock of her own body, draped over his shoulder.

Cymm pouted and remained silent until a flash of amber light caught his attention through a small clearing in the red fluid.

"What was that?" Azreala had moved the avatar's head, tracking its movement.

No one replied.

Dwarves fled before their gruesome parade. Not even a squad of Red Axe soldiers stood their ground.

"I am surprised you are not more excited to retrieve your trusty companion," Azreala stated nonchalantly.

His interest perked up. *"Is he okay?"*

"You should have paid the stableboy for more than two days of boarding."

Cymm moaned. He surveyed his surroundings as best he could. They were already in The Maker's Square. The army of dead met no resistance as they marched through the center, heading for one of the large staircases.

"Not to worry. I sent a faithful servant to pay for one month's boarding for both animals," Azreala said comfortingly.

Cymm's happiness at the news drifted slowly toward paranoia. *"I know who you are. Why are you being so nice to me?"*

"Do you have any idea what we could accomplish together? Both of us could have whatever we wanted."

"How could you know what I want?" Cymm did desire something she could help with: the eradication of all dragons. *Could she raise enough dead to kill a dragon? Absolutely, if she can kill a god. Could she raise a dead dragon to fight on our side? This is worth exploring.* Her silence made him regret what he said, and he visualized Bria's necklace once again around his neck. *"I'm sorry. I appreciate everything you have done for me and my friends. I don't understand what you want in return."* Cymm watched the dead soldiers climb the staircase in front of them.

"You are one of the oldest in your family, so you might not understand. Feldarius and I are the youngest, and everyone considers us incapable of attending the council, let alone leading it. You are a power magnifier. If we could be friends or lovers—or both—our joint power would ensure my position as head of the council and allow me to claim the Mantle of the Gods." Azreala cleared her throat, uncomfortable. *"Cymm, make no mistake, I am a good liar, but our future relationship means a lot to me, and I promised to never lie to you."*

A jumble of thoughts flooded Cymm's mind. *"I—we . . . well, you—"*

"Hold your thoughts." Azreala came to a halt behind her undead army; the gates were closed. "Open these gates now, or you will regret it."

Cymm could not see anyone manning the gates nor hear any response.

Azreala lifted her avatar's arms and red mist swirled around her hands. It coalesced into half a dozen misty skulls, which she threw at the openings in the gate towers. The ghostly heads wailed as they zipped through the air and reconnoitered both levels of each building. The thin wisps attached to the skulls fed back to her fingers and palms, like spider webs.

Cymm's fascination grew as the wisps became engorged with energy, and waves raced back to their origin. The first pulse overwhelmed Cymm's mind. He screamed in fear from the pure intensity. *"Stop. Please stop!"*

Azreala did as requested. "Last chance. Open these gates now."

Two loud clunks preceded a groan, and the gates swung open. The red wisps evaporated, and the dead soldiers shuffled forward.

Cymm's mind cleared, but his body felt strange. Raw energy surged through his limbs to the extremities. *"What am I feeling?"*

"The life force of the gatehouse soldiers," Azreala replied.

"I feel like I could rip the city gate off its hinges!"

"Yes—intoxicating, isn't it?"

"More like disturbing. The soldiers' thoughts and fears are running rampant through my mind." Cymm glanced up ahead and a lump formed in his throat. *"My horse!"*

The dead soldiers had formed a two-sided receiving line, extending from the gates to the stables.

"Will you allow the dead to return to their former resting place, or maybe you could command them to?" asked Cymm.

"Only those standing will be able to, but I will give the command. Now, our journey is almost complete, and I owe you a second story. I will warn you in advance, the answer you seek will shake you to your core. Are you sure you want to know who killed your friend?" Azreala extricated herself from Cymm's body.

"DragonSin, what do you think?" asked Cymm.

"I think Azreala is correct. Let's focus on saving Semper's father and sister, and not worry about Hardre." DragonSin's voice had a new rasp in it.

"You already know. Don't you?"

"I've known since I was trapped in Bardonril's mind."

Azreala had fully transitioned to her own body. "Have you decided? We need to keep moving."

Cymm was already moving toward Brogan to heal him. "I want to know . . ."

Azreala scanned the vicinity, but waited until he completed his task. She bit her lip and projected the name into his mind. *"Terazhan."*

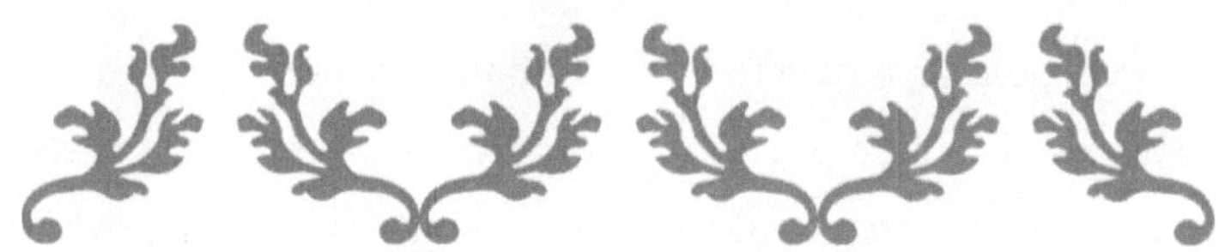

73

Fury

Cymm

Cymm's face turned as red as Azreala's robes. "How dare you claim Terazhan murdered his own disciple!"

Azreala remained resolute against his fury. "I told you it would be hard to accept this truth, but that does not make it any less true. I will share the facts without any speculation, and the rest you must confirm on your own."

"What facts do you have?" Cymm demanded.

"The sword you possess is quite powerful. It spoke to us while we were binding—"

"While you were what?" asked a familiar voice behind him.

Cymm spun to find a golden, ethereal figure. "Lykinnia!"

With hands on her hips, the priestess of Terazhan replied, "You were binding?"

Cymm flushed. "Not like that."

"Who or what is this thing?" asked Azreala.

Lykinnia ignored the comment. "Like how?"

Cymm's face screwed up in confusion. "As an avatar, like Terazhan—"

"Which is why he was unable to gain access. He wanted to use you to heal the injured," said Lykinnia.

Something about the way she said *use* did not sit well with Cymm, but he bit his tongue.

"We did fine without him." Azreala flipped her hair behind her shoulder.

"And who are you?" asked Lykinnia.

Cymm stepped between them. "Lykinnia this is Azreala. Azreala—Lykinnia."

"His girlfriend."

Cymm smiled at the declaration, then cleared his throat uncomfortably. "Azreala was telling a story to prove who killed my friend, Hardre." He turned to the red priestess. "Please continue."

Azreala sighed heavily. "I fear we have lingered here too long. So, I will tell you the abridged version. To create your miraculous sword, you needed the green dragon head to imbue it with the ability to resist and cure poison as well as deal devastating damage to green dragons. However, a second head or spirit is required to give the sword an ego, allow it to speak telepathically, and provide it with the capability to use psychic powers such as levitation or mental blasts. The second head used was Hardre's."

Semper placed his hand on Cymm's shoulder. "What is she saying?"

Cymm turned to Lykinnia. "Tell her you don't need two heads, and Lord Terazhan would never do such a thing."

Lykinnia shook her head slowly back and forth several times, and Cymm breathed more easily. "She is right, Cymm." It looked like she had bitten into a lemon.

"What?"

"The power of your sword could never have been created with only a green dragon—Ahh!" Lykinnia groaned in pain.

"Lykinnia, are you okay?"

"I have stayed too long. Come to the Peak of Power immediately, and we will figure this out together." Lykinnia faded away.

Ibor ran up to them. "The guards are massing. We need to go!"

Everyone jumped on a horse or pony, secured and positioned by Semper and Brogan, except for Azreala. She raised her fist into the air, spoke three words of magic, and summoned a black cloud of smoke. The plume swirled and pulsed, and a chilling shriek emanated from within. From the haze leaped a massive black steed of hellfire in the vague shape of a horse. Its eyes blazed with an eerie red fire as well as its hooves. Although it stood three hands taller than Cymm's warhorse, Azreala swung up on its bare back with ease.

Brogan was the first to recover his wits. "Let's go!" He led the riders out of the stables and through the channel of sentinels. The party of eight rode hard, heading back toward The Crossroads.

Cymm glanced at Azreala, riding next to him. "Please tell me the truth."

She fixed her gaze on him. "Cymm, if I am lying, may I suffer a pain so great Marekai himself would cry."

"Marekai?"

She sighed and rolled her eyes. "The God of Pain and Suffering."

74

Family

Lykinnia

With her hands on the altar, Lykinnia tilted her head back and screamed. Her eyes flared as an insidious wave of jealousy rippled through her body.

"We did fine without him," she said in a mocking tone. "Who in the nine hells does she think she is?"

"That is inappropriate for a young lady to say," came a tired but familiar voice behind her.

"Solar!" She whirled around to find him collapsed and haggard, resting against the back edge of the platform. She jumped down and grabbed his hand. "You are back."

"Yes. I waited for you to finish at the altar. You were on there for a while."

"I have been doing your job for you. Keeping an eye on Cymm—"

"You mean spying?" he deadpanned.

Lykinnia let out a low growl, fighting to keep from laughing. "Why does it look like you almost died again?"

Solar sighed. "Because I almost died again."

Lykinnia wagged her finger in his direction. "Even marsh cats have a limited number of lives. I am not sure you have any left."

Solar lifted his shoulders. "So, how is my ward, Cymm, doing?"

Lykinnia's face scrunched and her fists clenched. "Not good. And if he makes it back here alive, I might kill him."

"Troubles in paradise?"

"Your question is insulting, and therefore ignored. Cymm decided to run through the city of Delge with his friend and sword, killing assassins until he was thrown into the dungeons." She paused to gauge his reaction.

Solar staggered to his feet. "Then we must get him out."

"The story has only begun. Somehow, he escaped with a party of fifteen to twenty others. What is so funny?"

Solar met her gaze. "The young man is resilient. I assume the priestess, Grendella, was with him."

"Father contacted her, but I do not think she found him. Anyway, the escape party was cornered and almost wiped out when Uncle Bard made his appearance to finish them off."

"What? This is horrible!" Solar hobbled back and forth.

"Stop brooding and heal yourself already."

"I exhausted my power—"

"You could have asked." Lykinnia cast her most powerful heal spell, then continued the story. "Before Uncle Bard could attack, a red witch named Azreala arrived—"

"Azreala?" Solar's jaw hung open.

"You know her? She was able to control Cymm's body and distorted it. He claims it was similar to what Father does."

"Of course, it was. She is your aunt, twin sister to Feldarius, and not much older than you. She probably used him as an avatar."

Lykinnia sighed. "I do not like her. How old is she?"

"Around eighteen hundred lifeyears. Much too old for Cymm," Solar stated.

"Exactly! I—that is not why I dislike her—Father tried to make Cymm his avatar to heal the wounded but could not. She must have blocked him."

"So, your father knows all of this?"

Lykinnia shifted uncomfortably. "Most of it. Did I mention she raised an army of the dead to fight for her? They marched right through the city and out the front gates."

"None of this is surprising to me. She is the goddess of death."

Hmphff. "Any other relatives I should know about?"

"A few, but that is a discussion for another time. We should summon your father. We both have information to share with him."

75

DraKarrion

Hardre

Hardre sat on the top of a hillock in the middle of a meadow. Although the landscape stretched out in every direction to his visual limit, Hardre knew better. An invisible barrier blocked his exploration, and he could walk from side to side in less than one hour. The encapsulated space he was confined to was beautiful, a beautiful prison.

This was a recently developed sentiment, and his internment would have been unbearable without his friend TetraQuezar, the small green dragon resting on his lap. They had been friends for a long time, as long as Hardre could remember. The dragon regarded him as a father, and Hardre endeavored to care for him.

The skies were forever clear, the sun never set, and the temperature was perfect. A carefree Hardre lounged most days in the same spot, because there was not much else to do. He had no food to eat or water to drink, then again, he did not need any.

This day began the same as every other day, but the tremors coursing through TetraQuezar's body were the first sign today would be different.

A chill ran the length of Hardre's body. "Do you feel the temperature changing little buddy?"

TetraQuezar continued to shiver. "Yes, but I sense something else I cannot describe."

The words did not sit well with the dwarf, and he detected a deeper rasp in the dragon's voice. "Let's take a walk and see if we can find the source."

When they reached the bottom of the hummock Hardre's eyes grew wide. "TetraQuezar you're—growing."

The green dragon scratched the ground irritably. "Stop teasing me Da. You know I can no longer grow."

"I do not jest. I tell you, something strange is afoot in the land of DragonSin." Hardre ran ahead with the dragon bounding behind him.

By the time they completed the circuit, TetraQuezar had grown from the size of a small dog to the size of a large pig. Before Hardre could comment, the dragon's gaze caught his attention. A solitary figure with his hands on his hips stood on the top of the hill where they usually lounged.

After exchanging a glance, Hardre and TetraQuezar ambled up the hill, already exhausted from their trek.

The dwarven stranger never moved, even when they crested the slope, except to puff on the pipe hanging from the corner of his mouth.

Hardre huffed from exertion and his lack of activity. "Who—are—you?"

"You will no longer be constrained by the boundaries of this land." The stranger snapped his fingers, and an audible *pop* reverberated off the nearby hills.

Hardre glanced at TetraQuezar to find him staring back. "What?"

"You're not my father! TetraQuerahn is my father." The eyes of the young dragon, now the size of a large wolf, narrowed to thin slits.

"Why would you say something so hurtful? What has this stranger done to you?"

"You should not have been playing in my mind. Now you will regret it. I suggest you run before DraKarrion arrives," said the newcomer.

"TetraQuezar, we should leave this fool to his own games." Hardre turned to leave, expecting the dragon to follow.

"Da, you should run! I can't control these emotions." The dragon's voice had grown deeper and raspier.

76

The Prisoner

Lykinnia

Terazhan was already aware of the battle and its outcome before Lykinnia summarized the chain of events. She then turned her gaze to Solar.

Her guardian swallowed a large, visible lump in his throat. "I found Jakarrak, chained to a thick iron pole, next to a black granite altar."

"Why did you not rescue him? Is he dead?" pressed Lykinnia.

Solar shifted uncomfortably. "He was haggard, but far from dead, and in no immediate danger. Ledaedra wants something from him, and questioned him several times while—"

"Out with it, Solar. What did you discover?" boomed Terazhan.

"Ledaedra was there the entire time. I could not get close enough to speak with Jakarrak or signal him of my intent, and if I could have rescued him, I would—"

"Solaaaar!" Terazhan's impatience escalated.

Lykinnia was perplexed by his demeanor. Her warden shot furtive glances from side to side, determining his escape route.

Solar closed his eyes and exhaled slowly, then popped them open with a steady glare at Terazhan. "On the other side of the altar was another prisoner, similarly restrained. I observed this captive for days, knowing weeks were transpiring on our plane, but they never moved. I reached out telepathically and failed to form a connection; they are neither living nor dead. I crept out of the hole I hid in, inching forward, when a pack of hellhounds materialized from nowhere and attacked."

Lykinnia rolled her wrist and flared her hand in a flourish. "It may have been a warding spell. Once you broke the barrier, you triggered the—"

"Solar, why would you waste any time on this prisoner while Jakarrak remained lashed to a pole, enduring mental anguish?" asked Terazhan.

Solar shifted his gaze to Lykinnia. Her stomach lurched, and her confusion continued, but she listened intently to his words.

Twin tears washed down Solar's face, clearing a path in the ash and soot. "The only thing I could discern for certain is the prisoner is an elf, a female elf. Terazhan, it could be Sendaria."

77

Separation

Cymm

Azreala sat astride her hellsteed, keeping pace with Cymm. He pushed his warhorse at times, trying to shorten the travel time to the Peak of Power. He had no intention of delaying any further. After leaving Delge, their party had been harassed and harangued all the way to Copper Rise, where they had parted ways.

Even three days later, Cymm was still seething. "I can't believe you came with me, instead of going with them to Stallion Rise to get the gems."

Azreala shrugged. "I know they are important to you, but your safety is of the utmost importance to me."

"They better make it back to Copper Rise to meet us. Your proposed future relationship depends on it, and not as lovers, as friends," Cymm shot back. "I don't think I could ever love a Scarlet Priestess of the Phoenix."

Azreala's nostrils flared. "If anyone else spoke to me this way, I would drain their soul in an instant."

"Well prepare yourself for more. Lykinnia is livid about us traveling together. Although, you won't be allowed up the Peak of Power anyway."

"I kinda care, and kinda don't. I've never been allowed to visit the Peak of Power." Her eyes blaze with hatred.

Cymm steering away from the sensitive subject. "Then why do you travel this way?"

"I already told you. To ensure your safety. Besides, I have no interest in going back to Delge." She smirked.

Cymm could feel the heat escaping off the back of his neck. "I wanted you to accompany them to Stallion Rise—"

"By the look in your friend's eyes, he had no intention of returning home. My guess is he convinced them to enter through the escape tunnel you planned to use." Azreala slowed her hellsteed to match Cymm's speed.

"No, they wouldn't go back. Brogan would stand out . . ." Cymm brought his warhorse to a stop with a click. "Not if he wears Semper's ring. Why didn't you say something sooner? We must go back."

"By the time we arrive, it will be too late to help."

"What about your magic? Can you get us there quicker?" Cymm pleaded with his eyes.

"No. I do not possess that kind of magic."

"DragonSin, is she telling the truth?"

"Hmm—the problem with this one is she believes the lies she tells. It is difficult for me to separate fact from fiction. I think she is."

"Are you done searching my mind so quickly? You could have simply asked me the name of the boy I shared my first kiss with, or the girl." Azreala's eyes flashed wild like a lunatic.

Cymm's face flushed. "Do you enjoy embarrassing me?"

"Yes. You are even cuter with red cheeks."

"We should keep moving. I am getting the same foreboding feeling," said DragonSin.

"You've been getting these feelings since we left Delge. Maybe you continue to sense Bardonril's or Azreala's presence." Cymm urged his warhorse forward at a slow trot.

Azreala sidled up next to him. "Only two nights remain before we arrive. Since you let me enter your body so willingly, maybe tonight I can return the favor."

A new rush of blood raced to his face, and he half groaned, and half growled, then clicked three times. His horse surged forward instantly.

"DragonSin, can you put her to sleep or cramp her tongue or something?" Cymm pleaded.

DragonSin's haunting laugh echoed through his mind. *"Even if I could, I doubt I would be powerful enough."*

"Yes, you are weak. I could knock her unconscious if given control," whispered the familiar voice from behind.

Startled, Cymm nearly fell off the side of his saddle. "*DragonSin?*"

"That was not me," replied the sword.

"I am DraKarrion!"

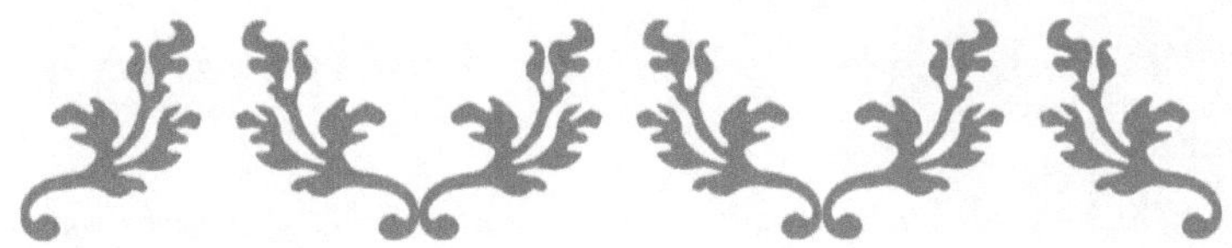

78

Aligned

Lykinnia

The following day, Solar and Lykinnia reconvened at the altar. There had been no discussion yesterday because Terazhan had immediately disappeared and blocked all attempts to connect telepathically.

Lykinnia rubbed her red puffy eyes. "I could not sleep at all last night. If my mother has been a prisoner for four centuries—"

Solar rubbed her back. "There is no way we could have known, and we are not certain of the captive's identity."

A booming voice from behind gave them both a start. "It is Sendaria. I was able to validate her identity this morning."

Solar puckered his lips. "How?"

"I spent all night traveling back until I could see her face."

"How far back?" Lykinnia asked with excitement.

A tremor infiltrated Terazhan's strong baritone voice. "Two hundred years, Ledaedra lifted her chin to stare at her face."

"What are we waiting for?" asked the young lady.

Solar shook his head. "Lykinnia, Ledaedra killed Phindazar and captured Jakarrak. This is not a time for hasty actions."

Terazhan breathed in deep and exhaled. "I am not strong enough. I ran through many scenarios and none of them had a good ending."

"Cymm is on the way. He will help us," Lykinnia stated proudly.

"Lykinnia, that *was* with Cymm's help." Terazhan opened a portal.

Lykinnia reached for her father. "Wait! What are we going to do?"

"If Ledaedra has not killed her in four hundred years, she must have other plans for her. For now, I will bide my time and wait for the right moment. I have gained more believers in the past year than ever before, and my power grows." Her father seemed pleased with himself.

Solar flared his wings. "Lord Terazhan, the objective is to be more powerful than Ledaedra, correct?"

"Yes . . ." replied Terazhan.

Solar glanced sideways at Lykinnia. "There is another option we have not considered. How do we make Ledaedra lose power? Take away her believers? Destroy her altar?"

Lykinnia put two hands in the air. "That is brilliant!"

Solar beamed from the praise momentarily before his face drained of color.

Lykinnia followed his gaze over her shoulder to the edge of the platform where ZaphMordakai stood staring at them.

79

Chase

Hardre

Hardre's legs burned with an internal fire. He had been running for days, or at least it felt like it. TetraQuezar continued to stalk him, not allowing him to rest for more than a few minutes. He could not sleep. The boundaries of his former land, DragonSin, had dissolved as the strange dwarf had claimed. So, he ran over and around hills and meadows. He had doubled back twice, around the blind side of a hill, but TetraQuezar had not been fooled.

Hardre paused momentarily at the summit of the hill he was cresting. *Where am I getting the stamina to continue?* he wondered. Ahead of him, a few hillocks away, loomed a dense forest. *I will try to lose him in there.* He glanced back quickly and glimpsed his pursuer a few hills back.

Tears welled in his eyes. *How could my little buddy turn into a monstrosity? A wicked, dreadful creature.* Hardre estimated the dragon's new size to be bigger than a warhorse.

He swallowed the lump in his throat and ran straight for the forest. Before he reached the next hill's pinnacle, a screech mixed with a roar resonated throughout the valley. A black shape in the sky behind him confirmed his fear. The dragon had taken wing.

A voice spoke in his mind. It sounded distant and dreamy. *"You must run faster. If he reaches you before the forest, all will be lost."*

Hardre bore down and leaned into the run, redlining his system immediately. *"Who—are—you?"*

"Focus! If you make it to safety, we will talk more then."

Hardre built up a tremendous amount of speed on the descent and had a challenging time maintaining his balance. His short, stubby legs worked double time when he stumbled to keep from falling.

As he climbed the final hill with his heart pounding in his chest, a thought occurred to him, *If I don't require food or water, and I don't require sleep, maybe I don't need air.*

The rhythmic beat of wings flapping overhead penetrated his introspection. He dove to the side, and clicking talons buffeted a breeze against his neck. He rose before his roll completed, already at a full sprint. *In the hundred years I have been here, why have I never noticed these inconsistencies?*

An emerald streak from the left caught his eye, as TetraQuezar bore down on him, blocking a repeat of his sideways roll. *Has it been a hundred years?*

He neared the top of the hill and planned to roll forward to dodge the attack, but at the last second, he instinctively jumped up with all his might.

80

Cold Reception

Lykinnia

Lykinnia fumed as she watched Cymm wind his way up the switchback trail alone. *It is about time. Where is the red witch?*

ZaphMordakai silently arrived next to her and followed her gaze to the traveler below. "Cymm?"

"Yes, sneaky cat. You should probably leave or wait at the springs."

Zaph snorted like a furious bull. "Do you need privacy to consummate your reunion?"

Lykinnia fixed the dark elf with a penetrating gaze. "Your jealousy is unattractive. I would prefer to speak to Cymm in private when he arrives."

Lykinnia strolled toward the entrance of the trail as Cymm maneuvered around the last switchback. He dismounted and completed the remaining stretch on foot, presumably to give his horse a break. She caught herself smiling, even though her anger had not abated.

Cymm crested the final rise, released the reins, and dashed forward, beaming.

Lykinnia's arms never left her sides, and she allowed him to hug a statue.

He withdrew slightly, and his smile faded, replaced by a concerned expression.

She punched him a little harder than planned. "Where is your new girlfriend?"

"My new—Lykinnia, *you* are my girlfriend," Cymm proclaimed, rubbing his shoulder.

Involuntary twinges tugged at the corners of her mouth. Nevertheless, she folded arms over chest. "Five nights alone with the seductress would be too much for most men to resist."

Cymm reached out and rubbed her arm. "I'm not most men, and besides, Terazhan requires me to remain chaste if I want to be able to channel more powerful spells."

"Of course, he does. Why am I not surprised?"

Cymm's nose crinkled. "Doesn't he require the same of you?"

Lykinnia stared off into the distance above his left shoulder. *If you only knew. Intimacy is highly frowned upon at my age, and children are not even possible for another thousand years.* "My boundaries are slightly different. Let us save this conversation for later." She swiftly moved to embrace him. "I apologize for the frosty reception. It was difficult to observe the two of you traveling together."

Cymm vigorously returned the hug for several seconds, then pulled back.

His visage caused an ache to manifest in the pit of her stomach. She knew who approached. Trying to get ahead of the awkwardness, she turned with a flourish. "Cymm, this is ZaphMordakai."

Cymm slowly extended his hand. "Nice to meet you."

Zaph's arms remained behind his back, ignoring the offer. "Yes, I would imagine. I have heard a lot about you and your *magic* sword."

Cymm quickly glanced at Lykinnia.

She rolled her lower lip and shook her head.

Zaph replied with slow, drawn-out speech, the words dangling on the end of his tongue before releasing. "Your friend has become quite famous, or infamous, depending on your perspective, I imagine. Have you displayed any new trophies lately?"

Cymm locked eyes with the dark elf. "Ahh, I see you don't agree with the dragon heads at the gates of Armak. It is only the beginning. More will join them."

"A very bold statement. How did you come by that magnificent weapon? Did mommy and daddy give it to you?"

"You are out of line, Zaph. His parents were slain heedlessly by dragons," reprimanded Lykinnia.

Cymm's eyes narrowed. "The very dragons you are so quick to judge me over."

Lykinnia noticed a fraction of the animosity evaporate from Zaph's visage, and she released a short sigh. "Is anyone hungry?"

"Yes. I can take care of my horse after. So, how did you meet?" asked Cymm.

"Zaph was in Armak and saw the battle with Dego. Then he came here, snuck past the sphinx twins, and found me." Lykinnia walked next to Cymm heading toward the stone table.

ZaphMordakai sauntered up next to Lykinnia, placing her in the middle, and walking three abreast. "Tell him about the game we played."

This is going better than I thought, but how will Cymm react to my age? Lykinnia's gaze switched to Cymm. "We wagered on who is old—"

"No. We played a game called bath-time rescue." Zaph opened his eyes wide.

"You did what?" asked Cymm.

Lykinnia gaped, then folded her arms over her chest. "We did not."

"Well, one of us played while the other lay there naked." Zaph leered past her at Cymm.

"I think I'll eat later." Cymm stormed toward his warhorse.

Lykinnia tried to grab his arm, but he quickly twisted out of it. She turned and glared at the dark elf. "Why Zaph?"

With a curled lip, he shrugged. "I don't like him."

"You do not know him," she said in a soothing voice, trying to repair the damage.

"I don't need to. I know his type. Plus, he is too young and immature for you."

"You are going with immature, after what you did? Really? I need to talk to Cymm alone. This is the second time you have noiselessly appeared in the middle of a conversation where you do not belong. There had better not be a third."

Zaph turned a cold shoulder and walked away.

She found Cymm brushing his horse while speaking to him in hushed tones. Cymm glanced back, then ignored her, and moved to the far side of his horse.

"Cymm, can we talk?"

Cymm continued to sulk. "I don't think there is much to talk about. Your time might be better spent playing naked rescue games."

She took a step closer to him and placed her hand on the horse's flank. "That is not what happened or how it happened. Do you not trust me?"

He stared at the ground. "I should ask you the same question?"

About to respond, she froze. The realization of her own hypocrisy startled and flustered her for many seconds. "I do trust you. Unfortunately, I have no faith in Azreala."

Their hands briefly brushed against each other while they pet the horse.

Cymm shot an accusatory glare at her until he realized it must have been an accident. "I was so excited to visit you—"

"Was?"

"We haven't seen each other in three or four months, and this is not how I expected to greet each other." Cymm released the horse and put away the brush.

Lykinnia took a half step closer. "Nor did I."

Cymm turned to face her. "This is on you. You take issue with me traveling with Azreala, while you have a guest staying with you. Trust needs to flow both ways."

Lykinnia surged forward and kissed him hard on the mouth. It only lasted for a couple of seconds before she pulled slowly away, but her arms remained wrapped around him.

"That—well that—I like—surprising," Cymm stammered.

Lykinnia grinned. "I did not know you could speak two languages."

He squeezed her tight. "Are you afraid I might pass you by, miss fifty-six languages?"

With attitude, she replied, "My count is now fifty-seven."

81

Investigation

Cymm

Cymm walked with Lykinnia toward the altar. "Have you been able to determine if Azreala was correct about how the sword was made?"

"I think you should watch the Rights of Melding for yourself. I placed a marker, so we can easily find the beginning." Lykinnia glanced at him sideways.

Cymm gulped. "I can already tell it's not good by the expression on your face."

Lykinnia shuffled her feet. "How long are you planning to stay?"

"It depends on a few things. After you show me the ritual, can we check on my friends? Azreala thinks they went back to Delge without me." Cymm noted the sour expression on her face. "Also, how my conversation with Terazhan goes, assuming I need to speak with him, and lastly, how long your friend is staying."

Lykinnia stepped up on the platform, placing her hands on her hips. "Are we going down this path again?"

Cymm followed her, his hand coming to rest near the once-damaged corner. "Who fixed the crack?"

"What?" she replied, irritated.

"The corner, it is no longer chipped." Cymm rubbed each flawless edge and surface.

"The Altar of One heals itself over time. Are you ready to start?"

Cymm stepped up next to her. "Yes."

She spread her hands and instantly recreated the ritual from the past in a viewing window.

A bolt of lightning descended from a clear blue sky and blasted a stone shard from the altar. The scene continued with him questioning Terazhan about doing more honorable deeds, the safety of his body during a flash travel, and when he would be allowed to cast spells like a priest. Ominous black clouds rolled in bringing lightning and thunder with them. He purified and cleansed the surface of the altar while chanting in a booming voice.

Cymm peeked over at Lykinnia, but she showed no reaction in her trance-like state. The sword pierced through the dragon's eye socket, exiting the back of its skull before he had raised the weapon above his head. The leathery skin tore free, and eventually, formed the throbbing green ethereal ball he remembered so vividly.

Lykinnia adjusted the view, pulling back to reveal more of the surrounding area. Small tremors ran down the length of her body.

Cymm was about to place his hand on her shoulder, when a portal opened in the scrying window, and Solar stepped out carrying a bloody burlap bag. Cymm gasped. Solar had emerged behind his back during the ceremony and next to Terazhan. The winged man gently placed the sack on the ground and rolled the sides down around the head contained within. There was no mistaking the previous owner. Hardre.

The blood rushed to Cymm's face in red-hot waves, and he struggled to breathe through pursed lips and clenched teeth.

A massive shudder of Lykinnia's body caused the image to waver.

Cymm was there immediately to comfort her as she sobbed. He placed a hand on her shoulder and whispered, "I'm here. Focus." The signal strengthened and the picture cleared.

Terazhan and Solar directed their palms toward his friend's decapitated head. It throbbed several times before levitating into the air, a synchronized movement with the now floating shard from the altar. The towering men's hands remained pointed at Hardre's head, and it slowly lost substantial form. After ten seconds, the remains, a misty wraith with tentacles, shot forth to merge with the vortex of particles revolving around the sword.

Solar scooped up the bloody bag and disappeared into a new astral gateway.

Terazhan spun and retreated, not waiting for the completion of the ceremony.

Lykinnia ended the vision from the past and cried into her folded arms on the altar.

Cymm's compassion overrode his anger. He patiently rubbed her back while she wept. When the tears came to an end, he finally spoke. "You had to watch that twice?"

She nodded without lifting her head.

Cymm pulled her into his chest and hugged her fiercely. "What in the nine hells is going on?"

"I do not know." She stood with her shoulders back, anger replacing her sorrowful expression. "But we must find out."

He backed away from her wrath, unbuckled the belt attached to the scabbard holding DragonSin, and held it in front of him. "I don't think I can wield this any longer."

"Cymm! Please do not abandon me. I need your help," the sword poignantly replied.

"Why didn't you tell me about Hardre?"

"I only recently found out. Bardonril destroyed the barrier protecting Hardre and TetraQuezar—"

"Tetra who?" asked Cymm, confused.

"The baby dragon, whose head was used to create the sword."

"They're alive?" Cymm's confusion remained.

"No. They are both dead, but the Rights of Melding combine their souls, creating my subconscious. Now Bardonril has corrupted TetraQuezar, and he hunts Hardre with the intent to kill him. If he succeeds, DraKarrion will take over, and I will cease to exist."

"Cymm?" called Lykinnia.

"What can I do?" Cymm asked.

"You need to explain this to Terazhan and ask him for guidance."

"No. Not going to happen—"

"Cymm, Hardre will eventually fall. You are my only hope." The sword went quiet.

The young man detected a hint of fear in DragonSin's voice. *"What you ask is too much. I do not want to speak to him right now."*

"You may not have a choice," said the sword.

Lykinnia rubbed his arm. "Cymm? Are you okay?"

Cymm peered down at her hand. "Yes. DragonSin is in trouble. Give me a moment to—"

Terazhan loomed over Lykinnia's back, staring at him.

The young man took a deep, steadying breath and exhaled. *"I'm doing this for you."* He locked eyes with the demi-god. *Ok Cymm, be nice and get help.* "Lord Terazhan, DragonSin believes Bardonril has jeopardized the link binding him to the sword. Is there any way to recreate the protection barrier?"

Terazhan nodded slowly. "The sword told you this?"

"Yes. He is worried he will cease to exist, and a creature called DraKarrion will take over."

Terazhan's eyes went wide. "Quickly! Put the sword on the altar and get off the platform. You too, Lykinnia." Terazhan stepped into position.

82

Assistance

Hardre

The stranger's voice echoed in Hardre's mind again, *"Help is coming. Head for the forest."* Hardre had narrowly escaped the most recent attack by jumping over the dragon. It was an impressive jump, and the height he attained defied reason. As he soared through the sky, he located his destination, and when he hit the ground, he rolled to his feet and kept running.

Ahead of him, the dragon banked right and circled back. A brilliant figure hovered in the sky above the dragon, approaching swiftly. The being did not appear to be moving, except for its robes and cowl fluttering about it. The awe-inspiring image brought him to a slow halt.

"Keep moving. Run to the forest!"

His reaction was slow and mechanical, and his mouth was agape, because the figure was flaring like a sun. An unexpected peace flooded his mind.

The same stranger's voice shook him from his reverie. *"Run. Run you fool!"*

Hardre took a hesitant step forward, then another. Lightning snapped and crackled in front of him, and he shielded his eyes as the figure's brilliance intensified.

Before TetraQuezar drew within fifty feet of him, forked bolts lanced out, striking the dragon. He roared, then shrieked, and finally mewled before the lightning relented. The dragon crashed to the ground, skidding a dozen feet, and ultimately resting ten feet in front of Hardre.

Another round of lightning amped up around the floating stranger.

TetraQuezar raised his head and glared at his attacker in a pitiful display of defiance.

Hardre's heart pounded in his chest, not out of fear, it was sympathy and his need to protect his best friend. He rushed forward and dove on top of the dragon, placing himself between the two of them. He raised his hands as if to ward off the stranger, begging him to spare his life.

TetraQuezar's warm, wet, pulsing tongue palpated his neck and face, removing the salty tears trickling down both sides.

The stranger's visage, barely perceptible among the bright halo, registered a smile. A gesture leaving Hardre bereft of words and confused. Almost as if he had expected him to protect the dragon.

"I told you help was coming."

Hardre scanned the vicinity to validate the voice was in his head. *"Who are you?"*

"I am DragonSin. It is hard to explain, but we are a part of each other."

"I will try to rebuild your sanctuary. In the future, you need to be more wary of visitors. You should never have any." The floating stranger rocketed into the sky and disappeared.

Hardre inspected his friend's wounds, and a lump formed in his throat. *"He isn't going to make it."* Large patches of skin were charred black, instead of their normal emerald iridescence, and two puncture wounds were bloodied and oozing. His breathing was ragged and forced. "If only I could heal you, my friend. I would do any—"

Hardre's hands began to glow.

83

Hard Truth

Lykinnia

Her father's eyes popped open, and he glanced slowly at the corner of the altar. He lifted his palms, spanning both the sword and stone surface, then turned to face them. "I have temporarily restored the balance. DragonSin is no longer in imminent danger. However, I must rebuild the barrier to protect them against the dark creature, DraKarrion, before he regains his power."

Cymm cleared his throat. "How?"

Terazhan pursed his lips. "I will need the head of another green dragon. It can be a young adult, but not a hatchling—"

"And another human, Terazhan?" Cymm bristled and he clenched his fists.

"Cymm!" Lykinnia admonished.

The demi-god stared with a deadpan face for several moments. "Terazhan? Not Lord Terazhan?"

Cymm shifted uncomfortably while sneaking a quick peek at her. "I thought we were the good guys. Now, I'm not so sure. I want to know why you killed Hardre?"

Now it was her father's turn to glance at her. "I am not sure what you *think* you know, but I can assure you, you know *nothing*."

Lykinnia craned her neck around, then telepathically reached out to her friend. *"Kamac, where is ZaphMordakai?"*

"He left, shortly after Terazhan joined you."

"I know his head was used to create the sword. I know—"

A darting wave of Terazhan's hand silenced Cymm. An enormous scrying window appeared overtop of the altar. "Come."

"Take your brother and follow Zaph for a day, then return." She broke the link, ending the discussion.

Lykinnia and Cymm stepped up onto the platform and peered into the window.

Hardre sat in his bedroom, in Old-Man Semper's house at Stallion Rise. Solar stood before him.

"I met him," Hardre whispered.

Solar nodded.

Tears streamed down Hardre's face. "I met him. He summoned me with a Divine Quest to the Peak of Power."

"I know. I was there," replied Solar.

Hardre had a gleam in his eyes. "It was beautiful—the altar, the pool, the view of the surrounding mountain peaks—I will never forget it."

Cymm had never seen him so happy.

Solar shifted from side to side. "Terazhan thought you might have questions. Do you want to talk about it?"

Hardre stood. "What will Semper and Cymm be told?"

"What do you want them to be told?"

"They won't understand. I don't want them to know. Let them assume the assassin's guild finally got me." Hardre sighed deeply, his shoulders slumped. "Missing them is going to be the hardest part of this decision."

"Those memories will cease to exist. A new life and friendship will be waiting for you. You will even forget about this conversation. The bond you form with your new friend will be the basis for the sword's conscience."

Hardre paced the floor. "Yes, Terazhan went through the process, but I don't understand. The sword can communicate with both Cymm and I, but I can't speak directly with Cymm?"

"Correct. All your core values and thoughts will guide the sword, and the sword will have constant interaction with Cymm. The sword will protect him from dangers he cannot even see," replied Solar.

Hardre pulled his shoulders back. "I love that boy, as if he were me own family. So, how are we going to do this? With a sword? Will it hurt?"

The nine-foot-tall Solar knelt before the dwarf and grabbed his hand with his own. Compassion filled his eyes, and he pointed toward the bed in the corner. A portal flared to life with a *buzz*. Solar had conveniently placed it between the pillow and the rest of the bed. He cleared his throat uncomfortably. "Once you lay down with your head on the pillow, and you are ready, I will give you the command word to close the portal. It will happen in less than a second and will not be painful."

Hardre took a deep breath and mumbled to himself. He sat on the edge of the bed, swung his feet up, and leaned back on his elbows. "What's the command word?"

84

Next Step

Cymm

Terazhan closed the scrying window with a wave of his hand before any displeasing and unforgettable images were generated.

Cymm wrapped his arm around Lykinnia. "Why would he . . ."

Lykinnia turned into him and wrapped him with both arms. "Cymm, I—I am sorry. I did not know."

"How could you? I'm so confused. Lord Terazhan, please forgive me." Cymm struggled to make eye contact.

"Apology accepted. In the future, I recommend you have all the facts before you pass judgment." Terazhan tilted his head down and raised an eyebrow.

Lykinnia smirked. "Unlike your friend."

Cymm nodded to Terazhan, then shot Lykinnia a scowl. "Before I embark on another dragon-hunting mission, I must check on my friends. Did they safely arrive home or head back to Delge?"

Lykinnia shot a furtive glance at Terazhan. "I can help track them."

A dour expression settled on Terazhan's face. "Cymm, I understand your concern, but the knowledge you gain regarding your friends should not change your destination. If the barrier inside the sword is not permanently restored, DragonSin *will* fall, and you will no longer be able to wield it. Furthermore, it will become a weapon of evil, strengthen our enemies, and can be used against our cause."

"What is our cause? We should be working to destroy the Dragon Queen and her evil horde. If this isn't our path forward, then my friends are my primary concern."

"DragonSin and Hardre need your help. Cymm, there are more lives at stake than you can imagine." Terazhan extended his arm with his palm up. "I will send Solar to assist your friends, and direct Grendella to aid your cause in Delge."

"Grendella?" asked Cymm.

"Grendella Ironcore. Paired with Solar, they would be a formidable force," stated Terazhan.

"Semper's sister," said DragonSin.

"We should validate where Semper went. We are relying on information from Azreala, who has already misled us once." Lykinnia nodded and pursed her lips.

"Good idea." Cymm shook his head. "I don't blame Azreala for the misunderstanding. She specifically told me she only knew half the story, and I would need to discover the rest for myself."

Lykinnia's eyes flared. "Fine. Shall we find out where Semper is?"

"Cymm, before I take my leave, I need to explain your mission. You need to travel south to the city of Norfolk. The King's daughter has been taken captive by a green dragon. Save the Princess and return with the dragon's head. I will send you a Divine Quest once you are en route to help you prepare for the battle." Terazhan turned to leave. "And

Cymm, you will not find many friends to our faith, so be careful. If you can, be an ambassador, win their hearts, and convert them to our cause."

Lykinnia folded her arms over her chest. "Save the princess? Seriously? How cliché."

A portal opened at the back of the platform and Terazhan disappeared into it.

Cymm closed his eyes and gritted his teeth. *Our cause? Our cause better be to eliminate the dragons.* Cymm returned his attention to the altar. "I'm mentally and physically exhausted."

Lykinnia's expression softened. "This might take a while. You should lie down, sleep if you can, and I will wake you as soon as I find them."

Nothing else mattered except his friends. Cymm wrapped his arms around her from behind and gently kissed her cheek. "Thank you."

85

Captains Meeting

ZaphMordakai

ZaphMordakai roared to announce his arrival, then entered the lair of BelCharius. He strutted down the tunnel and sashayed into the cave in his dark elf form. His reconnaissance missions to the Peak of Power continued to draw interest from the Queen.

The green dragon lifted his head and narrowed his eyes. "Where have you been for the past week?"

"On official business for the Queen. I cannot share the details; the mission was classified." ZaphMordakai relished the brief display of emotional anguish on BelCharius's face and wished it had lasted longer.

"I'm surprised you were gone for so long, what with the Captains Meeting upon us," the smug green dragon replied.

He almost took the bait. *Maybe I can trap him into admitting Ledaedra told him.* "How would you know about a Captains Meeting?"

BelCharius sneered and craned his neck closer. "Not *a* Captains Meeting, *the* Captains Meeting. The one occurring a week after the sky is full with four moons, which I believe was yesterday."

He is playing with me. A burst of electricity exploded in Zaph's brain. He envisioned the many ways he could kill him. His eye twitched. He knew his fantasies could only exist in his mind. Ledaedra would punish him with death. His breathing regulated He could be lying. Zaph narrowed his eyes. "We don't usually tell lieutenants about our Captains Meetings; how did you find out?"

The green dragon's neck slithered back and forth like a snake. "Because I have attended a few."

"A few? And yet I have never seen you—"

"ZaphMordakai, I know you are not invited to them."

The dark elf took a step forward, lightning crackling in his raised hand.

BelCharius's head withdrew rapidly. "The Queen."

Zaph's hand closed into a fist, and he bit it, then turned and headed for the exit. "I am invited. I choose not to attend!"

86

Southbound

Cymm

Cymm mounted his warhorse, prepared to leave, when Lykinnia had presented him with a ring. He fumbled the ring and almost dropped it. He inspected it from all angles and finally realized it was the ring from the dragon's treasure. "What does it do?"

She rubbed the side of his leg. "It is a ring of protection. It will shield you against swords, claws, and magic, reducing the effect they have on you. However, it is not a ring of invulnerability. Even a baby dragon could kill you."

He spun the ring now around his finger, reminiscing about her touch on his thigh three days ago. *Why would her parents allow her to leave home at such an early age? Apparently, Semper's sister had left home as well, but Grendella had been much older. How old was Lykinnia? She claimed her coming-of-age lifeday was only two months away. If she were a Plainsman, she would be turning thirteen, the same as Tanya, but that was unlikely. For most other humans in the realm, he had heard it was sixteen. Is it possible she is only sixteen lifeyears?* He found it hard to believe she could be a high-level priestess at the age of sixteen.

Cymm recognized how little he knew about Lykinnia. *When I see her again, I need to ask her how many lifeyears she has, where her family is, and whether she has any siblings.* He nodded, pleased with his plan. *If I were a better boyfriend, I would know the answers to these questions already.*

He grabbed at his abdomen as a wave of nausea coursed through him. He closed his eyes in agony, but with the darkness came a monstrosity. The enormous head of a green and black dragon lunged for him with a gaping maw. He opened his eyes and the image disappeared as quickly as it came. A chill ran down his body, causing him to glance in every direction. His stomach pain quickly abated, and even though he tried, he could not recreate the image in his mind.

"What in the nine hells was that?" Cymm scanned his surroundings again. The forest seemed a little darker, a little denser, and for the first time ever, he thought, *Where is Azreala?*

87

Tracker

Lykinnia

It had been three days since Cymm left the Peak of Power, and Lykinnia had finally located Semper Ironcore. She had hoped to find him before Cymm departed, but Terazhan had appeared one day into the search with high-pressure tactics, and Cymm had relented.

Lykinnia had no idea where to search for the secret entrance to the dwarven mines, north, south, or east of Delge, but even if she had, she never would have guessed it was over five miles away from the city.

She came upon their camp, almost ten miles south of Delge, in the forest among the foothills of the Knife-Edge Mountains. There were six of them huddled around a tiny campfire.

"Old-Man Semper do not be alarmed. It is Lykinnia."

Nevertheless, all six jumped to their feet with weapons drawn.

Semper waved his group off, and they lowered their weapons. "Lykinnia, what are you doing here?"

"I am looking for you. Azreala told Cymm you headed back to Delge. He was worried about you. I beg you to go home or come to the Peak of Power and wait for his return."

Semper returned to his seat by the fire. "Cymm can pretend he doesn't, but he understands what drives me. Ibor thinks my father and sister are in grave danger, with the Assassin's Guild aware of the connection. The longer we wait, the greater the chance they'll be dead before we can free them."

Lykinnia drew up close. "*You* are in grave danger. It is not safe. Why did you venture so far south?"

All six men cast glances at each other, then Ibor spoke, "We were trying to avoid the regular patrols from Delge. So, we circled far south of the mine entrance to double back and sneak into it."

"How much farther is it? Can you make it to the tunnel tonight?" Lykinnia asked.

"No. It's hard enough to find during the daylight. Impossible in the moonlight," replied Ibor.

"Okay, my time is short. Stay here and make the fire bigger. I will send Solar to help you." Lykinnia zipped away before they could reply.

88

Nighttime

Semper

The five dwarves and human remained on high alert long after Lykinnia abruptly left them. They had argued profusely about the wisdom of her final statement, "make the fire bigger." In the end, Semper's adamant position and stubborn personality prevailed, and they spent half an hour hauling fallen branches and logs close to the fire.

Brogan surveyed the results of their labor. "I'm not sure this will last all night, but the ring of brush also acts as a defensive wall."

"Or a prison," said the taciturn dwarven fighter, Dregur Cavernseeker. "Mark my words, this fire is a mistake."

Orlen, the last of the convicts to make it safely out of Delge, was already quivering. "Yes, it is."

Brogan waved them off. "The decision's been made. We'll set watch in groups of two till dawn. Dregur and I will go first."

However, no one laid down, and for a while, the only sound was of the crackling bonfire. A loud *pop* rang through the silence, the audible protest of a burning branch as the trapped gas inside it combusted.

Everyone jumped except for Bardur Kragrock, the other dwarven warrior, but Semper was convinced he was partially deaf.

After midnight, the wind picked up, causing a sporadic flicker of the campfire flames. Within the hour, howling gusts of air randomly materialized out of nowhere. The swaying treetops creaked and groaned overhead, unable to resist the blustery breeze.

Ibor turned to Semper sitting next to him. "Did you see that?"

"See what?" Semper stood to add more wood to the fire.

"A green pulsing light. It's gone now."

"There's one over here too." Bardur quickly rose and pointed.

"I saw it." Orlen's head swiveled from side to side.

Dregur hefted his axe. "It's over here now."

"Quiet," Brogan hissed in a muffled voice. "It could be circling us."

"No need for silence. It knows we're here," grumbled Dregur.

"There's more than one. I saw two flashes at the same time." Semper tossed more fuel on the fire.

"The wind is gone. It disappeared with the coming of the lights," stated Bardur.

A chill ran down Semper's back. *He's right. What are they waiting for?*

Brogan circled the fire, peering into the dark. "The flashes are occurring in the same spots. There's at least five of them."

The wind howled directly overhead in the treetops, despite there being no air flow to accompany it.

Semper grasped his warhammer tightly with both hands. "What in the nine hells—"

The leather on Bardur's battle axe creaked as he wrung his hands around it. "The green lights approach."

The wind wailed above them from the west then answered from the north, but again no movement of air. Every flash of light brought them closer, and now two small green glowing balls hovered above each one.

"What do we do?" Tremors infiltrated Ibor's normally calm voice.

Semper waited for someone to answer, but no one did, not even Brogan, who always had a plan.

A voice sounding like death, low and raspy, and laced with slight reverberations said, "Build the fire!" It came from in front of Ibor.

No one moved.

"Build the fire!" screeched a haunting voice directly in front of Orlen.

Orlen shrieked, scanning in all directions. "You people are cursed!" He ran sideways toward Semper, then attempted to leap the gathered brush. He tripped and fell. Before he could scramble to his feet, the howling wind descended from above, followed closely by an identical, echoing howl.

The dim light from the fire cast deep shadows, but Semper saw them, giant bat-like creatures with blood red skin. Engorged indigo veins ran through the membranes of its wings and across the surface of its hairless body. Six tentacles dangled from its abdomen like a wasp, and each ended in a hooked barb.

The monstrosity turned its gaze on Semper, and he gasped. "Orlen, get back here!"

Its head resembled a squid, mini feelers surrounding its mouth, and it had bulbous black eyes.

The first one struck Orlen with two tentacles as he attempted to hurtle the last of the branches. The hooked barbs speared into one side and out the other, latching in place. Orlen shrieked in agony, his feet barely lifting off the ground before the second flying terror attacked.

Two more barbed appendages lanced through his body, causing a continuous scream of pain.

Both creatures flew off in slightly different directions until the length of their tentacles blocked further movement. A tug-of-war ensued, and with a final croak, Orlen's screaming ceased as his body tore into two separate pieces.

Semper lurched backward, covered in gore. "Make the fire bigger!"

A new howl descended, streaking toward Brogan. He dropped his branch, leaped into the air, and brought his mammoth greatsword to bear. It ripped through the creature's face and out the side of its body, removing half of its wing.

They worked one-handed with a fervor. The bonfire reclaimed its glory and blazed anew, bringing the owners of the green lamps into view. Craggy tree trunks of various girths surrounded them. They stood twelve feet tall, had gnarled arms with crooked fingers, and two slits in the bark near the top containing green orbs. The most disturbing feature was their torso. Roots had grown up the base and arced out, forming a protective rib cage around a large green pulsing sphere, which deformed with each pulse.

Semper gasped. "It has a heartbeat."

Dozens of howls and screeches pierced the night sky from above, drawing Semper's attention. His heart sank, every tree surrounding them had at least four of the five-foot-long beasts screaming down at the fire.

"Keep feeding the fire," commanded Brogan. "They're afraid of it!"

The firelight exposed the tree beings, and they no longer concealed their movement, pushing forward into the remaining branches and logs.

Brogan grabbed Semper by the arm and dragged him over to Dregur and Bardur, with Ibor trailing behind. “Circle up and pray Cymm’s god helps us.”

89

Stench

Lykinnia

It was the following day, and Lykinnia had passed out trying to find Solar. She arose already at the altar. *I cannot wait for my lifeday in two months to release me of my confinement to the Peak of Power. Then, I will be able to help, that is, if Father allows me to.*

She scanned in every direction. Solar was nowhere to be seen.

Lykinnia sighed. *He must be in Delge, which is too far for my telepathy to reach.* She placed her hands on the altar and flash-traveled straight to the city gates.

Her intuition told her he would head straight for the dungeons of Delge, but she did not know how to get there. In desperation, she prepared to ask someone for directions in her ethereal form. As she flew from the main platform down to The Maker's Square, she saw Solar.

Ah-hah, that was easy. Although he had shrunk himself to six feet tall, he towered over everyone around him.

When Solar saw her coming, he pulled his hood up. "Go away. I am trying to be discreet."

"There is no time for discretion. When did you arrive?"

Solar clenched his jaw. "Now. I had other matters to deal with. Why are you here?"

"If they survived last night, Cymm's friends would have already entered the secret tunnel. We need to head toward them, not the dungeons. I was there when they were fighting. There are massive smelters and the tunnel we are searching for is rough-hewn and leads down into the depths from the southeast corner of the square."

"Smelter's Square? Follow me." Solar's pace quickened.

Lykinnia hurried to catch up. "My time is limited, but I will get you as far as I can."

"I am sure I will be fine. When you return, you need to let your father know, so he can redirect Grendella." Solar picked up the pace again.

"This is not being discreet. Why are you rushing?" Lykinnia hastened after him.

When Solar entered the next square, he slowed to a walk. "A cool breeze would be a welcomed friend right now."

Lykinnia could not experience the temperature, but all the smelters were running, full bore and imagined a wall of heat greeted him. "It is around this corner and almost at the end of the lane."

Solar glanced back at Lykinnia; sweat beaded his brow.

"Watch out!" Lykinnia screamed in horror.

A dwarf with a large metal rod charged out of the alley between two smelters. Solar spun forward and the rod hit him square in the face. He hit the ground like a sack of potatoes, out cold. The dwarf grabbed him by the collar with one hand and dragged his limp body back into the alley.

Lykinnia flew in after him. "What do you think you are doing? Let go of him."

About thirty feet in, the dwarf dropped Solar back to the ground, then turned to face her.

Their eyes met and locked in a contest of wills.

Lykinnia saw an insane happiness bundled up in those eyes, and fear overwhelmed her like a tidal wave. "Dego?" Panic set in, and before he could grab her again, she fled over the stone and cast-iron chambers, out the same tunnel they entered from. She could fly all day and not break a sweat, but she found herself hyperventilating. She paused before entering the tunnel to peek back. Dego had not followed.

Back at the Peak of Power, real tears streamed down her face, dripping on the altar. "What do I do?" Her mind swirled, unable to process through any ideas, instead of the dozens normally coming to her in the first few moments. Frustration competed with her fear for control of her mind. *I should release my ethereal form and call Father, but if I do, I am done for the day. No more travel.*

The pressure her hands exuded on the surface of the altar lessened. *Wait. Why can Dego grab me? If he walks between planes that would explain why he can touch me. Which means—I can touch him!* She forced her attention back to her amber unearthly body and raced back to the alley.

Solar's screams of pain echoed out of the narrow backstreet into the main corridor. She halted at the corner and peeked around. *This had better work. It must.*

Dego stood over Solar with both hands on her friend's head. The fingers had morphed into black tentacles, each one boring into Solar's head. Her steward for the past millennium could tolerate no more pain. Drool dripped from his lips, his eyes rolled into the back of his head, and his screams had degenerated into a moan.

Lykinnia wound up her courage, toughened her resolve, and sprang forward to help. *Please work. Melandri, I could use some luck.*

Her body shrank to a foot long and shot forward, transforming into a golden projectile.

He never saw her coming, and she struck him in his right temple. As she entered his heads, for they were on top of each other, she flashed a brilliant light. Her momentum slowed, but she continued to bombard his brain with a glowing illumination.

Convulsions coursed through Dego's body as she traveled from one side of his cranium to the other. One last flash and she focused on escaping. Lykinnia exploded out of the side of Dego's head, bringing half of his brains along with her. She shook and quivered trying to rid herself of the remnants clinging to her.

Lykinnia glanced down at Solar's collapsed body, now free of the black tentacles. She shot straight up, resuming her normal size, and hovered while scrutinizing the results. Her head tingled softly in warning. *No. Not yet.*

Dego stumbled and lurched, attempting to grab Solar, but his hands passed several feet over top of his sprawled body.

He is blind! She zoomed back down to Solar's side.

"You came back, golden bird. Be as quiet as you want, but you have a stench I could track to the far ends of the world. Both of you reek of it. As soon as you entered Delge, I could smell you." Dego swung again.

Lykinnia examined Dego's milky white eyes and the black ooze dripping down the left side of the dwarf's face. Her fear returned. She shrieked, "Run Solar!"

Dego changed tactics and stomped in a circle. "Even if he could run, it does not matter. I extracted the location and name of where you both live with Terazhan. Once my body heals, I will be coming for you."

The pain in her head surged much stronger. It was time to go. She smiled as Solar crawled on all fours toward the main passage. Lykinnia tried to help one more time with a bit of trickery. "Solar! Wake up, you have to wake up." She released herself to return home.

She removed her hands from the altar and sighed. "I guess it is up to Grendella to save her brother Semper and his friends."

90

Red Sunrise

Semper

Brogan held out his massive two-handed sword toward Semper. "Hit my sword with your hammer."

Semper wound up and paused. "What if I break it?"

Brogan growled, "I don't—"

A massive gout of fire rocketed out of the bonfire and into the sky, scorching two of the flying creatures.

Semper stayed his swing and investigated the area for answers. The five tree beings hummed a low guttural noise, while their gnarled hands and arms wove intricate patterns in the air.

Two more columns of fire shot forth, followed by two more, picking off more of the flying squid-faced creatures.

The largest of the apparent allies bellowed, "Build the fire. Kill the moonloks."

Semper jumped to comply. The others followed shortly after, and the bonfire grew again. The moonloks howled in unison and took wing. The group continued to haul branches with a wary eye.

A scream of pain came from Ibor. With a tentacle driven through his thigh, he failed to engage the moonlok in battle.

Dregur reacted first, severing the appendage on the upstroke, and disemboweling the creature on the downstroke.

Dozens of moonloks glided in, close to the ground, trying to avoid the deadly fire. Brogan and Bardur stood back-to-back fighting off two more, and Semper dove for cover as one swooped overhead. Smaller columns of fire continued to connect with flying targets all around them.

Two moonloks crashed into a tree being, tipping it off balance. The continuous beat of their wings drove it into the fire.

The largest tree creature yelled, "No!" and it sounded like a foghorn.

Brogan appeared out of nowhere, catching the tree as if they were dancing, and he was merely dipping his partner. Muscles bulged in his arms, legs, back, and neck, and he pulled the thing to him in a bear-hug maneuver. However, the weight and momentum were too much for him to control, and he lunged for the side of the fire. Brogan rolled away quickly, searching for his dropped sword.

Moonloks were dropping quickly now, the four standing tree beings furious with the near-death of their companion.

Semper charged Bardur's adversary. The dwarf had already been pierced by two tentacles, and the other four flailed around him like striking pit vipers. The appendages proved too elusive for Semper's hammer, but the abdomen was an easy target. Held in a fixed position by its connection to Bardur, his second swing took its wing off and half its flank.

Ibor almost took a pillar of fire to the face when he dumped a large load of fuel on the bonfire. His anger dissipated quickly when the blazing column struck a moonlok only five feet behind him.

Brogan and Dregur darted around the tree creatures, protecting their backs from incoming moonloks.

Semper shook his head in respect. *Now I see why the boy admires you.*

His attention returned quickly to his own issues. Another squid-head was mounting an attack on both him and Bardur. He failed to keep all the tentacles at bay, and one lanced through his calf, radiating pain up his leg and into his mind. Semper wound the rope-like appendage around the shaft of his warhammer, then used it to drive the creature to land.

Bardur dispatched the moonlok with two swift swings of his battle axe.

Semper nodded his appreciation and scanned the battleground while catching his breath.

Two moonloks speared Brogan simultaneously, but unlike Orlen, they could not lift him off the ground. He pulled down, and Dregur severed a wing of each, then took their lives.

The bonfire burned low from lack of fuel and length of time, and three of the tree beings had toppled over. Yet, the battle raged on.

Semper bowed his head, hope and energy running low, when the sounds of battle abated. He surveyed the area. The moonloks were gone.

Brogan tried to help the fallen trees rise, but they dug their roots in and stood on their own.

Ibor stoked the fire and pushed the charred ends of branches into the middle. He took a seat and worked on removing a tentacle.

"No," the largest tree creature exclaimed to Ibor.

Everyone gathered around the fire to listen.

Ibor hesitated with his hand grasping the tentacle. "I need to remove these."

"No." The tree's deep baritone voice resonated through the small clearing.

Ibor rose with a red face and his battle axe high. "If you say no again, I am going to chop you into pieces."

Brogan held his hands up. "Stop. Let's start again." He walked over to the tree standing by Ibor. "My name is Brogan. Thank you for your help."

"You are welcome. Mother sent us to protect you. She calls us caretakers of the forest. Others call us tree revenants."

Semper approached. "Thank you. I am Semper. What is your name?"

The big tree leaned forward. "You no listen to good. I am caretaker of the forest."

The exasperated expression on Semper's face made everyone laugh, including Ibor.

After the merriment subsided, Ibor said, "Caretaker, what should we do with these?" Ibor had three stuck inside him, and Brogan had seven.

"Cut off hook, trim long part, and leave inside," replied The Caretaker.

"For how long?" asked Ibor.

"Leave inside. You no listen to good either." The Caretaker's body creaked as he shifted.

The forest darkness was lessening, and Ibor's blood-red face was clearly visible. Brogan interceded quickly. "Why would anyone want to leave these things in their body?"

"I show you. Come." The Caretaker shambled over to another caretaker with two tentacles sticking out of it. A triangular rock appeared in his gnarled hand. "Cut off hook, trim long piece, and leave rest." He performed the action as he said it, and the result was astonishing.

Semper gasped and stepped closer to inspect the wound. The tree bark had reappeared, and the hole disappeared. “It turned to wood?”

“It turn to wood and bark, but in you it turn to flesh and skin.” The Caretaker proceeded to lance the other tentacle. “Moonloks not try to kill. They try to mate. If your friend had survived, he be moonlok now.”

Dregur wrinkled his nose. “I am going to be sick. This thing sticking in me is a—”

“Let’s cut them off. I will try one first.” Brogan drew his dagger and tried to replicate the process he saw.

The Caretaker’s gnarly hand grabbed Brogan’s massive bicep. “No. No pull hard. Already healing inside.”

Brogan sliced off the hook and trimmed the excess tentacle from the other side. Instantly, the remaining moonlok flesh transformed to an exact match of Brogan’s skin color. “What happens inside?”

“It becomes one like your body,” replied The Caretaker.

The four dwarves and one human excised the tentacles from themselves and each other, while the caretakers congregated near the fire.

Semper’s leg felt better already, and he was not limping anymore. “I can’t believe we survived.”

Ibor rubbed the back of his neck. “Except Orlen.”

Everyone nodded in silent agreement.

The Caretaker called out, “The one named Brogan, approach. We would like to bestow a mark upon you for your valor in battle.”

Brogan sought the support of his comrades. “What is a mark, and why only me?”

“Not only did you protect during battle, but you saved this caretaker from certain death. If she had fallen to fire . . .” The Caretaker trailed off.

Brogan approached with more confidence. "What will the mark do?"

"None of the caretakers will ever harm you or allow you to be harmed. Come." The Caretaker waved him over.

The trees formed a semicircle around him, and the smaller caretaker he had saved ambled forward. Her chest opened like a clamshell, the roots no longer protective ribs around the heart. She gently placed her gnarled thumb into the cavity and brushed against the glowing green orb. It pulsed and left a shiny residue behind. She withdrew her hand and placed her thumb on the thickest part of Brogan's shoulder. The mark throbbed several times before it was absorbed into his skin and disappeared. Her abdomen reformed and she stepped back into line with the others.

"She thanks you for your actions. We must go now, and you should not dally," said The Caretaker.

Brogan met the eyes of the caretaker who bestowed the blessing and thanked her.

Overcome by the ceremony and camaraderie, Semper wished Cymm could be there with him. This thought made his heart ache and he vowed that when they saw each other again, he would introduce him to his father and sister. This buoyed him, the idea of his old family and new family being together. He gazed into the heavens to say a prayer and realized dawn had broken. The sun's rays struck the moon Phoenix at the perfect angle, radiating the sky in his field of vision. "How beautiful. A red sunrise."

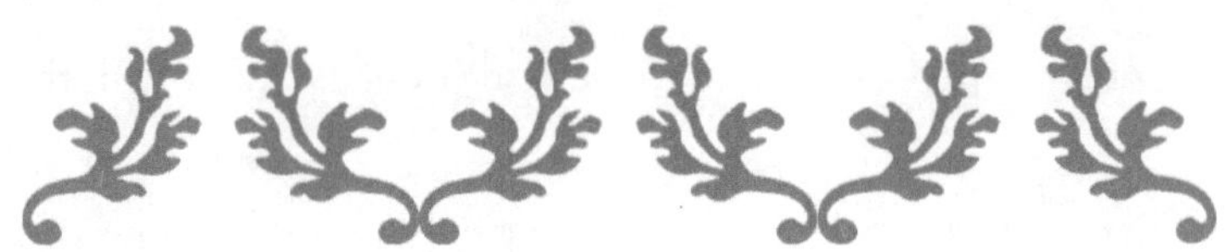

91

Norfolk

Cymm

A young girl's scream pierced the air. Cymm walked toward the barn. A second more urgent scream followed.

"Bria?" Cymm called, already knowing the answer.

"Help me, Cymm!"

Cymm burst through the barn doors with his sword in hand. "DraKarrion, if you touch her—"

A sinister laugh cut him off. "Touch her like this?" One razor-sharp talon sliced across her—"

Cymm sat bolt upright, drenched in sweat and hyperventilating. For the past nine days, the green and black dragon spirit had invaded Cymm's mind whenever his thoughts drifted, turning fanciful daydreams into nightmares. Or in this case, raided his dreams. The same monster plagued him every night, chasing him, killing him and his loved ones, only to recur with the same inevitable conclusion. He could not endure much more.

Cymm arrived at the gates of Norfolk physically and mentally exhausted.

Two guards approached with a greeting. "Hail traveler. State your business in the great city of Norfolk."

"I seek a king with your audience, concerning the princess." His prepared response had been slightly different a few hours ago.

The guards shared a glance and shrugged. "Follow me."

A guard secured a horse and led the way. The city was enormous. They rode toward the palace gates. "Fair warning, the King has executed false messengers and clowns with regards to his beloved daughter. Take care with your words."

Cymm nodded silently. When they arrived at the palace gates, they dismounted.

The escort spoke privately with the new guards, then returned to mount his horse. "You are in their care now. I must return to duty."

Four more sentries appeared from the barbican forming a procession. The captain, a gruff old man, spoke, "You have news concerning the Princess?"

"Yes," replied Cymm.

The captain grumbled to himself. "This way."

They ascended the marble steps and entered the palace. The first room was a grand entrance with a ceiling rising two stories high. Statues and paintings filled the room. Sitting in the center rested a large ornate table.

The captain motioned to the table. "Leave your weapons here."

"I'm sorry, but not going to happen. I'm here to help, not assassinate your king."

"Kill the king," whispered DraKarrion.

No one moved for many seconds.

"What did you say?" asked the captain.

"I didn't say anything." *Blessings to Terazhan, I'm not going crazy.* Cymm waited in silence, then shrugged, and turned to leave.

"Wait." The captain motioned to a guard, who sped off down the corridor.

An hour transpired, and finally the guard returned with several friends. One of them a hulking man with a fierce scar on his face. "Why do you refuse to leave your weapons here?"

"I am a holy paladin of Terazhan and have no ill will for your king. Given recent circumstances, I cannot be parted from the sword."

The warrior gawked at him, then shook his head. "Give me the message and I will see it delivered."

"This message is for the King only."

The warrior led the way down the hall, followed by Cymm and four palace guards.

They entered a large chamber with twenty armed guards outlining the walls of the room. Heavy crossbows were loaded and pointed in his direction. On a throne, against the far wall, sat the King, an old, wizened man.

Do I look that intimidating? The paladin bowed deeply. "I am Cymm Reich, First Paladin of Terazhan. Lord Terazhan, the One True God, has sent me to rescue your daughter and your people from the dragon."

The King feigned interest before stifling a yawn. "And how much gold does Cymm Reich and his god want in return for this good deed?"

"None, Your Majesty. If you tell me where to find the lair, I will kill the beast and return with the Princess and your citizens."

"Your words betray you. It is the hand of the Princess you seek. If you rescue her, you will expect me to offer her up as your bride," accused the King.

"No, Your Majesty. I am sure your daughter is exceptionally beautiful, but I am not interested in marriage." Cymm felt his patience waning.

"How do you plan to defeat a dragon with raggedy leather armor barely covering your chest, Cymm Reich?" The King led a chorus of laughter that ended with a look of disdain.

"Slaying a dragon is never easy, but I have already killed three enormous green dragons in the past two months." Cymm did not smile or shift his gaze, even as he fended off an attempt from DraKarrion to push into his mind.

The King appeared dubious. "Really? And how many men will you need to fight with you?"

Cymm rubbed his temples. "None, and I will even split the dragon's hoard with you."

The soldier standing next to him, the escort with the scar on his face, cast him a doubtful glance, then approached the King. "Up!"

The withered man sitting upon the throne, stood. "Yes, Your Majesty." He bowed and moved to the side of the room.

The warrior guard claimed the throne. "Femerik."

A plump man in white robes emerged from a hidden alcove behind him. "Yes, my King?"

Cymm glanced from one man to the other, confused.

The King clenched one fist inside of another and almost rose from the throne. "You know very well what I want to know."

The cleric rushed his words out. "Everything he said is true."

Many of the guards were whispering.

"Silence!" ordered the King. "How can that be? Even the part about the three dragons?"

"Yes, even the timeframe of two months." The cleric anticipated the King's next question.

The King's eyes bore into Cymm's. He traced the scar on his face before standing. "I am King Varacek, a Royal of the Realm of Legerdemain, Guardian of the Southern Border, and the Protector of Jannibar Pass. I am at your service Cymm Reich."

"Thank you, Your Grace." Cymm bowed again.

The King selected two guards. "Take this man to the armory and fit him with any suit he chooses." His gaze drifted toward Cymm. "We will dine together tonight and discuss the mission."

"Thank you, Your Grace, but even when I eat, the sword is strapped to my back."

"Very well. We dine at opposite ends of the table." The King grinned and left the chamber through a door behind the throne.

Cymm lingered, staring after the departing man. His eyes shifted from side to side, examining the remaining people in the room.

A guard broke the silence. "This way, sir."

"Cymm, please call me Cymm. Is he really the King?" He shuffled after the guards.

One replied, "Unless he's been fooling us for the past fifteen years. Come along, Sir Cymm. Our destination lies on the far side of the castle."

Cymm entered the royal armory like a wizard opening another's spell book. He knew he should not be there, and he realized he might not ever be there again. Many sets of armor rested on cross racks, some were stacked on shelves, and others were strewn on the floor.

The first guard volunteered the following, "The best armor is on the cross racks. I would choose from one of those."

Cymm searched the multitude on his own. His heart pounded in his chest when he found the full and field plate sets, the armor of his childhood dreams. With trembling hands, he sorted through them, selecting a field breastplate matching his physique. The holy symbol of Terazhan flashed through his mind's eye. The image, a warhammer parrying a sword over an ornate intercross, was emblazoned on his chest. The back of his head ached from the continuous smile splitting his face, but it was fading slowly. He collected the rest of the set and hoisted it in one large double arm load and strained his back from the surprising weight. *Nah, it won't be so bad when I am wearing it.* Refusing to concede, he snaked his head through the pauldrons and rested them on his shoulders.

He bent over to slip his greaves on and lost his balance. He recovered and turned his back to the guards. With only half of the armor on, it already restricted his movement and breathing. His gaiety was replaced with a large lump in his throat. His eyes welled with tears as his childhood dream smashed to pieces.

The friendly guard called out, "Looks good on you, and it's magical."

Cymm forced a smile. He removed it and shuffled away toward the simpler armor.

The same guard waved him over. "No. No. No. If you want chainmail, come here."

In the corner, on a cross rack, was a beautiful set of chainmail, glistening like a jewel. Cymm glanced up and pointed at it. "Is this made of mithril like my sword?"

"Yes. It's elven chainmail." The guard helped him remove it from the cross rack unceremoniously.

The dazzling light reflecting off it returned the smile to his face. Images of the village of Salvation and the creation of his sword came to mind, and he hastily slipped on the first piece from the rack. He donned the entire set, including pauldrons, gauntlets, greaves, leggings, coif, and helmet. He did not plan to wear every piece, but even if he did, it was not much heavier than his leather jerkin.

He turned to face his new friend.

The guard shifted the coif around his neck to form a proper union between the pauldrons and the helmet, then stepped back with a nod. "It looks like you've made a decision."

Cymm beamed. "I have. This is my choice."

"I don't know if it's magical, but it's lightweight and beautiful," said the guard.

"Let's go." The other guard grumbled on his way toward the door.

Cymm placed his leather jerkin on the empty cross rack and followed them out of the room.

ꝏꝏꝏ

Later that night, he dined with the King, the grandest feast Cymm had ever had. They sat at a long table, one at each end, with enough food between them to feed twenty men.

King Varacek hoisted his goblet of wine. "Cymm, is this your first time in the city of Norfolk?"

"Yes, Your Majesty."

"Did you happen to see the Temple of Terazhan on your way to the palace?"

"No, Your Majesty."

"Can we dispense with the pleasantries? Or should I address you as Lord Reich?"

Cymm choked on the food he was about to swallow. "Cymm will be fine."

The King nodded. "For tonight, you will address me as Varacek."

Cymm shifted uncomfortably. "Varacek, why did the dragon take your daughter hostage?"

The King wiped his mouth with a napkin. "The beast attacked a peaceful caravan over two months ago, killed more than half of the people, and took the rest captive, not only the Princess."

"Forgive me, but how do you know she's alive?"

Varacek set his fork down and steepled his fingers. "Myndar, a tracker among those captured from the caravan transporting the Princess, was released by the dragon to deliver a message. If I set one foot in the valley, my daughter will be executed. He has confirmed Jenaleya is alive and can explain where the dragon's lair is. What disturbs me is no ransom demands have been made."

"Is ransom an option? Will you give me authority to negotiate?"

Varacek scratched his head. "Yes, but I thought you came to kill him?"

"I am trying to plan for all possibilities, even the unlikely chance this dragon is not evil."

The King pushed his plate away and rose. "Cymm, follow me."

An advisor quickly stepped forward to intervene. "Your Majesty?"

"Silence." Varacek fixed Cymm with a penetrating gaze. "Coming?"

Cymm rose and followed him into an adjoining room.

It was a smaller room with bookshelves lining the walls, a hearth with a roaring fire, and two plush chairs set before it. The King stood between the chairs and pointed to the portrait above the mantle. "My Jenaleya, the Princess. Cymm, please bring her home to me."

Cymm empathized with him, especially when his voice cracked. "Last year, I experienced a great loss of loved ones. I would never wish that upon you. I will do my best."

Varacek clapped him on the back. "I can ask for nothing more." He motioned to the seats.

Cymm took a seat. "Varacek, I would like to talk to Myndar before I leave in the morning. Is it possible?"

The King waved servants over with snifters and an ornate decanter, which they placed on the small table in front of them. "A tall order, but I will send my men out immediately to search."

"Maybe his family could help?" Cymm suggested.

Varacek poured liquid into the two small cups. "Recent events have led to a deep investigation into his background. He has no family in this city and hails from Calp. My royal guard hired him as a wagoneer in Tinel."

Cymm grabbed the offered snifter, hoisted it in respect, and took a swig. It burned his mouth, then throat, and now his chest. "Whoa! What is this?"

"Blackberry brandy, but a little stronger than most," the King sniggered.

The two chatted like old friends for the next hour, while Cymm sipped at the alcohol. Two servants appeared at the King's summons and escorted the paladin to his room for the night.

ooooo

In the morning, Cymm awoke to servants bustling around his room, and when they left, two guards peeked through the doorway at him. *I wonder if they've been there all night.* He shook his head, embarrassed. *They probably heard me screaming, as DraKarrion had attacked repeatedly.*

The sweet smell of pastries drew his attention. A small table had been brought in, ladened with bread, cakes, pastries, and fruit. Drawn like a dwarf to gemstones, Cymm stood in front of the table hoisting his first selection. Servants swarmed him and tugged the clothes and armor he wore to bed off his body.

Halfway through his meal, a knock sounded at the door before it banged open and a man was forced through it, being manhandled by two of the five guards escorting him.

Half-naked, Cymm turned to face them. "Stop! Who is this?"

"Lord Reich, this is Myndar. The King said you wished to question him," replied one of the guards.

Cymm scowled. "Let go of him. I wanted to speak to him, not interrogate him."

Myndar shook the last remaining hand off his arm.

Cymm beckoned him over. "Have you eaten anything this morning?" He motioned toward the table. "I have plenty."

Myndar edged up next to him, gave a quick glance, and grabbed a cake. "What do you want?"

"I *want* to know about the dragon and its lair. Let's start with the location."

"I can draw a map, or for a small fee, I could guide you to the trailhead. Once on the trail, you can't miss it." Myndar stuffed another cake in his mouth.

Although Cymm was no longer hungry, he continued to take small bites to make his informant feel more comfortable. "A map will be fine. How many prisoners are there besides the Princess?"

Myndar licked his fingers. "There were ten alive when I left, plus the Princess."

Cymm shook his head slowly. "Wow. How is the dragon feeding everyone, especially during the growing season?"

"Most of the food we brought from the caravan is gone by now. Fortunately, we had a palace priest conjuring food from the beginning."

"He was wise to do so. Can you describe the lair?"

"It is a cave with only one entrance. A tunnel slopes down into a huge chamber, large enough to hold twenty dragons, with a makeshift cell constructed of stacked boulders. We could have easily escaped, but we didn't dare try. He was looking for a reason to kill us. The only time we were allowed out of the pen was to go to the bathroom outside. He didn't want to *smell* our disgusting odor." Myndar poured himself juice to drink.

"You have been most helpful and are free to go. Terazhan's blessings upon you. Take whatever you would like with you."

The guards escorted a smirking Myndar away.

Cymm pulled a guard aside. "Before I leave, I need a palace priest's robe."

92

Informant

ZaphMordakai

"Master Elf," a voice called down from above the cave opening. "I have been waiting several hours to speak with you."

ZaphMordakai glanced up, then scanned the tunnel with his sharp elven senses before beckoning his informant away from the opening. "What are you doing here?" he whispered, his voice barely audible.

Dyfar shifted nervously. His eyes darted back toward the tunnel. "I bring news from the city, master. A formidable warrior has arrived, claiming to be a dragonslayer. He intends to kill your fr—the green dragon and rescue the Princess."

A burst of laughter erupted from ZaphMordakai.

Dyfar winced, then continued, "His name is Cymm Reich."

The dark elf's laughter subsided, replaced by a menacing hiss. His eyes narrowed as he surveyed Dyfar.

"You know him?" The human's voice was tinged with curiosity.

Zaph hesitated for a moment before answering. "Well enough to know his sword is the source of his power."

Dyfar's expression turned contemplative. "I see." A gleam sparkled in his eyes. "Now you can plan for his arrival."

ZaphMordakai folded his arms over his chest. "I already know exactly what I'm going to do. Your message has been delivered. You may leave."

The dark elf stared after the retreating form of the human for a while. *You travel through treacherous lands, to deal with devious captors. Your days will be numbered Dyfar if you are not more careful.*

93

Palace Priest

Cymm

Cymm entered the mountain pass on horseback later, the same evening, under the watchful gaze of the crimson moon, Phoenix. Wearing a scarlet priest robe over his new elven chainmail, which seemed more vibrant as the sun rays diminished. The timing of his departure from the city had been late, and now he would need to make camp, trudge on at first light, and plan to attack in the morning.

He did not actually sleep. He had been warned of owlbears and kept a watchful eye. The deathly silence hung over the forest like a thick fog, and an ill-timed nightmare scream could have been catastrophic. When dawn finally broke, he was stiff, cold, and miserable. After a quick breakfast for his warhorse and himself, he continued down the trail, pulling a wagon.

He scratched his horse behind the ear and wondered if Jalko missed him. "When we are done here, and deliver the head to Terazhan, we are heading home buddy. Extra apples for you and berry bread for me."

Cymm received a whinny in reply. "Lykinnia needs to teach me how she taught you the common language."

The warhorse nickered.

Cymm shook his head and pushed on down the path. Within a couple of hours, a valley opened to the left, while the trail continued forward. *This is where Myndar said to leave the trail, and the cave is down in the dale.*

Cymm dismounted and grabbed his horse's muzzle. "I'm not going to lash you to a tree in case an owlbear is in the area, but I want you to stay here because we may need to leave in a hurry. Do you understand me?"

The horse's head bobbed up and down.

Cymm grabbed his neck, hugged him, laughed, then quickly sobered. "I'm going to fight another dragon. I should be serious." He stroked his horse's flank for a few moments, then slunk down into the vale.

At the bottom of the vale, Cymm crouched behind a tree, inspecting the entrance to the cave.

After ten minutes, DragonSin broke the solitude in his mind. *"He is in there. I can sense an evil presence."*

Cymm did not respond.

"Why do you wait?"

Cymm scratched the side of his head. *"If I climb above the cave to maximize your search—"*

A ruckus spewed out of the tunnel, and he tucked in closer to the tree. Roughly a dozen prisoners ran out of the cave for the bushes, like dogs being let outside by their master.

Cymm spotted the Princess immediately. Her long blonde hair remained surprisingly vibrant after two months of imprisonment. He turned his attention to the priest and walked swiftly toward her.

Most of the prisoners gawked at him, especially the priest, who stared at her doppelgänger. Finally, she said, "May the Mistress bless you."

"Yes. Azreala is a wonderful—"

"Do not blaspheme as if you know her!" The priestess's face turned as red as her robes.

Other prisoners gathered around them to listen.

Cymm glanced back impatiently at the cave entrance. "This is a disguise. I'm Cymm Reich and here to rescue everyone. Take the trail up out of the valley and wait for me at the top with my horse and wagon."

The Princess, wearing a tattered white dress, joined the group. "If we are not back inside in the next two minutes, the dragon will come crashing out of that hole and slaughter us like sheep."

"That is the plan. Not the slaughtering part. When the dragon comes out, I will take his head off." Cymm scanned the crowd of frowning faces.

The Princess waggled her finger in his face. "And what about his friend?"

Cymm discovered this was a shared concern. "What friend?"

"The dark-skinned elf that shoots lightning bolts from his hands," replied the Princess.

Cymm rubbed the back of his neck. "He's in there now?"

The captives exchanged glances, then collectively shook their heads.

The paladin scanned the sky for answers. "Any idea when he'll return?"

Twisted faces and shrugs were the only responses he received.

He pointed at the priestess. "I wish Myndar had mentioned you were a woman. Anyway, I need you to stay outside and take cover while we go back inside."

"Cymm, what are you doing?" asked DragonSin. *"You know I cannot protect any of them from his poisonous breath. Stick with the plan and wait for the dragon to leave the cave."*

"We may not have time. I can't take the chance." He took stock of the brave men and women standing around him. "Slight change in plans. Princess Jenaleya, you will remain with the priestess. I need five volunteers to go inside, and when the battle begins, run for the exit."

Cymm recalled the Divine Quest Terazhan had sent him on his way to Norfolk. He had noted significant differences already. A deep sigh escaped his mouth as he resigned himself to this course of action. "Let's go. Try to act normal as we walk down the tunnel."

Even though sunlight poured into the valley beneath the cloudless sky, by the time he reached the bottom of the tunnel, only a modicum of light came with him. Cymm crossed the threshold from tunnel to cave and veered right instead of left toward the pen.

The green dragon's head lifted off the cavern floor with a hiss. "Get in your cage before I kill you. Why are the rest of you milling about?"

Cymm continued to close the distance. "They don't take orders from you anymore."

The dragon's bulk shifted, cascading coins clinked off the floor and each other. "Where is the Princess?"

The paladin's eyes tried to adjust to the limited light, but the walls continued to elude his detection as well as the floor more than five feet in front of him. Most of the dragon's body remained indistinguishable from the shadows, except for its eyes, which glowered in the gloom. He halted and reached back behind his neck, placing two fingers in the small tear he had strategically cut in the robe. The snapping of fabric threads filled the silence.

DragonSin launched his mental assault.

With Cymm's free hand, he cast a light spell straight for his enemy's eyes. Unseen in the darkness, the ball of light struck a low ridge of short stalactites running along the ceiling, and the cavern burst into view.

The light was blinding, and the paladin recoiled from the effects of his own spell. Fortunately, his enemy did as well. For several moments, the only sound was pounding footsteps retreating up the tunnel.

Both combatants recovered their vision simultaneously and took measure of one another.

"I thought you'd be bigger," taunted Cymm, walking closer. "The two female dragons I killed last month were much larger."

DraKarrion lashed out, sending a piercing pain through the paladin's mind.

The serpent in front of him roared at the insult. "My size won't matter much to you when you're dead!" A thick cloud of toxic gas spewed from the dragon's maw.

Cymm lingered a few moments, cloaked in the yellowish green fog, listening to the dragon's hearty laugh, and recovering his senses. He stepped out of the cloud holding his belly, with a boisterous, mocking hoot of his own.

The large lizard's laugh subsided.

In the blink of an eye, Cymm charged with DragonSin held high. The sword descended in a wicked slash across the dragon's neck, chest, and left shoulder. The deep laceration smoked and sizzled; the surrounding skin folded over and flapped against his chest, revealing breast and shoulder bone.

The dragon shrieked in pain. Its talons scrabbled against the stone floor, seeking purchase to retreat.

His enemy blasted him again with another ineffective gout of noxious fumes. Cymm slowly stalked his quarry, pressing it back against the far wall.

Like a trapped badger, it lunged forward. Its emerald serpent head hurled to the side by DragonSin as if hit by Melcorac's Hammer.

With fear-filled eyes, it began to plead. "I am BelCharius, a lieutenant in the Dragon Queen's Army. I can—"

"Blah, blah, blah. I have heard this speech before." Cymm could feel the swagger in his step.

"Drive me deep into his heart and end this swiftly."

Cymm passed through the swirling pockets of chlorine gas like a wraith. *"No, not yet."*

"Yes, let him live," said the raspy voice of DraKarrion.

BelCharius mewled, then whispered a chant-like phrase to himself.

Cymm chuckled. "Your spells will have no effect on me either. Where is the arrogance and boldness from before?" He rotated the sword and lunged forward, cutting a perpendicular trough in the dragon's chest. This second cut, slightly higher on the neck, lacerated an artery, and blood spurted over the floor and nearby wall.

A dark phantom with the shape of a humanoid appeared. "Why do you summon me?" a harsh voice hissed.

"Ledaedra, help me," whined the green dragon.

After taking in the scene, the baleful eyes of the shadow fell upon Cymm. "You insolent worm. Your life is forfeit!" With a wave of its insubstantial hand, a torrent of spraying blood flew at his face.

It ran into Cymm's eyes, blinding him. Frantically, he wiped at it, creating a red hazy view. The color made him briefly wonder why Azreala had abandoned him.

The desperate dragon surged forward, its claws cutting deep into Cymm's left arm and shoulder. The power and surprise of the attack knocked the paladin off balance.

"Yes. Feel the power of the green dragons!" hissed DraKarrion.

Cymm fell to his back, knocking the wind from his lungs. Searing pain erupted from multiple locations on his body, causing him to cry out.

The drake's paw slammed into him, driving a talon through his collarbone, breaking it. His mithril armor deflected the rest of the claws, but the crushing weight pinned him to the ground. The wind rushed from his lungs. *"DragonSin, I need help!"* There was no reply. *"DragonSin?"*

It was then he realized his hand was empty. The sword lay on the ground, inches from his outstretched fingers. He clawed at the stone floor reaching for it to no avail. His mithril armor and magical ring continued to provide him protection as snapping fangs and raking claws careened off his torso. A blood red scratch appeared on the other side of his neck from ear to the armor's collar.

DragonSin called out, "Fight. Don't give up!"

Anger gave him a new surge of adrenaline. "I am!" He kicked up and out with both legs at the arm pinning him down. Both feet struck, inflicting little to no damage, but he inched closer to the sword.

The dark shadow chuckled. "Even a talking sword will not help you now."

Cymm kicked wildly again, a frenzy like never before, taking over him. He stretched again and his longest finger brushed the hilt. The eerie green mist blazed to life and DragonSin rocketed into his hand like two strong magnets calling each other. In one fluid motion, he brought the sword to bear, lopping off the arm with the talon impaling him.

The dark shadow screeched like an enraged harpy. "Where is ZaphMordakai?"

ZaphMordakai? Are you kidding me? Cymm's mind churned.

The tide of battle had turned yet again, and BelCharius lunged in desperation, its jaws snapping together inches from his face. Although DragonSin was pushing against the beast's head with all his might, what thwarted the attack was the mithril blade plunged deep within its heart.

"No. No. I cannot absorb anymore!" wailed DraKarrion.

Cymm did not have time to withdraw the blade. He hugged the dragon's arm still attached to him and swiftly rolled to his left, barely escaping the crushing bulk of the creature as it slammed to the floor. He had become separated from the sword once again.

The ebony shadow's form lost definition. "Pathetic human. Your life is forfeited. I will track you to the ends of the—"

94

Waiting

Lykinnia

In the past two fortnights, Lykinnia's free time had been non-existent. She obsessively studied the language of The One, when she was not searching for Semper, entertaining Cymm or ZaphMordakai, saving Solar from Dego, or watching over Cymm in Solar's absence. Through it all, her thoughts frequently drifted back to her mother; she was not ready to give up.

Solar had returned to the Peak of Power four days ago, but it had been twice as long since the encounter with Dego. His normal radiance had not yet returned, and he appeared lethargic and pale. He did, however, take his fair share of watch detail at the altar, rotating with Lykinnia, as they waited for Semper to exit the tunnel and enter Smelter's Square.

He rested his hand on Lykinnia's shoulder. "I assume there has been no development."

Lykinnia closed the scrying window. "Correct. No sign of Semper or Dego."

Solar shook his head. "Get some rest. I will take it from here."

Lykinnia, heading for her abode, paused, and glanced back over her shoulder. "As soon as this is over, we need to free my mother and Uncle Jakarrak. I will not sit by and wait for my father's power to grow and allow my mother to suffer any longer. I have a few ideas we can discuss."

Solar cleared his throat and appeared to recover his regal demeanor. "Young lady, we should focus on the ring and the scheme Jakarrak and Sendaria had concocted. It may shed new light and offer more options."

Lykinnia waved her hand at Solar with a derisive look. "The ring is no longer relevant."

Solar folded his arms over his chest. "Do not dismiss my comment so easily. It is no coincidence Ledaedra took them both captive."

"She captured my mother, waited four hundred years, then captured Uncle Jakarrak. What a dreadful plan."

"I have work to do, before Semper slips by us." Solar turned away from her and opened a scrying window.

She considered sneaking up behind him and plucking a feather from his wings while he was distracted, but quickly discarded the idea. *You will see, when this is over, I will rescue my mother.* Lykinnia returned to her abode.

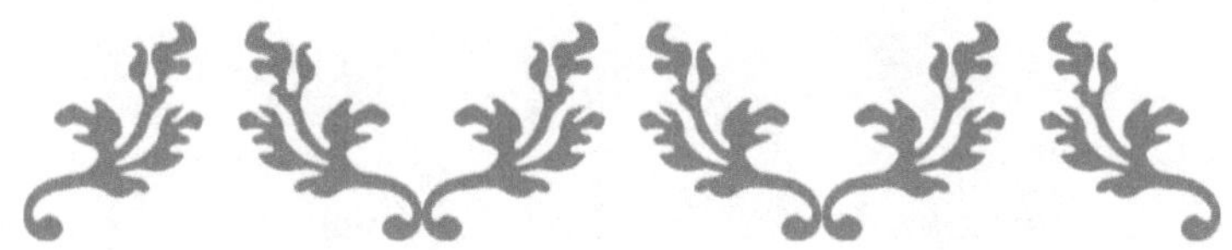

95

New Orders

ZaphMordakai

"I gave you one assignment—to watch over BelCharius— and you can't even do that right. And now he's dead!" The dark shade of Ledaedra scanned their surroundings. "Where in the seven heavens are you?"

ZaphMordakai transformed from a black panther to a dark elf. "I am almost to the Peak of Power to continue the assignment you gave—"

"I did not *give* you this assignment. You gave it to yourself! I asked you to watch BelCharius and the Princess. Now both are lost." The Dragon Queen continued to rage on incoherently.

You also asked BelCharius to watch over me. What would you do right now if I called you out? He is dead; no one cares, and I say good riddance, mused ZaphMordakai.

The Dragon Queen's bluster evaporated. "Why were you in the form of a panther?"

"What?" he asked, confused.

"Before, you were in the form of a panther. Why? If you are so close to the Peak of Power, why are you not in dragon form?" she hissed.

He instantly transformed and took wing, launching himself off a foothill. He circled as he gained altitude, then hovered, facing the Peak of Power. "As I said, I am close, not even an hour away. I do not deceive you. The raw power of the cat lets me think better," he lied. "How did BelCharius die?"

Her fury was mounting again. "It had to be the same human who killed TetraQuerahn. He had a talking sword. What was his name?"

ZaphMordakai clenched his jaw. *He is mine to kill.* "You mean Cymm Reich? No, he is at the Peak of Power, and there has been no mention of his sword talking. Perhaps Terazhan is creating an army of dragonslayers. I will try to learn more about this while I am there."

Her silence revealed her seething inside, and she did not speak until he landed. "You will return to Norfolk and hunt down this murderer. Get what information you can and kill him."

"Yes, my Queen. I will also see what facts I can glean at the Peak of—"

"You will return immediately!" she screamed.

ZaphMordakai's back straightened. "Yes, my Queen. I will kill the human, recover the Princess, and wait in the cave for direction. You will not even notice the loss of BelCharius."

"I was grooming him to be a general. I have tolerated one failure after another from you. You're a huge disappointment, and not half the dragon he was."

Turmoil swelled within ZaphMordakai, but he held his tongue. This was not a time to be impetuous. Why did the scar on his neck itch so bad? He resisted the urge to scratch it while he created an imaginary death scene for the little green worm. His pathetic wyrmling cries brought warmth to his heart, which exploded with happiness when he took his last breath. A beautiful thought came unbidden to the forefront of his raving thoughts—*maybe a dragonslayer will come for the Queen.*

96

Jenaleya

Cymm

Cymm lay on his back dying. At least it felt like it. He had tried numerous times, unsuccessfully, to remove the claw embedded in his chest, through his clavicle and out his back. Therefore, the dismembered dragon arm clung to him as he moved. He had reason to believe the tip of the talon piercing him was hooked in the fine mesh of his mithril armor. He could not rise or even roll again without a wave of excruciating pain racking his body, so he prayed from his back.

"Lord Terazhan, the mighty healer, please give me the power to restore my body!" Sweet relief coursed through him, and he set the back of his head on the stone floor. The light spell he cast before the battle remained, but he was not sure for how much longer. Wisps of green smoke streaked overhead, catching his attention. *How fascinating.* The patterns they formed as they undulated along with an unseen air current. His heart skipped a beat. *The poisonous gas, I have no protection from it!* He scanned from side to side, relieved to find two and a half feet of clean air along the floor.

Once again, he heaved on the parasitic appendage with no success. Unsheathing his dirk dagger, the gift from Old-Man Semper, he sliced, sawed, and hacked at the closest joint to the talon. When most of the scales, flesh, and tendons had been eliminated, he slipped the knife into the joint and pried it apart, severing the finger.

He rolled toward the dragon into a pool of sticky blood. Pushing his hand under the carcass proved difficult, but he forced his hand, scraping knuckles and ripping fingernails, until he felt the last two inches of DragonSin's pommel. The rest was buried deep in the beast's chest, driven there when it hit the ground. *"Do you have any ideas?"*

"Yes, next time don't be an overconfident orc's ass! We could have killed him within the first two minutes. Since when is winning the battle not enough? Why did you feel the need to taunt and ridicule him?"

Shame overtook Cymm. He would have hung his head if he were not lying on the floor.

"We are the good guys. We do not act like them. The killing is necessary to eliminate the evil, to eliminate the threat; it should not be enjoyed," DragonSin scolded.

Cymm growled. *"A little hypocritical, don't you think? I am surprised you didn't sing this time when we killed the dragon."*

"Get me out of here!"

"I'm not sure how, but I will." Cymm crawled to and up the tunnel, staying clear of the gas. When he was a half a dozen horse lengths away from the opening, he turned around and stood. Putrid green gas poured from the top of the crevasse. "The smoke from the cave looks like the mouth of a giant exhaling grass of the djinn."

"Yeah, it does." The Princess had silently walked up behind him.

Cymm jumped with a start. "Princess, I told you to wait for me by the horse and wagon."

The young lady screwed up her face, pulling her chin tight to her neck. “I don’t take orders from anyone, especially you.”

His jaw fell open.

She pushed him gently. “I’m kidding. So, is it dead?”

Cymm turned to face her. “Yes, but we can’t leave yet. I need—"

“Lady Taker help us. How did you survive?”

He followed her gaze to his chest and the near fatal wound. “I can’t lift my arm. Help me remove my armor, please.”

Although he was covered in blood and gore, Jenaleya did as requested.

Cymm cried in agony. “I can feel the broken bone shift every time you lift.”

“Don’t be such a baby.” She smirked. “It’s stuck on something back here.”

He glanced over his shoulder. “The talon pierced through my body. The tip may be entangled in the mesh rings. The other claws were slightly hooked at the ends. Try to work it—"

“I got it! Look forward,” she commanded.

He was half tempted to tell her he didn’t take orders from anyone, but he left it alone. He whistled, three short bursts, calling for his warhorse to join him. “The dark elf could return at any time. I know him. His name is ZaphMordakai, correct?”

“Yes, then we are safe?” she asked.

“Far from it. We need to keep moving.” As if on cue, his warhorse arrived with the wagon and the rest of the captives. He wished for Lykinnia’s presence, so he could inform her of the dark elf’s actions, and—because he needed her there. It had been a while since she visited. She would be able to discern the dark elf’s intentions immediately.

The Princess continued to work on the stuck armor. “The dark elf was unpredictable and moody. He even let one of us go, many weeks back.”

"He did wha—oww!" Cymm's cries of pain cut his question short.

The prisoners swarmed him, but like a mother hen, the Princess chided them back. "Stop jostling him! Am I the only one seeing the spear through his body? Sheeaza, help me get this armor off."

He assumed he knew the answer, but he asked anyway, "Who is Lady Taker?"

Amusement spread across her face. "The Mistress, or The Goddess of Death."

"Does everyone in Norfolk worship Azreala?" Cymm hunched over with a grimace.

The scarlet priestess grumbled to herself.

"No. There is a small temple dedicated to Terazhan."

"I remember your father mentioning it. After the toxic gas clears from the cave, I will go back in. We need to leave by midday, so we can get clear of the forest before dark." Cymm roared in pain as the two women attempted to lift the armor. Tears rolled down his cheeks.

"Sorry, I thought we had them all. There we go." The Princess lifted the armor over Cymm's head with the help of her handmaiden as he dropped to all fours. She gently caressed his skin with watery eyes. "How did you survive?"

"I will show you after we remove this talon. It needs to be pulled out or pushed through. I will trust your judgment." Cymm placed his hands on his thighs, bracing himself for the pain.

Jenaleya, however, did not trust her own assessment and glanced at the old man in the group.

The old man grabbed Cymm's neck and shoulders with a strength he did not appear to have. He pushed and pulled on the talon. "Neither solution is good. The hook will damage more flesh coming out if pulled, but pushing the talon through will widen the hole in your back and tug dragon flesh through your body." He waved the other prisoners over. "Hold him."

ꝏꝏꝏ

Cymm's eyes fluttered open. Several faces hovered over him. "What happened?"

"You passed out." The Princess held his head in her lap.

He tried to sit up, but Sheeaza was pushing on his chest. "It won't stop bleeding."

"Let me up." Cymm rolled to his knees. "Watch. Lord Terazhan, the merciful healer, please provide me with the power to heal myself." Brilliant white light exploded all around him.

Everyone shielded their eyes. When the light was gone, so was his wound.

No one spoke.

Cymm rose and donned his armor in the silence, while examining the sun's position. He did not like what he saw. They should have been on their way a long time ago. He must have been unconscious for a while.

He returned to the dark cave with whispers and murmurs behind his back. At the bottom of the tunnel, he expended his last daily spell by casting light into the ceiling again.

He hefted the dagger in his hand, then glanced at the carcass. The dragon treasure caught his attention. Amidst the coins and gems was a sword. "Terazhan be blessed."

With the short sword in one hand and his dagger in the other, he went to work. "I have butchered deer, wolves, and bears. It can't be much different." But it was. The hide of the young dragon was thick and tough. He sawed into it, then switched to wedging the tip of the sword under bone and using leverage to slice through its skin. After removing the entire right side of its rib cage, the process became quicker. Soon after, entrails and organs lay strewn all over the floor, and he was currently segmenting part of a lung. He paused. "What in the nine hells is that?"

"What?" came a voice from behind him.

Cymm screamed, then turned to find Jenaleya. "I asked you to stay outside."

"No, you didn't." She had both hands on her hips.

"It was implied! You scared me to death."

Jenaleya put both hands together and next to her head like a pillow. "How adorable. For someone who can kill a dragon, you scare easily."

He shot a sardonic smile her way. "The sac attached to the lung is not normal." He leaned in closer to examine it. "Aww, by Ledaedra's bones, it smells worse than the rest of it, which is saying something."

"The sac is probably how it creates the toxic gas it shoots from its mouth."

"Hmm. How do you know?" he asked.

"I'm surmising. It's what you do when you only have some of the facts." She shot him a mocking smile.

Cymm clasped the ogre ring around his neck. "You know—I already have enough sassy women in my life. I don't need another."

"Maybe. But are any of them a princess?" She puckered her lips and batted her eyelashes.

"That is so ridiculous." He laughed. "Why would you—" He could not stop laughing and Jenaleya joined in. He finally controlled himself and asked her to step back. Gingerly, he removed the sac by spearing it with both the sword and dagger, unsure what it might do to his skin if he touched it. Shortly after removing the lung, metal clanged against metal. It was DragonSin.

With one mighty swing of his friend, he cleaved through the dragon's neck, decapitating it.

"Princess, can you please get everyone ready to leave, and find someone to help me tie down the dragon head on the wagon?"

"I can do that." Jenaleya jogged up the tunnel.

After collecting all the gems and placing them in a bag, Cymm returned to the severed head. *"Can you lift this head up off the ground? Then I will push it up the tunnel."*

"It should fall beneath my weight limit," replied the sword.

"You will pay for this. With the additional strength this kill gave me, you won't be able to contain me much longer. I will destroy you both!" railed DraKarrion.

The head levitated, and Cymm found it easy to push through the air. When he emerged from the cave again, the former prisoners cheered.

Princess Jenaleya walked next to him on the way to the wagon, inspecting the floating head. "How is this possible?"

"As a paladin, Terazhan provides me with many skills, spells, and tools. This is one of them." Cymm gently maneuvered the head into the center of the wagon before DragonSin lowered it.

The expression on Jenaleya's face became serious. "Why not a paladin for the Lady Taker?"

"She has asked, and I am considering her offer. However, I would not be a paladin, more like a necromancer."

"You jest?" she asked.

"I do not."

97

Coincidence

Semper

Ibor rejoined the party after scouting ahead. “Smelter’s Square is close by. Everyone is back to work, and the patrols are limited. I waited until the next wave of workers was due, to provide some cover.”

“How does it look in there?” asked Dregur.

“I didn’t see any signs of the battle. The area was thoroughly cleaned,” replied Ibor.

Semper was the first to rise. “Lead the way.”

Ibor’s chest puffed out and he pointed his finger at Semper specifically. “I’m in charge from here on out. Don’t second guess me, or I’m done.”

Grumbles of confirmation followed from Semper, Dregur, Bardur, and even Brogan.

“Okay. Let’s go. In the unlikely chance we get separated, meet at Karaz’s shop.” Ibor took the lead.

A red glow brightened the tunnel ahead, indicating the entrance to Smelter's Square.

I didn't think we were this close, thought Semper, then double-timed his step to catch up with Ibor.

Workers were coming and going and loudly chatting with one another. They seemed to have forgotten all about the massive battle only three weeks ago.

Walking quickly, Semper fell in line like a duckling following his mother. Off to the side, a beggar sitting with his back to the wall caught his attention. At first, Semper imagined the vagrant was staring at him until he saw the milky white eyes and passed it off as coincidence when the dwarf's head turned to follow his passage.

98

Hero's Welcome

Cymm

The trek through the forest was uneventful, even though they had only made it halfway before it became dark. When they broke out onto the main road, a small cavalry unit awaited them and provided an escort back to the city.

Dawn broke by the time they passed through the gates, and the procession grew as they wound their way toward the palace. The King's Guard escorted Cymm and Jenaleya directly to the same chamber where he initially was received. This time only a few guards were present.

King Varacek rose from his throne, trembling with excitement. He winked at his daughter, but immediately returned to his regal demeanor. "Cymm Reich, First Paladin of Terazhan, the realm owes you a great debt of gratitude, as do I. Your valor and bravery are comparable to none. How may I repay you?"

Cymm bowed. "Your Majesty, I am quite fond of this suit of armor. May I keep it?"

The King raised an eyebrow. "It was yours the moment you donned it. Anything else?"

"The dragon amassed several thousand coins. Could you send a team to retrieve them? Not for myself. I ask for the crown and the temple of Terazhan to split them evenly."

"As you wish, Lord Reich. You have given to me yet again. What boon do you ask of me?" King Varacek could wait no longer and rushed down the steps to hug his daughter.

"You flatter me, but I am no lord. The favor I request is to have four guards and a wagoneer transport the dragon's head on the Great North Road to the Peak of Power."

Princess Jenaleya sighed deeply, causing Cymm and the King to glance at each other.

King Varacek clapped the paladin on the back. "Done! Now let us retire to a more comfortable room, where we can share food, drink, and stories with each other."

Cymm allowed himself to be led to the dining room. "Your Majesty, several prisoners overheard the dragon speak of abducting children from the royal families. We should send word to those in danger immediately."

The King puzzled through this for a moment. "What could they possibly want with the children?"

"I'm not sure. One of the prisoners might recollect more if questioned. Either way, we need to know why they destroyed other cities, but spared yours." Cymm reached for the door handle to open it for the King and Princess, but an attendant beat him to it.

"It would appear we have many things to discuss tonight," said Varacek.

"Add to the list, a dark elf was working with the dragon and is the one who released Myndar."

The following morning, Cymm visited the Temple of Terazhan feeling well rested. He had decided to wrap his sword in layers of cloth, and place it between the layers of the bedding, preventing DragonSin or DraKarrion from mentally contacting him. He had intended to leave today, but the wagon would travel quite slow, and he could easily catch up. King Varacek had been true to his word, and expeditiously assembled a team to deliver the dragon head to the Peak of Power.

A priest rapidly approached him. "You must be Cymm Reich."

"You—know me?" Cymm glanced about trying to determine the source of his information.

"Everyone in the city knows you, or at least of you. The King's courier delivered the good news yesterday. The temple needs many repairs, and the gold and silver coins are much appreciated." The priest extended his hand exuberantly.

Cymm gripped his hand and returned the firm shake. "You should receive over two thousand coins by my estimation. Lord Terazhan would want you to expand and glorify the temple."

The priest nodded with a tear trickling down his cheek. "Thank you, Cymm." His face brightened, and he put a finger in the air. "Oh, I almost forgot. You have a guest waiting for you in the back by the fountain."

"A guest?" He walked hesitantly out the back archway, grasping DragonSin. *"Scan for evil."*

A dark cloaked figure stood motionless in stark contrast to the bright surroundings. Were they contemplating the mysteries of faith or how to plunge a dagger in his back? Cymm strode forward to roughly grab and spin the person about.

"Cymm, wait."

"Hello Cymm."

"Princess Jenaleya? You shouldn't be outside the castle."

"The mighty Cymm Reich will protect me, even my father would agree. I came to pray. Will you join me?"

Cymm caught movement out of the corner of his eye. Two palace guards waited in the shadows. *So, she is not alone.* "I have time to pray."

Princess Jenaleya allowed Cymm to guide her back into the temple. "Do you think the Lady Taker will be upset with me?"

Cymm squinched up his face. "I haven't known her for long, but she is accommodating to my needs. I will put a good word in for you the next time I see her. Does that mean you believe in Terazhan's existence?"

"How can I not, after what I have seen with my own eyes," she replied.

Cymm chuckled. "I told Hardre the same thing when he asked me that question."

They knelt before the altar together, and Cymm asked, "Ready?"

Jenaleya slowly and gingerly slipped her hand into his. "Cymm?" She cast doe eyes upon him.

"Jenaleya . . ." Cymm slowly shook his head and retracted his hand from hers.

"Why didn't you ask for my hand? My father said you could ask for anything."

Cymm considered his words carefully. "Your father and I discussed this before I rescued you, and I told him I wouldn't ask for your hand."

"How did you know you wouldn't like me?" Emotion crept into Jenaleya's voice.

Cymm lifted her chin with his forefinger. "You misunderstand. Your father *accused* me of trying to save you only to gain your hand in marriage."

"Nah. He already calls you Lord Reich. Once I talk to him, he'll come around."

"Jenaleya, you are beautiful and witty, but I'm in love with another." Thinking of Lykinnia brought a smile to Cymm's face.

A devious smile crossed her face. "Maybe you could stay for a few—"

"No. Now, are we going to pray or not?"

She faced forward and interlaced her fingers. "Will you promise to visit?"

"Yes, whenever I'm in the area." Cymm also prepared to pray.

Jenaleya knocked into him with her shoulder. "So, who is this lucky girl?"

99

Divination

Lykinnia

Semper and his crew had entered Smelter's Square earlier this morning while Solar was on watch and headed straight out the other side. By the time Lykinnia joined her mentor at the altar, the beleaguered band was hiding out in a dwarven merchant shop on the other side of the city.

Looks like they have settled in for a while. Lykinnia's mind drifted to thoughts of her mother and her condition. *I might not be able to send an astral projection of myself to the Plane of Ashes, but with the language of The One, I should be able to see what is happening there.*

Lykinnia observed Semper one final time, then glanced over both shoulders. She closed and reopened the scrying window, using her newly gained language. Nothing appeared in the frame except for the swirling hypnotic mist. She adjusted her hand and finger position, and intoned her speech more accurately, without success.

After many attempts, the priestess wrinkled her nose and checked on Semper's group. They remained in the same place, and most had fallen asleep. This back-and-forth process continued for several hours. Lykinnia's frustration climbed in sync with the sun as it achieved its zenith.

"What are you doing?"

Lykinnia closed her eyes and cringed, then turned to face Solar.

"Why are you not watching Semper?" he asked.

"I am, but they are sleeping." She stretched and stifled a yawn.

Solar glanced at the space above the altar. "What were you trying to do?"

"Open a scrying window in the Plane of Ashes."

"And where were you looking?"

She pointed in the general direction. "By the map I saw, this way."

Solar guffawed so loud, he snorted. "I thought as much. It is too far away. You must open a portal first, otherwise, all you will see is mist."

Lykinnia's face turned red, and her eyes welled. "I want to see her."

Solar's hand snapped up and his wrist flicked. A portal opened above the Pool of Ages. "Be quick about it, before anything tries to come through."

Lykinnia gave him a lasting glance before initiating a window and sending her mind through. The smoky clouds parted, and barren wasteland stretched in every direction, meeting a blood red sky. Rocky outcroppings erupted randomly across her field of vision, and the land was covered in a layer of ash, which currently drifted down in large lazy flakes.

"Head to your right. I will guide you," came Solar's voice down a long invisible corridor.

It did not take long for her to figure out where they were heading. An enormous volcano leaked slow rivers of lava and belched out plumes of smoke.

Solar no longer provided directions. *"If you think it looks like the volcano on Fire Island, they are identical. Lykinnia, how is your divination coming along?"*

"Not now. Let me focus."

"Lykinnia, the hypnotic trance you feel will get worse if you do not listen to me. Answer the question."

"Fine. I was able to divine a simple event one hour into the future. A strawberry fell off my plate at my dining table and rolled in a semicircle. Otherwise, my efforts have been fruitless." Lykinnia snickered, then gulped. *"Is that the altar?"*

"Yes. Ledaedra will sense your presence. Keep moving, circle around your mother, then head back to the portal. Do you understand?" Solar's intonation had an edge.

"I understand." Lykinnia panned her head as she revolved around the female chained to the post.

A deep hissing voice assailed her mind. "*Would you like to see her face?*"

Excitement percolated within her, and instead of circling around and heading back to the portal, Lykinnia swooped around for a second loop.

Solar's voice rose an octave. *"What are you doing?"*

Ledaedra materialized out of nowhere, huge and menacing, a snarl on her face, towering over the prisoner. The lava flowing down the side of the volcano radiated through the membrane of her flared bat wings. The dark, misty head of the shadow dragon loomed above her when she dropped to one knee so she could twirl a talon in the captive's hair. "*Come a little closer.*"

Lykinnia hesitated, trying to stay in front of the prisoner. Ledaedra's green arm had not regenerated after being severed by closing the gate.

"Keep moving! Head back to the portal," yelled Solar.

The young priestess sustained her movement, orbiting to the back side, where her vision became blocked by the Dragon Queen. She reached the decision point in her journey and began a third loop.

100

Indecision

ZaphMordakai

ZaphMordakai arrived at BelCharius's lair last night and entered in the form of a dragon for the first time ever. Curled up with his head on his tail, he stared at the decapitated body, finding comfort in a morbid way.

"Grooming him to be a general." Give me a break. Green dragons are too weak. I need to find his head and summon his spirit, so he can remind me when the next Captains Meeting is. The black dragon chortled, his throat vibrating excessively this time. *If I can find Cymm, I can kill him and talk to BelCharius.*

ZaphMordakai's mirth ended abruptly. He had no clue how he would recapture the Princess. The likelihood of him landing on the palace grounds, amidst the warriors and wizards, demanding they turn over the Princess, then flying away was miniscule and absurd.

A tremor swept through his head, startling him. A summons from the Queen.

"Report!"

ZaphMordakai positioned himself between her and the carcass. "I have arrived at the lair; the killer is nowhere to be found. I will deal with the body before—"

"I do not care about the corpse. Find the killer and retrieve the Princess. I will be back tomorrow." Ledaedra craned her neck, trying to catch a glimpse of the background.

He shuffled his massive bulk to block her view until she disappeared.

ZaphMordakai rubbed his scar against a sharp edge in the stone wall. *No need for her to see his head is missing. Back to the problem. I can sneak into the city as a dark elf, sneak into her room, and threaten to kill her entire family if she doesn't come with me. Not bad, but how do I get her out of the city?* He sighed again, pondering the dilemma.

"Master elf! Are you in there?" a familiar voice called down the tunnel.

A growl rumbled in his chest. *Dyfar, you twit.* ZaphMordakai transformed himself into a dark elf and walked up the tunnel. "My patience with you has come to an end." He exited the shaft to the sun's rays bombarding him, temporarily causing blindness. "When my vision comes back, you had better be gone."

"You should choose your words more carefully when speaking to a friend. The only friend you have right now. I bring news from the city." Dyfar remained seated on the rock to the side of the opening.

"What is this news?"

"The King has sent a contingent to retrieve the treasure. I suggest you take what you can and leave quickly." Dyfar absently whittled a piece of wood.

"I care nothing for this treasure, or any treasure for that matter. Did the Princess return safely to the city?"

"Yes, along with her warrior escort, the one who I warned you was coming. Why?" Dyfar paused his carving and leaned forward.

ZaphMordakai turned to leave and waved dismissively. "You have delivered your message. Don't come back."

Dyfar returned his dagger to its sheath, and he hopped down from the rock he was resting on. "I asked *why*?"

Lightning crackled from fingertip to fingertip. "Dyfar, you forget yourself."

Dyfar took two steps forward and blinked. Not with his outer eyelids and not up and down. One inner eyelid swept across each eyeball, removing microscopic debris and moistening the surface.

ZaphMordakai's head pulled back, and his feet followed. "What are you?"

"Why do you want the Princess?" Dyfar's lip curled, and his eyes narrowed.

The lightning returned instantly to the dark elf's hands.

Dyfar smirked. "I guess you are down to no friends."

A barely perceptible footfall from behind drew ZaphMordakai's attention. He spun into a descending staff from a familiar face. It cracked him in the head. "Myndar?" The force whirled his head around toward Dyfar.

Dyfar now stood within arm's reach. His skin had taken on a platinum hue. A forceful exhalation of steamy hot breath raced toward him with silvery motes dancing in the sun's rays.

ZaphMordakai hit the ground hard and lost consciousness.

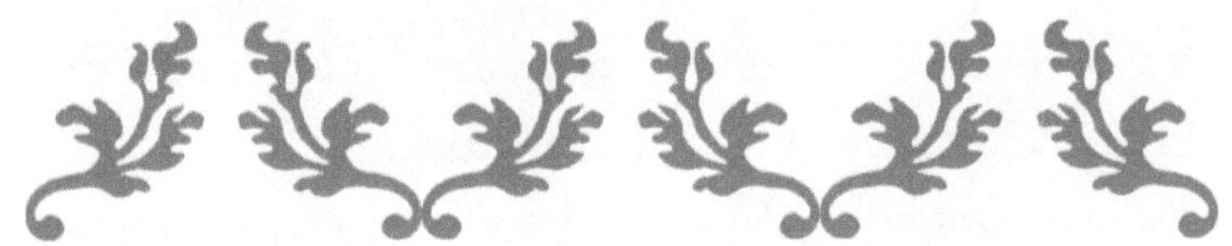

101

A Better View

Lykinnia

The velocity of Lykinnia's third loop decreased significantly, because she intentionally dragged her incorporeal feet to maximize her time before swinging to the back of the prisoner again.

Ledaedra stared in her direction as if sensing her.

"Lykinnia! You are in grave danger. It is time to leave," pleaded Solar.

You said to keep moving, and I am, albeit slowly. Her heart raced. How long had it been since she had seen her mother in person?

She knew exactly how long.

Four centuries, four hundred years, two thousand four hundred of Terazhan's Twilights. She missed four hundred lifeyear celebrations, well three hundred and ninety-nine. How special would my millennial lifeday be if both my mother and father could be there?

The radius of her arc never wavered, nor did her slow, monotonous pace, but she was already halfway to the front and center position.

"Lykinnia? Lykinnia!" Solar's voice sounded muffled and far away.

Her attention snapped back to Ledaedra. *What are you waiting for? Pull her head back. Four hundred years, five thousand six hundred months, since my mother's abode exploded in hell fire.*

Her hands were sweating as she arrived directly in front of the captive. Feeling a little warm, and parched in her mouth, she willed the demon to listen. *"Show me her face!"* Her palms were itching.

Ledaedra yanked on the twisted clump of hair, and the head rocked back, revealing a face.

Her own.

No. No! It cannot be. Father saw Mother's face. In her confusion, she came to a halt.

The sinister gleam in Ledaedra's eyes met hers, and the demon's nub shot forth, emitting hunter green waves of energy.

The undulating power struck Lykinnia like a tidal wave, pummeling her body. The bitter, iron taste of blood filled her mouth as she struggled to draw sufficient breath, to the point of hyperventilating.

Ledaedra released the prisoner's hair, pulled her black arm back and shot it forward with talons splayed. Another wave of black magic hurtled toward Lykinnia.

The impact was so forceful an audible *crunch* filled the air. Her body lurched forward, continuing its revolution around the prisoner, gaining speed with each passing second. A strange sensation of being held filled her with comfort.

"You are going to get us both killed," a voice whispered in her ear.

"Solar? I can barely breathe, and my hands are on fire," sobbed Lykinnia.

"My hands are burning too, but we have experienced this before. It will be okay if I can make the portal." Solar cleared his throat.

"I am sorry Solar. I wanted to see her." Lykinnia wept freely. She could feel the pace pick up yet again.

"I know Unie. I know. Hold on."

"The taste of blood in my mouth is overwhelming. I cannot—"

"Lykinnia?"

Her body went limp, and she lost consciousness.

102

Confrontation

Cymm

The wagon arrived at the base of the Peak of Power almost three weeks after it pulled through the gates of Norfolk. Cymm had traveled most of the way with the four guards and wagoneer, enjoying their company, but he was glad the journey was over.

The frequency and power of DraKarrion's nightmares, even in the waking hours, had grown since leaving the city. He could not afford to lose DragonSin as a watchdog while he slept, so he kept the sword close.

Cymm dismounted. "I can take it from here guys, and you can take the wagon back with you."

The guards followed suit. "Are you sure? We can help take it to the top. It's no problem."

Cymm nodded. "The people who live up there do not like strangers. It'll be easier if we part ways here."

While the men untied the ropes securing the dragon head, Cymm fished around in one of his saddlebags. He presented the four guards and wagoneer a gold coin each. "I want to thank you for your assistance and compensate you for your time away from your family."

"Thank you, Lord Reich," each said in turn.

Cymm endured the title with a half-smile." Travel safe." He waited until they had mounted and rode out of the small clearing before asking DragonSin to levitate it.

ꝏꝏꝏ

Cymm positioned the dragon head close to the platform. He sheathed his sword and glanced around, eager to see Lykinnia. "Anybody here?"

The sphinx brothers landed heavily on either side of him. Kamac roared. "Cymm, what are you doing here?"

Cymm's head flinched backward. "What are you talking about?"

Camak tucked his wings, his feline musculature taut and rippling. "Now is not a good time."

Cymm's stomach churned. "Why? What happened?"

Kamac stepped forward with another roar. "Leave now!"

Cymm drew his sword. "I will not leave until I see Lykinnia. If you try to stop me, I will cleave you in half."

"I have taught you well," came DraKarrion's raspy voice.

Camak bound over to stand shoulder to shoulder with his brother. "You can try, but you will die."

"What is going on here?" Solar tucked his wings slightly and landed between them. "Kamac?"

"Me?" Kamac bellowed. "You said no intruders, no visitors, no exceptions!"

"Cymm is not a visitor. Be gone and do your real job." Solar waved them away with a flick of his wrist.

Kamac snapped at the air in front of Solar and shot Cymm a sneer, then took flight with his brother in tow.

"Thank you," said Cymm.

Solar spun on him. "Do not thank me! What were you thinking? Drawing your weapon on an ally is unacceptable. You will—"

"They wouldn't let me see Lykinnia," interrupted Cymm.

"Your lack of maturity is shocking." Solar's arms and wings went up together.

Cymm followed suit and his hands shot up in the air. "What should I have done?"

Solar pointed at Cymm in anger. "Walked away. Asked to speak to me. Or prayed to Terazhan, who always answers you. Instead, you instigated a fight."

The anger drained from Cymm in an instant, leaving him weak in the knees. He collapsed, holding the sides of his head. "I don't feel right. The dragon from the sword is growing in power and haunting me more and more each day."

"Terazhan has everything he needs to repair the sword and release you from this burden. Never draw a weapon on our allies again. Understood?" Solar offered his hand to help Cymm rise.

Cymm nodded but rose on his own.

Solar sighed. "Do you want to leave the sword on the altar? It will be—" A glare from the paladin gave him the answer. Solar cleared his throat, and his face softened. "I do not know how to tell you this Cymm, but Lykinnia had an accident and has been in a coma for three weeks. Do you want to see her?"

Concern washed over his face. "Yes."

Solar placed his hand on the paladin's shoulder. "You must be strong for her. Maybe your voice will bring her comfort."

Cymm's voice croaked. "What happened?"

103

Fear

ZaphMordakai

ZaphMordakai had not eaten in almost three weeks. His captors seldomly provided liquids. When they did, it usually came in the form of sour wine. He examined the cave once again for anything to help him escape. BelCharius's carcass had been removed along with all the treasure. The only moveable objects remaining were the boulders they had used to construct the prisoner pen for the humans.

How ironic. Now I'm a captive in the same cave. ZaphMordakai, in dark elf form, rose to stretch his legs. He unconsciously rubbed his neck where the thick metallic collar chaffed him and irritated his scar. His captors had not been back to question him in days.

On the second day of captivity, he had had the brilliant idea of transforming back into a dragon and shattering the collar and shackles on his wrists and ankles. The metal was much stronger than it appeared, and he barely reversed the process before choking himself out and losing consciousness.

The chains ran into the wall as if the stone had formed around them. Magic was the only logical explanation. He rattled his restraints in frustration. "You will pay for this," he said to no one in particular.

"Not likely." Myndar chuckled, materializing from around the corner leading to the tunnel.

Dyfar followed behind him holding a small keg. "Are you ready to talk yet? We can drink this dryad dark while you explain the plan."

ZaphMordakai licked his dusty lips with his dry tongue. "I have no intention of telling you anything."

Dyfar's fake smile evaporated. "We are running out of time. Last chance before we move to more stringent measures."

The dark elf cast a derisive glance. "Torture? My tolerance for pain is exceptional."

Myndar disappeared up the tunnel with a nod from Dyfar.

Dyfar returned his attention to Zaph. "You misunderstood me. I have been watching you for quite some time. Torture might not work on you, but *fear* will."

The dark elf chuckled. "Fear? I fear no one and nothing."

"Liar." Dyfar glanced over his shoulder, then set the cask of wine and goblets on the cavern floor.

Myndar approached and set a small coffer down next to it.

Dyfar fixed his gaze on the dark elf and pointed at each object in turn. "Last chance, option one or option two."

ZaphMordakai was curious. "You think I'll be scared of the contents in the box?"

The smile on Dyfar's face was unsettling. "No, not scared—terrified."

Zaph put on his best amused face and longed to stroke his neck. *How could he possibly know?* He swallowed the lump in his throat. *Could it fit in that small box?*

104

The Dale

Hardre

It was difficult to keep track of time without a setting sun, and Hardre had given up trying long before the strangers came. The dwarf stood on an outcropping overlooking a dale below. A stream flowed through an old growth forest before entering the lowland between two hills, where it burbled in response to the boulders impeding its movement.

"You need to be wary of visitors. You should never have any," the second stranger had told him, which Hardre found humorous and hypocritical since the one giving the advice was a visitor.

TetraQuezar's wounds had healed nicely. Not even a scar remained.

Life had returned to the way it was . . . with a few exceptions. There was no longer a barrier blocking their movement and they could migrate when and where they wanted to, which helped with the second change. Every few days a dark cloud would settle over the surrounding area, and no matter how long they waited, it would not dissipate. In fact, the longer they waited, the darker it became.

After several moves, they came upon the dale below, with a magnificent view from both hilltops. They enjoyed the area immensely, and for the last few relocations, they had decided to rotate in a circular pattern to escape the shadow but remain in the area.

Hardre glanced back at TetraQuezar. "Come on, time for our daily walk."

The green dragon, now larger than a warhorse, bound over to him exuding energy. "Maybe we could head into the forest today?"

Hardre changed directions. "Sounds like fun." He rubbed his eyes and forehead. "By the nine hells, not again."

TetraQuezar followed his line of sight and croaked.

Hardre stepped in front of his friend and swallowed hard. "Don't worry, I will protect you." Then he called aloud, "What do you want?"

"It is good to be wary. I am here to repair your barrier as I committed to you before. I will be able to make a much larger sanctuary this time. Are you satisfied with this location?" asked the stranger.

"Yes, except for the shadow," replied Hardre.

A low growl rumbled in TetraQuezar's chest.

"A shadow? What do you mean?" asked the stranger.

Hardre waved his hand back over his shoulder. When he finally looked, it was gone. He scanned the horizon in every direction. "It was there a moment ago."

The visitor performed a midair somersault, rolling to his right as a massive greenish black dragon claw shimmered into view and raked the air where he had been.

The surrounding area reverberated with loud pops and snaps, and the attacking appendage disappeared.

Hardre glanced at his friend and found him staring.

Folding himself into a ball, the hovering man shot his arms and legs out wide. A burst of radiant light exploded in a spherical shape, revealing the outline of an enormous dragon. He struck with the element of surprise, sending gigantic bolts of lightning careening into his adversary.

A large amber shield appeared in the human's hand in time to block the descending, raking claw. Several more forked bolts rained down upon the dragon, and it yelped. The stranger showed no mercy and attacked again as the greenish black dragon retreated, then chased him until they were specks in the sky.

Hardre stood in shocked silence well into the aftermath, completely engrossed in the show. "I think we should get to the forest before they come back."

TetraQuezar did not reply but took three running strides and leapt into the air.

Hardre's feet were pounding the ground to keep up, but the stranger returned before they made it halfway to the tree line. "Leave us alone!"

The stranger's face screwed up in confusion. "I am not your enemy. I will restore your haven and rid you of the shadow."

TetraQuezar hissed at the traveler from behind the dwarf.

Hardre's hands found his hips. "What do you need from us?"

"Nothing. I will begin the process now with the dale below at the center." The stranger repositioned himself several hundred feet above the epicenter.

Thunder rumbled in the distance.

Hardre scanned the bright sky for clouds, but the sound was unmistakable as it reverberated through the area.

Fractures formed in the sky above, a symphony of eggshells cracking, running slowly at first toward both horizons. Chanting filtered through the broken heavens overshadowing every other sound. The acrid, putrid scent of rotting flesh permeated the air.

Hardre gagged multiple times and nearly vomited. When he recovered his stomach, he peeked up at the stranger and quickly shielded his eyes. The aura around the human had grown so bright, it was painful to behold. "By the seven heavens, and all that is good."

One final explosion knocked Hardre and TetraQuezar off their feet. In the seconds it took for them to sit back up, everything had been restored, including the peaceful silence.

Hardre waved goodbye, but the stranger was already gone.

105

Benefactor

ZaphMordakai

The ground shook. Dirt, debris, and small stones rained down upon them in their cavern home. A bestial roar echoed off the nearby mountains. ZaphMordakai had become accustomed to it.

"Zaphling, go outside and play with your brother and sister while I clean up in here," instructed his mother.

ZaphMordakai hesitated. His father had died twenty years ago, shortly after they had arrived in this world when he was only five lifeyears. Now, he clung to his momma. "I want to stay here, with you."

"You aren't a little wyrmling anymore. We need to prepare you for your future. Now, go outside like I asked. Your siblings are waiting for you." His mother nudged him toward the rear exit.

He crawled down the face of a short cliff and followed the stone trail a hundred yards to a circular area surrounded by boulders. His siblings rested against the far wall in their favorite spots. When he entered the ring, they perked up, as if rousing from a slumber.

Zaph strode into the center. "All you two ever do is sleep. Let's do something fun."

His brother, the bigger of his two siblings, was half his size. He rose on his hind legs with his snout twitching.

Zaph did not expect a response, neither of them ever talked much. "How about we practice shooting our lightning bolts at—"

"Zaphling!" came a voice from behind the boulders.

"Zaphling!" called a second voice, also on the other side of the rocks but further down.

ZaphMordakai turned and ran for the opening he had entered through.

A young red dragon only a couple of decades older than him, but twice his size blocked the exit. The other two dragons crawled over the boulders and perched on top of them.

"BrimStrakenstone, let me pass. My mother calls for me." Zaph lied.

"It is not you she calls for," sniggered Brim.

The other two chortled in response.

ZaphMordakai's eyes narrowed. "What's that supposed to mean?"

"Your momma has a twisted neck," a dragon behind him taunted.

"Her neck is so curled, squirrels use it for a fun slide," the other bully behind him said.

BrimStrakenstone stepped forward, staring into his eyes. "I think he's going to cry. You going to cry, little wyrmling?"

Zaph was on the verge of tears. He held them in check and stared back in defiance.

Brim's lip rose several inches on the right side of his snout. "Everyone knows your mother rubs necks with every captain and general hoping to secure you a high position in the Queen's Army."

ZaphMordakai rocketed forward, razor talons and fangs bearing down on the bully. The rock-hard scales deflected his claws, but his maw sunk into Brim's neck and blood washed over his tongue.

The red dragon shrieked in surprise and retreated. He quickly reversed directions and fell forward bringing his full girth down upon the black dragon.

Zaph lay there stunned, all the air forced from his lungs. The snapping, cracking noise could only be his ribs, but he felt no pain.

Brim rolled him over, facing his brother and sister, and lay on top of him. "I should kill you, but my papa would flay me. He says you inherited the crazy gene from your mother, and you will be a fierce warrior for the Queen. However, he never mentioned your friends."

"No!" Zaph croaked, squirming with the new reservoir of strength welling inside him.

The other two bullies slunk down from their perch to stand next to one sibling each.

Brim hooted. "That crazy drakaina has done a number on you. They aren't your family. They're not even dragons."

Tears streamed down Zaph's face. "Yes, they are."

The first to die was his brother. One talon slid slowly across his neck and blood gushed out.

Zaph went wild, flailing in a berserker-like frenzy, but he could not break free.

Brim bore down harder. "Have you ever seen dragon scales cut so easily?"

His sister suffered the same fate, and ZaphMordakai screeched in anguish.

BrimStrakenstone sent three gouts of flame into the air. "And now you have no friends once again."

The pack of three red dragons chortled and congratulated each other while Zaph lay on the ground blubbering.

An obstreperous death cry pierced the air, startling everyone, and drowning out Zaph's misery.

The black dragon seized the opportunity and lurched, toppling the already teetering Brim. His smoldering eyes drilled into Brim's as they squared off. Zaph spared a moment for a brief glance in the direction of his home.

Brim backed away and climbed up on the ring of boulders. "Zaph, don't go up there."

Zaph bound through the opening and rushed up the trail.

Brim flew over him. "ZaphMordakai, you crazy drake. Don't go up there!"

Zaph ignored him, scaled the short bluff, and slipped into the rear entrance of his home. While his eyes were adjusting to the dark, he bumped into the massive head of a black dragon. Its tongue lolled to the side collecting dirt from the floor. His heart skipped a beat until he realized the head was too big to be his mother's.

A low moan came from further inside the cavern, followed by his mother's struggling voice. "He has no father. Now you are required to raise him."

"Don't tell me the law, crooked neck!" the unfamiliar voice yelled, using the most disparaging phrase you could attach to a drakaina. "I came for the drake. You disgrace yourself and your family and poison his mind with weakness. No longer will he be the laughingstock of dragonkin."

ZaphMordakai had crept up behind them silently. An enormous black dragon towered over his mother. Then he noticed the deep lacerations across his mother's side and back, pumping blood onto the floor. "Momma."

Both heads swiveled toward him.

His mother's eyes rolled into the back of her eyelids momentarily. "Zaphling, you should be outside."

Zaph stared at the familiar monstrosity. "Did you hurt her?" The smirk gave him all the confirmation he needed. He attacked in a similar fashion to the assault he used on BrimStrakenstone. Not even a scratch appeared on the rugged scales of his forearm.

"You're braver than I thought. There are ancient dragons who don't have the guts to attack me." The large black dragon shook his arm and flung Zaph into the nearby wall as if he were a flea.

Zaph rose immediately and charged.

"ZaphMordakai!" yelled his mother.

His mother never used his formal name. It was enough to halt the young dragon.

"Come here," she continued. "I don't have much time left."

"No. You will be all right." Zaph was by his mother's side fawning over her.

"Not everyone has your tolerance for pain and injury. You got that from your father. Your Uncle DetonKonraber will raise you and teach you the way of a warrior."

"No. No. I don't want to leave you," Zaph whimpered.

"Shhh. Shhh. Listen. If you work hard, I know you can become a general in the Queen's Army." His mother's voice was losing strength.

"I don't want to join the army." Tears poured down his face.

"Hush." Her raspy voice transitioned to a whisper. "Zaphling, make your momma proud. Work hard and learn . . ."

"Momma? Momma!" He shot a death glare at the larger dragon. "I will kill you!"

"We don't have time for your fantasies, or the Queen's army. It's time to go," replied DetonKonraber.

Zaph bolted for the rear exit. A tunnel he knew was too small for the massive black dragon.

"ZaphMordakai, come back here now!" raged the older dragon.

Zaph nimbly raced out the back and down the path, intending to maneuver around the ring of boulders and launch himself into the air. He took one last glance around for his siblings. Their bodies were gone. Time was of the essence, but he veered into the ring, coming to rest before an incomprehensible sight.

An enraged roar echoed off the mountain tops.

Chained to the boulders—where his siblings had been—were two rabbits. Each one had its throat slit, and a small pool of blood had soaked the ground.

DetonKonraber landed heavily behind him. Without a word, he approached and latched a silver collar with a bright blue sapphire around his neck. It instantly adjusted to fit. "I had hoped not to use the collar, but you leave me no choice. Let's go."

A wave of ice-cold agony pierced his body like a hundred needles, and Zaph scratched at his neck to relieve the pain. Something he had never felt before.

106

Attenuation

Cymm

The Rights of Melding and the creation of DragonSin had been completed almost seven months earlier with a dragon head the size of a cantaloupe. This version of the process also resulted in the explosion of the rotting head, but it was the size of his warhorse.

Cymm's arms hung diagonally from his sides, dripping with blood, facial fragments, and fetid flesh. "I need a bath."

Solar shook his head. "Sit before you pass out. You are in desperate need of healing."

Pain replaced the subsiding adrenaline rush. Cymm palpated his face and quickly withdrew his hands. His nose had been nearly ripped off and two huge gashes in his cheek and forehead were the sources of greatest pain. The flying bone shards had also sliced his arms and legs, but fortunately, his elven chainmail had protected his torso.

"Solar . . ." Cymm swooned.

The winged man lunged forward to catch and gently lower him. He cast multiple healing spells in succession.

The light-headed feeling subsided, and Cymm sat up on his own.

"I will be conjuring containers of water to clean the altar and platform. I suggest you use one to clean yourself before you take a bath. If Lykinnia wakes to find bone and chunks of flesh in her springs, I will have wasted my time healing you." Solar set about his task.

Cymm sighed and nodded. He would welcome a good tongue lashing if it meant Lykinnia was awake and all right.

107

Progeny

ZaphMordakai

Dyfar gently kicked the keg then the coffer, bringing ZaphMordakai out of his reverie. His foot stopped on the coffer. "You already know what's in here. I can see it on your face."

The image of the two rabbits with slit throats faded slowly from his mind's eye. *How could momma have tricked me for so long? I never had a brother or a sister, only a mother who liked to cast spells on wild animals.* Zaph ignored his captors.

Myndar unlocked the coffer, flicked the latches, then peered up at Dyfar, who nodded. He flipped the lid open and even in the dismal light, the blue sapphire emitted a brilliant sparkle.

ZaphMordakai's lip quivered. *The collar. How? How did he know?* The answer came to him at once. *Uncle DetonKonraber. This is how he retaliates for me joining the Queen's Army.* "My grandsire gave it to you, but my attachment to it ended when I joined with the Queen," replied Zaph calmly.

"DetonKonraber the Devastation thought otherwise. It is hard to argue with the largest black dragon to have ever lived. But he did not give it to us. We waited until he left his lair and stole it." Dyfar knelt to admire it before hoisting it into the air. He approached the dark elf with it raised high, as if it were a crown. "Let's see who is right."

ZaphMordakai recoiled involuntarily and received a smirk in return from both his captors. His mind swirled as several thoughts stormed through his head. For fifty years, he had endured torture and brutal punishment disguised as lessons to make him tough. "Your momma has made you weak and pathetic," was his uncle's favorite saying.

The mental abuse was much worse, and more difficult to handle than the physical pain. On one occasion, he had held his arm down and threatened to slice off his talons a digit at a time. He cried, sobbed, and begged until finally Uncle Deton had released him, only to grab his arm moments later and slice his entire paw off. Zaph had wailed while staring at his nub with wide eyes. His uncle had chortled, enjoying his misery, then placed his own paw on the chopping stone and lopped off two talons. He had said, "My sire line has salamander blood in it, and your paw will eventually grow back." It took over a month to regenerate an identical replacement.

Dyfar was only a few steps away, and Zaph's thoughts turned to his mother. *She sacrificed everything for me, her sanity, her reputation, even her life. I thought of her death every single day I wore that infernal collar.* Her final words, "Make your momma proud," had become a mantra for him, especially in his darkest days.

Dyfar fumbled with the latch.

The scar on Zaph's neck prickled. "Wait." Although the collar somehow delivered an intense pain to him, he could endure it. His biggest fear was having DetonKonraber back in his life. The choker would instantly deliver its payload, but more terrifying, it would provide a clear signal to his whereabouts. A beacon to track. There would be nowhere to hide, and his lack of a lair would no longer matter. The grandsire of the family line would come to collect him, even though he had released him three hundred years ago when he feared the order of the Queen. However, his recent successful refusal to join the army had made him bold. DetonKonraber would come to finish his training.

Beads of sweat dotted ZaphMordakai's brow. He angled the crown of his head as far from the collar as possible. "My throat is a little parched."

Dyfar retracted the collar with a sinister smile. "Let us begin with a simple question. Why does Ledaedra want the royal children?"

"Not a simple question, and not even the right question. I will take that drink now."

Dyfar returned the collar to the coffer, propping it against the back lid to be clearly visible. Myndar was already pouring the wine.

ZaphMordakai licked his lips. *They have no clue what is going on. Ledaedra will kill me if she finds out I spoke, but DetonKonraber will make me wish I were dead, and the collar will guarantee he finds me.*

He accepted the goblet and hoisted it toward his captors, then continued to his mouth, taking two large gulps. "Ahh. Delightful. Some of the royal families are affected by Ledaedra's plan, but most of them are not." Interspersing much smaller sips, he continued. "Did you know the King of Norfolk isn't the father of Jenaleya?" The dark elf paused and examined the beauty of his drinking vessel. "But the Queen is the mother."

Dyfar's hands flew in wide circles. "I don't believe this."

Myndar rushed forward with his finger wagging. "You are a liar!"

Zaph saw his captor glance at the collar, and he swallowed the lump in his throat. "Wait! Jakarrak claims he beguiled the Queen of Norfolk in the form of her husband, while the King was occupied. So, The Trickster is the father."

Myndar drummed his fingers on his own forehead. "It does sound like something the God of Mischief would do."

"What proof do you have?" asked Dyfar.

"None. You didn't ask for proof. You asked why Ledaedra wanted Jenaleya. Do you want me to continue, or shall we debate the validity of my story?"

Dyfar's eyes narrowed. "Continue."

ZaphMordakai let the wine dance across his tongue. "In fact, several of the demi-gods have had children with mortals. The Dragon Queen calls them Descendants of Twilight. The most prolific is Jakarrak with four. Hymnoch has produced two, and Marekai one. Terazhan had two children, but only one survived: Lykinnia. She is the key to the next step in Ledaedra's plan."

108

Selection

Semper

Semper had lost track of time. It had been at least three weeks since they had been captured without bloodshed while they were asleep in Karaz's shop. Their party of five had been reprimanded to the dungeons of Delge immediately.

As they were being processed at the entry to the mines, a guard had poked Semper. "What about this one?"

"Meh. Move him over here away from the warriors," replied the captain.

Semper remembered his face burning red hot. "I am more of a warrior than you'll ever be."

"If he wants to fight in the arena, let him." The captain moved down the line continuing his inspection. Ibor was separated from the group.

Semper gave Ibor the eye and motioned for him to join them. Their guide hesitantly shook his head with wide eyes. Semper had insisted with an angry face and a finger pointed at the floor next to his boot.

Brogan shifted his position, and the chains around his ankles rattled in response, bringing Semper out of his self-reflection. "I'd rather be mining."

Semper elbowed him light-heartedly. "If they hadn't removed my magic ring from your finger, you would be. This is much better."

"No, it isn't. You've never seen Bardonril's Progression. It's brutal. Few survive." Brogan glanced over Semper's shoulder at the arriving guards.

Bardur rose to his feet, rolling his shoulders to loosen them. "He's right, Semper. You were foolish; Ibor had it right. He will live to fight against the evils of the Dungeon."

Dregur also stood. "Hold on. The winners are hailed as local heroes, and stand among the mages, clerics, and officers as they receive their accommodations at the Carnival of Progression."

"And the assassins, or administrators, receive their promotions too. Don't get your hopes up. It is unlikely we will be participating this year." Brogan remained in an unpleasant mood.

Semper finally rose. "This event is new to me. It was never celebrated before I left Delge."

"Roughly fifty years ago, the King of Delge decided to honor the dwarven mages graduating each year from the University of Mystics. This year there will be eight, the most ever. The parade commences when they arrive from the City of Mystics at the gates and ends at the arena. Bardonril's Progression commences immediately, and there is always a surprise."

Everyone nodded in agreement with Brogan's comments, except Semper, who simply sighed.

109

Choices

Cymm

There had been no change in Lykinnia's condition since Cymm arrived. His concern grew by the hour. Solar had eventually told the story about the latest encounter with Dego, and how Semper and some of the crew had entered Delge and made it to a dwarven silversmith shop. Solar had lost track of them as a result of Lykinnia's accident and the overheating of the altar.

Late in the afternoon on the third day, Solar entered Lykinnia's abode in a huff. "Cymm, I found them."

Cymm was half dozing by her bedside. "What?"

"Semper and his friends. They are in the dungeons, but not where I expected. Most of them were moved to the training pits below the arena. It seems like a major battle is looming." Solar inspected Lykinnia's face. "Cymm, there is nothing you can do here. You should go and help your friends."

Cymm's face tightened in painful consternation. "I want to be here when she wakes. It doesn't seem like they are in immediate danger."

Solar fluffed her pillow and tucked her in. "Terazhan is fervently searching for a cure, but he is uncertain how long it will take. If anything happens to your friends, you will never forgive yourself."

Cymm stood and sighed. "I don't know." But he was already walking toward the door and his horse. "When she awakens, I want you to promise me the three of you will find a way to destroy the dragons."

Solar's face registered surprise. "It would appear our goals have aligned once again."

110

A Lesson

Semper

"Swing like you mean it!" Brogan yelled.

Semper gave a feint left and swung again at his practice partner, knocking him to the ground. Semper extended his hand to help him up.

Brogan grabbed his arm roughly and pulled him to the side. "Don't get too friendly with him."

"Why?" asked Semper.

"Because . . . if there are too many of us left at the end, we will have to kill each other." Dregur frowned.

"What? You're kidding, right?" asked an exasperated Semper.

"No. Now let's get to work." Brogan's sword arced in high toward Semper's head.

Semper blocked it with a growl and a stinging in his hands and arms. "These wooden swords are too light. The ones I had made to train Cymm and—"

Bardur smacked Semper on the hamstring with his wooden sword. "Does that feel light?"

"Oww!" Semper swung in blind rage at his attacker, who ducked under it.

Dregur came around behind him, hitting him with the broadside of the sword across the back. "How about that?"

Semper drew upon his many years with the humans, fighting against his dwarven temper. With a heaving chest, he asked, "Why are you ganging up on me?"

"You are the weak link," replied Brogan.

"Nah." Semper noticed the other two dwarves nodding in agreement. The numbing, draining feeling ran through his body. The wooden sword clattered to the stone floor; his hand too weak to hold it. He walked to the nearest wall, put his back against it, and slid to a seated position. *I am not the weakest link. I have been through tough situations before. It takes more than strength and skill with a sword.*

"I told you it wouldn't work," an angry Bardur whispered.

"Semper, get your ass over here! We need to train before they arrive," yelled Brogan.

My mind is more resilient than most. Semper wrung his hands with a bowed head. *They want to give me a lesson?* "What's the use? We're all going to die anyway, like you said."

Dregur and Bardur cast the big man a disapproving glare.

Brogan groaned, then growled, "Fine. Yes, I said it, when I was feeling sorry for myself, but I have no intention of dying. How about you?"

With a sorrowful voice and slumped shoulders, Semper said, "What can I do? I'm the weak link."

Brogan drew within arm's length, knelt on one knee, and placed his hand on Semper's shoulder. "Come on, I—"

Semper could not contain his smirk any longer. His head shifted back to a normal position, and he locked eyes with Brogan. "I may have the least fighting experience, but you are the chink in the armor mentally. Two hours ago, everybody dies, now everybody lives. Which is it?"

Brogan remained motionless for several seconds, then lunged for him with a growl.

Semper scampered away. "Now, it's time for a hug?" He picked up his discarded sword.

Brogan charged.

Semper's eyes widened. *By the nine hells.* The tension in his shoulders subsided when the glimmer of a smirk registered on the big man's face. He easily side-stepped the lumbering charge and smacked him on the belly with the sword.

Brogan pulled up short. "Oww!"

Semper smacked him on the ass.

"You're dead." Brogan lurched to grab him.

ꝏꝏꝏ

Metallic hammering filled the air. "Everyone up! Come on you lazy half-orcs, get in line. The neophyte wizards return."

Many of the dwarven guards guffawed at the disrespectful terms being used.

The midday meal had only finished an hour ago. More food had been brought in than usual, and everyone had eaten well.

Brogan stretched like a giant bear. "That was the last meal you will get until the event is over."

"Which is?" asked Semper.

"Could be two hours or two days. One year they brought in a basilisk for the second battle and turned every remaining warrior to stone in less than ten minutes. Bardonril's Progression ended in less than one hour," said Bardur.

"I remember. There was rioting for days, until the King distributed hundreds of ale kegs, placing them in every square to calm the commoners," added Dregur.

Bardur waved them over in a bluster. "Come on. The first in line gets their choice of armor and weapons."

Brogan lurched toward the exit. Even the guards did not stand in his way.

The twenty would-be-gladiators solemnly walked as they were escorted to the armory. All shackles and chains were removed before the iron gate to the room was closed and secured, locking them in the chamber.

Brogan secured four swords, the best of the bunch, while the others strapped on mismatched armor.

Semper approached the big man, fully clad, holding an extra pair of gauntlets. "Here. Try these on. They might fit."

Brogan squeezed a massive hand inside the first one. "Almost. If the fingers were a little longer."

"Snap the ends off," Semper said in jest.

"What a great idea." Brogan removed the glove and easily popped one off at the first joint.

Semper's eyes went wide. "Wow."

Dregur arrived at his shoulder, holding an extra set of bracers, and Bardur raced over excitedly holding a set of studded leather.

"Hey, that's my armor." Brogan ripped it out of his hands.

"I thought so. It was at the bottom of the pile," replied Bardur.

A commotion at the iron gate interrupted their celebration.

"We were told not to open this door for any re—" The guard speaking was thrown into the wall.

"Open this door now," came the commanding voice of an unseen speaker.

Another guard crashed into the gate, the iron bars pressing deep into his face. "Okay. Okay." He was released and the jangling of keys commenced immediately. The gate swung open.

Dregur whispered, "This can't be good."

Other warriors shared the same sentiment. Several took defensive postures.

Five more dwarves strode into the holding cell with matching black armor and a swagger. Three of them were armed with swords and shields, another had a warhammer. The apparent leader sauntered in last, carrying a black metal mace and had a seven headed scourge strapped to his hip.

The same commanding voice as before said, "We are here to fight with you, not against you. Besides, it looks like you could use the help."

Dregur issued a low growl and stepped forward.

Bardur quickly horse-collared him. "Don't."

Brogan whispered, "Watch your backs in there. I don't think they are here to help."

Semper gasped at a loss for words while pointing at a dwarf.

The dwarf was the shortest of the five, had a full shield helmet on, and carried a warhammer. Semper's warhammer.

Dregur growled louder and pulled against Bardur's restraining grasp. "Thief!"

The leader of the newcomers brandished his mace, the head of it turning red with an intense heat. "If you can't control your dog, I will. Let him go."

Dregur was foaming at the mouth like a rabid dog, inciting laughter among the other contestants.

Brogan placed his meaty hand on Dregur's chest. "Not now." Then in a low voice, "We will deal with them in the arena."

Dregur was not placated. He had almost broken free when a metallic latch released. A loud grinding, screeching noise echoed in the nearby arena and into their chamber. Everyone froze.

"It's time!" one of the guards yelled from behind the closed gate. "Enter the arena." He pointed toward two tunnels leading from their current chamber in the opposite direction from where they entered.

No one moved.

"Let's go weaklings," ordered the dwarf wielding the mace while locking his eyes on Dregur and fondling the scourge with a sinister smile.

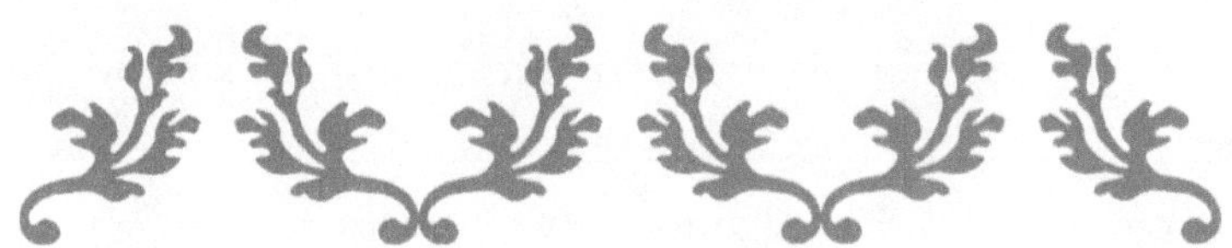

111

Ash Worm

Lykinnia

Lykinnia glanced unconsciously over her shoulder at Ledaedra, even though every movement and sound she had made the past five days had gone unnoticed. She had flown through Ledaedra, blown in her ear, and screamed in her face, but nothing garnered a reaction. Thinking the monster was playing a trick on her, she sought out other denizens of the Plane of Ashes. They too could not sense her presence.

She focused her attention back on the prisoner. The one she believed was her mother. The one who had possessed Lykinnia's face. Had she though—possessed her face? Everyone had always said she looked like her mother. It had been quick and stressful. Maybe she was mistaken or Ledaedra was playing a mind game on her. How could she have seen something so different from her father?

Her frustration was mounting. She ducked under the long cascading locks of hair and stared at the prisoner's face. In the dim light,

Lykinnia could not be certain of anything. It could have been her mother, herself, or any other beautiful woman. This made her giggle.

With a sigh, she moved back to her original vantage point and scrutinized the female captive. "Assuming you are my mother, your robes are a little soiled. You need to change them immediately, young lady. Unfortunately for you, my humor does not get any better than this."

Lykinnia continued her charade. "Now, where was I? Oh yes, your hair needs to be brushed and cut, you need a bath, your fingernails are as long as daggers, and when was the last time you practiced the lute?"

She decided at that moment to believe it was her mother and silently gazed at her for an indeterminable amount of time. "I wish I could see your eyes. Having faith you were alive without proof was mentally taxing, but being this close to you and incapable of touching you is torture."

Lykinnia searched the rest of her mother's body for the hundredth time, finding nothing new. The skin on Sendaria's hands and wrists was the only exposed area. The restraining chains ran up her sleeves and the hem of her robes to manacles she presumed.

Movement in her peripheral vision drew her attention. She turned her head. Nothing moved. She drifted closer to the rocky knoll where it had originated and waited. A round nub poked above the horizon. She had discovered several ash worms as thick as her leg and longer than she was tall. This was probably another one.

She floated higher into the air to investigate and noticed a deep depression behind a partially buried boulder. With each passing second, more of the hollow was revealed including the man hiding inside it.

Solar had arrived.

112

Arena

Semper

The roar of the crowd assaulted his ears before they exited the corridor. Semper took one step out of the tunnel and paused, awestruck. When he left Delge many years ago, this had been a massive natural cavern. Now, it was a reworked monolith. The walls surrounding them were twenty-five feet high and built to keep the spectators safely removed from the action. Nine other entrances, evenly spaced around the perimeter, were the only breaks in the otherwise perfectly smooth wall.

Semper shook his head in wonder as thousands of excited faces screamed down at them.

"Keep moving." Brogan lightly pushed him toward the closest side wall.

Standing high above the coliseum floor, a dwarf dressed in regal attire struck an enormous gong. The crowd went wild. He hit it two more times and the tumult did not abate.

The King arrived with his entourage, including the eight mages to be honored, on the viewing platform and patted the air to settle the crowd, but the clamor reached a new crescendo.

Dregur chuckled for the first time in a while. "They don't want to hear your lying mouth, *king*."

The King of the Dwarves waved his hand at the crowd in frustration, while turning his back on them.

The Hearth Council arrived next, temporarily silencing the mob. Another loud metallic snap rang through the air. The rattle and clatter of gears and chains commenced, and the turmoil returned with a vengeance.

Twenty-five heads in the arena turned toward the rising portcullis under the King's platform. Every combatant braced himself. Before the gate had lifted halfway, another latch released, and an additional portcullis lifted off the ground.

Semper noted the glance Dregur and Balduer exchanged, and realized this was unusual.

Scores of orcs came pouring out of the first opening, howling and hooting. They too wore helms and pauldrons, jerkins and bracers, in addition to the swords they carried. Without hesitation they charged their mostly dwarven opponents. A thunderous clash of metal on metal mixed with grunts, groans, and screams of pain followed.

The orcs already outnumbered them two to one in the arena, when the boisterous roar of their second, unseen enemy rolled across the battlefield.

Semper's attention shifted to the second tunnel when six large ogres exited and joined the fray. *And this is only the first battle. Terazhan help us!* A sword slipped through his distracted defense and clanged against his helm. He stumbled backward, his ears ringing, then lunged forward, impaling the orc who hit him.

Bodies hit the ground all around him, some never to rise again, others scrambled back to their feet immediately. Brogan and the ogres towered above the sea of chaos, and Dregur's boisterous voice rang out above the din.

Semper detected movement behind him and spun, coming face-to-face with the black-armored dwarf carrying his warhammer. They stared at each other. The thief's eyes were barely visible through the narrow slits, but when his gaze shifted to the weapon, his nemesis charged. He raised his sword to block the descending hammer and braced himself for an impact that never came.

His opponent leaped past him and sunk the warhammer into the face of an orc intent on attacking Semper from behind, saving his life.

Confused, Semper whirled back around to find his next target and realized he was surrounded by the black-armored company. Fortunately, two ogres currently had their attention, so Semper slid toward the distant Brogan until a third ogre blocked his path.

The last time he fought an ogre he spent days in a coma, until his brother arrived to heal him. Hardre would not be able to save him this time. Semper barely dodged the wooden club and it cracked against the stone floor. He rolled forward, sprang to his feet, and opened a gash on the ogre's thigh. He tried to retreat out of the ogre's reach, but a second ogre fell at his feet, trapping him.

The black-armored leader smashed the head of the fallen ogre with one swing of his red-hot mace. The ogre's blood smoked and sizzled on the crown of the weapon and left charred flesh behind from its impact.

Semper's back pressed against the side of the corpse, and he ducked under the swing of the beast he was fighting. The ogre then tried reaching down to grab him.

A black mass flew by in a blur. It was the mace wielding leader, launching himself off the dead body. His mace hit the ogre attacking Semper in the head so hard, its eyeball flew out, and a second ogre's body hit the floor. Semper squatted next to the first body to avoid getting smothered.

"Thank you." Semper watched his rescuer jump down next to him.

The mace wielder scanned the battlefield. "Where is he?" A shadow of insanity passed over his face.

The dwarf with his warhammer arrived at his leader's shoulder instantly.

Semper straightened his posture and searched the perimeter. He sighed in content; his friend was out of sight. *Dregur, you picked the wrong enemy this ti—*

The leader kicked him in the chest, blasting the air from his lungs. "Where is he?" he screamed.

"I don't—know," Semper gasped, leaning heavily against the dead ogres.

The leader took a menacing step forward, then his eyes were drawn up above Semper's head.

Semper's gaze followed his, landing on another ogre looming behind him. He quickly refocused on the leader's face as the bloodlust returned. His gaze shifted to the dwarf with the warhammer, and he backed into the makeshift tunnel formed by the last ogre body lying crisscrossed with the first. He scurried to the other side, sliced the ogre's calf on the way by, and ran toward Brogan. So many bodies blocked his path, he found himself weaving and leaping to advance forward.

Brogan had three orcs surrounding him, and Semper barreled into the closest, knocking it to the ground. He rammed his sword down into its neck and withdrew it when frothy blood bubbles appeared on its lips. Semper fell in line next to the big man. "Have you seen Dregur?"

Brogan's sword arced high and fast, decapitating an orc. "No. Why?"

The remaining orc lunged at Brogan's exposed side.

Semper parried the attack, and countered, scoring a minor wound to its arm. "His new *friend* is looking for him. We should try to regroup."

Brogan kicked the orc in the midsection, knocking him to his back, then finished him off with one thrust. “Good idea. I’m sure he is with Balduer.” Brogan turned in a circle, searching. “This way.”

A well-organized group of orcs barred their way.

Semper pulled up short next to Brogan and glanced back over his shoulder. “By the nine hells, we got company.”

Before Brogan could comprehend the source of his frustration, the black-armor brigade barreled past them and collided with the orcs.

Brogan and Semper skirted the outside of the battle, barely helping.

Semper noticed one of the black-armor warriors was missing. His attention shifted to a staggering Balduer, surrounded by an arc of dead bodies. It looked like Balduer was about to join them. Two orcs pressed their advantage, unaware Brogan was bearing down on them. He swept them away like the undertow of a current, and Balduer collapsed to one knee, straining to catch his breath. Semper patted him on the shoulder, then took a defensive position next to him. “Where’s Dregur?”

Balduer shook his head slowly and shrugged.

Semper took stock of the waning combat. The company of black armor had made short work of the eight orcs. The few remaining orcs were slain throughout the arena and every ogre had been dispatched, but the gladiators had paid a hefty price for this success. Gravitating slowly toward Brogan and Semper were the surviving warriors, including the black-armored dwarves.

Semper shot Balduer a non-verbal warning.

Balduer rose immediately and headed in the opposite direction.

The leader wielding the mace stared at Semper. “Where is your friend?”

Brogan rested his sword up on his shoulder and puffed his chest. “What is your problem?”

The leader shot Brogan daggers of disdain, then shifted his gaze back to Semper. "Why isn't your friend here?"

Semper quickly glanced over his shoulder and located Balduer frantically searching through the bodies for Dregur.

Brogan leaned in threateningly. "We have a couple of battles to fight, then you can try to settle your petty score."

The leader's nose flared, and his eyes radiated hate. "I wasn't talking to you."

"Brogan, I need your help!" yelled Balduer.

Other gladiators were forming small groups in the vicinity, trying to catch their breath.

Brogan gave one long, baleful gaze at the leader, then took off running.

"I am only going to ask you one more time. Where is your friend?" The leader stared at Semper, slowly twirling his glowing red mace.

The crowd's bloodlust had been temporarily satiated and the lull in the cacophony became obvious when the next latch released. The metal *snap* startled Semper and others, causing them to flinch in response.

The portcullis was rising.

113

Plane of Ashes

Lykinnia

Solar had not moved for over an hour, except for his intermittent head bobbing. Lykinnia could not determine his motive, but she had nothing else to do, so she continued to watch him. Finally, he stirred, popping his head up over the rim.

A golden sun rose on the horizon, directly opposite Solar's position, a stark contrast to the constantly dismal gray sky. The brightness and size grew rapidly causing Ledaedra's chanting to cease.

The Dragon Queen stepped through the ebony altar as if she were made of smoke, positioning herself between it and the light. "What in the seven heavens is that?"

Lykinnia had the same question and glided over next to Ledaedra. She glanced down at the monster's missing arm and felt grim satisfaction. Her smirk dissipated. The golden ball was not a sun, and floating at its epicenter was her father. "No. You said you were not strong enough to fight her. What are you doing?"

"You dare challenge me on my own plane? In front of my own altar?" Ledaedra cackled wildly.

Terazhan shrugged and spoke slowly, "I do not wish to fight you. I came only to collect my brother and my wife."

Ledaedra's haunting laugh bellowed forth. "You fool. You think I am going to give them to you?"

Terazhan remained at a distance. "No. I wish to negotiate or even barter if—"

"You have nothing I want or need!" she replied sharply.

"Nothing?" Terazhan glided toward the female prisoner. "My wife is a mere mortal, and of little value to you. There must be some arrangement we could come to."

Ledaedra shifted her position to keep herself between Terazhan and the altar. "You sentimental fool. She does not want to leave with you."

Solar raced toward Ledaedra's back.

If Lykinnia had a material heart, it would have been pounding in her chest. "No. What are you doing?"

Terazhan continued drawing Ledaedra, rotating her body toward the captive he believed was Sendaria. "How do you know?"

Ledaedra snorted. "I know."

Lykinnia hovered over the altar, marveling at Solar's audacity, even as he stopped charging and worked the knots on Uncle Jakarrak's restraints.

"Would you mind waking her? I would like to ask her myself."

"This is never going to work." Lykinnia glanced back in her father's direction.

"Your negotiation skills are horrendous. You insinuate I'm a liar, and now you expect me to let you speak with her?" Ledaedra knelt next to the prisoner.

"Hurry Solar, while she is distracted." She moved closer to her guardian. "But how will you get my mother?"

Terazhan cleared his throat. "If I can speak with her, and she is willing to come with me, I will give you my phylactery."

"What?" asked Ledaedra.

"What!" Tears streamed down Lykinnia's face. Without his phylactery he would die within a decade, if not sooner.

Terazhan showed Ledaedra his empty palms. "This is not a unicorn, but I think you will like it."

Lykinnia's nose wrinkled. "What did he say?" It was a common phrase her father used before he introduced his favorite magic trick. Lykinnia visually tracked Solar. Even though he carried Uncle Jakarrak, he was already hundreds of feet away and moving rapidly.

"You *can* wake her, right?" asked Terazhan.

"This is one big ruse. I should be following Solar." Lykinnia slowly drifted in Solar's direction while battling her indecision.

"I can wake her . . ." Ledaedra slid one sleeve of the captive's robe up. The chains embedded in the crook of her elbow. "The chains go in one arm, through her chest, and out the other arm." Ledaedra smiled wickedly.

Lykinnia wanted to scream until she ran out of breath. They could not save her mother, not now. Ledaedra was playing games with her father, the same games that had been played with her. She raced after Solar. "She has no intention of waking her." Lykinnia growled in frustration. "Please Father, this one time, think with your head and not your heart."

Solar had been a speck in the skyline, but as an unencumbered ghostly form, Lykinnia was gaining fast. As she drew closer, she discovered they were heading toward another mark in the sky, a portal.

A shriek of death reverberated through the air, surrounding them. Lykinnia intuitively knew the source—Ledaedra. The ominous howling droned on incessantly.

Her father materialized in front of them, and Solar and Lykinnia plowed into him. They all piled through the gateway and fell to the ground.

Lykinnia rolled to her back and pushed herself up on her elbows, searching the portal for movement. Ledaedra's big red head streaked toward them, wailing like a banshee.

With a quick wave of Terazhan's hand, the doorway closed.

114

Bone Spikes

Semper

Before the portcullis found its apex, creatures swarmed out of the opening. At first Semper thought they were human, given they possessed the head and torso of one. Upon closer inspection, their pallid skin was pulled tight over prominent cheekbones creating a permanent snarl. Dozens of long needlelike teeth protruded from their mouth, and shoulder-length, jet-black hair framed their faces. The naked humanoid torso was attached to the body of a black widow spider and stood over six feet tall.

Eleven gladiators formed an arc and prepared to receive the eight monstrosities charging them. The boney spikes protruding from the ends of its eight legs scraped on the stone as they moved.

The skittering intensified as they ran and sent a shiver down Semper's spine. A dwarf pushed up next to him, giving him a start. "Dregur, you should be resting."

Dregur shrugged. "No need. He healed me."

Semper craned his neck, trying to find out more, when the enemy smashed into their line, now twelve strong. They leaped from sixty feet away and descended upon the warriors, using their legs as spears. Three dwarves fell immediately, and the line of defense was broken. Among the fallen were Balduer and a black-armored dwarf.

The bloated abdomens of the spider creatures had a tough, chitin-like shell, but Brogan's powerful swing cleaved into one, and it exploded. A black ichor flew ten feet in every direction, saturating the big man and the dwarf on either side.

Two more creatures burst apart near the black company, followed by their cursing and swearing. The innards of the creatures not only smelled horrendous but created an exceptionally slick surface on the stone. A dwarf two positions from him keeled over, moments before Semper collapsed with a spider leg speared through his chest.

He rolled side to side to avoid being impaled by the other seven legs. A second one pierced his stomach, and a third penetrated his neck. He lay prone on his back, waiting for the next assault, gurgling in his own blood, when Dregur's sword ripped through its body. The spider thing stiffened, and its human half slid to the floor.

Semper closed his eyes, knowing death was at hand, and accepted his fate.

He was tired. Tired of fighting. Tired of caring. Maybe sleep would be a welcomed reward.

A gentle voice whispered below the din of the raging battle. It was soft, gentle, and mostly unintelligible, except for the name of Terazhan. His eyes popped open. Golden snowflakes fell in lazy patterns from the ceiling. A flake struck his nose, and a tingle radiated through his body. More flakes struck, and like an avalanche, a wave of energy built then surged through his entire being. The spider leg through his lower abdomen remained inside him, while the others had separated when the spider fell. He forcefully extracted the spear before the last of the golden snowflakes disappeared.

Other warriors rose as well, but not all. The healing precipitation had been too late for some. In contrast, the golden flakes striking the four remaining monsters caused a searing hiss. The spider creatures shrieked in pain and horror, immediately evacuating the area. Red angry welts appeared on their human skin and small puffs of smoke drifted up from them.

The black-armored leader charged after the monsters, howling and screaming. He pulled up abruptly when his armor and exposed skin began to smoke. He scanned the standing dwarves and Brogan. His gaze came back to one of his own, the dwarf holding Semper's warhammer. "Did you do this?" He withdrew to the edge of the flake zone, waiting, seething, ignorant of the fact he had turned his back on the spiders.

He stepped forward as the last flake descended, and a sinister smile bloomed upon his face. Two spider legs erupted from his chest, then three more. His eyes went wide before he gritted his teeth and snarled.

Semper stared in mute horror as the black-armored-leader's face liquified along with the rest of his body. It swirled around his orifices like miniature whirlpools. The downdrafts sucked hair, skin, flesh, and finally bone into each vortex. Within seconds, he turned himself inside out, and now stood facing his attackers.

The crowd went insane, screaming, yelling, and stomping.

The deafening noise rang Semper's ears, and he was tempted to cover them.

One of the spider creatures roared and spit in the leader's face before his red-hot mace caved the side of its head in. Another leg speared through his chest. He could not get at the second attacker, and after multiple failed swings launched into a berserker-like frenzy.

The remaining two monsters had fought less aggressively up until now as they stalked in. This time the gladiators were ready and fanned out to envelope their opponents.

The leader's mace swung furiously at the legs of the dead spider, and finally kicked the dismembered body away. Then he returned his attention to his second attacker.

Semper, Brogan, and the others hacked, slashed, ducked and dodged, working together to slay the two monstrosities they had surrounded. Dregur cleaved two adjacent legs off the beast in front of him, and Balduer raced in to finish it. A spear penetrated the muscle between his chest and shoulder, ending his charge. Balduer's sword sliced through the attached leg, and he stumbled backward. Brogan filled the gap, producing a powerful overhead chop and bursting the body of the spider.

The final creature retreated slowly, fighting with a renewed vigor and crazed disposition. Dregur roared in frustration after a bone spike sliced across his cheekbone. He sprinted behind the spider and raised his sword to strike. The monster spun with lightning speed knocking him off balance. Four swords descended from behind on the exposed back, exploding the abdomen and killing it.

The leader with the red mace had already defeated his second enemy and stalked back toward the group.

Semper heaved on the bone spear penetrating Balduer's chest, then paused when the leader approached the group.

"While I wait for your friend to arrive, I will deal with this one." With his mace, the leader indicated the dwarf holding Semper's warhammer.

Semper involuntarily glanced at Dregur.

"Not him, idiot!" The leader continued to walk toward the dwarf with the warhammer.

The only other dwarf wearing black armor stepped in between them, blocking his leader. "Nargdin, you have been acting strange. What are you doing?"

A latch released on the far side of the arena, and a portcullis clanked and clinked as it rose.

The leader pushed past the mediator with a flick of his wrist. "How did I not see your deception? You're one of them. Aren't you?"

The besieged dwarf wrung his hands on the handle of the warhammer.

A second latch released, drawing everyone's attention, including Nargdin.

The first portcullis was halfway up when an enormous bulk crashed into it, sending the iron gate and huge chunks of stone flying into the arena. When the dust settled, the colossal head of their next adversary pushed through the opening until its shoulders were wedged on the side walls. It wailed and cried like a baby stuck in a birth canal. After squirming and struggling, both shoulders erupted from the tunnel, skinned and bloodied.

The behemoth completed the crawl to freedom and rose to its full height of fourteen feet. Long, wispy strands of hair fell across a chubby-cheeked face with a deep gash in it. The mostly gray skin was conspicuously different from the large, green, wart-covered arm and shoulder banded and stitched in place. It was barrel chested with a belly wider than its shoulders, and a deep purple scar ran up its midline, partially covered with old sutures and steel bands.

The monster hoisted a large leather sack over its shoulder and yelled with its tongue stuck between his teeth, "Wed!"

At the same time a lone humanoid figure exited the other portcullis, walking steadily and surely.

Nargdin chuckled and spun his mace. "Well, hello friend. I've been waiting for you."

115

The Dance

Lykinnia

Terazhan jumped to his feet. "Even though time passes slower there, we must hurry."

Solar reached down and pulled Lykinnia up into a bear hug. "Nice to have you back.

Lykinnia, partially in shock, gaped down at her material body. It had been waiting for her when she returned through the portal. Her father's jarring voice pulled her back to reality.

"You need to be steadfast and trust me." Terazhan's face wavered and a brief glimpse of fear darkened his features. "The easy part is over. We need to get ready."

"Your timing was perfect on the teleport spell, Lord Terazhan," said Solar.

A glimmer of a smile breached the demi-god's stoic façade and was gone in a flash. "This arduous task has fallen on our backs to carry. It will not be easy."

Solar motioned toward Jakarrak. "What about him?"

A haggard Jakarrak, covered with soot and ash, and on the brink of death, moaned in response. Deep gashes traversed his torso and legs, leaving red-stained skin below them from the ooze seeping out of the wounds.

Lykinnia did not wait for an answer. "Uncle Jakarrak!" She knelt beside him and immediately cast a healing spell. The familiar golden lattice sealed the wounds and gradually converted to new skin.

Uncle Jakarrak's countenance softened for a moment, but his peaceful expression was replaced with a shriek of agony. The previous wounds ripped open and instantly festered. A large knot deep in the muscle of his thigh expanded, pushing out more ooze, then subsided and disappeared.

Terazhan pushed up next to his daughter. "Watch out dear." Concentration washed over his face. A huge column of golden light shot forth from each hand. He targeted both sides of the largest wound and brought the light beams together. The skin rippled, and the muscle quivered, before an eight-inch-long black leach slithered out of the gash. When it flopped onto the ground, Terazhan raised his foot to stomp on it, and it struck like a snake. It sunk its mouth full of razor-sharp fangs into the bottom of his sandal. His foot struck the ground, splattering the vicious parasite across the stone.

"Lykinnia, back up a little more." Solar joined in on the leach extraction.

Lykinnia retreated. "How long was I gone?"

Solar considered her question. "Time moves much slower in the Plane of Ashes. Here it was about five weeks. You missed Cy—"

"Cymm was here? Why did he leave?"

Terazhan shot him an angry glare. "We have our own situation to deal with. Quite dire, I might add." He completed the exorcism of the eighth and final leach. "Adorable little creatures."

"I will heal him." Lykinnia dropped to her knees next to his head. Her healing spells proved much more effective this time, and her uncle finally opened his eyes. She expected her actions and his recovery to be acknowledged and was confused when it was not.

Terazhan and Solar both stood at the altar, the former in a trance-like state, the latter facing the opposite direction playing lookout. Pulses emanated from the demi-god in rapid succession, disturbing the air and causing concentric rings to roll past Lykinnia. The disturbances had the properties of a liquid and gurgled as they propagated forward.

"Lord Terazhan, I see it!" Solar turned toward Lykinnia. "Get him up. He needs to help." The winged man leapt from the back of the platform and glided into a run.

Her father had already turned his back on the altar. "Lykinnia, move it. You too, Jakarrak!"

Lykinnia trailed behind her father, taking the longer route around the platform, and helping her uncle keep his balance for the first dozen strides. A wave of immense pain shot through her mind. The three-day reprieve while on the Plane of Ashes was over. The snap and crackle of a fire ahead caught her attention. She peered around the three giant-sized men and gasped. A new rift had opened, growing larger by the second, and deep within it, a fire raged.

Even more bizarre, Ledaedra's severed green arm stood upright in front of the growing rift, performing an intricate dance.

Terazhan and Solar flanked each side of the rift, feet firmly planted and both palms extended toward the fracture. Golden columns of energy shot forth from their hands repairing the damage and attempting to close the aperture.

Uncle Jakarrak jogged up to stand shoulder to shoulder with his brother. With a flick of both wrists, two shiny claymores hovered in front of the fissure. Sunlight glinted off the edge of each sword and an orange aura danced around it.

Lykinnia's heart climbed into her throat. She retreated a couple of steps, marked her palm with coal and recalled the verbal component of her fireball incantation. Her concentration was limited by her pounding headache, but this was a spell she had performed hundreds of times. The aperture grew to eight feet tall, and a shimmering figure appeared in the gateway. The priestess gasped and released a miniature ball of fire at the green appendage. It struck the arm and flung it halfway to the rift.

The golden light from Terazhan and Solar continued to bombard the edges, healing it from both sides. While the arm struggled to stand, the two men completed their work and healed the rift. They gawked at each other simultaneously, both shocked to speechlessness.

Lykinnia glanced down at the final throes of Ledaedra's green arm. It quivered, it trembled, it rolled over, and her headache disappeared, then the world exploded. The young priestess recalled Uncle Jakarrak's wounds after she healed them the first time as the rift violently tore itself asunder. Recreating a gaping black hole, ten feet tall and four feet wide. A wave of energy threw everyone backward. Her father grabbed her arm and yanked her to the side as a claymore whirled past her head. Lykinnia cried out, reaching for her father's hand. He grasped it and pulled her behind him.

In the same amount of time the rift groaned, pulsed, then doubled in size. The crackling and roaring of a blazing fire emanated from inside the dark void. Ledaedra's green stump forced itself through the ether. In response the severed green arm became reanimated and jumped toward the fissure.

Uncle Jakarrak was the first to act. He motioned the claymores back into position, then put the heels of both palms together and extended the union toward the rift. A gale force wind pummeled the opening and the creature inside. The severed scaly arm lifted off the ground and sailed through the air. Wisps of tangerine smoke marked its passing. As if magnetized, the appendage collided with the nub and fused together.

Terazhan and Solar resumed their attempt to reseal the fracture.

"Healing it is pointless. It is too big!" Lykinnia released a fireball, targeting the green arm again. It barely missed one of the flying swords converging on the same spot. The ball of fire dissipated as it hit the foggy ether.

A black, taloned, scaly arm grabbed the edge of the rift, as if it were substantial, while the green arm slowly undulated in the center of the void, flexing, and testing its mobility before also latching onto the fringe.

With the green and black talons pulling on the edge of the fissure, it tore several more feet in both directions, and the head of a red dragon emerged from the void, its eyes blazing with hatred.

116

The Scourge

Cymm

The patchwork flesh golem took two giant strides forward. "Wed," it said with its tongue hanging out. It paused, put down its leather sack, then squeezed both fists tight, causing its body to tremble. After partially hoisting the bag, it was set back down. "Wed," He opened the sack, retrieved a small round boulder, and heaved it. The rock sailed over the heads of the gladiators and struck the wall right below the King's platform, almost hitting a decorative red silk banner. "Wed!" he screamed, then charged.

Cymm immediately located Semper, then Brogan. *Terazhan be blessed. Two of Brogan's warriors are with them too.* He was unfamiliar with the rest of the combatants, including the crazy-eyed dwarf walking toward him. This was the first time he had donned the complete set of mithril armor, and he lowered the visor into place before charging into battle.

The lead dwarf with black armor holstered his mace and uncoiled the scourge strapped to his waist as he approached. He tested the action and reach with a couple of easy flicks, then fixed Cymm with a sinister stare. Each of the seven thongs ended in a barbed hook, to inflict maximum pain, not death.

Semper nudged Brogan and pointed. "Cymm's here."

"Nargdin, watch out!" a black-armored dwarf yelled moments before the giant simulacrum trampled him.

The crushing blow to Nargdin weakened the resolve in the defensive line, and all seven gladiators fled before the juggernaut. The patchwork giant ignored them as if they were ants and crashed into the wall under the King's platform. It reached as high as it could toward the silk banner, falling three or four feet short. "Wed!"

Three of the honored mages leaned over the railing preparing to cast a spell.

The black-armored dwarf who issued the warning, hurried to his comrade's side, but Nargdin had already risen to a seated position. Skin was missing from his left cheek, and on his right side, his elbow was dislocated, and his ankle broken. He forcefully grabbed his right arm, and with a bone crunching twist, reseated his elbow.

The other black-armored dwarf shoved Semper with the shaft of the warhammer across his chest.

"Are you kidding me? You better step back." Semper raised his sword.

Dregur moved to intercede. "Hold on."

Cymm rushed forward the remaining five steps to break it up.

"Semper, take it. Quickly!" The dwarven warrior pushed the weapon into his chest again, then glanced back at the two approaching forms.

Nargdin hobbled closer, dragging the side of his right foot on the stone, his ankle at an unnatural angle. "I have been waiting for your arrival, holy warrior."

The gladiators repositioned themselves, forming a line with Semper to defend against the black-armored warriors.

"How do you know my name?" asked Semper suspiciously.

Dregur pushed in between them. "This is who healed me."

"It's true Semper the gold digger." The black-armored dwarf stared him down.

"I am not a gold—" Semper's mouth flopped open.

"What's true?" Nargdin stroked the handle of the flail.

"Wed?" The giant flesh golem snatched Balduer by the head. It hoisted him up to its face, then poked his back with a finger. "Wed!"

Balduer twisted his body and sunk his sword into the monster's forearm.

The patchwork giant roared, then grabbed Balduer's legs with its other hand and dismembered him into two pieces with one swift motion. Blood sprayed everywhere. "Wed!"

"No!" Brogan sunk his sword into the leg of the giant.

Cymm followed suit, swinging DragonSin, and opening a large gash in the simulacrum's side. Seven scourge thongs wrapped around his arm, ripping flesh from his forearm and bicep. Cymm howled in pain, turning toward his dwarven attacker. "What are you doing?"

Nargdin reeled back for another strike, delight on his face. "You have something I want."

DragonSin unloaded with a violent push, sending Nargdin forty feet head over heels to land among the dead bodies.

Five swords and a warhammer chopped at the abomination. The dwarves resembled lumberjacks trying to fell a tree. Flesh and blood flew like wood chips about the area.

The simulacrum kicked out, connecting with Brogan's chest, then punched down and caved in the head of another dwarf, the last independent gladiator.

"I—can't—breathe." Brogan dropped his sword and grabbed his chest.

DragonSin threw Nargdin for another loop as he tried to approach Cymm. *"He is blocking my mental blast."*

Semper, Dregur, and the two black-armored dwarves hesitantly continued their attacks, not knowing what else to do.

Cymm drove his sword deep into the monstrosity's lower back.

Brogan's face was redder than the moon Phoenix, and he dropped to his knees.

Cymm circled cautiously to help the big man, but the black-armored dwarf blocked his progress.

The giant flesh golem lifted his leg to stomp on Brogan.

The dwarf next to the big man froze, with a horror-stricken face.

"Red!" yelled Dregur.

The simulacrum glanced over its shoulder at Dregur, with its foot in midair, and DragonSin pushed as hard as he could. The giant slipped on the blood and gore coated stone, crashing to the floor on its back.

Cymm surged to the head of the creature and drove his sword deep into its eye socket.

The patchwork golem twitched several times, then lay still.

The crowd went into another frenzy. The ruckus beat down on the floor of the arena from every direction.

Semper extracted his buried warhammer from the brute's chest. He glanced at his young friend to acknowledge his efforts. His eyes widened. "Cymm, watch out!"

A red-hot mace grazed the side of Cymm's helmet and struck the top of his pauldrons, breaking his left collarbone. His arm went limp and hung useless at his side. Out of the corner of his eye, an amber glow blossomed over Brogan.

A chant from the spectators gained momentum with each passing second. "Live—live—live."

DragonSin pushed Nargdin.

The black-armored leader shook his head, glaring. "Not this time." He swung again.

Cymm barely rolled out of the deadly arc, then struggled to rise to his feet with only one arm. He backpedaled, remaining one step ahead of his assailant with the broken ankle. Scanning over his shoulder provided him with a view of Dregur charging to his defense, as well as a black-armored dwarf, and he witnessed Brogan rise on wobbly legs. The scene was comical, the short healing dwarf helping the giant man catch his balance. Cymm continued to wind his way back and forth, trying to create enough distance to heal himself, but the dead bodies were causing him more problems than Nargdin.

Dregur arrived with a sweep of Nargdin's good leg. The black-armored leader went down in a heap.

The chant continued, "Live—live—live," until the King took the platform, and it lost some energy.

Cymm immediately healed himself.

Nargdin's comrade reached down to help him up. "The battle's over. We won!"

Nargdin accepted his hand without comment. Cymm received a death stare. "Your reputation is unfounded. You are a coward. Stop running and fight."

Magically amplified, the King demanded silence.

Semper, Brogan, and the healer joined the loosely packed group.

From thirty feet away, Cymm rolled out his shoulder, pleased with the mobility and the thoroughness of the healing process. "Why am I your enemy?"

Nargdin chortled. "Foolish I see, and you took the bait. You still haven't figured out who I am?"

Cymm's confusion lasted only a moment. A second shadow head briefly phase-shifted to the right, creating a familiar two-headed monster. It was gone as fast as it came.

"Dego?" Cymm quickly raised his sword and took a defensive posture.

The King proclaimed, "The battle for Bardonril's Progression is over!"

Nargdin charged.

His compatriot reached for his arm but missed. "Nargdin, stop!"

Cymm braced himself for the attack, timed his swing, and unloaded as his enemy did the same.

The clamor of the crowd surged again, reaching its previous volume.

Cymm's sword pierced the black armor as if it were cloth, right through the heart and out the back.

Nargdin's mace descended full force, hitting Cymm on top of the shoulder.

By the nine hells! The same shoulder? Although it felt numb, this time it did not feel broken. Cymm pushed him to get away and extract his sword. He failed to do either.

Nargdin had wrapped his free arm behind Cymm's elbow, locking him in place or forcing him to leave the sword. His smile grew. He raised his mace to strike again, his body shuddering involuntarily.

Dregur's sword thrust into Nargdin's armpit.

Semper's warhammer sunk into the back of the leader's hamstring.

Both attacks damaged his body, but he did not seem to notice.

The dwarven healer shot a column of golden light at Nargdin's back.

Nargdin howled in pain. When he tried to turn, the embedded weapons held him fast.

"Wed!" came a familiar and poorly annunciated word. The flesh golem grabbed the head of the mace. The smell and sizzle of scorched flesh instantly permeated the air. The simulacrum released its grasp immediately with a pitiful wail. "Wed?"

Everyone froze, shocked, until the giant creature raised two fists high above its head.

"Hold on tight!" DragonSin warned before violently pushing against Nargdin.

Cymm flew backward with his bastard sword in hand.

Dregur abandoned his sword and scampered back, along with Semper, while the healer continued to shower Nargdin with amber light from a distance.

Each fist was bigger than a stone giant's club, and when they struck the top of Nargdin's head and shoulders, the snap and crack of numerous bones resounded above the cacophony of the crowd.

The healer was relentless with the light. "Cymm, help me!"

Cymm recovered to his feet. "How?"

"Wed!" yelled the simulacrum while inspecting the blood dripping from its fists.

"You need to heal him," the healer yelled.

"What?" Cymm shook his head.

A dark, two-headed body appeared, rising from the puddle of flesh and broken bones.

"Do it!" the healer demanded.

Cymm shuffled uncomfortably. "I can't unless I touch him." Cymm recalled the first time he encountered Dego inside Dirk Darkmane. Although it was many years ago, he remembered the searing pain as Dego entered his leg and tried to overtake his body. *I can't do it.*

Dego took a step toward the healer.

117

Forked Lightning

Lykinnia

"I am sorry Father. I have doomed us!" Lykinnia wailed.

Terazhan placed his hand on her shoulder. "Trust—"

A fiery inferno blasted forth from Ledaedra's maw.

Her father made a quick gesture and recited a few magic words. The air shimmered and a ten-foot golden shield appeared in front of them with a static charge snapping about it.

Solar took flight with blue electricity pulsing in his wings.

Lykinnia wrapped her arms around her father's waist, before burying her face in his back, feeling small and vulnerable.

The column of fire struck the shield with the force of a titan. The detonation hurled the pair backward sixty feet, where they landed in a heap.

The twin claymores struck the red dragon head repeatedly; the orange aura leaving streaks in the air where it had been. The performance was dazzling, but it had no physical impact.

Solar released the energy from his supercharged wings by flapping them together toward his target. Double bolts of blue lightning raced forward. Ledaedra's eyes widened, revealing some concern. They struck with enough force to knock the enemy halfway back into the void and blacken the skin on the right side of her face.

Her uncle touched the index finger on each hand to its matching thumb and linked them together, then forced the union toward Ledaedra. The air shimmered. A thick, sturdy chain shot forth with links as big as Lykinnia's hand. It hissed and howled, the racing air enhancing the magma color. It twisted around the dragon-like neck, wrapped itself around the bicep of the black arm, then hurtled around the neck again. When the chain's length had been exhausted, it immediately cinched itself tight.

Terazhan struggled to his feet first, hoisting his daughter to hers. "Are you hurt?"

Lykinnia took stock of her scrapes and bruises. "Nothing serious."

"Then fight beside me. This is our home," her father said fiercely.

Her father's validation fueled the power surging within her.

Terazhan's golden bolts of lightning sailed off the fingers of both hands, caroming into the giant snout, causing Ledaedra to blink.

The Dragon Queen kept coming, using the edges of the rift for leverage to pull the rest of her bulk through the crack in a slow, agonizing birth. The fissure ripped several more feet in each direction. A second head erupted from the black hole with an ear-piercing roar, the unique trait of a shadow dragon.

In response, Lykinnia's head swirled with random thoughts while her ears rang like a bell.

Terazhan seemed unphased and cast repetitive lightning bolts at their adversary, with no effect.

Uncle Jakarrak continued to control the chain, cinching it tighter and tighter, searing the flesh and choking Ledaedra. The black taloned claw pulled closer to her head, and finally popped off the edge, releasing her grasp.

With an enraged roar, Ledaedra thrashed against her incarceration, driving the chain links deeper into her own flesh.

The acrid smoke wafted past Lykinnia's nose, causing her to wiggle it, shake her head, then sneeze.

The chains snapped.

The red dragon roared again, but this time in pain.

Lykinnia quickly examined the scene, to find Kamac soaring past Ledaedra's snout, and several tail spikes embedded in the dragon's eye.

The sphinx banked around, a spectacle of aerial precision.

She shrugged off the remnants of the paralysis, prepared to cast her favorite spell.

The smoky shadow dragon wailed again, its ear-piercing shriek deafening at close range, but Lykinnia resisted the effects this time around.

Kamac was not so lucky. His body went rigid, and with wings extended, he plummeted to the ground.

Camak and the giant men appeared to be impervious to the screech.

Camak rushed to his brother's aid, unsuccessfully trying to break his fall. The audible sound of bone snapping filled the air, and Kamac's wing folded over on itself.

"No!" An enormous ball of flame swirled before Lykinnia. She thrust it angrily at their adversary. It accelerated with tremendous speed and exploded on impact, forcing the monster to involuntarily retreat further into the void.

Terazhan cast a golden ray of healing at the fracture's top gash. An amber lattice filled several feet of the gap, then the annealed area turned white hot, pulsed, and stretched.

The red dragon head twisted and shuttered, trying to regain the position it had lost. A roar of frustration bellowed forth, followed by misdirected blazing gouts of flame.

Lykinnia and her uncle successfully dove to different sides avoiding all but the outskirts of the fire.

Camak barreled into the side of the shadow dragon's head, clinging like a bat to a cave wall. The sheer force of the impact laterally shifted the beast's head ten feet to the right.

Lykinnia observed the blazing speed of Camak's claws and teeth from her prone position. The pure savagery caused a ripple of fear to course through her, as the sphinx ripped and shredded the attacker's neck on its way up toward the face.

Terazhan, his cowl in place, remained in a defensive posture while he cast the next healing spell on the rift.

Solar's wings had recharged sufficiently to release another blast. Blue lightning forked into the injured eye of Ledaedra, rupturing the orb and cascading a gelatin-like ooze down the side of her face. Ledaedra's head reeled back violently into the neck of the shadow dragon, leaving long parallel gashes from the horns on top of the red dragon head.

Lykinnia regained her feet and recalled the incantation for her explosive fireball. She hesitated, her concern for Camak's safety delaying the completion.

Six tavii warriors zipped past her, forming a protective semi-circle.

"Lykinnia, cast your invisibility spell!" Solar screamed.

His insistence on putting her safety before all others did not bother her as much as it normally would have because it seemed to have merit. It forced her to reevaluate the situation. She locked a steady gaze on Ledaedra while running several new calculations through her mind at the speed of light. "You shall not enter our home!"

Ledaedra cackled. "Who's going to stop me?"

"The three of us can heal the fracture faster than you can tear it." Lykinnia quickly cast a light spell at the edge of the rift.

Solar immediately joined her, but Terazhan was reluctant.

"Father, I do not have time to explain. Cast your heal spell, now," pleaded the young lady.

Terazhan stared at her dumbfounded. "But you are not—"

"Trust me. Now!" screamed Lykinnia.

Terazhan's golden light raced forward.

Uncle Jakarrak strode to his brother's side and sent a vortex of wind at their enemy. "What is she doing?"

Ledaedra's raspy voice rang out, "You are weak. You—"

"No, you are weak. You will never break through now!" Lykinnia charged the rift. *"Father, as soon as she tries to come through, stop healing."*

Terazhan blanched and barely nodded. A tear rolled down his cheek and he glanced at Solar.

Ledaedra roared, then surged forward with a massive display of strength and power. Her wide shoulders doubled the width of the rift and tore it violently, top and bottom.

"Now, Father!" Lykinnia ended her light spell and instantly cast invisibility. She blinked out of view.

Solar continued his charade with the non-healing light spell, and Terazhan ended his effort.

A metallic groan, deep and drawn out, echoed from the rift as the arms attached to both clawed talons bulged, propelling Ledaedra forward. She howled in delight and burst through the fracture quickly and powerfully in her full glory.

Lykinnia positioned herself directly in front of the rift, in harm's way, and even though she was invisible, Ledaedra's momentum brought her bulk crashing down toward her. The second part of Lykinnia's spell kicked in instantly, and with her new calculations, a mammoth void opened. The same void she would normally send all noise to when trying to sneak past Solar.

Ledaedra howled again, this time cursing and screaming as she plummeted through the void and back into her own plane.

Lykinnia temporarily considered closing the portal early, cutting her body in half, but reconsidered after the arm incident.

Solar switched his spell from light to healing, and Terazhan did not need to be asked.

Lykinnia joined them. Together they managed to seal the rift much faster without something pushing its way through.

Her father had pride etched upon his face. "You little genius."

Lykinnia winked at Solar. "Not yet Father. We cannot let her get even one talon into the crack. With her severed arm no longer on this side, she will not be able to reopen the portal."

The last vestige of the rift converted from a golden lattice and faded into non-existence, as if it were never there.

Lykinnia and her father exchanged a smile.

The tavii warriors cheered and the sphinx brothers sat on their hindquarters, licking their wounds.

Terazhan splayed his fingers and shot five golden bolts into Kamac's body from where he stood. The sphinx's wing moved of its own volition, repairing itself.

Lykinnia scanned the battleground, satisfaction blooming on her face.

Terazhan glanced at Solar with dread, then sprinted for the Altar of One.

118

Healing Light

Semper

Cymm and Semper stood motionless next to each other, although the dwarf assumed it was for different reasons. Semper was in shock from the verbal exchange with the healing dwarf, and what he believed was revealed to him. His gaze shifted from the flesh golem behemoth to the two-headed shadow creature, and a wave of helplessness washed through him. The giant simulacrum continued to admire the red blood on his fists, and the one Cymm called Dego, stalked closer to the dwarven healer, cutting tangents to reduce the gap.

The golden rays emanating from the healer's hands continued to streak toward the shadow creature, smoking and sizzling upon impact.

Dego roared in pain and frustration. Small embers took hold of large swathes of his body.

Semper grabbed Cymm's arm. "You have to help her."

Cymm glanced over, absorbed in his own thoughts. "I can't touch him. If I do, he will try to enter my body again."

Semper scanned the vicinity for a solution. His eyes came across the tunnel the golem had emerged from while blasting the iron gate off its hinges. "Cymm, help me get everyone over to the opening."

Cymm instantly complied with the request. "Rally to me!" He hastened to the position, dodging the hurled upper torso of an orc.

"Wed!" The simulacrum picked up another dead body and ripped it in half.

The crowd generated a mix of groans and cheers, degenerating quickly to the morbidly obsessed.

Brogan ran to Cymm with Dregur in tow. "It has a troll arm. It will heal any wound we deliver."

The paladin clasped his hands together and tilted his head skyward. "Terazhan, I need your help."

Semper returned his attention to the healer. Her steps had slowed, and her eyes had glazed over.

Cymm yelled, "Don't look in Dego's eyes!"

The smoke emanating from Dego's body burst into flames as the healer continued to ravage his body. Although, as soon as the flames erupted, the healer's arms dropped, and the healing light extinguished.

With a sinister howl of glee, Dego wound his arm back, as if to throw a rock, and released his invisible payload. His arm hurtled forward, stretching as it went, covering the forty-foot gap in a split second.

The healer's head snapped to the side as an unseen force propelled her out of the way.

Semper silently thanked Cymm and his sword while rushing to assist the stunned dwarf.

"Red!" yelled Dregur, extending his lungs.

The flesh golem's head snapped to the side. "Wed?" it replied in return, then charged.

Dego, much closer now, wound his arm back for another throw.

Semper grabbed the healer's arm. Before he could turn her around, they were both struck by the black tentacle arm and thrown backward. The healer went limp and fell almost immediately, but Semper fought to keep his balance. He took several awkward strides before colliding with the upturned bars of the portcullis. Two penetrated his back like spears and erupted from his chest.

"No." Cymm was by his side in an instant. "Terazhan, give me the power to heal my friend!"

"Wed!" The golem bowled over Dego, unable to slow his charge. He bent over the prone, burning form and pointed down. "Wed!" He attempted to touch Dego's weapon and recoiled once again in pain.

Semper could taste blood in the back of his throat and laughed at the irony of his position. He rested his warhammer on the metal bars around and protruding from him. He had intended to use the portcullis, but not as a shelf.

"Terazhan!" Cymm cried with a tight jawline. He wrapped his arm around Semper's back, attempting to push him off the impaling bars.

"No." Semper coughed, producing blood flecks on his lips. "Get everyone behind me."

Brogan pulled Cymm back. "He'll bleed out."

Cymm resisted and lunged back to Semper's side. "I don't know why he isn't answering."

Semper beheld the young man he had met at five lifeyears and marveled at the man he had become. "I am very proud of you Cymm, and I know your father would be too."

Anger washed across Cymm's face. "Stop talking like you're dying!"

Semper coughed up more blood. He raised a slow hand and pointed at the dazed, dwarven healer. "Cymm, that is my sister, Grendella. Protect her and save my father."

"We both will. Terazhan, give me the power to heal my friend!" Cymm cried.

Semper put on a brave face with a smile. "Hey, half-pint, promise me."

"I will." Cymm blubbered, stumbling back behind Semper while guiding Grendella.

With a rapid surge, Dego stood and delivered an uppercut to the stooping giant's jaw. The sheer power in one punch snapped the golem's head back and sent his remaining teeth flying. The simulacrum stumbled backward a few steps, then sat heavily on its massive behind.

Dego immediately stretched his arms out to the side with palms down, then turned them over.

Semper had no intention of letting him complete his nefarious action and smacked his warhammer as hard as he could on the portcullis. He thrust the weapon in Dego's direction and warbling waves shot forth.

Cymm yelled from behind him, "Terazhan, please help!"

The smirk on Dego's face disappeared. The definitive outline of his shadow lost form. He grunted several times before screaming in agony.

The simulacrum, already dazed, sprawled on its back, out cold.

A black fly landed on Semper's lip, and a second one on the back of his hand. He spit in disgust to chase the insect away while noticing a faint buzz in the air. He struck the portcullis with the hammer even harder and leveled the weapon at the two-headed demon.

Dego emitted banshee-like shrieks from both mouths as his body lost shape again.

A scream from above caused Semper to glance over his shoulder in confusion.

A dwarven mage hurled himself off the King's Platform, and hollered as he descended, "No hurt Durby!" He landed on the portcullis with a *clang*.

The rock fragments wedged under the iron gate and propping it up, absorbed some of the force, but Semper felt the bars rip down through his abdomen. He groaned in response.

"Not this time." Cymm brought DragonSin to bear, decapitating the dwarven imp with one swing.

Semper's knees buckled, and he gasped. The damage had already been done. His life force poured from the elongated gashes down the front of his body. He thought of his brother Hardre as the warhammer slipped from his lifeless fingers.

119

The Plague

Cymm

Cymm's mouth fell open for only a second before two black flies entered and bit his tongue. He ground them with his teeth and spit out the remains. "Terazhan, Solar, why won't you respond? I already lost Torak and Torc, I can't lose him too."

Hundreds of flies swarmed through the air, bouncing off his face and exposed arms. A few of them landed, generating sharp, irritating bites.

Cymm noticed the dead bodies were desiccating unnaturally fast and were the source of Dego's plague of flies.

Dego and Grendella recovered simultaneously and eyed each other like two roosters about to fight.

Thousands of flies buzzed through the air, creating black clouds obscuring his sight. Many of the dead bodies had withered into dry husks, then simply disintegrated, including the bones.

Brogan stood in the opening of the arena wall created by the simulacrum. There was no sign of Dregur or the remaining, black-armored dwarf.

Grendella attacked first. Her arms shot forth to cast the healing light, and Dego flinched involuntarily. Nothing happened. She tried again with the same result.

Dego grinned and stepped toward them.

Cymm grabbed the warhammer and pulled it away from Semper's partially decayed body, then slammed it into the portcullis. He lifted it toward Dego. Again, the demon cringed, but the telltale warbling did not come forth. Cymm tried a second time to no avail.

Dego shook his head slowly, taunting him.

Tens of thousands of flies now swarmed through the air. One tried flying into his nostril. Spectators shrieked in panic, and their screams of bloodlust turned into cries and shouts of fear as they shoved and pushed toward the exits.

Flames shot forth a dozen feet from each of the mage's hands, scorching flies by the hundreds, protecting the King and his family as they retreated. The smell was vile, and something Cymm would never forget.

Brogan called from behind him, "Cymm, come on! Dregur opened the prison gate."

Cymm and Grendella locked eyes, knowing each other would refuse to leave Semper's body behind. As they stared at each other, his remains exploded into thousands of buzzing flies. Horror stricken, he turned to run.

Dego screamed in frustration and leaped forward in pursuit. "Cymm, I have your girlfriend."

Cymm paused at the opening. Grendella pushed him into the tunnel. He shrugged off her grasping hands and turned. "You're a liar. She is far from here."

Each of Dego's fingers grew six inches and wriggled like a worm in the sun. "She came here to help you." Dego walked forward slowly, as if stalking his prey and trying not to spook it.

She can't leave the Peak of Power. Now I know you're lying. Cymm turned to leave once again.

"I have proof." Dego chased after him.

Cymm hesitated for only a second, and when he glanced back, five finger tentacles hit him in the face. The appendages penetrated his ears, nostrils, and mouth, boring deep into his head. He tried to resist, but his efforts were futile.

"I really do have proof. The red mace was hers. I intercepted her while roaming through the dungeons." Dego paused as if waiting for a response.

Cymm was miserable. The pain from the tentacles was becoming unbearable, and the flies landing on his exposed skin took small painful bites.

The fingers on Dego's second hand morphed into rope like structures, then entwined themselves around Cymm's neck, arms, and legs, locking him in position. "I guess I will never know what you see in her. Is it the way her eyes match her fingernails? Anyway, goodbye Cymm. The white shard will not save you like the first time we met."

Cymm's agony erupted in one long, shrieking wail. His heart was being ripped from inside him. No, his soul. The fibers of his very being were delaminating, the seams were popping, and something was being torn from inside him. *Torn or separated? Torn, this was far from surgical.* The pain was excruciating, even his hair hurt. *What does he want?* With a growing fear, Cymm already knew, *My white aura! The gossamer-winged dragonfly.*

The pain had passed its crescendo, and Cymm realized he was passing from this life. He did not want to die; he had reasons to resist, but if he did complete this journey, his mother, father, and sister would be there to console him. Additionally, he could resume his training lessons and philosophical discussions with Semper. He could ask Semper, "What in the nine hells were you thinking, by going back to the dungeons of Delge without me?"

His thoughts wavered, and he visualized himself walking along the bank of a river, similar to when he met Azreala the first time. *The only one I know with red eyes and red talons is The Goddess of Death. If Dego had taken her captive, that would explain her absence. I wonder if she will have Feldarius detain my soul, at least until Jalko and my warhorse can join me. I might even rejoin with Torak and Torc. What about Lykinnia? I may never see her again. She may never awaken from her coma.* He sighed deeply, a great weight settling on his chest. *I can't accept this outcome.* He snorted derisively. Tanya's spirited personality came to mind, revitalizing him. *I'll miss the opportunity to train her as a paladin and give her this short sword I cut the dragon apart with. She should be turning fourteen in the next couple of months. And Talo*—an invisible hand squeezed his heart—*won't understand what happened here. Hell, I don't understand what happened here, and I—*

A warbling echoed in the recesses of his mind, pulling him back from the final leap into the waters of oblivion. A wave of nausea washed through him, and he almost passed out. The burbling river next to him winked out of view and the hideous, stark reality stood before him.

Brogan and Dregur lay motionless beside him, cast aside like split wood.

The sinister red orbs on Dego's faces bulged out of their sockets, intensifying the energy-draining effect.

The warbling assaulted Cymm's hearing again, but Dego's tentacles shoved deep into his canals subdued it. His gaze dropped and behind his oppressor stood Grendella hoisting Semper's warhammer while standing over the portcullis.

She hit it again.

All five fingers on Dego's second hand instantly uncoiled from Cymm's body, and the two-headed demon hurled his arm at Grendella.

The dwarven priestess leaped back defensively, and his tentacle fell short, hitting the portcullis. The appendage promptly latched onto the iron gate, and Dego hurled it onto the King's Platform. Grendella remained motionless for several seconds, watching in amazement. The tentacle retracted, then immediately whipped out again at the healer. She blocked it successfully with the shaft of the hammer, then lost a hasty tug-of-war battle.

Cymm continued to avoid Dego's eyes and focused on Grendella. He could not yell, could barely breathe, and only the occasional muffled sound broke through the droning hum in his ears. She was the last one standing, their only hope, but she appeared indecisive. After taking two steps to her right, she turned and ran back to the left. She never made it to her destination before Dego's long arm wrapped around her ankles, and she crashed to the floor.

Foot by foot, Dego hauled her back. She fought for purchase against a floor that did not provide any opportunities. About halfway back, her hand drew across a helmet. She grabbed it, rotated to a seated position, and pummeled the tentacle. It was a pointless attempt, as her progress only slowed for a moment.

A wave of pain shot through Cymm's back, causing him to arch in response. His suffering was about to get worse; he could feel it. The same pain ran from his lower back up through his neck to the base of his skull. His body curled backward, and the ceiling of the coliseum came into view, descending upon him were twin bolts of lightning. They struck him in the head, right through the eyes, and an upsurge in power racked his body. His vision clouded and Grendella faded from view. Her scream echoed through his mind. The stretching of his body persisted to the point of snapping.

The pain subsided. He could breathe easier, and his ears were only slightly plugged.

Grendella screamed again. This time it sounded more celebratory.

Lightning crackled all around Cymm, and his confusion continued. With his newfound strength he rose to a standing position, but he did not remember telling his legs to do so. When the golden liquid pooled in his eyes, the blinding sensation came as sweet relief.

"Terazhan, don't attack! Heal him," yelled Grendella.

A voice sounding like Solar's said, "Heal, are you sure?"

Cymm's mouth involuntarily bit down on the tentacle shoved down his throat, then he retracted the severed piece. His hands shot out, latching on to two distinct necks. "You will not escape this time, Dego."

Dego thrashed and flailed, instantly withdrawing the appendages deep inside the ears and nostrils. "No. No. You can't be here. You should be fighting Ledaedra!"

An intense energy raged inside Cymm, bouncing off imaginary walls like a caged tiger. On the verge of exploding, it released a wild, multi-pulsed surge. The fanatic screech from Dego hit Cymm like a wave of ice-cold water. The scream of agony endured for many seconds, and he enjoyed it almost as much as the droning moan that followed. From the sounds and other context clues, he imagined all three of them, Terazhan, Solar, and Grendella, were simultaneously blasting him with their own amber columns of healing light. As Terazhan's avatar, he too was participating.

"Father, you cannot kill him. Father!" It was Lykinnia's voice.

She had awakened. Cymm wanted to call out to her, but he could not. His heart shouted in jubilation, then abruptly stopped. *Her voice had a tremor in it. Why is she so scared?* Fear crept into his mind. *"Father, you cannot kill him."* Her words replayed in his mind. *Why would she care if Dego died? He hurt her, he almost killed Solar, and he threatened to attack the Peak of Power. Is she talking about me? If he drains too much of my energy, could I die?* He tried to swallow the lump in his throat, or wipe the sweat off his brow, but he still had no control over his own body. *He wouldn't kill me, would he? I am too valuable for—*

"Wed?" cried a familiar voice.

You've got to be kidding me, thought Cymm.

"Father?" came Lykinnia's sorrowful voice.

"Quiet. I am not killing anyone," replied Terazhan.

Dego went abruptly silent, followed by *clink, clink, tink.*

"Leave it." Terazhan compelled Cymm's body to rise and walk several dozen feet. His body levitated, and his hands grasped a soft, silky fabric. Threads popped loudly as he tore it in half. Cymm's body descended back to the floor, and he extended his right arm holding the material.

"Wed?" asked the simulacrum.

"Yes. This is for you," replied Terazhan.

"Wed!"

The fabric was yanked from Cymm's hand.

"Wed." The flesh golem issued a content sigh. His footfalls indicated he was withdrawing.

Terazhan vacated his body.

A veil of silence dropped over the area. Cymm basked in the peaceful serenity. Even the buzz of the flies had dissipated. He dropped to his knees, weak and exhausted, listing to his right side. *I hate this part. It was so much better after Azreala left my body.* "We have to find Azreala." Cymm passed out.

ꝏꝏꝏ

"He is coming to."

Cymm could not determine which of the multiple faces hovering over him said it. His vision slowly came into focus, revealing Solar, Grendella, Brogan, and Dregur. Cymm moaned. "You two—are alive?"

"Semper's warhammer knocked us out," replied Brogan.

Grendella shrugged. "I had no choice."

"Semper?" asked Cymm half-heartedly.

No one replied at first, and Dregur shook his head.

Solar cleared his throat. "We tried, Cymm. There was nothing to heal, not a body to bring his soul back to. Besides, Lykinnia has never tried her resurrection spell. There is no guarantee it even works."

"Maybe Azreala can help us. We need to find where Dego imprisoned her and save her." Cymm was forcefully restrained from rising.

Solar glanced over his shoulder. "Terazhan can cast a trace spell to find her, but I would not say her name—"

"Azreala." Lykinnia's voice materialized from thin air.

"—because Lord Terazhan and Lykinnia are watching us through a portal," Solar finished.

"You asked about Semper, then Azreala, in that order. Not how Lykinnia is doing after she was unconscious for five weeks?" The young priestess giggled. "I heard you were sitting by my bedside for days holding my hand."

"I didn't want to leave. It was hard to decide between friends. I'm glad you've recovered." Cymm's gaze shifted to Brogan. "Why didn't you stick with the plan and wait for me?"

The big man hung his head, and his voice cracked. "I don't know. We got caught up in the adventure."

"Cymm, we lost Balduer too. Can you also ask her to help him?" asked Dregur.

The paladin's eyes welled. "Lykinnia, I know how smart you are. You're a genius, but I don't think your resurrection spell would work even if we had their bodies."

The young lady cleared her throat. "Why?"

Cymm gazed in the direction of her voice. "I remember Azreala telling me she made life and death decisions every day for others, but even she could not bring someone back from the dead without the assistance of her brother, Feldarius. He is the Keeper of Souls and determines what branch in the River of Binding they journey down. Does your spell invoke the approval of Feldarius?"

Lykinnia stammered uncomfortably. "I only recently learned of his existence. It does not."

Cymm nodded, accepting what he already knew. Semper would never be there for him again, with his sage advice, or as a training partner, or with his rare knee-slapping laugh. He walked on his knees toward Grendella, a woman he had never met before, and hugged her. The agony building inside him finally broke, and it hit him like Melcorac's Hammer. He hugged her fiercely, with tears running freely down his cheeks, and his body heaved with racking sobs.

Through his blurry, teary-eyed vision, he caught a glimpse of the golem over Grendella's shoulder. He remained sitting with his back against the wall caressing his face with the red silky banner. "Wed," he said passionately.

120

The Ebony Shard

Lykinnia

Uncle Jakarrak took a long pull from his wine goblet, compliments of Lykinnia, who had conjured food and drink on her stone table for everyone to celebrate their victories. "How did you know?"

"I did not know until after Grendella advised us to heal him. I figured it out after I saw the effect it was having, and he continued to lose his shape." Terazhan lounged comfortably against a boulder. "What did Grendella decide?"

"After we talked about Cymm's missing girlfriend, Azreala," Solar cast a sideways glance at Lykinnia with a wink, then dodged the bread she threw at him, "Grendella and I had a long talk about her future. She wants to be involved in the coming war and will accompany Cymm to the Peak of Power. She believes this path to be the greater good."

"And what of the ebony shard?" asked Terazhan, referring to the foot long cylindrical crystal, the only remains of Dego.

"They wrapped it in a thick leather sheet, placed it inside a bag, and took it with them. I told Grendella not to let anyone touch it, especially Cymm," replied Solar.

"Yes. He could set off the recombining of the shards and kill himself." Terazhan adjusted his robes.

"We need to tell him. He has proven himself to be trustworthy many times," Lykinnia said emphatically. *And before another incident occurs! According to Cymm, Grendella had awoken in the middle of the night with a stranger in her room. Cymm had come running at her call to find Dirk Darkmane with the shard bag in his hands. Dirk had apparently been sleepwalking and had no recollection of it the following day.*

Terazhan and Solar nodded in agreement to telling Cymm.

Uncle Jakarrak scowled at his wine. "What if Azreala gets her hands on it?"

Terazhan sipped his wine, a rare indulgence. "The ebony shard has already rejected her. If she tries to take control of it, it will kill her. It seems to only want Cymm, or more specifically, the white shard."

Solar grabbed several refreshments and seated himself on a large rock nearby.

Lykinnia grabbed more bread and also found a comfortable seat. "Father, how are we going to save Mother?"

Terazhan chewed his food slowly. "I am not sure we can, but maybe Jakarrak can shed some light on your research concerning the ring."

Lykinnia shot Solar a death stare.

"I did not say a word. Your father already knows most of what I tell him anyway."

"How?" Lykinnia directed her question to her father with hands on her hips.

Terazhan pondered the request for a moment. "Consider the scrying window Solar uses to watch Cymm. Imagine if he could open four at the same time."

Lykinnia's eyes widened. "You can open four?"

"Not in this world, but in the Plane of Mists, I can open twenty-seven simultaneously. Unfortunately, my interests are much greater, so it does not allow me to observe everything." Terazhan moved toward the table for a second round of refreshments.

Lykinnia shook her head in disbelief. "So, you spend your entire day spying on people?"

Solar and Uncle Jakarrak rose uncomfortably, intent on making an exit.

Terazhan's voice boomed, "We are not done. Find your seats!"

Lykinnia remained undaunted. "Uncle Jakarrak, is this how you spend your time?"

"Not exactly." He forced a smile.

Solar interjected, "*Uncle* Jakarrak does not spy, he manipulates people in a real-world game of altagee. Even if he does not have two others to play against."

"Even though you released me from prison, I will retaliate birdman—painfully," retorted her uncle.

"Altagee?" Lykinnia asked, confused.

Solar explained, "It is a three-dimensional game of good versus evil versus neutral, based on strategy—"

"I know *what* altagee is!" Lykinnia's hands flailed in the air. "How does it bring any value to the conversation? What does it mean?"

"It means your Millennial Lifeyear is almost here, and it is time to grow up," replied Solar.

Uncle Jakarrak jumped in. "He wants you to see my faults. He has always been jealous of the bond you formed with Fun-Uncle Jakarrak."

"You are bound to tell the story of the ring and why you were being held captive. We had a deal." Solar's wings flared and flushed with tiny lightning bolts of anger.

Her uncle cleared his throat. "Do not get your feathers ruffled. Lykinnia, my princess, can you conjure another flagon of wine?"

"Of course." Her hand was already twirling.

"Start with the ring. Everything else follows," demanded Solar.

Uncle Jakarrak poured the wine slowly, in no apparent hurry to comply.

Terazhan cleared his throat and peered at him through the top of his cowl.

"My big brother wants me to get to it." Uncle Jakarrak took another sip of wine. "I knew your father would arrive at the graduation ceremony dressed as an elf, and the lovely Sendaria would beguile him, so I gave her the ring to even the playing field."

"I think you left out your ulterior motive." Lykinnia folded her arms over her chest.

Her uncle glanced from Terazhan to Solar, then back to Lykinnia with a smile. "And what might that be?"

Lykinnia stared at him. "You asked her to report—"

"Oh child, that was to—"

"Distract my mother from your true motive," Lykinnia said.

"Which was?" countered Uncle Jakarrak.

"To get my father to fall in love with my mother so you could manipulate him, and his decisions. You found it easy to control my mother. She was completely driven by power, a trait you understood well and could exploit." Any kindness in her voice had dissipated.

The corners of Solar's mouth practically touched his ears.

Her uncle's face paled. "You make me sound so evil."

"No, not evil. Devious and unscrupulous for certain. Why would you do it? To what end?" asked Lykinnia.

Uncle Jakarrak glanced sideways at his brother. "A demonstration of power and because I can."

Terazhan shook his head. "Twenty millennia I have had to deal with this."

Solar prodded again, "Now explain why you were imprisoned."

Her uncle drained his glass of wine and poured another. "Ledaedra searches for my phylactery and plans to kill me and take it."

"It is of no value to her. She already has one," said Terazhan.

"Maybe she figured out how to combine their powers to increase her own," replied Uncle Jakarrak.

Solar turned his gaze to the younger brother. "I do not think so. She had no interest in trading for Lord Terazhan's. The reason you were a prisoner was the theft of a valuable book."

With a red face, her uncle shifted uncomfortably. "I had—we had—Ledaedra and I made a deal. When she failed to deliver, I took the book in recompense."

Terazhan's head tilted. "What deal?"

"What book?" asked Lykinnia simultaneously.

Her uncle set his empty wine glass on the table. "The deal was of a personal nature. As for the book, it was bound in mahogany brown leather with moondust images on the front. One of Sendaria's high-level spell books."

That is the book! Aloud, Lykinnia asked, "What does this have to do with saving my mother?"

"How could anyone survive chains running through their body in such a manner?" Terazhan took another small sip of wine, deep in thought.

"And yet, my brother, she is alive. I saw her move, and I heard Ledaedra talking to her." Uncle Jakarrak grinned sympathetically.

Solar drew air in through his teeth, drawing everyone's attention. "Why were the chains not running through your body? I saw identical chains curl up next to the post."

Jakarrak gazed skyward as if the clouds had the answer. "I do not know. The shackles she used drained my strength. Maybe she wanted you to try to rescue me."

Terazhan's nostrils flared while taking a deep breath. "She has been a step ahead of us the entire time. Dego knew we were battling Ledaedra. They must have coordinated their attacks."

Solar's attention was drawn away from the conversation, and he made a small head motion. "The altagee game continues. Here comes more pawns."

An orange aura swirled around Uncle Jakarrak's index finger. "Do not test me," he hissed. He rose with outstretched arms to greet the three approaching figures. "DyFarastine and MynDartain, welcome! Have you met everyone?"

Lykinnia inspected the third visitor with interweaving shackles on his black wrists, ankles, and neck. She met his eyes and choked on her food. "ZaphMordakai?" She turned to his captors. "Release him at once!"

"My lady, don't you want to know what he is guilty of?" asked the captor named DyFarastine.

"*My lady*? In other words, you are too *young* and too *stupid* to understand what is going on here?" Lykinnia asked forcefully, "Is that what you are implying?"

Uncle Jakarrak's eyes darted from one party to the other, apparently unsure who to side with or how to end the conflict.

Solar popped an enormous strawberry in his mouth and chewed with a huge red smile.

Terazhan allowed his daughter to proceed without admonishment or assistance.

DyFarastine fumbled his next words. "I—no, well—you . . ." He sighed. "You might not be aware, but he is a—"

"Black dragon, yes I know," interrupted Lykinnia.

The captor jerked back. "You already knew?"

"How long have you known?" ZaphMordakai tried to contain a smile of amusement but failed.

"Does anyone else think I am an idiot, besides these two?" Lykinnia pointed her finger at them.

After several seconds of silence, Solar said, "I do," then popped another strawberry in his mouth, thoroughly enjoying the discussion.

Lykinnia gave him a sideways glance, then returned her attention to the captor. "Remove the chains now. The altar will disintegrate him before he can complete the transformation."

ZaphMordakai rubbed his emancipated wrists, while the other manacles were removed. "Thank you Dyfar." He smirked at Lykinnia. "May I approach, my lady?"

"Do not push your luck, Zaph. What are the charges against him?" Lykinnia raised her eyebrows.

DyFarastine threw his shoulders back proudly. "The most egregious accusation is he conspired with Ledaedra to capture all eight Descendants of Twilight, including you, especially you."

"Descendants of Twilight? Lykinnia turned the phrase over in her mouth like it generated a bad taste.

Terazhan shifted his position, taking an interest in the conversation for the first time.

MynDartain interceded. "Anyone born to a demigod. There are eight of you, and none are protected by a phylactery. Your *friend* was assigned to gain your confidence then betray you to the Dragon Queen. Your life force would be drained and given to Ledaedra."

Lykinnia's gaze bore into Zaph. "Would you like to defend yourself?"

ZaphMordakai cleared his throat. "Yes, but I am afraid you will eviscerate me like you did to my friend, Dyfar."

DyFarastine scowled.

Zaph continued, "Unfortunately, everything they claim is true. I agreed to this assignment before I knew you."

"And did you agree to this *assignment* before or after you overheard us talking about destroying Ledaedra's altar?" Lykinnia paused, but there was no response. "This is why you have no friends, Zaph. Even when you finally get one, you betray them."

ZaphMordakai's smug smile vanished.

DyFarastine found his. "So, what shall we do with this traitor?"

Zaph hung his head in the ensuing silence, as if ready to accept the fate he knew was coming.

Everyone else stared at Lykinnia while she finished her internal deliberation. She reached out telepathically to her father, *"I know there is good inside him, and he does not know how to embrace it. He has had a harsh life with no role models. I want to give him a chance."*

Terazhan made no movement. *"I will trust your judgment."*

Lykinnia's head came up. "We will let him go."

"What?" Jakarrak and ZaphMordakai both said with equal shock.

Lykinnia continued, "He saved my life and Solar's as part of the ploy, but maybe he does not know how to act toward a friend because no one has ever shown him."

"DyFarastine and MynDartain of the Silver Dragon Order, the information you have gathered may give us the advantage we need in the war to come. Is there any more you require from ZaphMordakai?" asked Terazhan.

One shook his head, while the other said, "No."

Terazhan nodded perfunctorily to his daughter.

Lykinnia considered her wording. "Very well. Zaph you are free to go, but I want you to think about something. The Dragon Queen is no fool, and she will know you betrayed her."

"I know. Can I choose to stay here?" asked Zaph as if he were dipping his toe in the water.

"Not until you have had sufficient time to consider your options. You know a war is coming, so it is time to pick a side. Once you have figured that out, we will know if we are friends or not." Lykinnia motioned toward the only path.

ZaphMordakai appeared ready to argue, then scanned the scowls surrounding him. His shoulders slumped, and he left, transforming into a black panther before taking his third step.

121

Dragons

Cymm

Cymm and Grendella made their way up the final switchback to the Peak of Power's plateau on their trusty steeds. It had been three days past a fortnight since leaving the dungeons of Delge and competing in the arena for Bardonril's Progression. Brogan and Dregur had said their goodbyes and remained in the city of Delge to enjoy their new fame as 'survivors of the golem.' The fighting was being touted as 'the battle of the ages,' 'the best arena battle ever,' and 'an honorable brawl for the mages.'

When Cymm had mentioned the search for Semper's father, Grendella shared the story of his peaceful passing three years earlier. Cymm shook his head, his eyes welling. "Then this whole thing was for nothing?"

To make matters worse, Grendella informed Cymm she was doing missionary work. She was in the dungeons by choice to ensure the workers always had food, and she could heal their injuries from working in the mines.

Cymm had assigned Dregur with the task of informing Melkerie, Semper's dwarven ex-fiancée. As for the dwarf's two prized possessions, his warhammer and ring, he had a plan for their rightful disposition. His sister inherited the weapon, and his widow would receive the ring. His stomach churned when he thought about telling Semper's wife.

It had only been three weeks since his last departure from the Peak of Power, but it seemed like a year had passed as he approached the Altar of One with Grendella by his side.

Lykinnia, as usual, was already there. "Hi, Grendella. Welcome back. Have you seen my boyfriend? He promised to be here for my lifeday celebration, which is tomorrow."

"Grendella, if my girlfriend is looking for me, could you tell her I have arrived, and I am visiting with the court jester by the altar?" countered Cymm.

Lykinnia wrinkled her nose with a mocking smile. "Grendella—"

"Grendella hasn't seen anyone! Take your game elsewhere so I can pray at the altar."

Lykinnia stepped off the platform while Cymm dismounted. They ran to each other, and he wrapped his arms around her, lifting her off the ground and spinning. He placed her down and while giggling, she threaded her arm through his and led him to her dining table. "I was getting worried. Many people have already arrived."

He noticed several beings, including a unicorn, gigantic dog-like creatures, several humanoids with large feathery wings, a flying snake twelve feet long, two giants over eighteen feet tall, and, of course, the sphinx brothers and six praying mantis warriors.

"People is an interesting word choice. I don't see many *people*." Cymm's attention was drawn to the sky, and he gaped in awe as an enormous silvery beast progressed through a spiral descent. "Is that a dragon?"

"Yes, a good dragon."

Cymm pointed at the majestic creature. "There are good dragons?"

The priestess nodded before frowning sympathetically. "How are you doing?"

"Better. I still can't believe he's gone . . ." Cymm's voice faded away. He stared into the distance. *Good dragons? Huh.*

The silver dragon landed. Its body shimmered to the point it was difficult to determine any of its features. He transformed into a handsome man of approximately forty lifeyears and walked with purpose directly to Lykinnia. After taking her hand, he knelt and kissed it. "My Lady Lykinnia, you are even more beautiful than the last time I saw you."

She flushed and attempted to withdraw her hand. "NilaCapton, this is Cymm Reich."

The silver dragon maintained perfect posture. "It is my pleasure to meet you, Cymm. I have heard remarkable things about you."

Cymm nodded mutely.

NilaCapton pulled Lykinnia toward him. "May I have a moment to discuss urgent matters with you?" He bowed his head toward Cymm and led her away.

She glanced back at Cymm apologetically and shrugged her shoulders.

"Hey DragonSin, did you know dragons could transform into humans?"

"No. It is a foreign concept to me."

"Is there any chance Lykinnia is a silver dragon? Because it would explain a lot of things." Cymm continued to stare after them for a few more moments, then went to retrieve his warhorse. Ruminating over the existence of good dragons, and with his head down, he walked into a gaggle of sprites and pixies hovering six feet off the ground.

"Whoa, watch where you are walking," said a pixie.

"No more sprite wine for him," said another to the merriment of his entire group before they flew off in a tizzy.

Cymm whistled and his warhorse cantered over, then followed him to his favorite resting place back along the tree line by the Altar of One and the Pool of Age. Lykinnia had placed a cabinet, a small table, and a wooden stand for a saddle in the area.

He removed his weapons, backpack, and armor, then proceeded to care for his horse by removing the saddle and brushing him down. As he came around the backside of the warhorse, he came face to face with a scantily dressed, stunning being. There was a permanent glow emanating from his body, and enormous white feathered wings sprouting from his back.

Cymm jumped away, startled.

"You are Cymm Reich. I am Solar. It is my pleasure to meet you," said the winged being.

"Your name is Solar?" asked Cymm skeptically.

"My name is no longer relevant. I am Solar to Sehaleah. The tales of your miraculous deeds have me anxiously awaiting more."

Cymm beamed with happiness. "Thank you. I—"

Sehaleah's Solar turned and walked away.

How strange. Solar is a title, not a name? Cymm finished brushing his horse, grabbed a clean priest robe from the cabinet Lykinnia had stocked, and headed for the warm springs to bathe and clean up for the party tomorrow.

The pools were vacant when he arrived, so he quickly disrobed and slipped into the warm water.

"Take care not to splash me," said a voice in his mind.

Cymm panned the vicinity. "Who said that?"

An eighteen-inch-tall red dragon stood on top of a large boulder above him. The setting sunrays enhanced its gossamer wings as the light glittered and sparkled off them.

"If my wings get wet, I will not be able to fly." The miniature drake settled back into position.

"I am going to soak for a while, and I will try not to splash. Doesn't the steam make your wings damp?"

The little dragon stared unflinchingly, then blinked out of sight.

Incredulously, he laid his head back on the mossy rocks. *This event is crazy. Why would so many different creatures and beings come to celebrate Lykinnia's lifeday?* While staring into the cloudless sky, he contemplated his question until a huge golden body soared overhead. "By Melcorac's Hammer, another dragon?"

It was enormous, yet graceful and beautiful, and when it landed, the ground trembled from its girth. This dragon would have towered over TetraQuerahn, the green dragon he slew.

He quickly scrubbed his body with the small stones and sand at the bottom of the spring, rinsed his hair, then decided to search for the golden dragon.

122

Love and Friendship

Lykinnia

The following morning, Lykinnia woke at the break of dawn. It was the fourth day of the fourth month, also known as the month of The Initiate. It was her lifeday, her millennial lifeday. She was brought into this world one thousand years ago. Her excitement about the day's events prevented her from falling back to sleep. She got dressed and headed over to find the only one awake at this hour to share the moment.

I have waited a long time for this. My confinement to the Peak of Power has ended. Now I can travel to the Lower Darken Wood and see my creations with my real eyes. If Cymm or Solar need help, I can be of use. And I can finally travel to the other planes of existence.

There was no movement in Cymm's minicamp. "Hey—" She abruptly cut herself off.

Cymm was sleeping.

She almost giggled aloud as she tiptoed over to his cabinet, grabbed a leather bag, and put her fist in it. then nudged his well-defined bicep while trilling her lips like a horse would.

Cymm rolled away from her.

Lykinnia moved up to his shoulder with a more forceful prod and nickered softly.

"Happy lifeday, horse breath." Cymm rolled toward her with one eye open. "I will get even."

"You will try. Get up. I want a lifeday hug." Lykinnia was practically dancing in place.

Cymm sat up and extended his hand for assistance in rising. When they clasped hands, he tried to pull her down on top of him.

Caught off guard, she almost lost her balance, but she recovered and heaved him to his feet. She hugged him fiercely. "I am so excited for today."

Cymm stood motionless. "How did you do that? A strength spell?"

"If it makes you feel better, then yes." She squeezed him one last time, then grabbed his arm and pulled the confused young man toward the altar. Several moments of silence passed. "After giving me the spell book and escorting the six tavii warriors to the Peak of Power, I hope you did not get me another gift." Lykinnia observed Cymm's expression change from confused to mortified. She sighed. *Why did I say that?*

Cymm swallowed hard. "Of course, I did. It is your lifeday gift. It can't be a previous gift."

Lykinnia giggled. "You are a horrible liar. You should never play Medusa's Gaze with Solar and I, we will eat you alive."

"Well, I take that as a compliment." Cymm's feelings appeared to be hurt.

"How about we pray, then eat breakfast together?" the priestess asked, knowing she was too excited to pray.

Cymm nodded and took his position.

She tried, but her focus was restricted.

"Happy Lifeday to my little girl!" came her father's booming voice, making her head swoon.

"Thank you, but I am not so little anymore."

"I know, I know. Although, you pray like a little girl."

"I cannot concentrate this morning. Did you know it is my Millennial Lifeday?" Lykinnia did a pirouette next to the altar, drawing Cymm's attention.

"Stop distracting Cymm. Did NilaCapton share with you that he intends to begin the courting process?"

"No. He is a little too old. I hope you politely declined."

"He was asking for his sons, and besides, you cannot marry for another millennium," her father said with humor in his voice.

"I will not be able to bear children for another millennium. However, the laws do not prohibit me from matrimony after I have come of age."

Her father stopped laughing and broke the link.

Lykinnia's mind continued to drift while she waited for Cymm to finish at the altar. Her gaze fell upon him. *I need to be more honest with him. He does not deserve all these half-truths and intentional omissions that have been a part of every conversation.* She sighed. *It has become a pattern in our relationship. How will he react when he discovers who my father is, and why I live here, or when I tell him how old I am and how long I will live for? At breakfast, I am going to tell him my age.*

It was a baby step, but she was trying to determine how to build and maintain a friendship based on the relationships she had with animals and creatures.

Cymm finally finished. He stared at her with disapproval.

"What? I finished early today. Eat breakfast with me. I have something I want to tell you." She pulled him off the platform and led him to the stone table.

Cymm's brow wrinkled. "Is everything okay?"

"Yes!" she squealed. "I am thrilled about today, and I am happy you are here to celebrate it with me."

"Me too. What did you want to tell me?"

She screwed up her courage and nonchalantly cast a spell to bolster her telepathic powers. Images immediately bombarded her from Cymm's mind. "Today is my coming-of-age day. Do you know how old I am?" Lykinnia manipulated the tentacles of her spell, linking into his thoughts.

"I have tried to figure it out. I honestly have no idea."

Her mind probe revealed a quick glimmer of a plainsman's wedding ceremony, and she was exuberant to find herself as the bride. Her heart skipped a beat, and she continued forward. "Cymm, today is my millennial lifeday."

Cymm let out a raucous laugh. "Millennial? As in one thousand?" Her visage stopped him abruptly. "How?"

His thoughts of marriage were fading or at least changing. Now, he visualized himself as an old decrepit man standing next to a young, beautiful woman.

She struggled to control her breathing. "Let me explain. I am part high elf. My mother, Sendaria Moonbeam, crafted the spell book you brought me from the dragon's hoard."

"Lykinnia." Solar waved her over to a group of newly arrived guests.

She held up her index finger, then turned back to Cymm. "Come with me?"

"I'm going to eat and wait for you here," he replied, trembling.

What did I do? What did I do? I should have waited till later. "It is going to be like this all day. Promise me you will not disappear, and we will talk more about this tonight when we are alone again." Lykinnia chewed on the inside of her cheek, awaiting his response.

Cymm reached out and rubbed the side of her arm. "Of course."

ꝏꝏꝏ

The lifeday celebration commenced at midday with dancing, singing, and storytelling, but mostly small groups gathered to talk and eat. Lykinnia was pulled from one group to the next.

True to his word, Cymm mingled freely, introducing himself to several guests. Lykinnia kept her eye on him, amused by his courage, and wondered if he would dance with her.

Cymm broke from the main group, heading toward the gold dragon.

"Would you please excuse me?" asked Lykinnia of a guest she had only begun to speak with. She rushed over to intercept Cymm, but she was detained several times on her way. She excused herself each time, politely, arriving in the middle of a conversation.

". . . cannot take the human form naturally. I would need to cast a spell. You are confusing gold and silver dragons."

"My apologies," replied Cymm.

"Hello Talon. Are you enjoying the party?" asked Lykinnia, causing Cymm to jump.

"Yes, Daughter of Twilight, but you didn't come over here to talk to me. Did you?" asked the gold dragon.

Lykinnia smiled at the new nickname and shook her head. "The polymorph dance is coming up soon, and I want Cymm to dance with me. You should join us, Talon."

"I think not. I have not danced in four or five hundred years." The dragon raised his chin in mock aloofness.

Cymm's eyes were wide open. "I'll keep Talon company."

"We will return after the dance." Lykinnia hooked Cymm's arm and pulled him toward the dance area. She caught Cymm glance back at Talon for help, but none was forthcoming.

"This is not a promising idea. I don't know how to dance."

"I will instruct you on dancing later. This is more of an event, and it is my favorite, most anticipated part of the party," Lykinnia said excitedly.

Cymm continued to resist, even pulling against her arm to return toward Talon.

Lykinnia stopped and locked eyes with him. "Did I mention it is my lifeday. My Millennial Lifeday."

Cymm sighed, bowed his head, and shuffled to the dance area. "What do I have to do?"

Lykinnia cheered and shook his arm fervently. "It is simple. When everyone claps their hands, you change shape."

"What?" Cymm's face screwed up in confusion.

Lykinnia picked up a vial of liquid from a table and handed it to Cymm. "When it is time, you drink this potion, which enables you to change yourself into an animal or creature by thinking about it. The last person to polymorph is eliminated and the dance continues until there is a winner."

"That's not so bad. What does everyone do in between claps?" asked Cymm.

"Move around swinging their arms and hips," she replied sheepishly.

"So, dancing. Ughh." Cymm kicked at the ground.

"Come on. It will be fun." Lykinnia was already moving to the rhythm in her head.

Cymm lifted the vial and stared at the contents through the milky glass. "Where is yours?"

"I do not require a—"

"Of course, you don't. Are you up to eighty-two languages yet?" Cymm delivered a grand smirk.

Lykinnia giggled. "Go ahead and drink it, so you can practice a couple of times before we start."

Three centaurs, each with a musical instrument, made up the band. The familiar, upbeat tempo of the polymorph dance song engaged and so did her body. Her hips had a mind of their own, her arms and hands wove intricate patterns as if she were casting a spell. Soon, she would be, as she reformed the shape of her body into her favorite characters.

Clap.

Lykinnia became a unicorn.

Cymm changed into an orc.

The music thrummed and boomed for a bit, while the participants swayed and bounced.

Clap.

Lykinnia morphed into a pegasus, and Cymm a flesh golem.

Cymm yelled, "Red!"

Clap.

Lykinnia turned into a red pixie, spinning and twirling about.

Cymm faltered and was removed from the competition.

Clap.

Twenty minutes later and dozens of claps, only Lykinnia remained with her nemesis, Solar. It took five lightning rounds to determine the winner, and she exploded with a rapid succession of ten polymorphs after she was proclaimed the victor.

"Show-off!" yelled Solar before hugging her. "I thought I had you this time."

She hugged him back. "I love this game."

The music turned slow, and a few bodies became doubled.

"Where is Cymm?" She scanned in every direction until she found him slinking away. "Cymm Reich come back here!"

"I will dance with you," came a voice from behind.

Lykinnia spun into the arms of a hulking minotaur. "Is this your costume or a game of guessing?"

"Yes, and yes."

"I accept. Four questions and a guess?" she asked.

"Yes. You have three left," answered her dance partner.

She accepted the challenge with vibrant eyes. "Have we met before?"

"Yes. Two more."

Lykinnia tousled her hair. "Have we seen each other in the past three months?"

"Yes."

Lykinnia's eyes narrowed. "Should you be here right now?"

After a long pause came the response, "No. I wanted to wish you a Happy Lifeday."

"Interesting. ZaphMordakai wants to be friends—"

"No. You misunderstand my intentions. I have made my decision. As long as Cymm lives, we cannot truly be friends. Therefore, I am forced to choose the other side. I won't disturb your celebration."

Lykinnia glanced over her shoulder, then back to Zaph with a clenched jaw. "She will kill you."

"I will take my chances. Happy Lifeday, *friend*." ZaphMordakai the minotaur scoffed, then turned and left.

Lykinnia stared after him until the dancing couples blocked her view. Only then did she realize she had blasted a hole in the ground near her foot.

ꝏꝏꝏ

As the night wound down, and the stars appeared, Lykinnia found Cymm in a quiet spot staring up. Four full moons dominated the beautiful night sky, eclipsing the stars but not each other. The dazzling brilliance bounced off his armor and hair.

Most of the partygoers had departed before sunset, and the last few stragglers were in a small group saying their goodbyes.

She snuck up behind him and wrapped her arms around his waist.

He jumped, then relaxed in her embrace. "Hi, beautiful. The perfect ending to your special day." He made a grand flourish toward the night sky. "Was it everything you hoped for?"

"And more. Beautiful? Have you been drinking the pixie's wine?" she asked.

"No. Why does everyone assume I have?" Cymm rubbed her arms wrapped around him.

She put her head on his shoulder and gazed into the sky. "Does this mean you are willing to accept our age difference?"

Cymm did not answer.

"What if we were the same age and would live relatively the same length of time?"

Again, he did not answer.

She released him and walked around to face him. "Have your feelings changed for me because I am not human?"

"No! Not at all. Why are you doing this?" he said with sorrow in his voice.

She fell into his arms. "I do not want to lose you."

Cymm hugged her and buried his face in her hair. "I am not going anywhere. We will be good friends for—"

"Friends? I do not want to be friends; I want to be together forever. Do you?" Lykinnia sniffled.

"Of course, I do, but some of us don't live two thousand years."

Finally. She cleared her throat and prepared to study his reaction while nestled in his arms. "What if you could? Would you want to be with me?"

Cymm pushed her away in frustration. "Why do you torture yourself with dreams of madness?"

"They are not dreams of madness. Answer the question!" Lykinnia's stomach churned with fear and hope as she waited for his reply. Too afraid to scan his thoughts, but too insecure not to, she opened the door to his mind and walked in. She could not help herself. What she saw was powerful and confusing, to the point it almost overwhelmed her.

"Yes, I love you! But that does not mean we should act on our feelings. We will both get hurt in the end." Cymm's voice cracked.

"You have told me what I need to know. I am exhausted from today's events. I will see you in the morning for prayers. Good night." Lykinnia gave him a big hug.

"Good night," he said slowly.

"We will talk more in the morning." She rushed away, knowing what she must do.

∞∞∞

She returned to Cymm's camp a couple of hours later, hoping he had fallen asleep. To make sure he did not rouse in the middle of the process, she cast a sleep spell on him. Every phase of the process would be complex. She had to harvest a core seed from her own heart, then plant it deep within his. The seed would grow into an energy shard that would stay with him forever and extend his life hundreds, possibly thousands of years.

If it were ever needed, she could replenish the energy in the shard when their life forces were synchronized. This was the part of the equation her father had missed. It had taken a lot of research to understand how and when sinusoidal life force curves coincided, and she had intended this to benefit her mother. In theory, her discovery would allow her to perform small, frequent replenishments without impacting her own life expectancy.

Lykinnia's body transformed into pure amber energy. She hovered over Cymm's prone body, staring at him lovingly. Her humanoid form of golden energy sank slowly into his body, completely infusing with his, leaving no trace of her at all. The transference had begun.

Her work was meticulous. It had to be. Both of their lives depended on it. Any distraction, even the smallest, could be disastrous. She lanced the core seed from her own body without hesitation, then faltered, uncertain if she should proceed. She gritted her ethereal teeth, and plunged the seed deep into Cymm's heart, then fine-tuned its placement. Pleased with her artwork, she withdrew from his body.

Her essence coalesced into her material form, and the smile instantly faded from her face.

Terazhan stood before her. "Why did you disobey me, child?"

Lykinnia hung her head. "I love him."

"I know, but did you try to determine the ramifications of your actions?" asked her father.

She shook her bowed head.

"Turn and look." Terazhan's hand shot out, and Cymm's body convulsed briefly.

The pure white aura responded violently, surrounding him with a protective shield.

Before Lykinnia could question him, he said, "Look closer."

Then she saw it. She placed both of her hands over her mouth and gasped. At the center of his pure white globe of power was a pulsing amber blemish. She had tainted his aura. "No. I did not—that should not have happened."

"It gets worse. Follow me." Terazhan led the way to the altar. "Have you been practicing your gazing into the future?"

"Yes. Why?" Lykinnia bit her fingernail. A knot of muscle was forming in her back between her shoulder blades.

"Step up here and scry with me." Terazhan made several hand motions and verbal incantations. An amber globe of energy hovered before them.

Lykinnia stared into the ball and a smile immediately formed on her face. She had traveled to a populated city with Cymm, and they strolled down the street holding hands. Several large objects passed overhead, casting dark shadows upon them and the surrounding street. She continued to watch with wide eyes, and her mouth opened farther and farther.

Her eyelids blinked away the tears before a solitary tear dripped onto the Altar of One. "Oh, blessed Melandri. Cymm!—No!"

Synopsis

In the mystical world of Erogoth, dragons have reigned supreme for centuries.

At the age of seventeen, Cymm Reich, the First Paladin of Terazhan, embarks on a noble quest to liberate the realm from draconian dominance. His pursuit of justice unveils staunch allies and formidable foes, as the ghosts of his past decisions linger.

Meanwhile, Lykinnia, driven by the desire to resurrect her long-lost mother, navigates a perilous journey filled with duplicity and emotional turmoil. As her understanding of the magical Altar of One expands, loyalty and principles are put to the test as she comes of age amid a world teeming with intrigue, deception, and betrayal.

Ledeadra, the formidable Dragon Queen, deploys ZaphMordakai, a maverick captain in her Dark Army, to thwart the efforts of those who resist her reign. Zaph, cunning and charismatic, finds himself entangled with enemies like Cymm and Lykinnia, blurring the lines between loyalty and rebellion.

In the heart of the enigmatic "Dungeons of Delge," Lykinnia seeks truth, while Cymm becomes further entwined in his crusade against evil. They require each other's assistance to successfully complete their quests. Yet, the forces that bind them together are relentlessly strained by demons, dragons, and dark elves. As the saga unfolds, their decisions hold the power to save the world of Erogoth or plunge it into darkness.

Will their unity withstand the relentless onslaught, or will the very actions meant to rescue the world become the harbingers of its destruction?

Grab your copy now and get swept away as destinies collide, and the stakes are nothing short of the world itself.

www.ingramcontent.com/pod-product-compliance
Lightning Source LLC
Chambersburg PA
CBHW020616310726
48979CB00008B/1511/J

* 9 7 9 8 9 8 5 9 6 2 2 6 0 *